PIGS DON'T FLY

MARY BROWN

PIGS DON'T FLY

A Baen Books Original

Baen Publishing Enterprises
P.O. Box 1403
Riverdale, N.Y. 10471

ISBN: 0-671-87601-5

Cover art by Darrell K. Sweet

First printing, May 1994

Distributed by
Paramount
1230 Avenue of the Americas
New York, N.Y. 10020

Printed in the United States of America

This one for my little brother,
Micky-Michael,
and my half-sister,
Anna,
and their families.

Acknowledgments

Thanks, as always, to my husband Peter, for his care and patience.

Belated thanks—sorry, folks!—to Bobby Travers and his daughter Joanna for smoothing our way out here.

Thanks, too, to Margaret and Barry Shaw for their help with Christopher.

I am also grateful to our *alcalde,* Don Carlos Mateo Donet Donet, for his assistance and encouragement.

Last, but never ever least, thank you Samimi-Babaloo, my Sam—just for being yourself!

Part I
AN END

CHAPTER ONE

My mother was the village whore and I loved her very much.

Having regard to the nature of her calling, we lived a discreet distance away from her clients, in a cottage up the end of a winding lane that backed onto the forest. Once the dwelling had been a forester's hut, shielded by a stand of pines from the biting winter northerlies, but during the twenty years since she had come to the village it had been transformed into a pleasant one-roomed cottage with a lean-to at the side for wood and stores. Part of the ground outside had been cleared and fenced, and we had a vegetable patch, three apple trees, an enclosure for the hens, a tethering post for the goat and a skep for the bees.

Inside it was very cozy. Apart from the bed, which took, with its hangings, perhaps a third of the space, there was a table, two stools, hooks for our clothing, a chest for linen and a dresser for the pots and dishes. Above the fire was the rack for drying herbs or clothes, beside it a folding screen that Mama sometimes used when she was entertaining if it was too cold for me to stay outside—though as I grew older I preferred to sit among the pungent, resinous logs in the lean-to, wrapped

3

in my father's cloak, thinking my own thoughts, dreaming my own dreams, where witches and dragons, princes and treasure could make me forget chilblains or a runny nose until it was time for Mama to call me back into the warmth and the comfort of honey-cakes and mulled wine in front of the fire.

Then Mama would sit in her great carved chair in front of the blaze—a chair so heavy with age and carving it couldn't be moved—a queen on her throne, me crouched on a cushion at her feet, my head against her knee, and if she were in a good mood she would talk about Life and all it held in store for me.

"You will be all I could never be," she would say. "For you I have worked and planned so that you may have a handsome husband, a home of your own, and a dress for every season. . . ."

That would be luxury indeed! Just imagine, for instance, a green dress for spring in a fine, soft wool, a saffron-yellow silk for summer, a brown worsted for autumn and a thick black serge for winter with fresh shifts for each. . . . A man who could afford those for his wife would have to be rich indeed, and live in a house with an upstairs as well as a downstairs. Even as I listened the dresses changed colour in my mind's eye as quick as the painted flight of the kingfisher.

Mama's planning for me had been thorough indeed. On a Monday she entertained the miller, who kept us regularly supplied with flour and meal for me to practice my pies, pastry and cakes; Tuesday brought the clerk with his scraps of vellum and inks for me to form my letters and show my skills with tally-sticks; on Wednesday Mama spent two hours with the butcher and once again I practiced my cooking. On Thursday the visit of the tailor-cum-shoemaker gave me pieces of cloth and leather to show off my stitching; Friday brought the Mayor, who was skilled with pipe and tabor so I could display my trills and taps and on a Saturday the old priest listened to me read, heard my catechism, and took our confessions.

Sunday was Mama's day off.

She had other visitors as well, of course, besides her regulars. The apothecary came once a month or so, sharing with us his wisdom of herbs and bone-setting, the carpenter usually at the same interval, teaching me to recognize the best woods and their various properties, and how to repair and polish furniture. The thatcher showed me how to choose and gather reeds for repairing the roof, the basketmaker, also an accomplished poacher, instructed me in in both his crafts.

All in all, as Mama kept telling me, I must have been the best educated girl in the province, and she covered any gaps in my education with her own knowledge. It was she who taught me plain sewing, cooking and cleaning, leaving the refinements to the others. She insisted that as soon as I was big enough to wield a broom, lift a cooking-pot or heat water without scalding myself, that I kept us fed, clean and washed, and throughout the year my days were full and busy.

During the spring and summer I would be up before dawn—taking care not to wake Mama—and into the forest, cutting wood, fetching water, looking to my traps, gathering herbs and then home again to collect eggs, feed the hens, and weed the vegetables. Then I would milk the nanny and lay and light the fire, mix the dough for bread, sweep the floor and empty the piss-pot in the midden, so that when Mama finally woke there was fresh milk for her and a scramble of eggs while I made the great bed and heated water to wash us both; then I changed her linen, combed and dressed her hair and prepared her for her visitors. Once the ashes were good and hot they were raked aside for the bread, or if it was pies or patties I would set them on the hearthstone under their iron cover and rake back the ashes to cover them.

Once Mama was settled in her chair by the fire it was away again for more wood and water and once I was back there were the hives to check, a watch on the curdling goat's milk for cheese, digging or sowing or watering in the vegetable-patch and perhaps mixing straw and mud for any cracks in the fabric of the cottage. Then indoors for sewing, mending, washing pots and bowls, followed by any other tasks Mama thought necessary.

Once the gathering, storing and salting of autumn were over, my outside tasks during the winter were of a necessity curtailed, although there were still the wood- and water-chores, even with snow on the ground. There were the stores to check: jars of our honey, crocks of flour, trays of apples, salted ham, clamps of root vegetables, strings of onions and garlic, bunches of herbs, dried beans and pulses. That done, it was time for candle-dipping, spinning, carding wool, sharpening of knives, re-stuffing pillows and cushions, sewing and mending, mixing of pastes and potions and repairing of shoes.

Then came the time I liked best. While I dampened down the fire and made us a brew of camomile flowers, Mama would comb her hair and sing some of the old songs. We would climb into bed and snuggle down behind the drawn hangings for warmth, and if she felt like it my mother would either tell me a tale of wicked witches and beautiful princesses or else, which I like even better, would tell once more of how she had come to be here and of the men she had known. Especially my father.

I had heard her story many times before, but a good tale loses nothing in the retelling, and I would close my eyes and see pictures in my mind of the pretty young girl fleeing home to escape the vile attentions of her stepfather; I would shiver with sympathy as I followed the flight of the pregnant lass through the worst of winters and sigh with relief when she reached, by chance, the haven of our village, and my heart filled with relief when I re-heard how she had been taken in by the miller and his wife. Once her pregnancy was discovered, however, there was a meeting of the Council to decide what should be done with her, for now she was a Burden on the Parish and could be turned away to starve.

"But of course there was no question of that," said Mama complacently. "Once I had discovered who was what, I had distributed my favors enthusiastically to those who mattered, and all the important men of the village

were well disposed to heed my suggestion for easing their
... problems, shall we say? Of course much was tease
and promise, for there is nothing more arousing to a man
than the thought of undisclosed delights to come. . . .
Remember that, daughter. You had better write it down
some time. Of course I was far more beautiful and
accomplished than the other girls in the village, though
I say it myself, even though I was four months gone. I
still had my figure and my soft, creamy skin, and of
course every man likes a woman with hair as black and
smooth as mine. . . .You would say, would you not, child,
that my skin and hair are still incomparable?"

"Of course, Mama!" I would answer fervently, though
if truth were told her hair had grey in it aplenty, and
her skin was wrinkled like skin too long in water. But
she had no mirror but me and her clients, and who were
the latter to notice in the flattery of candles or behind
drawn bed-curtains? Besides, those she entertained were
mostly well into middle age themselves and in no position
to criticize.

"So by the time the meeting of the Council came
round it was a foregone conclusion that I would stay. It
was decided to offer me this cottage and food and supplies in return for my services," continued Mama. "Of
course I laid down certain conditions. This place was to
be renovated, extended, re-roofed and furnished. I was
also to entertain six days a week only: Sunday was to be
my day of rest.

"At first, of course, I was at it morning, noon and
night, but eventually the novelty-value wore off and my
friends and I settled to a comfortable routine. Your elder
half-brother, Erik, was born here and three years later
your other half-brother, Luke. . . ."

Erik now was a man grown with a shrewish and complaining wife. Dark, long-faced, with tight lips, he had
teased me unmercifully as a child. Luke I remembered
more kindly. He was apprenticed to the miller and had
the same sandy hair, snub nose and gap-toothed smile.
It was obvious who his father was and he even resembled
him in temperament: kind and a little dim.

And now came the part of Mama's story of which I never wearied.

"Some dozen or more years ago," she would begin, "your half-brothers were fast asleep and I was all alone, restless with the spirit of autumn that was sending the swallows one way, bringing the geese the other. It was twilight, and all at once there came a knocking at the door. It had to be a stranger, for there was fever in the village and I had forsworn my regulars until it had passed. . . ."

"And so there you were, Mama," I would prompt, "all alone in the growing dusk. . . ." Just in case she had forgotten, or didn't feel like going on. So vivid was my imagination that I felt the shivers of her long-ago apprehension, imagining myself alone and unprotected as she had been with the October mist curling around the cottage like a tangle of great grey eels, slither-slide, slither-creep. . . .

"And so there I was," continued Mama, "determined to ignore whoever, whatever it was. But again came that dreadful knocking! I grasped the poker tight in my hand, for I had forgotten to bolt the door—"

"And then?" I could scarcely breathe for excitement.

"And then—and then the door was pulled open and a man, a tall, thin man, stood in the shadows, the hood of his cloak pulled down so I could not see his face. You can imagine how terrified I felt! "What—what do you want?" I quavered, grasping the poker still tighter. He took one step forward, and now I could see his cloak was forest-green, and the hand that held it was brown and sinewy but still he said nothing. Then was I truly afraid, for specters do not speak, and of what use was a poker against the supernatural?"

I gasped in sympathy, crossing myself in superstitious fear.

"I think that my bowels would have turned to water had he stood there silent one moment longer," she said, "but of a sudden he thrust one hand against his side and held the other out towards me, saying in a low and throbbing tone: 'A vision of loveliness indeed! Do I wake or sleep? In very truth I believe the pain of my wound has conjured up a dream of angels. . . .'"

How very romantic! No wonder Mama was impressed.

"The very next moment he crumpled in a heap on my doorstep, out like a snuffed candle! What else could I do but tend him?" and she spread her hands helplessly.

And that was how my father had come into her life. At once she had taken him into both her heart and her bed—what woman wouldn't with that introduction?—and nursed him back to health. For an idyllic month, while the village still lay under the curse of a low fever, my father and mother enjoyed their secret love.

"He was both a courtly and a fierce lover," said my mother. "A trifle unpolished, perhaps, but not beyond teaching. He was always eager to learn those little refinements that make all the difference to a woman's enjoyment. . . ." and my mother paused, a reminiscent smile on her face.

"And what did he look like, my father?"

But here always came the odd part. Perhaps the passage of years had played strange tricks with my mother's memory for my father never looked the same for two tellings. At first he was tall, then recollection had him shorter. Dark as Hades, fair as sunlight; eyes grey as storm clouds, blue as sky, brown as autumn leaf, green as duck-weed; he was loquacious, he was taciturn; he was happy, he was sad; shy, outgoing . . . I was sure that if ever I loved a man I would remember every detail forever, right down to the number of his teeth, the shape of his fingernails, the curl of his lashes. But then Mama had known as many men as there were leaves on a tree, so she said, and always tended to remember them by their physical endowments rather than their physiognomy. In this respect she assured me that my father was outstanding.

I hated the sad part of my father's story, but it had to be told. One frosty day, as my mother told it, the men from the village came and dragged him from the cottage and carried him away, never to be seen again. "They were jealous of our love," she said, and she had never ceased hoping that he would return, her wounded lover who came with the falling leaves and left with the first frosts.

He had left nothing behind save his tattered cloak, a purse full of strange coins, and a ring. Mama said the coins were for my dowry, but that the ring was special, a magic ring. She had shown it to me a couple of times, but it looked like nothing more than the shaving of a horn, a colorless spiral. It would not fit any of my mother's fingers, and she would not let me try it on.

"He wore it round his neck on a cord," she said, "for it would not fit him either. He said it was from the horn of a unicorn, passed down in his family for generations, but it did nothing for him. . . ."

She had tried to sell it a couple of times, but as it looked so ordinary and fit no one, she had tossed into a box with the rest of her bits and pieces of jewelry— necklace, brooch, two bracelets—where it still lay, gathering dust.

My days were not all work and no play, though I mostly made my own free time by working that much harder. I had two special treats. If the weather was fine, summer or winter, I would escape into the woods or down by the river, lie under a tree and gaze up into the leaf-dappled sunshine and dream, or sit by the river and dangle my toes in the fast-running water. This would be summer, of course, but even in the cold and snow there were games to play. Skipping-stones, snowballs, imaginary chases, battles with trees and bushes . . . Away from the cottage I was anything I chose and could forget the confines of my cumbersome flesh and flew with the birds, swam with the fish, ran with the deer. Gaze up into the rocking trees in spring and I was a rook, swaying with the wind till I felt sick, my beak weaving the rough bundles they called nests. Dangle my fingers in the water and I was a fish, heading upstream into the current, the river sliding past my flanks like silk. Given the bright fall of leaves and I ran along the branches with the squirrels and hid my nuts in secret holes I would never remember. Winter and I sympathized with the striped badgers, leaving the fug of their sets on warmer days to search for the scrunch of beetle or a forgotten berry or two, blackened into a honey sweetness by the frost.

But the thing I loved most in the world to do was write in my book.

This had grown from my very first attempt at writing my letters, many years ago. Now it was thick as a kindling log and twice as heavy. At first the clerk had formed letters for me in the earth outside, or had taught me to mark a flat stone with another, scratchy one, but as I progressed he had shown me how to fashion a quill pen and mix inks, so it was but a short step to putting my first, tentative words on a scraped piece of vellum.

As parchment or skin was so expensive I sometimes had to wait for weeks for a fresh piece, but I practiced diligently with my finger on the table to ensure I should make no mistakes when the time came.

For the Ten Commandments, my first page, the old priest provided me with a fine, clear page, but by the time I finished it was as rough and scraped as a pig's bum. My next task was the days of the week, months and seasons of the year, followed by the principal saint's days and festivals of the Church calendar. Then came numbers from one to a hundred. This done, the elderly priest dead and another, less tolerant, in his place—he never visited Mama—I was free to write what I wished, whenever I could beg a scrap of vellum from the clerk. Down went recipes for cakes, horehound candy, poultices, dyes and charms.

I do not remember what occasioned my first essays into proverbs, saws and sayings. It may have been the mayor, once chiding me for hurrying my tasks. "Don't remove your shoes till you reach the stream," he had said, and this conjured up such a vivid picture of stumbling barefoot among stones, thorns and nettles that down it had to go. Not that it cured me of haste, mind, but it was an extremely sensible suggestion. Then there were my mother's frequent strictures on the behavior expected of a lady: "Do not put your chewed bones on the communal platter; reserve them to be thrown on the

fire, returned to the stock pot, or given to the dogs." Or:
"A lady does not wipe her mouth or nose on her sleeve;
if there is no napkin available, use the inner hem of your
shift."

She also gave me the benefit of her experience of sex;
pet names for the private parts, methods of exciting pas-
sion, of restraining it; how to deal with the importunate
or the reluctant, and various draughts to prevent concep-
tion or procure an abortion. Down these all went in my
book, for I was sure they would one day prove useful,
though she had explained that husbands didn't need the
same titillation as clients. "After all, once you're married
he's yours: you will need excuses more than
encouragements."

When the pages of my book grew to a dozen, then
twenty, I threaded them together and begged a piece of
soft leather from the tanner for a cover and a piece of
silk from Mama to wrap it in. A heated poker provided
the singed title: *My Boke.* At first Mama had laughed at
my scribblings, as she called them, for she could not read
or write herself, but once she realized I was treasuring
her little gems of wisdom and could read them back to
her, she even gave me an occasional coin or two for more
materials, and reminded me constantly of her forethought in providing me with such a good education.

"What with your father's dowry and my teachings, you
will be able to choose any man in the kingdom," she
said.

And that was perhaps the only cause of friction
between us.

A secure, protected, industrious childhood slipped
almost unnoticed into puberty, but I made the mistake
one day of asking Mama how long it would be before
she found me the promised husband, to be met with a
coldness, a hurt withdrawal I had not anticipated. "Are
you so ready to leave me alone after all I have done for
you?" I kept quiet for two more years, but then asked,
timidly, again. I was unprepared for the barrage of blows.
Her rage was terrible. She beat me the colors of the
rainbow, shrieking that I was the most ungrateful child

in the world and didn't deserve the consideration I had been shown. How could I think of leaving her?

Of course I sobbed and cried and begged her on my knees to forgive me my thoughtlessness, and after a while she consented for me to cut out and sew a new robe for her, so I knew I was back in favor. Even so, as year slipped into year without change, I began to wonder just when my life would alter, when I would have a home and husband of my own, as she had promised.

And then, suddenly, everything changed in a single day.

CHAPTER TWO

That morning Mama was uncharacteristically edgy and irritable. She complained of having eaten something that disagreed with her, and although I made an infusion of mint leaves and camomile, she still seemed restless and uneasy.

"I shall go back to bed," she announced. "And I don't want you clattering around. Have you finished all your outside jobs?" I had. "Then you can go down to the village and fetch some more salt. We're not without, but will need more before winter sets in. Wait outside and I'll find a coin or two...."

This was always the ritual. Our store of coins, which Mama always took from passing trade, were hidden away, and only she knew the whereabouts. I didn't see the need for such secrecy, but she explained that I was such a silly, gullible child that I might give away the hiding place. I couldn't see how, as I scarcely spoke to anyone, but she insisted.

I picked up an empty crock and dawdled down the path towards the gate. It was a beautiful morning, and I was in no hurry to go. I hated these visits to the village, but luckily only made them when there were goods we could not barter for—salt, oil, tallow, wine, spices. I

enjoyed the walk there, the walk back and would have
also enjoyed gazing about me when I got there, but for
the behavior of the villagers. When I was very young I
did not understand why the men pretended I didn't exist,
the women hissed and spat and made unkind remarks
and the children threw stones and refuse. Now I was
older I both understood and was better able to cope.
When I complained, Mama always said she couldn't comprehend why the women weren't more grateful: after all,
she took the heat from their men once a week. Like
everyone else, she said, she provided a service. But that
didn't stop the children calling after me: "Bastard daughter of a whore!" or worse.

"Here, daughter!" I turned back to where Mama stood
on the threshold. She would never come outside. In summer it was "too hot", in winter "too cold". In autumn it
was wasps and other insects, in spring the flowers made
her sneeze, and through all the seasons it was a question
of preserving her complexion. "I wouldn't want to be all
brown and gypsyish; part of my attraction to my clients
is my pale, creamy skin. You had better watch yours,
too, girl: you're becoming as dark as your father. What's
acceptable on a man won't do on a woman."

Now she handed me some coin. "Watch for the
change: I don't want any counterfeit. And if I'm asleep
when you return, don't wake me. I shall try and sleep
off this indisposition."

"If you're really feeling ill I could fetch the
apothecary—"

"Don't be stupid: I am never ill! Now, get along with
you before you make me feel worse—and for goodness
sake straighten your skirt and tie the strings on your shift:
no prospective husband would look at you twice like that!
Do you want to disgrace me?"

I kissed her cheek and curtseyed, as I had been taught,
and walked away sedately till I was out of sight, then
hung the crock over my shoulder by its strap, hitched up
my skirts and scuffed my feet among the crunchy, crackly
heaps of leaves along the lane, taking great delight in

disordering the wind-arranged heaps and humming a
catchy little tune the mayor had taught me for my pipe.

It seemed I was not the only one fetching winter
stores. Above my head squirrels were squabbling over
the last acorns. I could hear hedgepigs scuffling in a ditch
searching for grubs, too impatient for their winter fat to
wait till dusk, and thrushes and blackbirds were testing
the hips and haws in the hedges and finishing off the
last brambles, while tits and siskins were cheeping softly
in search of insects. A rat, obviously with a late litter, ran
across in front of me, a huge cockchafer in her mouth.

The sun shone directly in my eyes and shimmered off
the ivy and hawthorn to either side, making their leaves
all silver. I passed through a cloud of midges, dancing
their up-and-down day dance—a fine day tomorrow—
and on a patch of badger turd a meadow-brown butterfly
basked, its long tongue delicately probing the stinking
heap. My only annoyance was the flies, wanting the sweat
on my face, and the wasps, seeking something sweet, so
I pulled a handful of dried cow parsley and waved that
freely round my head.

I purchased the salt without much notice being taken,
for a peddler had found his way to the village, and the
women and children were crowding round his wares. So
engrossed were they that the miller passing by with his
cart had time to give me a huge wink and toss me a
copper coin. "Don't spend it all at once. . . ."

Money of my own! A whole coin to spend on whatever
I wanted! At first I thought to buy a ribbon from the
peddler, but that would need explanations when I
returned home, and somehow I didn't think Mama would
approve of her clients giving me money. Lessons and
food were different. Food! I had just reminded myself I
was hungry. I looked up at the sun: an hour before noon.
Still, if I bought something now I needn't hurry home,
and Mama could enjoy her sleep. I peered at the tray in
the bakers. Ham pies, baked apples, cheese pasties . . .
The pies looked a little tired and I had had an apple for
breakfast, so I carried away two cheese pasties.

One had gone even before I reached the lane again,

but I decided to find somewhere to sit in the sun and thoroughly enjoy the other. There was a bank full of sunshine a quarter mile from the cottage just where the lane kinked opposite one of the rides through the forest, and I seated myself comfortably and enjoyed the other pasty down to the last crumb, wiping my mouth thoroughly to leave no telltale grease or crumbs. I found a couple of desiccated mint leaves in the hedge behind and chewed those too, just in case Mama spotted the smell of onions, then burped comfortably and lay back in the sunshine, the scent of the mint an ephemeral accompaniment to the background of autumn smells: drying leaves, damp ground, wood smoke, fungi, a gentle decay.

I sniffed my fingers again, but the scent of mint had almost gone; strange how the pleasant smells didn't last as long as the stinks. I must put that thought down in my book. "Perfumes are nice while they last, but foul smells last longer"? Clumsy. What about: "Sweet smells are a welcome guest, but foul odors stay too long." Still clumsy; it needed to be shorter, more succinct, and could do with some alliteration. "Sweet smells stay but short: foul odors linger longer." Much better.

As soon as I had time to spare I would write that down. The trouble was that it took so long; not the actual writing, now that I was more used to it, but the preparation beforehand. First, I had to be sure I had at least a clear hour before me, then the weather had to be right: too hot and the ink dried too quickly; too wet and it wouldn't dry at all. It had to be mixed first of course to the right color and consistency, and the quills had to be sharpened and the vellum smoothed and weighted down and the light just right.

But then what joy! I scarcely breathed as I formed the letters: the the full-bellied downward curve of the *l*, the mysterious double arch of the *m*, the change of quill position for the *s*, the cozy cuddle of the *e*—each had its own individual pattern, separate symbols that together made plain the things I had only thought before.

Magic, for sure. First the letters themselves, precise in shape and order, then the interpretation into words

and meaning and lastly the imagination engendered by
the whole. The old priest had once given me a saying:
"God created man from the clay of the ground: take care
lest you crack in the firing of Life." I had dutifully copied
this down, but once it was there it took on a new dimen-
sion. In my mind I could actually see little clay men
running round with bits broken and chipped off them,
crying out that the Almighty Potter had not shaped them
right or had made the kiln too hot or too cold, and—

"Hey, there! Wake up, girl!"

Suddenly the sun had gone. I opened my eyes and
there, towering over me, was the awesome bulk of a
caparisoned horse, snorting and champing at the bit. Still
half-asleep I scrambled to my feet and backed up the
bank, wondering if I was still dreaming.

"Which way to the High Road?"

The horse swung round and now the sun was in my
eyes again. I dropped down to the road, and was seem-
ingly surrounded by a party of horsemen who had obviously just ridden along the ride out of the forest. Hooves
stamped, harness jingled, men cursed and I was about
to panic and run for home, when the face of the man
on the caparisoned horse swam into view and I felt as
though I had been struck by lightning.

He was the handsomest man I had ever seen in my
life. It was the eyes I noticed first, so dark and deep a
blue they seemed to shine with a light all their own.
Dark brows drawn together over a slight frown, a high,
broad forehead and crispy dark hair that curled down
unfashionably to his collar. His skin was faintly tanned,
his nose straight; there was a little cleft in his rounded
chin and his mouth—ah, his mouth! Full and sensual,
wide and mobile ... I remembered afterwards broad
shoulders, wide chest and long, well-muscled legs, but at
the time I could only stare spellbound at his face.

Someone else spoke, a man who was probably one of
his retainers, but the words didn't register. I couldn't
take my eyes off his master.

The mouth opened on perfect teeth and the apparition
spoke.

"I asked if you knew the way to the High Road."

"She's maybe a daftie, Sir Gilman. . . ."

I shook my head. No, I wasn't a daftie, I just couldn't speak for a moment. I nodded my head. Yes, I did know the way to the High Road. I was conscious of the sweat pouring from my face, an itch on my nose where a fly had alighted, could feel an ant run over my bare toe—

"If you follow the lane the way I have come"—I pointed—"you will come to the village. If you take the turning by the church you will have to follow a track through the forest, but it is quicker. Otherwise go across the bridge at the end of the village, past the miller's, and there is a fair road. Perhaps four miles in all." I didn't sound like me at all.

He smiled. "And that is the way to civilization?"

I stared. Civilization was here. Then I remembered my manners and curtsied. "As you please, sir. . . ."

He smiled again. "Thank you, pretty maid. . . ."

And in a trample of hooves, a flash of embroidered cloth, a half-glimpsed banner, he and his men were gone clattering down the lane.

I stood there with my mouth open, my mind in a daze. He had called me "pretty maid"! Never in my wildest imaginings had I conjured up a man like this! Oh, I was in love, no doubt of it, hopelessly, irrevocably in love. . . .

I must tell Mama at once.

I hugged his words to my heart like a heated stone in a winter bed as I raced home, near tripping and losing the salt. Flinging open the door and quite forgetting she might be sleeping, I rushed over to the bed where she sat up against the pillows.

I grabbed her hand. "Mama, Mama, I must tell you—Mama?"

Her hand was cold, and her cheek, when I bent to kiss it, was cold too. The cottage was dark after the bright outside and I could not see her face, but I didn't need to. She couldn't hear me, couldn't see me, would never know what I had longed to tell her.

My mother was dead.

CHAPTER THREE

At first I panicked, backing away from the bed till I was brought up short by the wall and then sinking to my knees and covering my head with my arms, rocking back and forth and keening loudly. I felt as if I had been simultaneously kicked in the stomach and bashed over the head. She couldn't be dead, she couldn't! She couldn't leave me all alone like this! I didn't know what to do, I couldn't cope. . . . Oh, Mama, Mama, come back! I won't ever be naughty again, I promise! I'll work twice as hard, I'll never leave you, I didn't mean to upset you!

My eyes were near half-shut with tears, my nose was running, I was dribbling, but gradually it seemed as though a little voice was trying to be heard in my head, and my sobs subsided as I tried to listen. All at once the voice was quite plain, sharp and clear and scolding, like Mama's, but not in sentences, just odd words and phrases.

"Pull yourself together . . . Things to be done . . . Tell *them*."

Of course. Things couldn't just be left. I wiped my face, took one more look just to be sure, then ran as fast as I could back to the village. Luckily the first man I saw was the apothecary. As shocked as a man could be, he hurried back with me to confirm my fears. He examined Mama perfunctorily, asked if she had complained of pains in the chest and shook his head as I described her symptoms of this morning, as best I could for the stitch in my side from running.

"Mmm. Massive heart attack. Pains were a warning. Must have hit her all at once. Wouldn't have known a thing."

Indeed, now I had lit a candle for his examination I could see her face held a look of surprise, as though Death had walked in without knocking.

"Will tell the others. Expect us later." And he was gone.

Expect us later? What . . . ? But then the voice in my head took over again.

"Decisions . . . Burial . . . Prepare . . . Food."

Of course. They would all come to view the body, decide how and when she should be buried, and would expect the courtesy of food and drink. What to do first?

"Cold . . . Water . . ."

The fire was nearly out and there was a chill in the room. For an absurd moment I almost apologized to Mama for the cold, then pulled myself together, and with an economy born of long familiarity rekindled the ashes, brought in the driest logs and set the largest cauldron on for hot water. With bright flames now illuminating the room, I checked the food. A large pie and a half should be enough, with some of the goat's-milk cheese and yesterday's loaf, set to crisp on the hearth. There were just enough bowls and platters to go round, but only two mugs; I could put milk into a flagon and what wine we had left into a jug and they could pass those round. Seating was a problem; the stools and Mama's chair would accomodate three, and perhaps two could perch on the table or the chest. The rest would have to stand.

The water was now finger-hot, and I turned to the most important task of all. Crossing to Mama's clothes chest I pulled out her best robe, the red one edged with coney fur, and her newest shift, the silk one with gold

ribbons at neck and sleeve, and the fine linen sheet that
would be her shroud.

The heat from the fire, which had me sweating like a
pig, had relaxed her muscles, so it was an easy enough
task to wash her, change the death-soiled sheets, pad all
orifices and dress her in her best. That done, I combed
and plaited her hair and arranged it in coils around her
head, but was distressed to see that the grey streaks
would show once I had the candles burning round the
bed. She would never forgive me for that, I thought,
then remembered my inks. A little smoothed across with
my fingers and no one would notice. . . .

I crumbled dried rosemary and lavender between the
folds of her dress for sweetness, then went outside and
burned the soiled sheets and the dress she had been
wearing when she died. Outside it was quite cool, the
sun saying nearer four than three, and the smoke from
the bonfire rising thin and straight: a slight frost tonight,
I thought. On the way back in I gathered some late
daisies and a few flowers of the yellow Mary's-gold, and
placed them in Mama's folded hands, then set the best
beeswax candles in the few holders we had around the
bed, ready to light once it grew dark.

I looked at her once more, to see all was as she would
have wished and to my amazement saw that Death had
given her back her youth. Gone were the frown lines,
the pinched mouth, the wrinkles at the corners of her
eyes. She looked as though she were sleeping, her face
calm and smooth, and the candle I held flickered as
though she were smiling. She was so beautiful I wanted
to cry again—

"Enough! Late . . . Tidy up. Wash and change . . ."

I heeded the voice, so like hers—but it couldn't be,
could it?—and a half-hour later or so I had swept out
and tidied, washed myself in the rest of the water, including my hair and my filthy clothes, hanging out the latter
to dry over the hedge by the chicken run, and had
changed into my other shift and my winter dress. Mama
would be proud of my industriousness, I thought. But
there was no time for further tears, for I could hear the

tramp of feet down the lane. My mother's clients come
to pay their last respects.

Suddenly the room, comfortably roomy for Mama and
me, had shrunk to a hulk and shuffle of too many bodies,
with scarce space to move. The only part they avoided
was the bed.

They had all come: mayor, miller, clerk, butcher, tailor,
forester, carpenter, thatcher, basket-maker, apothecary;
all at one time my mother's regular customers. The new
priest was the only odd one out. In spite of their common
interest I noticed how they avoided looking at one
another. At last, after much coughing, scratching and
picking of noses, the mayor stepped forward and everything went as quiet as if someone had shut a door.

"Ah, hmmm, yes. This is a sad occasion, very sad." He
shook his head solemnly, and the rest of them did likewise or nodded as they thought fit. "We meet here to
mourn the sudden passing of someone who, er, someone
who was . . ."

"With whom we shared a common interest?" suggested the clerk.

"Yes, yes of course. Very neatly put. . . . As I was saying, Mistress Margaret here—"

"Margaret? Isabella," said the miller.

"Not Isabella," said the butcher. "Susan."

"Elizabeth," said the clerk. "Or Bess for short."

"I thought she was Alice," said the tailor.

"Maude, for sure . . ."

"No, Ellen—"

"I'm sure she said Mary—"

"Katherine!"

"Sukey . . ."

I stared at them in bewilderment. It didn't seem as
though they were talking about her at all: how could she
possibly be ten different people? Then, like an echo,
came my mother's voice: "In my position I have to be
all things to all men, daughter. . . ."

The mayor turned to me. "What was your mother's
real name?"

I shrugged my shoulders helplessly. "I never asked her. To me she was just—just Mama." I would *not* cry....

"Well," said the priest snappily, "You will have to decide on something if I am to bury her tomorrow morning. At first light, you said?"

They had obviously been discussing it on the way here.

"It would be ... more discreet," said the mayor, lamely. "Less fuss the better, I say."

"Aye," said the butcher. "What's over, is over."

"What I want to know is," said the priest, "who's paying?"

They all looked at me. I shook my head. I knew there were a few coins for essentials in Mama's box, but not near enough to pay for a burial and Mass.

"I don't think she ever thought about dying," I said. This was true. Death had never been part of our conversations. She had been so full of life and living there had been no room for death. I thought about it for a moment more, then I knew what she would have said. "I believe she would have trusted you, all of you, to share her dying as you shared her living."

I could see they didn't like it, but there were grudging nods of assent.

"What about a sin-eater?" said the priest suddenly. "She died unshriven. Masses for a year and a day might do it, but ..."

More money. "There isn't one hereabouts," said the mayor worriedly. "I suppose if we could find someone willing we should have to find a few more coins, but—"

"I'll do it," I said. "She was my mother." I couldn't leave her in Purgatory for a year, even if I was scared to death of the burden. "What do I do?"

But no one seemed very sure, not even the priest. In the end he suggested I take a hunk of bread, place it on my mother's chest and pray for her sins to pass from one to the other. Then I had to eat the bread.

It near choked me, and once I had forced it down I was assailed by the most intolerable sense of burdening, as though I had been squashed head down in a small box after eating too much.

They watched me with interest.

"Is it working?" asked the priest.

"Yes," I gasped, and begged him for absolution.

"Excellent," said the priest, looking relieved. "We shall repair to the church, choose the burial site and you may confess your mother's sins and I shall absolve her."

It was cold inside the church for the sun was now gone and twilight shrouded the altar, mercifully hiding the mural of the Day of Judgment which, faded though it was, always gave me nightmares. To be sure, there were the righteous rising in their underwear to Heaven, but the unknown artist had had an inspired brush with the damned, their mouths open on silent screams as they tumbled towards the flames, poked and prodded by the demons of the Devil.

The priest led me through Mama's confession—it was very strange confessing unknown sins for someone else—and he told me to confess to absolutely everything, just in case. Some of those sins he prompted me with I had never even heard of.

"Now you may either say a thousand *Hail Marys* in expiation, or perhaps find it more convenient to make a small donation," he said hopefully.

As it happened I had the change from buying the salt still tied round my waist in my special purse-pocket, so he gave me a hurried full absolution to our mutual satisfaction. Immediately it seemed as though the dreadful heaviness left me, just like shucking off a heavy load of firewood after a long tramp home. Now Mama could ascend to Heaven happily with the rest of the righteous.

We came out into a dusky churchyard, and found the others grouped in the far corner against the wall.

"This'll do," said the mayor. Next to the rubbish dump. "It'll take less digging and is nicely screened from view. Why, you could even scratch the date of death on the wall behind. Pity she couldn't lie next to your father, girl, but of course his bones were tossed to the pigs long ago—"

"My *father*?" I could not believe what I was hearing.

My father had been driven away by jealous villagers and dared not return; my mother had told me so.

"Of course. Led us a merry chase, but we caught him about two mile into the forest, and—"

"She doesn't know," interrupted the miller, glancing at my face. "Happen her Ma told her something different." He looked at the others. "No point in bringing it up now."

I could feel something crumbling inside me, just like the hopeful dams I had built as a child across the stream, only to see them crumble with the first rains. I had cherished for years the vision of a handsome soldier-father forced to leave his only love, my beautiful mother, and now they were trying to say—

"Tell me!" I shrieked, the anger and bewilderment escaping me like air from a pricked bladder, surprising them and myself so much that we all jumped apart as though someone had just tossed a snake into our midst.

So they told me, in fits and starts: apologetically, belligerently, defiantly. At first it was just as Mama had related it; there had been fever in the village, the stranger had sought refuge at our cottage and they had enjoyed their secret idyll. Then everything had gone wrong. Houses left empty by fever deaths had been looted, and as they reasoned no one in the village could have been responsible, they had searched farther afield, and had found some of the bulkier objects hidden in a sack at the rear of our dwelling. My father had run; they had pursued him into the forest where a lucky arrow had brought him down. Although he was dead they had had a ceremonial hanging in the village, then had chopped him in pieces and thrown the pieces to the pigs.

So the man whose memory I had cherished, the father who my imagination had made taller, handsomer and braver than anyone else in the world, was nothing more than a common thief!

"I don't believe you, any of you! You're all lying, and just because Mama isn't here you're—you're—" I burst into tears. But I knew they were telling the truth; they had no reason to lie, not after all this time. But the anger and frustration would out, and I switched to another hurt. "And I won't have Mama buried next to the midden! She must have a proper plot, a proper marker, a decent service and committal, just as she deserves—"

"Now look here, girl," interrupted the butcher angrily. "Don't you realize we have to pay for all this? Now your Ma's dead you have nothing, are nothing. Of all the ungrateful hussies—"

"Easy, Seth," said the clerk. "She's upset. None of this is her fault. It's up to us to do the best for—for ... I'm sorry, girl, I don't think I remember your name."

"My name?"

"Yes," said the tailor. "Always just called you 'girl,' as your mother did."

There were nods, murmers of confirmation from the others.

"Well?" said the priest.

I stared at them all aghast. I could feel myself falling. . . .

"I haven't the faintest idea. . . ." I croaked, then everything went black.

CHAPTER
FOUR

They brought me round with hastily sprinkled font water.

I had never fainted before in my life and I felt stupid, embarrassed and slightly sick. Their faces swam above me like great moons, in the light from the miller's lantern. For a moment I could remember nothing, and then it came back like a knife-thrust: Mama was dead, my father a thief, and I had no name. In a way the last was the worst. Without an identity I was a blank piece of vellum, a discarded feather, the emptiness that is a hole in the ground. I felt that if I let go I should float up into the sky like smoke, and dissolve as easily. I was deathly frightened.

Then somebody had a good idea. "You must have been baptized." Of course, else would I not have been allowed to attend Mass.

They helped me to my feet and we all repaired to the vestry, where by the light of the lantern and the priest's candle, the fusty, dusty, mildewy parish records were dragged out of a chest.

"How old are you?"

But I couldn't be exact about that either, till the miller suggested the Year of the Great Fever, and there was much counting backwards on fingers and thumbs and at last the entry was found, in the old priest's fumbling, scratchy hand.

"Here we are. . . . Strange name to call anyone," said the present priest. Only the clerk, he and I could read, and I bent forward to follow his finger. There it was, between the death of one John Tyler and the marriage of Wat Wood and Megan Baker. The cramped letters danced in front of my eyes, but at last I spelled it out.

No date, but the previous entry was June, the latter July.

"Baptism of dorter to the Traveling woman: one Somerdai."

"Somerdai . . ." I tried it out on my tongue. "Summerday." And Mama had called herself one of the Travelers. All right, she had given me an outlandish name, but at least I now existed officially. And, according to the records, I was seventeen years old, and knew something more of Mama's origins. All at once I felt a hundred times better, and was able to invite them all back for the funeral meats almost as graciously as she would have done.

It did not take them long to demolish everything. I closed the shutters, made up the fire and lighted the candles around Mama; they threw our shadows like grotesques on the whitewashed walls and made it look as though Mama sighed, smiled and twitched in a natural sleep.

The mayor accepted the dregs of the wine jug, drained them and brushed the crumbs from his front. Clearing his throat, he addressed us all.

"I now declare this special meeting open. . . ."

What meeting?

"Having determined to settle this little matter as soon as may be, I think it is now time to for us to agree on our previously discussed course of action."

My! They had certainly been busy amongst themselves, either on the way here or in the churchyard. . . . But what "little matter"?

"Firstly, Summerhill, or whatever your name is—I

should like to thank you on behalf of us all for the refreshments." Everyone murmured their approval. "We have already agreed to attend to the burial of the—the lady, your mother, and to defray all costs." He cleared his throat again. "Now we come to the distribution of the assets. . . ."

"My hens," said the butcher.

"My goat," said the tailor.

"My bees," said the clerk.

"The clothes chest—"

"The hangings—"

And suddenly they were all shouting against each other, pointing at our belongings, even gesturing towards the padded quilt on which Mama lay and touching the gown she wore.

I was horrified, but as they quietened down it became obvious that everything I had thought we owned, Mama and I, belonged in some way or other to her clients. They were just loans. If I had ever thought about it at all, which I hadn't, I should have guessed that the finely carved bed, the elaborate hangings, some of the fine clothes, could not have been gifts, like the flour, meat and pulses.

Now the butcher was on his feet. He was the man I had always liked least of Mama's clients, not only because he sometimes tried to put his hands down my front.

"Comrades . . . Quiet! I know what we all have at stake here, but we cannot leave the new whore entirely without."

Surely they couldn't mean that I—

But the mayor took over, with an uneasy glance in my direction.

"Normally, of course, we could have left all this for a day or two until everything settled down," he said. "But under the circumstances—"

"With her losing her job and all—" said the butcher.

"—we shall have to make a quick decision," continued the mayor.

My heart gave a sudden lurch of thankfulness. They hadn't been thinking of me as a replacement after all.

But the mayor's next words hurt. "Normally we might have offered young Summer-Solstice here the job, as her mother's daughter, but under the circumstances I don't believe she would attract the same sort of custom. . . ."

"Oh, come on!" said the miller, always ready with a kind word. "She's not that bad! A nice smile, all her teeth, small hands and feet, a fine head of hair . . ." Even he couldn't think of anything else.

"Mama wished me to become a wife, not a whore," I said stiffly. Whores were special, but wives came in all shapes and sizes, so I had a better chance as the latter, especially with my learning and dowry—come to that, where was it? Mama had never said. And when I found the coins, how did I set about finding this elusive husband I had been promised? With winter coming on, it would be better to leave it until New Year. If what they had said about the furniture going to the next whore was true, the cottage would seem very bare. I had a few coins left of Mama's, and perhaps if they let me keep a couple of the hens and I could persuade the carpenter to knock me up a truckle bed, I could manage with what was laid aside. But I should have to buy some salted pork—

". . . so, if it is convenient, shall we say noon tomorrow?" asked the mayor. "Although your brothers are not here now, they will attend the interment in the morning, and your eldest brother let it be known his wife would not be averse to the dresses. . . ."

I had lost something in his speechifying, but that pinched-nosed sister-in-law of mine was not going to wear my mother's dresses, and I told him so.

"Why not? They're of no use to you. Your ma was tall and thin."

"I still would not like to see another in her dresses—"

"Nonsense! Why waste them? The new whore, Agnes-from-the-Inn, would fit into them nicely, too. No point in wasting them."

So that sandy-haired, big-bosomed wench was to be the next village whore! "No," I said.

"As she's getting everything else," said the butcher,

"including this cottage, why not chuck the dresses in as well? Not yours to dispose of, anyway."

"This place? But it's ours—mine, surely?"

The mayor shook his head. "Goes with the job. So, as I said a moment or two back, I can expect you out by midday tomorrow?"

"I can't! I've nowhere to go!" This just couldn't be happening! All in one day to lose my mother, the shreds of my father's reputation and also find I possessed a ridiculous name, then to be turned out into an unknown world with nothing to my name and nowhere to go—

I burst into tears; angry, snuffly, hurt, uncontrollable, ugly tears. Now Mama had always taught me that tears were a woman's finest weapon. She had also tried to teach me how to weep gently and affectingly, without reddening the eyes or screwing up the face, but all my tears produced were embarrassment, red faces and a rush for the door, just as if I had been found with plague spots.

"Back at dawn," called out the mayor. "We'll bring a hurdle for the body. . . ."

The priest was the last to leave. "Not even one coin for the Masses?" I shook my head.

I heard their footsteps retreating, then one set returning. The miller poked his head round the door.

"Just wanted to say—will miss your Ma. She was a lady. Sorry I can't take you in like your brother, but the wife wouldn't stand for it." He turned to go, then stopped. "Thought you might like to know; years after your dad—died—someone else confessed to planting those stolen goods. Said he was jealous. Dead and gone, now . . . Hey there: no more tears! Could never abide to see a lass cry. Here, there's a couple of coins for your journey. And don't worry, you'll do fine. I'll see the grave's kept nice." He sidled out through the door. "Sorry I can't do more, but you know how it is. . . ."

"Yes," I said. "I know how it is. . . ."

Alone, I sank to my knees beside the dying fire, my mind a muddle. Shock and grief had filled my mind to such an extent I was incapable of thinking clearly. All I wanted was for Mama to be back to tell me what to do, for I felt an itching between my shoulder blades that told me I had forgotten something, and could not rest till it was seen to.

A log crashed in the hearth and I started up. Mustn't let the fire die down, tonight of all nights—But why? Of course: tonight was All Hallows' Eve, the eve of Samhain. Tonight was the night when the unshriven dead rode the skies with the witches and warlocks and the Court of Faery roamed the earth. . . . Tonight was the night that, every year, Mama and I closed and locked the shutters and doors early, stoked up the fire and roasted chestnuts and melted cheese over toasted bread, thumbing our noses at those spirits who moaned and cursed outside, wanting to take our places and live again. But it was the fire that kept them away, so Mama said, that and the songs we sang: "There is a time for everything," or "After Winter cometh Spring," and "Curst be all who ride abroad this night."

I rushed outside and brought in all the wood I could gather. Why bother to save any for the new whore? Let her seek her own. And she had no daughter to fetch and carry as Mama had done: they would soon be sick of her. I even emptied the lean-to of our emergency supply, running back and forth under an uneasy moon, till the room was overflowing with faggots and logs. Tonight we would have the biggest blaze ever, Mama and I.

By the time I had finished I was quite light-headed, even addressing the still figure on the bed. "There you are, Mama! Enough to set the chimney alight!"

"And everything else . . ." came a voice in my head. "Everything must go with me. . . . Nothing left."

Was that what she wanted? Everything burned? But wasn't that what her people, the Travelers, did? Hadn't she told me once that when a chief died his van was piled with his belongings, his dogs and horses were sacrificed and all consumed in a great pyre? Then if that was what she wanted, that was what she should have.

I approached the bed again. "You shall have a bonfire

fit for a queen," I told the silent figure. "They shall not
have your bed, your dresses, your chair; I promise."

"Open ... Fly ..."

I frowned; what did that little voice mean: *Fly*? What
was to fly? There was a moth doing a crazy dance round
one of the guttering candles and I moved my hand to
bat it away, upon which it swerved over my head and
made for the shuttered window, beating frantically
against the wood. Then I understood.

"Sorry, Mama ..."

Ceremoniously I flung back the shutters onto the
night, then wedged open the door. Coming back to the
bed I blew out the candles, one by one, then knelt to
pray. I prayed for a safe journey for my mother's soul,
reminding God that her sins were all absolved. Then I
leaned over for the last time and kissed her brow.

"All ready, Mama. Go with God." As I did so it seemed
a little breeze stirred the hangings, and I distinctly felt
a rap on my head—the sort Mama used to make with
her knuckles when I had completed a task after a
reminder. A moment later the door crashed shut. She
had gone.

I refastened door and window, then bethought myself
of my own arrangements. If I were to be away from here
before they discovered what I had done, then I must
pack up all I needed for my journey quickly. Clothes,
food, utensils, blanket, money ... Money. Where had
Mama put my dowry? Frantically I searched all the
places it could be and came up with nothing. It must be
somewhere; Mama wouldn't have made it up. I wished
it was light again, for the cottage was full of shadows and
every corner looked like a potential hiding place. I must
find it, I must! I couldn't face the wide world with the
few coins left in Mama's box and the couple the miller
had left me.

Opening Mama's box, however, discovered her bracelets, necklet and brooches, and the horn ring my father
had left behind. I took them over to the bed, fastened
the brooch and necklet, and then tried to force the ring
onto her fingers, one after the other, but it wouldn't go:

her fingers were too fat. Strange, she had long, slim fingers. I put on the bracelets, deciding I would take the ring with me, wearing it on a string round my neck. It might bring me luck, I thought, and without thinking slipped it onto the middle finger of my right hand, while I bent forward to adjust the bracelets on Mama's wrists to their best advantage.

As I placed her hands once more crossed upon her breast, I noticed something strange; although I was certain I had washed her thoroughly there was what looked like a sooty residue caught under the fingernails of her right hand—All at once I knew where the dowry would be. Rushing over to the fireplace I felt high up in the chimney, first to one side, then the other. At first all I got were scorched fingers and a fall of soot, but at last on the left-hand side my scrabblings found a ledge, and on the ledge a bag of sorts, which I snatched out to drop on the floor with a clink and chink of coin.

I fell to my knees on the hearth and gazed with excitement at the pile of coins that had burst from the split leather pouch that had contained them. I had never seen so much money in my life! And all the coins looked like either silver or gold. . . . All in all, a fortune. Hastily wiping my sooty fingers I began to examine them, one by one. All but two were strange to me, the inscriptions and symbols utterly alien. A scrap of singed paper fluttered to the floor. It was so brittle with age and heat it crumbled to pieces in my fingers even as I read it: "Thomas Fletcher, Mercernairy, his monnaies." There followed a list I could not follow, then "Ayti coyns in all."

So my father had been named, and could write, after a fashion! That surely was where I had got my learning skills. But eighty coins? There were less than half, surely, for even with the confirmation of my tally sticks there were forty-seven missing. I glanced over to the bed where my mother lay in all her finery, extra dresses and shifts spread around her, and my eyes filled with tears, remembering the silver coins and a couple of gold that had purchased them. At the time I had wondered where they had come from, and now I knew. But how was I to know that my father hadn't wished it so? After all, she had been his beloved, and I shouldn't grudge a single coin. Before me lay enough still for a fair dowry, even if the coins would have to be weighed for their metal content only, as they were foreign. But there still a couple of our own coinage: I could manage for a while on those.

Before my eyes the piece of paper crumbled into ash, the pouch also, as if they had been just waiting for me to find them and were now dead like my mother. Carefully I packed the coins inside my waistband purse, determined as soon as possible to make them a separate hiding place.

As I tucked them away I noticed for the first time the ring upon my finger. I couldn't remember putting it there, and absent-mindedly tried to pull it off to tie round my neck, as I had originally intended. But it wouldn't come. There it was, settled snug on my finger as if it was part of the very skin. . . . Suddenly I tingled all over and everything became brighter and sharper, as if a veil had been pulled away.

As if a stranger I saw all the cracks in the wall, the shabbiness of the room; I heard the crackle of the fire, the creak of furniture as if were talking to me; for the first time smelled the sweetish-sickly odor of decay coming from the bed so strongly I had to pinch my nostrils and swallow hard. There was a taste of soot and ashes in my mouth where I had licked my fingers and the hearth beneath my hands was rough with grit and dust.

But there was something else as well. Not exactly hope, that was too strong a word, but a sort of energy I had not known I possessed. Something enforced the knowledge that I was alone for the first time in my life, but also that I would manage somehow or other, that I wasn't a complete idiot, that life held more than I had expected.

I rose to my feet. There were things to be done and as my inside time clock told it was near midnight, the sooner the better. Outside, when I went to check that the goat and chickens would be safe, the moon was riding clear of cloud, the stars were bright and a crispness to the air confirmed frost.

I loaded up the sledge I used for wood with what I thought necessary, did a last check, then piled wood around the bed, sprinkling it with oil the better to burn. I opened the shutters for a draught and left the door open. That done I made a last check, then gazed around the cottage that had been my home, expecting nostalgia.

Nothing. Nothing at all.

It was just a place that two people had lived in, an empty shell with now no personality left. A room, nothing more, as empty of life as the still figure on the bed, the living and memory seeping from it as surely as the body became cold in death. No, there was nothing for me here now.

"Goodbye, Mama," I said, and threw a lighted brand from the fire towards the bed.

Part II

SUMMER'S JOURNEY

CHAPTER
FIVE

Someone had opened both shutters and door, and pulled back the bedclothes; the light was shining in my eyes and I was freezing—

I came to with a start. I was in a forest, so had I fallen asleep while collecting wood? Realization came as bitter as the early morning taste in my mouth, as I struggled out of the blanket I had wrapped myself in.

I was in the woods somewhere between the village and the High Road, I was alone, and I was hungry and needed to relieve myself. First things first, and as I squatted down I glanced around the little dell in which I had hidden myself the night before. Last night's frost still silvered the grasses and ferns, but the rising sun promised a warm day. Already a cloud of midges danced above my head and a breeze stirred the almost leafless trees. A pouch-cheeked squirrel darted across the glade ahead, and I could hear the warning chink of a blackbird as I scrambled to my feet. Otherwise everything was quiet, except for the tinkle of a stream away to my right.

So, I hadn't been followed. So far . . .

I cringed when I remembered my escape of the night before. Once I had been sure the cottage was blazing merrily, the flames lighting up the night sky until I feared the conflagration would be spotted in the village, I had set off down the path, dragging the loaded wood sledge behind me. Sighting the way had been easy, with the fire behind and the moon above, so I had not needed my lantern. But where had my caution, my fear of the night, gone? As I remembered it I had strode through the village as if it were a midsummer day, singing some crazy song I couldn't now remember, almost asking those within doors to come out and discover the suddenly-gone-mad girl who had made the cottage a funeral pyre for both her mama and all those goods that now belonged to someone else, and who was now disregarding the terror of All Hallows' night and marching down the road with the demons at her heels and the witches swooping around her head.

But no one had appeared. Doors remained bolted and barred, shutters firmly closed. Those who had heard my wild passage had probably hid beneath the bedclothes, crossed themselves and been convinced that at last all their fears walked abroad in ghastly form and that to look on such would snatch what little wits they had away forever. And in the morning, when they saw what remained of the cottage, with luck they might think it had all been a ghastly accident, and that I had been immolated with Mama. Of course, once the embers had cooled down and they could rake through the ashes they would probably realize what I had done and make some sort of search for me—but by that time I hoped to be well away beyond their reach.

My stomach gave a great growling lurch, reminding me it had had nothing since I couldn't remember when. I didn't remember eating a thing last night, so those cheese pasties must have been the last thing to comfort it. I scrabbled among the wreck of my belongings on the sledge—it had tipped over twice last night and scattered everything—and at last found twice-baked bread, cheese and a slice of cold bacon. Washing it down with water from my flask, I refilled the same from the stream nearby, determined next to sort out the things I had brought. But I was still hungry. I couldn't think straight

without something else in my stomach. After all, to someone who was used to breaking her fast with gruel, goat's
milk, bread and cheese, ham, an egg or two and honey
cakes, this morning's scraps were more of an aggravation
than a satisfaction.

Searching among the debris I found a heap of honey
cakes I had forgotten about. I gobbled down one, two,
three.... That was enough; I should have to go easy. I
couldn't be sure when I would come upon the next village. Well, perhaps just one more: that would leave an
even number—easier to count.

Feeling much better, the stiffness of the night nearly
gone, I spread out my belongings on the grass. The
sledge looked the worse for wear; too late I remembered
it was due to be renewed as soon as possible: the carpenter had promised to make new runners. I should just
have to hope it would carry my belongings as far as the
High Road, then I would have to think again. Even now,
there must be at least something I could leave behind
to lighten the load.

An axe for chopping wood: I couldn't do without that.
Tinder, flint and kindling, also necessary. Lantern, candles, couldn't do without those either. The smallest
cooking pot, with a lid that would double as a griddle,
a ladle, large knife and small one, spoon, two bowls and
a mug. Essentials. Water flask, small jug, blanket, rope,
couldn't do without those, either.

Clothes? I was wearing as much as I could, but surely
I still needed the two spare shifts, ditto drawers and
stockings? My father's comfortable green cloak, pattens
for the wet, clothes for my monthly flow, comb, needles,
thread and strips of leather for mending clothes and
shoes. Packets of dried herbs and spices, seeds for planting when I finally reached my destination—onion, garlic,
chive, rosemary, dill, bay, thyme, sage, turnip, marjo-
ram—and a small pestle and mortar.

Which brought me to the food. A small sack of flour—
bread to eat if nothing else—a crock of salt, bottle of oil,
pot of honey, jar of fat, pack of oats. And for ready
consumption two cheeses, a hunk of bacon, two slices of

smoked ham, some dried fish, two loaves and twelve honey cakes.

Which left my writing materials, tally sticks and the Boke. Those came with me if nothing else did.

I surveyed the articles laid out on the grass with dismay. There was nothing, absolutely nothing, I could leave behind. Somehow or other I would have to pack them better, and trust the sledge would at least get me as far as the High Road. Then perhaps I could find a lift, or could repair the runners well enough to get me to a village.

The sun was already clear of the trees: I had better get moving. Setting to work I found the packing much easier and the result neater and better balanced, especially when I utilized one of the double panniers I had also dragged along for the eatables, salt and flour, and I reckoned I should get along much faster now.

Perhaps the pannier would be better balanced if I distributed the food more evenly: it must be ten o'clock, and I should travel better with a nibble of something in my stomach. That bread was already stale, so if I ate a crust and a slice of cheese—or two . . .

"Proper little piggy, ain't you?" said a voice.

I whirled around on my knees, sure I had been discovered. But there was no one in sight, the forest was in the same state of suspended alert and there was no sound of footsteps. I decided I must be light-headed and had imagined it. I took another bite of cheese, and—

"Some of us ain't eaten for two days," said the same voice. "Chuck us a bit of rind, and I'll go away. . . ."

Dear God! It must be one of the Little People, of which I had heard from Mama. I crossed myself hastily. What had she said about Them? Mischievous, usually only out at night, not to be crossed lightly. With shaking fingers I cut a piece of rind and threw it as far as I could, then hid my eyes, remembering that They don't like to be looked at either.

"Mmm, not bad at all," said the voice again. A very uneducated voice, I thought, then wondered if They could read minds. "How's about a bite of crust, while we're at it?"

Obediently I threw the crust, and this time there were distinct crunching noises, then silence. I decided I could risk a peep. Surely It had gone. . . .

At first I thought It was an Imp, a black Imp, then I saw that Whatever-it-was had taken the form of a dog. At least I think it was meant to be a dog. I shut my eyes again.

"Garn! I ain't that bad-lookin', surely?"

"Of course not," I said, still with my eyes shut tight. Heaven knows what would happen if I looked at it straight in the eye. "If—if there is nothing else, may I please go my way?"

"I ain't stoppin' you," said the Thing. "Though I thought as how you might like a bit of company, like."

"No thanks," I said hastily. "I'm fine, thanks."

"Pity," said the Thing. "Could be a lot of use to you, I could. Fetch and carry, spot out the way ahead, general guide, guard dog . . ."

"Guard dog?" I said, suddenly suspicious. "You did say 'dog'?"

" 'Course. Don' look like a cat, do I?"

I scrambled to my feet and stared at the apparition. "I've seen you before somewhere. . . ."

"Course you have, in the village; seen you a coupla times, too."

I stared across the diplomatic space that still separated us. Of course he was a dog, how had I ever thought otherwise? But dogs don't talk. Especially this one. He resembled nothing so much as a scrap of rug you might leave outside the door to wipe your feet upon. He was like a furry sausage, a black and grey and brown sausage. One ear was up, one down; there was a tail of sorts and presumably mouth and eyes hidden under the tangle of hair at the front. The nose was there and underneath four paws, big ones like paddles, but set under the short-est set of legs imaginable. I remembered now where I had seen him before: chased down the village street by the butcher, those stumpy legs going like a demented centipede.

All right, he wasn't a figment of my imagination and he wasn't one of the Little People, but there was still something wrong. Dogs don't *talk*. . . .

"Where you goin' then?"

"To—to seek a new home. My mother died yesterday."

"Makes two of us—lookin' for somewhere, that is. Never had a place to set down me bum permanent-like. Folks is wary of strays."

Dogs don't talk. . . .

All right, if he wasn't the Devil himself—which was just possible—and he wasn't of Faery stock, then this must be magic. A very powerful magic, too. Surreptitiously I first crossed myself again, then made the secular anti-witch sign, the first two fingers of my hand forked. Nothing happened; he still sat there, but now he indulged in a fury of scratching and nipping, then hoofed out both ears with a dreadful, dry, rattling sound.

"Little buggers lively 's mornin'. . . . Tell you what: I'll just come with you as far as the road—that's where you're headed, ain't it? Keep each other company, like."

"No . . . Yes, I don't know. . . ." I said helplessly.

DOGS DON'T TALK!

"Aw, c'mon! What harm can it do? You and I will get along real well, I know we will. 'Tween us we'll make a good team—"

The scream would out. It had been sitting there at the bottom of my throat like a gigantic belch and I could hold it back no longer. It escaped like the tuning wail from a set of bagpipes, only ten times as loud.

"Go away, go away, go away! I can't stand it anymore! Dogs don't talk, *dogs don't talk*, DOGS DON'T TALK!"

And I ran away across the glade, screaming like a banshee, until there was a *thud!* in the middle of my back and I fell face down in a heap of leaves, all the wind knocked out of me.

"Shurrup a minute, will you? Want the whole world to hear? Got hold of the wrong end of the stick, you has. Just sit up nice and quiet-like, and I'll explain. . . ."

I did as I was told, emptying my mouth of leaves and pulling twigs from my hair. The dog sat about six feet away, his head on one side. Close to he was even tattier. I felt like a feather mattress that has been beaten into an entirely different shape.

"Now then you says as how dogs don't talk. Well o' course they does. All the time. Mostly to each other, 'cos you 'umans don't bother to listen. You expects us to learn how you speak, but when we tries you tells us to shut up. Ain't that so?"

I nodded. I had had nothing to do with animals, except the goat, hens and bees—Mama wouldn't have a dog or cat in the house: she said they were messy, full of disease, and took up too much space. Some of the dogs in the village were used for hunting, others as guards, a couple as children's pets, but I had never heard anything from their owners save a sharp word of command, though I had seen kicks and cuffs in plenty. Certainly no one talked to them.

"We don' only talk, we sings, too. P'raps you heard us sometimes o' nights, when the moon is full and the world smells of the chase and we can hear the 'Ounds o' 'Eaven at the 'eels of the 'Unter?"

Indeed I had. Some nights it seemed that the dogs of the village never slept, and even where we lived we could hear the howling and baying and yelping.

"Lovely songs they are too," he said. " 'Anded down from sire to dam, from bitch to pup. . . ."

"But why," I said carefully, "can I now understand what you say?"

"Now, I could spin you a yarn as fine as silk and tell you as 'ow I was the magickest dog in the 'ole wide world, and you'd believe me. For a while, that is, till you found as you could talk with other animals, too. No, I won't tell you no lies, 'cos I believe we got business together, you and I—" He nipped so quickly at whatever was biting him that I jumped. "Got the little bugger. . . . Truth is, lady, that why I can talk to you and you to me is all on account of that there bit o' Unicorn you carries round with you." And he scratched at his left ear, the floppy one, till it rattled like dry beans in a near-empty jar.

I was lost. "Bit of a *Unicorn?*" Unicorns were gone, long ago.

"The ring you wear, you great puddin'! That what you got on that finger of yours. Bit of 'orn off'n a Unicorn, that is. Now you can understand what all the creatures say if'n you pays a bit of attention. Din' you know what you got?"

I sat looking at the curl of horn on my finger in bemusement. It still looked like nothing more than a large nail-paring, almost transparent. I tried to pull it off but it wouldn't budge. Indeed, it now felt like part of my skin. I tried again. "Ouch!"

"Once it's on, it's on," said the dog. "Only come off if'n you don' need it no more, or don' deserve it. Very rare, these days. . . . Come by it legal?"

I nodded, remembering my mother telling me how my father had worn it round his neck. So perhaps he hadn't needed it anymore—or hadn't deserved it. But I wouldn't think about that. Nor that it wouldn't fit my mother. But why me? Perhaps I needed it more than them, specially now I was on my own. Indeed, it had a comforting feel, like something I had been looking for for a long time and had found at last.

"Well," said the dog. "We'd best be goin'. Day ain't gettin' any younger, and we've a ways to travel to the Road."

"I'm not sure I want . . . What I mean, is . . ." However I said it, it was going to sound ungracious, but I had no intention of sharing my dwindling rations with a smelly stray dog with an appetite even bigger than mine.

"Come on, now: you *needs* me. I can be your eyes and ears, I can. Best thief for fifty mile. Nab you a bit o' grub any time; never go 'ungry with me around. 'Sides, I'll be comp'ny, someone to talk to. Nighttimes I'll keep watch, so's you can sleep easy. No one creeps up on me, I can tell you!" He put his head on one side, in what I supposed he thought was an engaging manner. "What d'you say? Give us a trial. We can always part comp'ny if'n it don' work. . . ."

Some of what he said made sense, if he stuck to what he said. And I wouldn't really be any worse off, unless he decamped with all the food. He made it sound, too, as if all the advantages were on my side.

"And just what do you get out of it?"

He hung his head, and I could scarcely hear what he was saying. "P'raps I'm tired o' bein' on me own. P'raps, just for once, I should like to belong. Never had a 'ome, nor one I could call boss." He looked up, and there was a sort of defiant guilt in the one eye I could see. He shook his head as if to free it of water. "Got me whinging like a sentimental pup, you has. C'mon, let's get started; with all that fat you're carryin' it'll take us twice as long. . . . Now what's the matter?"

Just exactly what he had said: that was the matter. The words were carelessly cruel but none the less accurate. He had put into words a fact that everyone—me, my mother, her clients—all knew but never mentioned. The children in the village shouted it out often enough, one of the reasons I hated shopping there, but I could always pretend they were just being malicious. That was one of the reasons the mayor last night would not have accepted me as Mama's replacement; the reason the kind miller had run out of compliments past hair, smile, teeth and the size of my hands and feet.

The fact was I was fat. Not fat, obese. No, admit it: gross. I was a huge lump of grease, wobbling from foot to foot like ill-set aspic. I couldn't see my feet for my stomach, hadn't seen them for years; I had to roll myself in and out of bed, was unable to rise from the floor without first going on hands and knees and grabbing bedpost or chair. I couldn't climb the slightest rise without panting like a heat-hit dog; had lost count of my chins and got sores on my thighs with the flesh rubbing together.

And I had been unable to stop eating, which made it worse. Surprisingly Mama had made no attempt to stop me: she had even encouraged my consumption of honey

cakes, fresh bread and cream after that time I had asked
her about a prospective husband—

"Missin' your Ma, eh?" said the dog sympathetically.
"Understand how you feels; felt the same myself once
. . . Are you all right, then?"

We had struggled on for perhaps another half mile
when the dog stopped suddenly, his good ear cocked.

"Shurrup, and listen."

Gratefully I put down my burdens. I could hear nothing. Perhaps a kind of rustling and stamping far ahead,
a sort of cry . . .

The dog was off through the undergrowth like a flash,
his legs a blur of movement. He was gone what seemed
like hours, but could only have been a matter of minutes,
and arrived back literally dancing with impatience.
"C'mon, c'mon! I got us transport!"

"A—a cart? Another sledge?"

"Nah! The real thin'! I got us a 'orse!"

CHAPTER
SIX

"That's—that's a horse? You're joking!"

A creature with four legs, sure, head and tail in the right place but the mess in between—was a mess. From what I could see, shading my eyes against the sun, it was swaybacked, gaunt, hollow-necked, filthy dirty and with a hopelessly matted mane and tail.

"Sure it's a 'orse. Got all the essentials. Needs a bit of a wash and brush-up, p'raps. . . ."

It would need more than that. As I walked cautiously forward, fearing it might run at sight of us, I saw that it wasn't going anywhere. It had got itself hopelessly entangled in the undergrowth by bridle, tail, hoof and the remains of a slashed girth and saddlebags that had ended up under its stomach. Its eyes widened with alarm as we approached and it made a token struggle against the bonds that held it, only to become more enmeshed than ever.

I halted a few feet away and spoke soothingly, using the words I had heard the villagers use to their work-horses, for I had never had cause to deal with one before and wasn't quite sure how to begin. The horse showed the whites of its eyes, as well as it could for the sticky tendrils of bindweed that clung to mane and ears.

"Speak to it nicely," said the dog. "Just like you would to me."

"You mean—it can understand me?"

"O-mi-Gawd!" he said. "Din' I tell you about the ring? 'Course it understands, but it's a bit scared right now and may not listen. Nice and easy, now." He walked nearer. "Now stand still, 'Orse, and 'er ladyship 'ere will see to you. . . ."

"Get away, get away! I'll kick you to death—"

"You an' 'oose army?"

I had understood this plainly enough, so I walked up to the horse more confidently and stretched out my hand. It made a halfhearted snap, but seemed quieter, though it still trembled till the branches and twigs which held it fast shook like wind-troubled water.

"Look," I said, "at my finger. I wear the ring of the Unicorn and that means we can understand each other. All I want to do is help. If I release you, will you promise not to run away till we have talked?"

It looked at the ring, at my face, and back at the ring. The shivering stopped, and I gathered it agreed, though I heard nothing definite.

It took a long time, and I was sweating as much as the horse by the time it was released and stood free. I picked away the last of the bramble and bindweed, and tried to comb out the worst tangles from mane and tail with my fingers. Standing free it didn't look much better. There was a long gash across its rump where someone had tried to slash the girths that held the now-empty saddlebags, but these had only loosened, not broken. I slid them up from under the belly and restrapped them.

"There, that's better. . . .Stand still a moment and I'll put some salve on the cut and the graze on your shoulder." In my belongings, dragged along behind as I followed the dog to his " 'orse," was a pot of one of the apothecary's favorite healing balms, a mixture of spiderwebs, dock-leaf juice and boar's grease. I smeared some gently on the broken hide, and found another gash on one hock, which I treated the same way.

"There," I said, standing back. "Near as good as new. . . ."

"I thank you, bearer of the Ring," said the horse. It had a soft, gentle voice, quite unlike the dog's raucous voice. "I am in your debt—"

"Then you can help us carry 'er things," said the dog, who had been remarkably quiet during the last half hour or so, not surprising when I found he was chewing on the rest of the cheese I hadn't packed well enough.

"Thief!"

"There was ants on it . . . All right, all right! Won't do it again. Well, what about it, 'orse? Gonna 'elp?"

The horse glanced from one to the other of us. "I don't know. . . ."

"Of course I can't ask you to help if you belong to someone," I said. "That would be stealing. Is your master hereabouts?"

"All gone, all gone . . ." It started shivering again. "I ran away."

Obviously some disaster. "Calm down! Well, if you don't belong to anyone, what did you plan on doing, boy?"

I was interrupted by a loud snigger from the dog. "Blind as a bat, you is! 'E's a she. . . ."

I felt as though I had been caught in a thicket with my drawers down, and apologized profusely.

"My name is Mistral," said the horse, "and among my own people I am a princess. I wish to go back to where I came from, of course."

Anything less like a princess of anything I had yet to see, but I hadn't had much experience of horses. "And where was that?"

The horse hung her head. "That I do not know. They stole my mother when she had me at her side, and would not leave me to escape. She told me of our people, of how we lived, and of my inheritance. But she died, they killed her with overwork, and I was sold as a packhorse. That was a year, two, ago. All I want now is to find my way back to my people. . . ."

"And you have no idea where that is?"

"No, except that south and west feels right."

"Well," said the dog, "if'n you goes on your own you could be picked up by anyone; best you can get from that is 'eavier burdens or a knock on the 'ead for the glue in your bones and a tough stew or two. Then there's wolves if'n you're thinkin' o' goin' the long way round. Now we offers you a bit o' protection-like, a step or two in the right direction, reg'lar food and all in exchange for carryin' a light load for this lady. What d'you say?"

"And you go south, south and west?"

The dog must have seen my mouth open to say we had decided nothing like that, for he jumped in before I could say anything. " 'Course we is! With winter comin' on, 'oo'd be idiot enough to go north? North there is snow, west there is storms, east there is icy winds, so south we goes. Right, lady?"

Weakly I nodded. Put like that it seemed like the only road to take.

"Right," I said. "And—and if you agree to come with us, then I will care for you as best I can and try and put you on the right road for your home. Is that fair?"

"Without you I should probably have starved to death, or worse," said Mistral. "I accept. And now, perhaps, we should load up. The sun starts to go down."

Indeed it was well past its zenith. Hastily I started to pack our belongings on the horse, only to be brought up short by her patient explanation of weight distribution, top-heavy loads, etc., so the light was already reddening as we set off. Even then she seemed curiously reluctant to go the way I wanted, the way the dog assured me led straight to the High Road.

"We'll have to go past *there*," she said. "*There*, where it happened."

"Where what happened?"

"Yesterday . . . sun-downing. Men, horses, swords. Panic, fighting, blood . . . No, I can't go that way again!"

"Windy," muttered the dog.

"They came out of the trees, the sun behind them. Couldn't see . . . Noise and pain. I ran this way. . . ."

Indeed I could see we were now following the road she

must have taken: branches broken, shrubs torn by her wild progress, grass trampled and leaves scattered.

"Look," I said. "Whatever happened, happened yesterday. It sounds as though it was an ambush, but they will all have gone by now. It's perfectly safe, I promise. . . . Go forward, dog, and reconnoiter."

"You what?"

I explained, and he ran on ahead. The ground started to slope downwards towards a little dell and Mistral was breathing anxiously.

"Down there . . ." she whispered.

The dog came running back, his tail between his legs. "You ain't goin' to like this, lady: 'old your nose. . . .'"

But I could already smell the stench of death, and hear a great buzzing of flies, the flap of carrion crow. There were four of them, lying sprawled in the random carelessness of sudden death, naked except for their braies. Their eyes had already gone, and the crows rose heavily gorged, the men's wounds torn still further by cruel beaks. I shouted and ran at the birds till they flapped to the nearest tree; they would be back, and there was nothing I could do about the clouds of flies, the ants, the beetles. I moved among the corpses, holding my nose, but there was nothing to say who they were, where they had come from, save a scrap of torn pennant under one twisted leg—

My heart gave a sudden, sickening lurch. Staring at the scrap of silk I suddenly recalled what I had completely forgotten until this moment: a tall, beautiful knight on a huge horse, who had smiled a heart-catching smile and called me "pretty." So much had happened since that encounter that he had not crossed my mind again—until this bitter moment. And I had sent him down this road. . . . No, no, it couldn't be! Life couldn't be that cruel!

Frantically I ran among the corpses in the dell, no longer squeamish, turning the lolling heads from side to side, seeking my knight. One head, already severed from the body, came easily to my hand, and I was left holding something that was shaped and heavy as a cabbage, but crawling with maggots. . . .

He wasn't there, he wasn't there! I ran up from the dell, farther into the forest, but there was no other stink of death, nor flies, nor carrion. I ran back to the horse, Mistral.

"What happened to him, where is he? Where is your master, Sir—Sir . . ." But I had forgotten his name.

"Who? What man?"

"He was a knight and rode a black horse—you must remember!"

"They killed the men and took the horses and the baggage. I ran away. That's all I know."

"All of them?"

"I don't know. I only saw my corner of it."

Maybe they had taken him for ransom. Perhaps they had ridden him away into the forest on his fine black horse, to bargain with his folks for far more than the horses and baggage they had stolen—I held the tattered piece of blue silk in my hand and prayed for his safety.

The dog nudged my knee. "Better find a place to kip for the night soon: near sundown."

I gestured towards the bodies. "We can't just leave them like this. . . ."

"You gotta spade and a coupla hours? No. Don't worry 'bout them. This track is used by those in the village; they'll deal with the remains. Bury them the way you 'umans do things. To my way o' thinkin', better leave bodies to the birds and the foxes to pick clean."

I muttered a prayer, crossed myself. "Right: lead on, dog."

About a half-mile farther along, as it grew too dark to see underfoot and my feet felt swollen to twice their usual size with the unaccustomed walking, the trees suddenly thinned and we found ourselves at the top of a steep bank. The moon rode out from behind some scummy clouds and there beneath us was a luminous strip of roadway, wide enough for six horsemen to ride abreast.

"Is that it?"

"Well, it's a road," said the dog. "Give or take . . ."

"It runs north/south," said Mistral.

"Come on, then," and in my eagerness I started to slide down the bank towards the shining expanse.

"Not so fast, lady," said the dog behind me. "You doesn't travel a road like this at night—"

"Scared?" and I slid down to the bottom, giving my right ankle a nasty jar, but determined to continue our journey now we had found what we were looking for.

"—'cos it's too dark to see," continued the dog, as the moon disappeared again.

"Neither do you travel alone," said Mistral. "There is safety in numbers. Look what happened to me."

A night-jar churred above my head and I lost one of my shoes in the scramble back. The dog retrieved it for me, all slathery from his mouth.

Scrabbling around in the dark, for I was now afraid of the risk of a lantern, I found the ham and the rest of the honey cakes, sharing a third, two-thirds with the dog. Afterwards, snugged down in my blanket, I listened to Mistral cropping the grass, sounding in the night like the tearing of strips of linen, and felt strangely comforted by the proximity of the two animals, even though the promised guard-dog, alert to every danger, the one who had promised to stay awake so I could sleep easy, was snoring heavily long before I closed my eyes.

I woke early and now that we had reached the road I was eager to be on my way. Not only impatience but also the knowledge that we were still within a half-day's travel of the village by foot, and those on horseback could travel much faster. I had no intention of being called to account for burning down the cottage and everything in it, and at mention of the villagers' possible vengeance the dog, too, looked thoughtful, then volunteered to scout out the road beneath us.

He was gone some twenty minutes, and arrived back to announce that all was clear as far as eyesight.

"Been a group of people past in the last twenty-four

hours," he reported. "Mule turds, dried piss. Doubt if there'll be others on the road today."

I decided we'd risk it, and the sooner we were away the better. A quick snack of cheese for the dog and me and we all scrambled down the bank and onto the road.

My memory of the highway from the night before had been of a broad ghostly ribbon winding away smoothly into the distance, but the reality was far different. The surface was stony and uneven, marred by wheel-ruts and loose flints big enough to turn one's ankle, and it twisted and turned like a pig's tail, to follow the contours of the land. Nor was it the same width all the way. Sometimes it narrowed to pass through a gully or across a bridge, like the one that spanned the river that flowed away from our village; at other places it widened or split in two where the ground was obviously boggy after rain.

After an hour of this I felt I had had enough, even though Mistral matched her pace to my waddle—the dog scurried about like an agitated beetle, up and down, back and forth, till it made me dizzy to watch him—and I called a halt. The sun was shining in my eyes, sweat running into my eyes until they stung; my feet were swollen, my thighs sore with rubbing together and my stomach was howling-empty.

But unpacking the food gave me a shock. I hadn't realized how much I—we, I thought, scowling at the dog—had consumed. All that was left that didn't need cooking was a rind of cheese, a slice of cold bacon and one squashed honey cake. I threw the rind to the dog and ate what was left almost as quickly, while Mistral munched philosophically among the scrub at the side of the road, lipping at leaves I wouldn't have thought edible. Obviously her wasted look was partly due to starvation.

The dog, too, found something edible: he crawled out from under a bush crunching on an enormous stag beetle. I felt sick.

"Better get goin'" he said. "Only done a coupla miles . . ."

"Oh, do stop grouching!" I cried in exasperation, all the more annoyed because I knew he was right. "Grumble

and grouch and eat, that's all you do all day! Matter of
fact, that's what I'll call you from now on: 'Growch'! So
there . . ."

He spat out stag-beetle bits, then hoofed his right ear
and inspected the results. "Never had a name before,"
he said. "Thanks." He tried it out. "Growch, Growch,
Growch . . . Not bad."

And I immediately felt mean: how would I have felt
if I had been christened "Grumble"? Even though "Somerdai" was odd, it had nice connotations. But the dog
seemed happy enough; I think he liked the subdued
barking noise his name made.

We progressed better for the next hour or so, heart-
ened by the various pieces of evidence that others had
traversed this way earlier—a scrap of cloth, more droppings, a midday cooking fire. I began to feel much better,
as if a great load had left my mind. I was no longer
confined by routine, everything was new and exciting and
different. All I encountered from now on would be fresh
to my senses and would have to be dealt with by me
alone, no one to tell me what to do. In a way daunting,
in another exciting. I hoped I was equal to the challenge.
But why not? With my education and God's help even I
could have a stab at Life. True, not everything was on
my side, and I now had the added responsibilities of the
horse and the dog, but the former at least was more of
a help than a hindrance.

So it was with a sense of lively anticipation that we
topped a rise shortly after midday to see, spread beneath
us, a huddle of roofs that meant safety and food. The air
was still, and the northerly drift of house fires stained
the deep blue sky like snarls of sheep's wool caught in a
hedge.

I forgot my discomforts and hunger as we wound our
way down into the valley beneath, and even though the
journey was longer than I thought, due to the bafflement
of distance in the clear air and the twists of the road, it
was not much after two in the afternoon by the time we
reached the outskirts of the sizable village. It must, I
calculated, hold at least five times as many people as

ours, if not more. Even without my tally-sticks that would mean well over a thousand: more people than I had ever seen in my life!

I stopped to enquire if a caravan of people had passed by of the first person I saw, an old crone catching the last of the sun outside her hovel.

"Went this way yesterday and on again this morning. Left the blind idiot behind."

My heart sank. The sun was now dipping away behind the hills to our right and there was no way we could hope to catch them up. That would mean we should have to shelter here for the night and think again in the morning. I asked if there was a traveler's rest place.

"Not as such. Ask at the inn down the road for stable space."

We trudged down the main street till we came to the tavern she had indicated, a mean-looking place with a tattered bunch of hops hanging over the doorway. I was not reassured by the surly landlord telling me he was short on both food and ale.

"Blame them as came through yesterday," he said brusquely. "More'n usual for this time o' year. Can do you a stew tonight and there's space in the stable out back."

"How much?"

He named an outrageous price, but Mama had taught me how to bargain and the matter was settled for a couple of coins. I begged a crust of bread in anticipation of the stew, which I shared with Growch, then bedded Mistral down in the dilapidated stable, collecting together some stray wisps of hay for her. Growch I left on guard, mindful of the packs I had stored away under the manger. I reckoned the threat of a horse's kick and a dog's bite would be enough to deter even the landlord or his wife, were they inquisitive enough to try and inspect my belongings.

I decided to take a walk through the village while it was still light. In the distance, from the direction of the church tower, came shouts of merriment and I made my way in that direction. Turning a corner I saw that the space in front of the church was crammed with people all apparently enjoying themselves heartily. Children were screaming and running about, playing tag, and over to my left folk were dancing to the strains of a bagpipe.

I caught the sleeve of a woman passing by with her friends. "Is it a festival? A Saint's Day?"

She stared at me and shrugged. "Not as I know. We just come to see the fun. Got a blind idiot in the stocks over there, been pelting 'im all day. Come night we drums 'im outa town, as the rules say."

I knew these "rules." Anyone liable to be a burden on the parish was got rid of, quick. I remembered what the old crone had said.

"Is this the man that was picked up on the road by the caravan yesterday?"

"The same. Now, if'n you'll 'scuse me . . ."

I peered over shoulders in the direction the woman went, but was too short. Might as well see what was going on. We had the small-brained in our village, more than one, but people were generally kind enough to them. After all they were part of the community, some-body's relatives. Of course the worst ones got smothered at birth. This one must be something special.

Using my elbows I squirmed through for a better view. A few minute later I was at the front, staring at the pathetic figure drooping over the stocks. He was naked except for a short pair of braies, and his hair and body were matted with filth.

Someone picked up a rotten apple, obviously used before for target practice, and chucked it, but it fell short.

I stared hard at the pilloried man. There was some-thing familiar about that tall figure. But what did some disreputable blind idiot in the stocks of an out-of-the-way village have to do with me? I edged nearer: now I was only a couple of feet away. Look up, I begged him silently; let me see your face. . . .

I found I was twisting the horn ring on my finger, unreasonably agitated, as if something unexpected was about to happen.

And then it did.

Someone threw a stone which struck the man in the stocks a painful blow on the shoulder and he lifted his head and howled like a dog at his tormentors.

"Leave me alone! What have I done to you that you should torture me like this?"

My gasp of horror and recognition was lost in the jeers and catcalls of the crowd. How could I have been so blind? That filthy, disheveled, near-naked creature in the stocks had been wearing silks and riding a tall black horse the last time I had seen him.

It was my beautiful knight, Sir Gilman!

CHAPTER
SEVEN

Horror, exultation, anxiety: all three emotions chased through my mind at the same time. Horror at his condition, exultation at his survival of the ambush, anxiety as to how I was to get him out of this terrible mess. Indulge in the other two later, I told myself: concentrate on the last. Come on, now: it's up to you. No one else can save him. You fell in love with him at first sight, remember? You never believed you would see him again, he was just someone to fantasize about. Well, here he is, just like all the stories you used to tell yourself. In those stories you got your hero out of the most impossible situations: what would your heroine do to save him?

I rushed to the foot of the platform on which stood the pillory and shouted up at him: "Sir Gilman! Sir Gilman? Can you hear me?"

But his face, bespattered with grime and with a two-day growth of beard, showed no recognition, his blue eyes staring past my right shoulder.

Behind me I heard ribald comments, requests to move myself, but my whole being was concentrated on the figure before me. I noticed a huge bruise on his right temple, extending from his hairline right down to his eyebrow; it was a livid, raised purplish-blue, and I

recalled what they had said of him: "Blind idiot." Had
the blow to his head robbed him both of his sight and his
wits? I tried his name again, but there was no reaction.

"Move aht the way, yer silly cow!"

"Shift yer fat arse, and let's get a sight o' the action!"

A hand grasped my arm. A stout man with a colored
sash round his waist frowned down at me. "Now then,
lass ..."

I twisted the ring on my finger in my agitation, opened
my mouth to say something, but found I was speaking
words out of the air instead.

"Are you in charge of—of this travesty, sir?"

"I'm the bailiff, yes, but—"

"Then kindly release my brother at once!" Now I knew
what to say, what to do; it was just like my stories. I
jingled the few coins in my purse. "I have been seeking
him three days now. I am sorry if he has been a nuisance,
but ..." and I tapped my forehead significantly. "You
know how it is."

He nodded. "And you come from ... ?"

I mentioned the name of our village and even spoke
the first deliberate lie of my life. "Of course, the mayor,
our cousin, has been worried sick! He has always been
very fond of—of er, Gill, and even lent me his horse to
seek him out, and I have bespoke stabling for us all
tonight at the 'Jumping Stag' down the road.... And
now, if you would please release him, I promise to be
responsible for the silly boy!" and I pressed a couple of
coins into his hand.

He glanced at me keenly out of eyes like currants,
pocketed the coins, and turned to address the restless
crowd.

"Listen here, my friends ..." and as he spoke I
climbed up to the pillory and whispered in Sir Gilman's
ear.

"Don't fret! I've got you out of this and we'll sort
things out in the morning...." I didn't want him dis-
claiming all knowledge of me.

He swung his confined head in my direction. "Who
am I!"

"I know who you are, but you must be patient. Say nothing, just take my hand when you are free, and I will lead you to safety."

The bailiff took keys from his pocket and I led my knight down from the platform and through a clearly discontented crowd, already armed with sticks and stones to drive him out of town. These expulsions often meant the death of the victim, I knew that; I also knew that the bailiff believed little, if any, of my story. Still, he had the coins in his pockets and it was too late to send a horseman to the village to check tonight. Tomorrow I determined to be away at dawn.

I led Sir Gilman through darkening streets to the stables behind the inn, lucky to be unfollowed.

"What the 'ell's that?" said Growch.

But Mistral recognized him and crowded back in her stall. "He brings danger! He led the others—"

"Rubbish! He's in need of care and attention. He's no threat to anyone. Just stay quiet while I see to him."

I went to the inn and begged a bucket of washing water, but had to part with another small coin. I gave my knight a strip wash, even taking off his braies to rinse them out, and he stood quiet as a felled ox, even when I rinsed his private parts, which I noted were ample. But Mama had always said that that the criterion was less in inches than in the performance.

Apart from his trousers he wore a pair of tattered boots, and that was all. I should have to make him something to wear, but in the interim I put my father's green cloak over his shivers and went to fetch the promised stew and a helping of bread. It was tasteless and stringy, but I added salt and a sprinkle of dried parsley and thyme to make it edible. I fed him with soaked bread until he pushed aside my hand and said: "Enough."

That was the first word he had spoken since his release, but as if a dam had been broken he now started with how's and why's and when's until I shushed him. "Enough for now. It's night and you should sleep. Rest easy. Does your head still hurt?"

"Very much. What happened to it?"

"I told you: in the morning. Lie still, and I'll put salve on it and give you a sleeping draught," remembering of a sudden the vial of poppy juice I had brought with me.

I led him out to piss against the wall, but two minutes later, after I had tucked him up in the straw, he was snoring happily. I fended off questions from the others, merely asking the more reliable of them to wake me at false dawn. That done, the rest of the stew shared between Growch and myself and a few strands more of hay scrounged for Mistral, I lit my lantern and settled down with scissors, needle and thread to turn the better of the two blankets into a tunic for my knight.

A round cut-out for the neck, plus a strip cut down the front for ease of donning; seams sewn down the sides, with plenty of room for arms; laces threaded through holes in the neckline and rope bound into an eye at one end, knotted and frayed at the other for a belt . . .

I opened my eyes, lantern guttered, stiff and sore, to find Mistral nudging me.

"An hour before dawning . . ."

We crept through the outskirts of the village till we found the road south and once out of sight of the village I cut an ash-plant stave from the roadside, thrust it into my knight's right hand, put his left on Mistral's crupper, and determined to put as many miles as I could between us and possible questions or pursuit.

We made about four miles before a growling stomach, the proximity of a nearby stream and the knight's questions decided me it was time to break our fast. As the thin flames flared beneath the cooking pot and the gruel thickened around my spoon, I answered Sir Gilman's questions as best I could. His name and station, the ambush, his blow on the head, that was all I really knew. And he knew no more. Even what I told him raised his eyebrows. "You are sure?"

I reassured him, but did not remind him of our meeting in the forest the day before, lest he remember a hideous fat girl he had courteously called "pretty." . . .

Indeed, I was careful to avoid any physical contact except by hand or arm, so that he wouldn't guess at my bulk.

After I had explained twice all that I knew of his circumstances he was silent for a moment or two, spooning down his gruel which I had sweetened with a little honey.

"So I am a knight. But of what use is my knighthood without sight or memory? Where can I go? What can I do? How can I manage without my horse, my sword and armor, money? How do I even know which road to take?" He flung the bowl and spoon away and buried his face in his arms. I longed to put my arms about him, to thrill to the feel of his helplessness, but I knew better than to try. Instead I went over to Mistral and talked quietly to her.

"All I know is this," she said slowly in answer to my questions. "I was hired as a packhorse to carry his armor—and heavy it was. This was in a town many miles north of here. In winter it was very cold in that town, and the people's talk was heavy and thick, not like yours or his. When he set off he said farewell with much of your human embraces and tears with a young woman who seemed reluctant to let him go. Since then we have traveled south by west, and I gather there were many more miles to go. That is all I know."

"Who are you talking to?"

"No one, Sir Knight," I said hurriedly. "I was thinking aloud."

"And what conclusion have you come to?" he said sarcastically. "I for one am tired of walking in this stupid manner and eating food for pigs. I demand you take me to someone in authority and see that I am escorted—taken . . . That I am properly cared for till I regain my memory, and can return to my home. Wherever that is . . ."

He was being rather tiresome. After his experiences of the last few days, how on earth did he think that anyone would believe his story, even with my word as well? Folk would think we were trying it on. If he could have remembered where he came from, even, it would have been a simple matter of sending a messenger to his

home, requesting assistance, and then waiting a week or
so for grateful parents or family to rescue him. As it was,
he was lucky to be still alive. Patiently I tried to explain
this to him, but he was not in a receptive mood.

"Still," he said magnanimously, "I am grateful for your
help, girl. You know my name: what's yours? And why
are you here? Where is *your* home?"

What a wonderful tale I told! The only really true fact
was my name. He learned of loving parents dying of
fever, leaving their only child with a huge dowry, traveling south to find her betrothed—

"But why did you not wait till he could send for you?"
he asked reasonably.

"Ah," I said, thinking rapidly. "The fact is, my parents
did not entirely trust his family, although they paid over
the dowry. They said, before they died—" I crossed
myself for the lie: he could not see me. "—that it were
better I arrive unannounced. Then they could not turn
me away."

"Sounds chancy to me. Which way do you go?"

"I was just coming to that," thinking again as fast as
light. "I am not in any hurry to reach my new home, so
I thought we might try and find where you live first. You
were traveling south, so why don't we both go that way
and hope you recover your memory on the journey? I
have very little money, but we'll manage—if you don't
expect too many comforts. As for walking—it will do you
good, help you recover. What do you say?"

"It seems I have little choice." He still sounded resent-
ful. "But you will promise to speed my return when I
regain my memory?" He sounded so sure.

"Of course! But in the meantime . . ." I could see so
many problems ahead if we continued as we were. "It
would seem strange if we travel together and I address
you as a knight and no relation. We may have to share
accommodation, so I think it best—until you regain your
memory—if we pretended we were brother and sister,
traveling south to seek a cure for your blindness. If you
didn't mind I could call you Gill and you can call me
Summer. . . . No disrespect intended, of course."

He sighed heavily. "Again I see no help for it. All right—Summer," and he suddenly smiled that heart-catching smile that had me emotionally groveling immediately. "Any more pig food? A drop more honey this time, please. . . ."

That night we were dry and cozy enough in a small copse off the road, with the slices of ham fried with an onion and oatcakes, but in the morning as I prepared gruel again, I had an argument with Growch. This precipitated another confrontation with Sir Gilman—Gill, as I must remember to call him. It still seemed disrespectful.

Growch:—"Is that all, then?"

Me:—"You've had as much as anyone else."

Growch:—"Gruel don't go far. . . ."

Me:—"We've all had the same."

Growch:—" 'E's 'ad more'n me. . . ."

Me:—"He's a man. He needs more."

Growch:—"You gave 'im some o' yours; I saw you."

Me:—"So what? I wasn't very hungry."

Growch:—"Favoritism, that's what it is. Ever since 'e joined us you been 'anging round 'is neck like 'e was the Queen o' Sheba, 'stead o' a bloody hencumbrance. Don't know what you sees in 'im. Can't see a bloody thing; can't hunt, can't keep watch, all the time—"

Me:—"Shut up! Otherwise no dinner . . . Go and catch another beetle."

"You're doing it again," said Sir—said Gill, irritably.

"What?"

"Talking to yourself." I loved the way he spoke, with an imperious lilt to his voice—I must practice the way he pronounced things—but I wasn't too keen on some of the things he said, especially when I had to explain something awkward, like now.

I decided the truth was best. Some of it, anyway; he didn't look the sort of man to believe in magic rings, unicorns and such.

He wasn't. "What you're telling me, Winter—sorry, Summer—is that you possess a ring your father gave you

that enables you to understand what the beasts of the
field say?"

I nodded, then remembered he couldn't see. "Yes,
more or less. It heightens my perceptions."

"What utter rubbish! There are no such things as
magic rings, and as for conversing with animals ... Does
not religion teach that animals are lower creatures, fit
only to fetch and carry, guard, or hunt and kill?"

I didn't think so. What did religion have to do with it
anyway? I knew that Jesus had shown his friends where
to fish, and had ridden on a donkey into Jerusalem but
I didn't remember him talking about hunting and killing.
And hadn't he somewhere rebuked one of his followers
for holding his nose against the stink of a dead dog in
the gutter, and said something like: "But pearls cannot
equal the whiteness of its teeth"? It showed He noticed
things, anyway.

But Gill hadn't finished. "I'm surprised you should try
and deceive me in this way! I had thought you to be an
intelligent girl, but now you're talking like a superstitious
village chit!"

He was so persuasive that for a moment I began to
doubt the ring, my own powers. Had I made up what
Growch and Mistral said to me, a mere delusion bred of
my loneliness and anxiety? I glanced down at the ring to
make sure it still existed, and found it no longer a thin
curl of horn but rather a sparkling bandeau, glittering
like limestone after a shower of rain.

"What's 'e on about?" asked Growch. I opened my
mouth, but daren't speak back. The dog cocked his head
on one side. "Like that, is it? Don't 'eed 'im. 'E'll get
used to the idea. You can think-talk, you know, long as
you keeps it clear. Easier for us, too. Try it: tell me to
do somethin' in your mind," and after I had successfully
demonstrated that Growch would turn a circle and Mistral nod her head up and down, I felt much better.

I remembered something my mother had once said:
"Don't expect them (men) to have any imagination,
except what they carry between their legs. Don't forget,
either, that they are always right; even if they swear

black's white, just agree with them. No point in aggravation . . ."

This exchange had only taken a few moments—that
was another thing: this communication by mind was
much quicker than speech—and I was able to answer
Gill almost immediately. "You are quite right, of course;
and yet . . ."

"What?"

"Would you not call the commands you teach your
dogs, horses and falcons a sort of magic?"

"Certainly not! Their response is limited to their intelligence. And they are our servants, not our friends and
equals."

He really could be rather stuffy at times, but I had
only to gaze across at him to renew my adulation. Torn
and bruised he might be, my beautiful knight, with a
three-day growth of beard and blind to boot, but he was
all my dreams rolled into one. Nay, more: for what
dreams could have prepared me for the reality! And the
very best thing of all was that he was so helpless he
needed me, fat, plain Summer, to tend him. And he
couldn't see my blemishes; that was perhaps even better.
To him I was just a voice, a pair of hands, and I could
indulge my adoration unseen. It was just as if Heaven
had fallen straight into my lap. All I could further hope
was that it would be a long time before he regained his
memory. In the meantime he was mine, mine, *mine*!

By midday we had made eight or ten miles and it
started to cloud over. It had been gruel again for lunch,
there was nothing else, and I was eager to press forward,
especially as Growch's nose told him of smoke ahead,
borne tantalizingly on the freshening breeze. Gill grumbled constantly and the weather worsened, so it was with
a real sense of relief that we glimpsed the roofs of a
village away on a side road to our right. I had given up
hope of catching the caravan ahead of us, and was now
resigned to spending the night in a stable. Money wasted,
but at least we could stock up on provisions, even if it
meant breaking into my dowry money. Needs must, and

I thought I could recall at least two coins of our denominations.

We still had a couple of miles to go when it started to rain, hard. Leaning into the wind, my cloak soaked, my feet slipping and sliding in the mud, dragging behind me a reluctant knight and complaining animals, I had to think quite hard about my blessings. But then, in which of the stories I remembered did the heroine have it all her own way? On the other hand, reading and hearing of privations was quite different from enduring them.

Three quarters of an hour later the animals were rubbed down and fed, dry in a warm stable, and my "brother" and I were esconced in front of a roaring fire, our cloaks steaming on hooks, our mouths full of lamb stew and mulled ale. I wanted nothing more than to nod off with the warmth and the food in my belly, but there were things to be done. Upon enquiry I found a cobbler and leather worker and a barber, and by suppertime Gill was washed, shaved, trimmed, and had mended boots, a leather jerkin and woolen hose, and we had paid for our food and lodging in the stable. That took care of the silver coin in my father's dowry, which left only the gold one of our coinage. The others were all strange to me, though mainly gold. These I would keep untouched, for unless I could find an honest money changer, as rare as bird's teeth, they would have to be handed over to my future husband intact. If I chose a sensible man, he would know what to do with them.

And when would I find this husband of mine, I wondered, as I lay quiet on my heap of straw, listening to the gentle snores of Gill and the snorting of Growch, who seemed to hunt fleas even in his sleep. When I had left home my plan had been to join a caravan, travel to the nearest large town, engage the services of a marriage broker and be wed by Christmas. Now I was promised to the service of a man who had lost his memory, had pledged assistance to a horse who had forgotten where she came from, and was lumbered with a dog nobody wanted—and they had preference over my plans, I realized. I was beginning to understand the meaning of the word "responsibility."

The weather had cleared by morning. By diligent enquiry I found that the larger caravans of travelers came past about once a week in either direction during the summer months, but far more rarely during autumn, scarcely ever in winter. The one we were pursuing hadn't stopped at the village, and I realized now that they had a two-day start and we should probably never catch them up. The nearest town, we were informed, was two days travel south—nearer three for us, I thought—but I wasn't going to waste money waiting for the next party of travelers or pilgrims. We had been safe from surprise on the road so far, and with Growch and Mistral as lookouts we could probably make it as far as the next town, where three roads met: a better chance to find traveling company.

But first I had to change my gold coin to buy provisions, and I knew it was a mistake as soon as I handed it over at the butcher's in exchange for bacon and bones for stew. He took the coin from me as though it were fairy gold, liable to disappear at any moment. He held it up to the light, turned it over and over, tested it on tongue and teeth, showed it to the other customers, then called his wife to a whispered conference.

Apparently satisfied it was real, he turned suspicious again and demanded to know where I had got it, implying with his look that no one as tatty-looking as I was could possibly have come by it honestly.

The real story was so preposterous—renegade father, a dowry of strange coins found stuffed up a chimney just before I sent my Mama's body up in flames and fled—that I realized I should have to make something up, and could have kicked myself for not thinking it out earlier. Embarrassed, unused to lying, I floundered.

"It's . . . it's . . . ." In my distress I found I was twisting the ring on my finger and all at once, so it seemed, a story came out pat.

"It is a confidential matter," I said glibly, "but I am

sure there is no good reason why I should not tell you."
I looked around: the place was filling rapidly, and even
the local priest had turned up. "My brother is blind, but
he heard of the shrine of St. Eleutheria where it seems
miracles have occured, and there was nothing for it but
that he must travel there. My father wished him to travel
in comfort of course, with a proper escort, but my
brother insisted that it must be a proper pilgrimage,
every inch on foot, dressed poorly and eating the meanest
viands on the way." I smiled at the priest. "You will
agree, good Father, that this shows true religious intent?"
The priest nodded, and I could see him trying the
obscure saint's name on his tongue: I hoped it was right.

"As the youngest daughter," I continued, marveling at
when I was ever going to find the time to confess all my
duplicity, "it was decided I should accompany him to
find the way. But my father was determined we should
not want on the way, whatever my brother said, so he
gave me a secret hoard of coin to smooth our passage.
But no one must tell my brother," I said, gazing round
at the assembled company in entreaty. "It would distress
him to think we could not manage on the few copper
coins he holds. . . ."

The priest gave us his seal of approval. "I shall pray
for you both, my child," he said solemnly. "Take good
care of the change: we are good, honest people here, but
farther abroad . . ." and he shook his head.

After a deal of counting and re-counting I pocketed a
great deal of coin, more than I had ever handled before,
and made sure to give the priest a couple of small coins
for prayers. On to the vegetable stall for onions, turnip,
winter cabbage; the merchant for more oil, the millers
for flour and oats and a small sack to carry everything
in, and lastly the bakers for a loaf and two pies for the
day's food. The cheese at the inn was of excellent quality
so I bought a half there, then had to shuffle all round
to get it packed tidily on Mistral's back.

Everywhere I went in the village I found my invented
tale had preceded me, and folks nudged each other and
nodded and smiled as I went past. It seemed everyone

came to see us off, just as if we were a royal procession. Quite embarrassing, really, especially as I couldn't explain to Gill what all the fuss was about.

We made reasonable progress, stopping a little later than usual for our pies and bread and cheese. I had indulged in a couple of flasks of indifferent wine, but it was warming and stimulating, so that when we resumed I endured the discomfort of a blister long after it would have been prudent to stop, so that when it finally burst I found I could hardly walk. Cursing my stupidity I unpacked salve and was just applying it when both Growch and Mistral pricked up their ears.

"Someone coming," said Growch.

I was ready to pull off the road and hide, but Mistral reassured me. "Cart, single horse, coming fast so either empty or certainly holding only one man . . ."

By the time I had put on my shoe again I could hear it too, and after a minute or two a simple two-wheeled cart came into view, carrying a few hides. The driver pulled up beside us.

"Got problems?" he asked.

I recognized him as one of the men from the village. He had been in the butcher's when I was trying to change the gold coin, and afterwards I had seen him outside the inn just before we set off. He had a cheerful open face, a smile which revealed broken teeth and eyes as round and black as bilberries. I remembered what the priest had said about the villagers being honest, and smiled back.

"Not really," I said. "We're slowed down a bit because I've blistered my heel."

"Well now," he said, "seems as I came by just when needed! Couldn't ha' timed it better, now could I? We'll all get along fine if you an he"—he nodded at the knight—"just hops aboard the back o' the cart and you ties your horse to the tailgate. That way we'll reach my cousin's afore nightfall. He's got a small cottage on the edge of the woods a few miles on, and he'll welcome company overnight. By tomorrow you'll be in easy reach of the next town. That suit you?"

It suited me fine. The heavy horse he drove seemed more than capable of taking our extra weight—after all the cart was nearly empty—so I tied Mistral securely to the back and guided Gill to sit so that his long legs dangled free of the road, then pulled myself up beside him.

It was sheer bliss to be riding instead of walking, and the countryside seemed to slip by with satisfying speed. The only complaints came from Growch, and after I saw how fast those little legs of his were working, trying to keep up, I leaned down and hauled him up by the scruff of the neck and sat him beside us.

I relaxed for what seemed the first time in days. Soon, with the sun already dipping red towards the low hills to the west, we should be snug in some cottage for the night, with perhaps a spoonful or two of stew to warm our bellies.

The driver pulled to a halt, and skipped down to relieve himself. "Best do the same yourselves," he said cheerily. "Last stop before my cousin's. I'll help your brother, lass, and you disappear in them bushes."

I needed no encouragement: I had been really uncomfortable with the jolting of the cart over the last mile or so. I clambered down and looked about me. The road was deserted and the land lay flat and featureless, except for a dark mass of forest a couple of miles or so ahead. The nearest shrubs were a little way off, and as I trotted towards them the ring on my finger started to itch: I must have caught one of Growch's fleas or touched a nettle.

Squatting down in blissful privacy I looked up as a flock of starlings clattered away above my head, bound for roosts in the woods. It was suddenly cold as the sun disappeared: even my bum felt the difference as the night wind stirred the grasses around me and I stood up hastily and pulled up my drawers.

Suddenly there was a shout from the direction of the roadway, a clatter of hooves, frantic barking and the creak of wheels. Whatever had happened? Had we been attacked? Had the horse bolted? Had my beloved Gill been abducted? Hurrying as fast as I could, all caution forgotten in my anxiety, I tripped over a root and fell flat on my face. Struggling to rise I was immediately downed again by a hysterical dog.

"C'mon, c'mon, c'mon!"

"What's happened?"

"Come-'n'-see, come-'n'-see, come-'n'-*see*!" was all I could get out of him.

"I'm coming!" I yelled back at him, skirt torn, face all muddy, shaking like a leaf. "Get out of the *way*!"

The first thing I saw as I arrived at the roadside were the long legs of Gill waving from the ditch as he tried frantically to right himself. I rushed forwards and grabbed an arm, a hand, and by dint of pulling and tugging till I was breathless, managed to get him back on his feet again, spluttering and cursing.

"Are you all right?"

"No thanks to that cursed carter! Just wait till I see him again—till I get hold of him," he amended.

"The carter? Oh, my God! Where is he?"

"Gone," said Growch, back to normal, his voice full of gloom. "Gone and the horse and all our food with 'im. Waited till you went behind those bushes then tipped your fancy-boy into the ditch. Chucked a stone at me and was off down the road like rat up a drain. Got a nip at 'is ankle, though," he added more cheerfully. "Now what we goin' to do?"

CHAPTER EIGHT

What, indeed! As for this "we," it was down to me really, wasn't it? So, I could cry, scream, yell, kick the dog, run off down the road in vain pursuit. I could refuse to go any further, abandon both my knight and the dog, do my own thing. I could tear my hair out in handfuls, creep away into the wilderness and die; I could become a hermit or take the veil. . . .

I did none of these, of course. Instead I sat down by the roadside and considered, steadily and calmly, the options left to us. I was aware that despair was only just around the corner; I was also aware just how much I had changed. A few days ago, while Mama was still alive, I would have been totally incapable of coping. Then, if even the smallest thing went wrong, my fault or no, I had run to her skirts and asked for forgiveness, aid, advice, whatever; I had been whipped, scolded, but given my course of action. Now I was on my own.

No, not on my own. I had the others to consider. Without me they would probably perish, except perhaps for Growch. Had the unaccustomed responsibility brought this mood of somehow being able to deal with it all? Or had my "magic" ring wrought the change? It had certainly tried to warn me of danger when it prickled and itched on my finger. I glanced down at it wryly. In the stories I remembered one twist and straw would be spun into gold, a table spread with unimaginable delicacies—But of course! I still had all my money safe, so we wouldn't starve. We might have lost our transport, food, provisions, utensils and, saddest loss of all to me, my Boke and writing materials, but what was that against our lives and some money?

And my ring did give me the power to communicate with Growch and Mistral: why not send out a call to her to escape back to us if she could, however long it took? Given the choice, I would rather have her back than regain our goods. If the carter turned her loose perhaps she would find us. Shutting my eyes and praying that my thoughts had the power of travel I sent her a message, wondering at the same time if I wasn't being foolish to hope.

And while I was about it, an ordinary prayer wouldn't do any harm. So I made one, and Gill joined in with an "Amen."

Rising to my feet I dusted myself down, retrieved Gill's staff, put one end into his right hand and took the other in my left.

"Right! Hang on tight. I'll try and keep to the smoother part of the road, but it will soon be dark and we must seek shelter."

"Where?"

"There are woods a mile or so down the road."

"And what do we do for food?"

"I'll find something."

"Not more of your stupid 'magic,' I hope!"

"If you must know, yes, I have tried to reach Mis—the horse."

"What rubbish! She's miles away by now. You'll never see her again."

"Wait and see. . . ."

And in this way we set off down the road in the gathering gloom, a sneaky wind fingering my ankles and blowing up my skirts indecently. Then just as we reached the shelter of the first trees, it started to rain. It was now almost too dark to see, and we sheltered uneasily, unwilling to lose our footing venturing father into the forest. But the rain came down harder, and while the firs and pines provided some protection, the oaks and beech had lost most of their leaves by now and were useless as shelter.

From the distance came a growl of thunder, a gust of wind shook the branches above us, increasing our wet misery with a few hundred more drops, and we struggled on, Gill falling on every tenth step and Growch tripping me up on every twentieth. If we didn't find better shelter soon we could die of exposure—

A vivid flash of lightning flared through the trees, followed almost immediately by a tremendous clap of thunder and—

And something else.

A frightened cry. An owl? Something trapped? Someone in distress? It came again. The high-pitched whinny of a terrified horse. This time I recognised it at once.

"Mistral!" I shouted. "Mistral, where are you?"

An answer came, but from which direction? I plunged forward, forgetting Gill, and we near tumbled together.

"Mistral, Mistral! Here, we're here!"

But it took a few minutes more of stumbling around and calling before she found us. I flung my arms around her trembling neck, dropping my end of Gill's staff.

"What happened? Are you all right? How did you escape?" I had forgotten about thought-speech, forgotten that Gill would hear me.

She told me that when the carter had rattled off down the road she had resigned herself to her fate, but once she heard my thought-call—yes, she *had* heard it—she struggled to free herself, but alas! I had fastened her too securely to the tail of the cart. Then she had tried to bite through the rope, with little success until the cart had bumped over a particularly deep rut, when the chewed rope had at last parted, and she had galloped back to find us.

"Brought the food back with you?" asked Growch hopefully.

"Everything is just as it was. He didn't stop to investigate." She paused. "But now I am so tired and wet. . . ."

"Now you're back everything will be fine," I said. "I'll light the lantern and we'll find a snug spot in no time at all!"

"And eat," said Growch.

For once I was in full agreement with him. "And eat."

I held the lantern high to try and get our bearings and saw what seemed like a reflection of our light off to the right. I blinked my eyes free of moisture and looked again. As I watched, the lantern or whatever it was swung slowly from side to side. Yes, it wasn't my imagination.

I stumbled forward, never considering any danger I might be heading for. "Is there anyone there? Help, we need shelter. . . ." and grabbing Gill's hand I made off towards the other light.

The trees shuffled away into the shadows on either side and we found ourselves in a small clearing. A flickering lantern held by a small man threw dances of light onto a queer, humpbacked building, no taller than me, that crouched for all the world like a giant hedgehog beneath the trees. It must be a charcoal-burner's hut, I thought, and certainly not big enough to hold us all. A wisp of smoke trickled from the roof.

The small man bowed. "Welcome travelers. It is not often I have the pleasure of welcoming visitors so far into the forest. Pray take advantage of my humble dwelling, for methinks the weather can only worsen." He spoke in a creaky, old-fashioned way, as though speech came seldom to his tongue. He was elderly, and looked to be dressed in skins; the hand that clutched the lantern was gnarled like a bunch of twigs.

"Thank you, sir, for your kind offer," I said formally. I looked at the low doorway. "But there are four of us, and I fear . . ."

"Plenty of room: You will see."

One of us wasn't waiting; Growch pushed past and disappeared behind the hides that covered the entrance and I found myself pulling Gill in with me. Inside it wasn't a bit what I expected.

Somehow the roof seemed higher—perhaps we had
come down a step or two—and the space far greater
than I had imagined. It was quite roomy, in fact. The
floor was clean sand, the walls wattle and daub; there
were piled skins to sit on and a merry fire burned in the
center, the smoke curling up tidily to a hole in the roof.
To one side of the fire a cauldron simmered and on the
other meat was skewered to a spit, browning nicely. A
pile of oatcakes was warming on a flat stone, a flagon of
wine stood by a jug and wooden bowls and mugs were
piled ready. The tantalizing smell of the food was almost
more than I could bear without drooling.

I guided Gill to a pile of skins and sat him down,
hanging his sodden cloak on a hook in the wall. Growch
was already steaming, as near to the fire as he could get,
and biting at his reawakened fleas. I heard a munching
sound and there was Mistral behind me, lipping at a
bunch of winter grass.

It was all rather unexpected, but then I was still
unused to much of the refinements of the world. Perhaps
houses could, and did, stretch to accommodate extra
guests; far more likely, I told myself, my eyes had
deceived me outside and I had thought the place much
smaller than it obviously was; if not, then we must be in
some underground chamber.

Our host came forward, rubbing his hands together
with a dry, whispery sound. "Help yourselves to refreshments, my friends. There should be more than enough
for all."

Indeed there was. Gill and I spent the next half hour
or so crunching into the delicious spicy meat, throwing
the bones to Growch, and chasing the last of a thick,
hearty broth with oat bread. Then with a mug or two of
wine to follow I leaned back and relaxed. The fire still
chuckled merrily, apparently without need of fuel,
although our host threw a handful of what looked like
powder into the flames and instantly the room was full
of the scents of the forest.

He was much taller than I had thought, nearly as tall
as Gill. How could I ever have thought him smaller than

me, I thought muzzily. It was difficult to make out his
features properly, too. He seemed to have greyish hair
and bushy eyebrows, big ears like ladles and small, round
eyes so deeply set I couldn't make out their color. I
thought at first his nose was as round as an oak-apple,
but in the firelight it suddenly seemed sharp as a thorn
and twice as long. His mouth was hidden by an
untrimmed beard, but one moment he seemed to have
long, sawlike teeth, then none at all.

The food and the wine and the fire were getting to
me, I thought: I must pull myself together. Glancing to
one side I saw that Mistral's eyes were closed, her head
drooping; Growch was staring vacantly at the fire and
Gill had his head on his chest. I pinched myself on the
hand, surreptitiously, to try and keep awake, catching at
my ring as I did so. It seemed very cool to the touch.

I looked up at our host. "I thank you, from all of us,
for your food and shelter."

"A pleasure, young traveler. As I said, it is rare for
anyone to venture this far into my territory."

"*Your* territory?"

"Indeed. I said so. This forest is my domain."

Surely all land and the people thereon were owned by
the lords of the manors? Even in our village we owed
ours work in his fields and tithings.

"You are a lord?"

He chuckled, a sound like wind in the trees. "Lord of
the Forest, yes. All around you are my trees, my shrubs,
my bushes. My birds, my wild creatures. Every living
thing . . ." He sounded quite fierce.

"It—it must be a big responsibility," I said weakly.

He shrugged. "Everything usually runs smoothly: I
see to that. Besides, who is there to challenge my
authority?"

Certainly not me, I thought, noting the scowl, the bee-
tling brows.

"And now," he continued, "I should like to ascertain
just how you come to invade my territory. You seem an
ill-assorted company, if I may say so. This young man . . ."

Gill was fast asleep, too far gone even to snore. ". . . is a relative, perhaps?"

In the silence that awaited the answer to his question, short though it was, I suddenly became aware of all sorts of sights and sounds that had been hidden before. The uneasy prickle of the ring on my finger, the rush of wind and thunder of rain outside, the fire that needed no wood, the unnatural stillness of my companions. Even the shelter in which we found ourselves was seeming to change: the walls were closing in, the roof becoming lower. It's all a big illusion, I thought; he is trying his magic on me and if I tell him the wrong thing—

Before there had been a great compulsion to tell the truth, but now outside reality and I had erected a kind of barrier between the Lord of the Forest and us. So, I told him the story I had told everyone else, lying as thought it were the truth.

At the end of it all he humphed! as if he knew it was untrue but couldn't fault the telling. I was beginning to relax again when he suddenly switched his attention to something else.

"That's an unusual ring you have on your finger. A pity it is so undistinguished. Not worth much, I should say."

"It is worth the love of my father, who gave it to me. Were it made only of thread, still would I treasure it. Of course, because it is part of the horn of a—" Horrified, I stopped myself, the ring itself now throbbing like a sore on my finger.

"The horn of a what? Some fabled creature who never existed, save in the imagination of man? I am surprised you believe in such fable. Still," and now his face was all smiles, benign, kindly, "I am willing to exchange it for something far more valuable, just because I am grateful for your company. See here. . . ." and from his pocket he drew out a handful of jewels; gold, silver, green stones, red ones, blue, purple, yellow. "Rings, brooches, necklaces, bracelets: take your pick! Just slide that old piece from your finger and I will give you two for one! How's that?"

"It won't come off," I said flatly. "Not even if I wanted it to. Which I don't. It was my father's gift, and I shall keep it. Sorry."

Of a sudden I felt a great squeezing, as though the breath were being taken from my body by an unwelcome hug, and the walls were so close as to squash me up against the others. Instinctively I took hold of Gill's sleeping hand and cuddled Grouch close. Above me Mistral's mane hung like a curtain before my face and I grabbed a handful with my free hand.

Then sleep came down with a rush like a collapsing tapestry.

A drop of rain plopped onto my nose, the aftermath of the storm. Opening my eyes, I blinked up at the trees above. I was cold and *very* hungry. I had been lying uncomfortably on a heap of twigs and stones and my hip and back ached. I sat up; where was the fire? A tiny charred ring in the grass. Walls had gone, roof disappeared. I let go Mistral's mane, Gill's hand, moved away from Growch. Whatever had happened? In a little heap beside the remains of the fire lay a pathetic heap of small, burnt bones: mouse, rat, vole? By them a small pile of dessicated skins crumbled to dust, and blew away on the morning breeze together with half a dozen acorn cups.

Gill stretched and yawned. "What time is it? I'm hungry."

"Hungry?" said Growch. "*Hungry?* I could eat an 'orse!"

"You can talk! I haven't eaten for twenty-four hours," said Mistral.

I gazed at them all. "But don't you remember last night? The food? The little man?" But none of them had the slightest idea what I was talking about.

CHAPTER NINE

After that, all I wanted was to get away back to normality, and I never thought I should be so glad to see a plain old ribbon of road again. We had no idea exactly where we were, but with the aid of a watery sun headed west by south; even so it must have been at least an hour of stumbling progress before we were free of the forest.

All the while I wondered about what had really happened during the night. As far as we four were concerned we shared the experience of seeing the flickering light between the trees, but after that the others remembered nothing but disturbed dreams. Only I recalled a gnarled old man first small then tall, a room that expanded then contracted, a fire that needed no fuel, food and drink. . . . And in the morning the Lord of the Forest had gone, if he had ever existed. So had his shelter. I might have believed myself the victim of hallucination, except for that tiny ring of charred ground, the little chewed vermin bones, the acorn cups. Magic of a kind, but not nice.

How many other travelers had succumbed, I wondered? If it hadn't been for my ring, the ring he had coveted, the ring that I realized had bound us all together as I gathered the others around me, we too might have been bones on the forest floor. I glanced down at the

circle on my finger: it was the color of my skin and
nestled quietly now. Whatever had threatened was
behind us now, but I wouldn't rest easy till we were away
from the forest completely. The trees still crowded the
road on either side, dank and dripping, their rain-laden
branches drooping down like disapproving faces, and no
birds sang.

A half hour later we were out in the open. Standing
once again in the blessed sunshine, I offered up a silent
prayer for our deliverance. It was a chilly morning, last
night's rain still lingering in pockets of mist that swirled
about our feet and slithered down into the valley below.
The countryside was spread out like a checkered quilt
beneath us, and some five miles or so distant I could
make out through the haze the snaking of a river that
curled round the smoke of a fair-sized town. I even imagined that I could hear on the freshening breeze the faint
ting-ting of a church bell.

There was little enough dry wood about, but with the
aid of the kindling in my pack I soon had a fire going,
and spread out cloaks on bushes as I hurried up the first
solid food we had eaten for hours—bacon, fried stale
bread, cheese and onions eaten raw. It seemed like a
feast, but I still mentally gagged when I remembered the
'food' of the night before and could swallow but little,
busying myself instead finding choice bits of fodder for
Mistral.

We reached the town by midday, and I managed to
find an inn which provided both stable room and pallets
in the attic. After hearing that a caravan from the east,
heading south, was expected within the next couple of
days—a rider coming through had reported passing it—I
determined to stay until they arrived. Far better to travel
in company after the misadventures of the last few days.
It meant spending money, but at least we could tidy
ourselves up and have the choice of provisions before
the others arrived.

I took our washing to the river stones and beat it clean,
bought hot water to cleanse ourselves and took Gill once

more to the barber, investing in a razor which I thought
he could use if careful. I also bought him a cloak with a
hood, at horrible expense, and a silken scarf to tie around
his eyes: although he could still see nothing, he complained of headaches and a cold prickling in the eyes
themselves. The bump on his head was scarcely visible
now, but I gave it more salve, just in case.

After decent food and a good night's rest I felt a hundred times better and much more optimistic. I sat Gill
out in the sunshine while I caught up with the mending,
and tried to jog his memory regarding his family, his
home, anything relevant, but he still shook his head sadly.

"I don't remember, Summer: I'm sorry." I could not
bear to see someone who should be so haughty and sure
of himself brought so low. I tried to recall anything I
could of that scene of carnage in the woods and suddenly
bethought myself of the scrap of silk I had rescued. Digging it out from the baggage I showed it to Mistral, who
sniffed at it, identified it as belonging to the knight's
train, but knew nothing of color or shape, as I understood
it. I took it to Gill, tried to describe the blue and yellow
and what looked like a beak, but he still shook his head.
I was sure I could recall a bird's head on the shield I
had glimpsed that first day when he asked the way, and
tried to combine it all in a drawing, but it was hopeless.
Still, I asked about the town as best I could with the
scrap of silk, but met with no success there either.

I was making my way back to the inn at dusk, after a
wasted afternoon's questioning, when I came across a
scuffle of small boys throwing stones up onto the roof of
a deserted cottage, shouting and yelling with enjoyment.
Looking up, I saw the feeble flapping of wings—
obviously they were trying to finish off an injured bird.
Even as I passed the bird fell off into the gutter, where
it was scooped up by greedy hands and held on high by
the tallest boy.

"Mine! Mine!" he chanted. "Pigeon pie for supper!"
He was a thin, starved-looking child of about nine, and
I couldn't blame him for capturing his supper, but as he

put his hand around the bird's neck something made me
put out a hand to stop him.

"Stop! Don't kill it. I—I'll buy it off you. . . ." I said
impulsively, cursing myself for a soft-pate even as the
words were out. What on earth did I want an injured
pigeon for?

The boy hesitated, his hand still ready to wring the
bird's neck.

" 'Ow much you givin' us, fatty?"

I flushed with anger—but then I was fat, wasn't I, and
he was as skinny as only starvation can make one.

"Twice as much as it's worth in the market. Only I
want it alive—to fatten it up." I reckoned an alley-wise
kid such as this would appreciate that argument. I pulled
some coins from my pocket and jingled them invitingly.
Immediately his eyes glowed fiercely, and I realized I
had made a mistake: I should have only produced the
two small coins I was willing to part with. I held out my
other hand. "Give me the bird. Please."

He clutched the bird closer. "Four pennies, then."

"Rubbish! It's only worth one in that condition, and
you know it." To my alarm I sensed the other children
closing in around me. There were at least a half-dozen,
and I knew I could never escape by running. The alley
we were in was narrow and twisting, and if they made a
concerted attack I would have no chance. They could
crack my head open with a stone with as little compunc-
tion as they would wring the bird's neck and share the
coins between them, and none the wiser.

If only I had thought to at least bring Growch with
me! Nothing to look at, he still had a fearsome bark, a
worse growl and very sharp teeth. I took a step back,
which was a foolish thing to do. "I—I'll give you another
half-penny on top, and that's my last offer."

But still they crept closer, so near that one child
nudged my elbow. I took a further step back till I was
up against the wall. My heart was beating like a tambour
at a feast, and I felt like chucking the money in my hand
away as far as I could and taking a chance on running.
If only I could reach the end of the alley . . . I lifted my

hand, but suddenly there was a small frightened voice in my ears.

"Help me!" The ring on my finger tingled briefly. "Help me. . . ." It was the bird. Suddenly I felt a surge of anger and stepped away from the wall. "Give me the bird! At once! Or I'll . . ."

"You'll what?" But it was the boy who backed away.

"Just wait and see! Well?" I spoke from a confidence I did not feel but even as he shook his head my deliverance was at hand.

A black blur erupted at the far end of the alleyway and charged towards us, bringing its own cloud of dust, the little legs were working so fast. Then there was a nipping and a snarling and a yarling and a yelping and a barking and a biting and boys were scattering everywhere to escape. The pigeon's tormentor dropped the bird in his flight and I snatched it up and made for safety, closely followed by Growch.

We fetched up near the inn and I paused for breath. He spat a fragment of cloth from his mouth, tail wagging. His eyes were bright as blackberries and he smelt as high as hung venison. I made a mental note to dunk him in water whether he liked it or not.

"Lucky I was only dozin' when you called," he observed. "Saw that lot off pretty sharpish, din' I?"

"I called you?"

"Yeh, you yelled 'help!' in my ear. Took off like a flea on a griddle I did. What's that you got?"

Once again the ring had worked, and only a thought this time. . . .

"A . . . a pigeon," I said, and loosened my fingers a little, aware that I was holding the bird far too tight. "I think it has a broken wing."

"Supper?"

"Certainly not! Don't you ever think of anything except food?"

"Yes, but I ain't seen nor smelt any likely bitches recent. . . . Don' I get anything for helpin'? A reward, like . . ."

He was disgusting, but I bought a pie and gave him

half, stuffing the rest into my mouth with relish. "Mmmm . . . Good."

"Might justa well been your bird. Pigeon pie, weren't it?"

"Of course not! Pork and sage," I said, before I realized he was teasing. The bird shivered in my hands.

Upstairs at the inn I examined it more closely. It was a handsome bird in an unusual coloring of soft pinky-brown and buff. On its leg was a tiny canister, locked tight. So, it was a homing pigeon. But from where? One wing lay splayed and crooked and I touched it gently, using slow thought for my question.

"Is this where it hurts?"

"Yes. Broken I think. Falcon strike, two days back. Hungry . . ." The voice in my head was faint but clear. A mug of water and some oats later and the voice was strong enough to guide me as I bound and strapped the wing with a splint of wattle and strips of cloth while he mind-guided my clumsy fingers into the most comfortable position.

"That'll take a while to heal," I said. "Where are you from?"

"South. A town tall with towers. I am a messenger."

"I can see that." I touched the canister on his leg. "How far have you come?"

"From north fifty miles or so. The same again three times to go."

"Well, you can't fly for a while. . . . South, you said?"

"Yes, and a little east."

"Is your message urgent?"

"It is a message of love from my mistress' betrothed."

Urgent enough to the one who waited. "We travel south," I said. "But not as fast as you could fly. I don't know how long you will take to heal, but you are welcome to travel with us if you choose. I can make a box for your transport."

Of course my dear Gill thought I was quite mad when he found out what I was doing sitting on the settle by the fire that night, weaving a little basket from withies I had gathered from the riverside by lantern light. (With

Growch for company this time.) When I explained about the injured pigeon he snorted most unaristocratically and asked whether I was thinking of gathering any more encumbrances to hold up our journeying.

Of course I loved my knight most dearly, and could not now imagine the day when I could not refresh my heart by gazing at his beautiful face; marveling at the high forehead, straight nose, and those darkly fringed eyes, so blue in spite of their blindness—but I did wish sometimes that he would grumble a little less.

"Anything the matter?"

"Of course not. I'll just finish this, then perhaps I could ask the landlord for some mulled ale. You'd like that?"

"I should prefer a decent bottle of wine."

"Certainly." Wine was twice as dear. "I know how you must hate all this idleness, but perhaps the caravan will arrive tomorrow. . . ."

The travelers straggled in at midday the next day, some fifty of them. The inn and all the other lodging places in town were full that night and we had to share our pallets and those spare with a husband and wife and their three half-grown children. I doubled up with the wife and Gill with the largest boy. The latter grumbled that Gill took up too much room, while I found myself on the floor a couple of times, the wife having a thin body but a restless one, and the sharpest elbows this side of a skeleton.

The caravan did not waste time and was determined to set off again next day. I had had the forethought to stock up with provisions the previous day, so not for me the frantic buying of everything eatable. I already had flour, oats, cheese, salt pork, dried beans, honey, a small sack of onions and vegetables and a dozen apples, but I did remember to buy some barley for the pigeon and a truss of hay for Mistral in the morning.

I judged there would be room for barter on our travels, for I noticed a couple of goats and a crate of hens were traveling with us, part of a merchant's entourage. Milk and eggs would be a treat, although it was late in the year for laying.

Like all so-called "safe" caravans, this one was in charge of a captain and men-at-arms, six of the latter in this case. The captain's job was to determine our rate of progress, decide when and where to halt and to keep us safe from marauders. Our captain was a very large man called Adelbert; he looked quite outlandish, wearing skins and a huge helmet decorated with a pair of bull's horns sticking out on either side. He had a habit of hunching his broad shoulders and thrusting his head forward if anyone dared to question his decisions, that made him look more taurine than ever. His men were a surly bunch, too. They conversed with their captain in a guttural patois I didn't recognize and kept themselves well apart from the rest of us.

Before we set off the following morning "Captain" Adelbert explained his terms. In return for his guidance and protection he demanded a penny a day from each traveler, or sixpence a week in advance. Wagon and carts double, but no charge for horses, asses or mules. I was only too happy to relinquish my worries to someone else, so handed over money for Gill and myself. A week at a time would do.

That first day there were forty-seven of us. Besides the captain and his men, Gill and me, there were the merchant, his wife and four attendants, five lay monks returning south after pilgrimage to another monastery, our room companions of the night before, another family consisting of four generations and thirteen assorted people, a trader and his assistant, a clerk and a troupe of jugglers going south for winter pickings. Captain Adelbert himself led the caravan, two of his men brought up the rear, and the other four patrolled out on either side.

Our pace was of necessity that of the slowest amongst us. We were ruled by a rigid routine imposed by our leader, who became increasingly autocratic the farther south we traveled. We rose an hour before dawn, broke our fast and were on the road as the sun came up. We traveled for four hours, then broke for a meal—not

longer than an hour: the captain had a very efficient
sand-glass, which to me always traveled faster than the
sun—then we were on the road again till dusk, another
three hours, perhaps a little more. We camped where he
stopped us, unless we were in reach of a town, then it
was first in, best served. If we were camping out then
we built fires for our evening meal, sometimes combining
with others for a joint meal, which was a nice change:
the merchant and his wife were too aloof, but the other
families and the jugglers became good companions. If
the weather was wet we supped cold and soon huddled
beneath what shelter we could find.

Luckily we had few really cold days; farther north by
now all would be huddled in front of roaring fires, waiting for the snow. I think this was the first thing that
made me realize how far we had already come, for by
the beginning of December I must have been at least a
hundred and fifty miles south of my old home, if not
more.

I began to enjoy my life outside, to look around me
more. I started to notice weather signs, to see trees,
rocks, stones, streams as separate entities. I delighted in
the colors of the falling leaves—red, yellow, brown, purple, orange—was forever running off the road to supplement our diet with mushroom and fungi, and was the
first of the humans to hear and see the skeins of geese
winging south, though I must admit it had been our little
pigeon who had alerted me.

He was healing slowly but well, and I didn't need to
alter the splint of his wing. Seen at close quarters he was
extremely handsome, his pinky-brown plumage set off by
creamy beak and legs and bright eyes as red as rubies.
He was in no doubt we were heading in the right direction for his home, though he found it difficult to explain
why.

"Don't know for sure . . . Something inside my head
pulls me the right way." He scratched behind his left
ear, or where I supposed it to be, with a delicate claw,
then followed the itch all around his neck. "You see,
when I am taken away from home and then released to

carry a message I climb slowly in spirals, looking all the while for familiar landmarks. If there are none, which means a long journey, I climb until the tug inside comes and I know which way to go." He settled down in his basket, fluffing out his breast feathers. "Of course if I am within ten miles or so of home, then I can see my way, and will be home, weather and hawks permitting, between strikes of the church of the tall tower, which is nearest my loft."

Three hours was the usual interval between strikes of the bell, if the priest was awake, to coincide with the church Offices.

"What does it look like, the earth, from so far above?" I asked hesitantly.

I had put his basket and our baggage on a rock while we took one of our halts, so that Mistral could graze unburdened, and now the bird looked up and then down and around. For a while he said nothing, then: "Stand you up and look down on this rock. This is a mountain. That clump of grass over there is a forest. Scratch a line on the ground and stick two or three twigs along it and you have a river with a town beside it. The ants you can see are the people . . ."

For an instant I could feel the currents of air beneath my wings, stroking my feathers, and glancing down watched the moving map beneath unfold, instinct pulling me farther and farther south—

"You all right?" asked Growch. "Got a funny look on your face, like you was goin' to be sick. If'n it's the bacon, I don' mind finishin' off that bit for you. . . ."

Gill had been remarkably silent about my exchanges with the animals ever since Mistral had found us in the forest; of course I now mostly used thought-communication, but sometimes forgot and used speech. I don't for a moment believe he thought I was really talking to them, or they to me, but he suspected there was something special between us and was no longer sure enough of himself to ridicule it.

The fresh air, plain food and walking miles every day did appear to be helping his memory a little; odd things, like: "I remember having my hair cut when I was a child, and the smell as the pieces burned on the fire," or: "My mother had a blue robe with a gold border," and: "I fell out of a tree when I was six and broke my arm." All endearing memories that made the child he was more real to me, but not really helpful as far as finding out where he lived. Still, it was a hopeful sign.

The caravan changed its character, size and shape as various travelers left or joined us. Among the former were the jugglers and the large family, but the farther south we went, the more our numbers swelled. There were more merchants, with or without wives and attendants, a merry band of students, a couple of pardoners, craftsmen and masons looking for work during the winter and even a dark-skinned man wearing a turban who had woven silk mats and hangings in his wagon.

Of course as the road became more traveled, the deeper the ruts and the more chance of being held up for repairs to wheels or axles. Then we would all stand round cursing the inaction while the Captain organized repairs and restless horses steamed in the chill of December mornings. In spite of this we still managed an average of some fifteen miles a day.

At this time we were traveling through broken countryside: small hills, stony heath, straggly old woods half-strangled with ivy, isolated coppices and turbulent streams. The road, from its usual width of twenty or thirty feet, had shrunk to a wagon's width. Earlier in the day we had come to a crossroads and Captain Adelbert had insisted on taking this narrower right-hand road, saying it was a short cut. I began to wonder if he had made a mistake. It had obviously rained heavily here in the last twenty-four hours, for in many places the horses were splashing through shallows and I had to lift my skirts to my knees and paddle. Once I actually had to carry the smelly Growch twenty yards when he pretended he couldn't swim—it was easier than arguing.

It was getting dark, with a lowering sky overhead, but there was no sight of a suitable camping site. The countryside looked even more inhospitable, outcrops of rock and tangled undergrowth crowding down towards the narrowing road. To make it worse Adelbert's men were harrying the train, trying to make us close ranks and we were soon almost treading on one another's heels. The wagon ahead of us snagged on an overhang and came to an abrupt halt. I was bursting to relieve myself, so dragged Gill and Mistral off the track and behind some rocks, just as the monks behind us closed up.

Our departure went unnoticed in the general hubbub, and I was able to squat down in peace. That was one of the only advantages of Gill's blindness: I had no need to hide myself. He took advantage of the break also, and I was just leading him back to Mistral when the ring on my finger started to itch and burn, and a moment later all hell broke loose in the direction of the road.

Shouts, screams, the thunder of hooves, the frantic barking of a dog, sickening thuds and crashes— Whatever in the world had happened? Making sure Gill had hold of Mistral's mane, I pulled at her bridle to lead her back to the road, but she dug in her hooves and refused to budge, wordless terror coming from her mind to mine. Well, if she wouldn't move I would have to come back for her, but I must see what was happening.

Just as I stumbled towards the rocks something thumped me hard in the stomach and down I went to my knees. Growch was tumbling all over me, stinking of fear.

"Get back, get back!" he barked over the increasing din. "Hide, quick! It's a massacre!"

CHAPTER
TEN

I woke with a sudden jerk, as though I had plummeted down a steep stair, and gazed around wildly. Mistral blew soothingly through her nostrils.

"All safe: sleep . . ."

I lay down again, chilled through to the core of my being, glad for once for the smelly warmth of Growch against my back. Gill was breathing heavily beside me and above the stars shone clear. I closed my eyes, tried to doze off again, but even if I managed a moment or two I soon jumped into wakefulness, fighting the hideous images that crowded sleep.

We had camped beneath an overhang of rock off the road—somewhere. It had been too dark to see, I had not dared light the lantern, and sheer luck and Growch had found this comparatively sheltered spot. We had eaten hastily of broken meats—some sort of pie, I judged—then had wrapped ourselves in the extra blankets and tried to sleep. Gill had dropped off first, but then he hadn't seen what I had. . . .

When Growch had cannoned into me crying "Massacre!" I had not at first believed him, despite the shouts and screams, the clash of weapons. At first I thought it was a minor ambush and that Captain Adelbert and his men were fighting off the attackers, glad that we were out of the way. I saw two monks flee past our hiding place, pursued by a man on horseback waving a sword. It was obviously not safe for us to emerge.

I crept back to Gill. "It looks as though the caravan has been ambushed. It's not safe to move until it's all over. . . ."

But the noise seemed to go on for ever. The screams of anguish and pain were the worst, and I held my hands over my ears; I saw Gill do the same. Perhaps through his dim memory he was reminded of the ambush in which he had been caught.

At last it grew quiet, as far as the screaming was concerned, but I could still hear the tramp of hooves, the crunch of wheels, men's voices, curiously exultant voices. The battle was over; someone had won. I crept forward for a better look. Nothing to be seen, just an empty road. I was about to step out for a better look when there was a fierce tugging at my skirt.

"No! Not yet," growled Growch. "Let me take a quick sken first."

"But—"

"No buts! You ain't got the sense of a newborn pup!" and he crawled forward on his belly and disappeared. I waited for what seemed an age, shivering a little from both fear and excitement, but he came back so stealthily that I heard and saw nothing until a wet nose was pressed into my hand, making me jump. He was shivering, too.

"What's happened? Is anyone hurt? Is it over?"

"S'over all right. They'll be movin' off soon, I reckon. Got what they wanted." He lay down, panting. "All dead."

"I can smell the blood," came the frightened thought from Mistral.

"Like a slaughterhouse," said Growch, still shivering. "Move back a bit: they'll be coming past in a minute or two."

"Who? Who will be coming past? You haven't explained anything! Who is dead? Who attacked us?"

"Never trust no one," was all he would say. "Never trust no one. . . ."

Impatiently I moved for a better view of the road, crouching down behind a rock, mindful through my curiosity of Growch's warnings. Two minutes later I nearly burst out of my hiding place with relief, for here rode our Captain on his stallion, leading behind him two pack horses laden with unwieldy packages. So we had beaten off our attackers! I opened my mouth to cry out, but then I saw the sword hanging from his hand, thick with congealing blood. Instinctively I shrank back; if I leapt out at him too suddenly he might use it without thinking. A moment later and his six men followed, one nursing a gash on his arm, but all chattering and laughing among themselves. Each one led two or three laden horses, and on one I saw the silken rugs from the dark merchant's cart. And surely those two piebalds were the ones who had pulled one of the other merchant's carts? And wasn't that mule the one belonging to one of the pardoners? Where were the others?

I craned forward; the horsemen passed, but there were no others behind. Their voices still carried clearly.

"Din' take too long. . . ."

"Pity about the younger woman—"

"Should'a thought o' that before you chopped her!"

"Whores aplenty where we're goin'."

"Why din' we take one o' the wagons?"

"Captain says as we're goin' cross-country."

"Three cheers for 'im, anyways! More this time than last!"

" 'E says enough to lay up for the winter. No pickin's worth the candle till spring."

"What about those that ran?"

"Two-three at most. One o' the monks—"

" 'Prentice—"

"Din' see the fat girl and 'er blind brother. . . ."

"Quite fancied 'er, I did. Like an armful, meself. . . ."

"Won't none of 'em get far. Not with the bogs all around."

"Shit! Dropped a bundle. . . ."

"Coupla blankets. Leave 'em. Got plenty. . . ."

Their voices faded as the road bent away, until there was only the dull clop of hooves and a tuneless whistling, and soon both were lost in distance and the growing dark.

I sat down heavily, my mind whirring like a cockchafer. Had I heard aright, or was it all some horrible nightmare? Had our captain, the man we all trusted, led us all astray and proceeded to massacre everyone for the goods we carried? And was it his living, something they did regularly?

Growch slipped past me. He was back in a couple of minutes, looking jauntier. "All clear. You can come out now. Not much to see, though. Or do . . ."

He was right, about the second part anyway. They were all dead, all our companions, strewn along the road for two or three hundred yards like broken dolls—

But dolls never looked like this. Gash a doll and you have splintered wood; wood does not bleed, and there was blood everywhere. My shoes stuck in it, clothes, faces, limbs were caked with it. Dark blood, pink, frothy blood, bright blood—my lantern showed it all. Who would have thought blood would have so many different shades?

And the flies—It was December: where had they all come from? Greedy, fat, blue-black flies crawling everywhere over the carrion that lay cooling in the dark. And in the morning would come the kites, the crows, the buzzards. . . .

Gill was at my side as we picked our way through the corpses, but of course he could see nothing. Growch sniffed his way from corpse to corpse, but there was no life left. We came to the end of death, and there, on the narrowest part of the roadway, a great tree blocked any further progress. At first I thought it had fallen, then I saw the axe marks. So, this had all been carefully planned, and by the look of the tree this way had been used before, this sudden death had come out of the dusk to other travelers.

I must leave word, warning, at the nearest town, I

thought distractedly, but first we must get away from
here ourselves. Mistral wouldn't come near, and the
pigeon cowered in his basket. Taking Gill's hand once
more I led him back through the obscenity of bodies,
the bile rising in my throat and threatening to choke me.
I found I was muttering: "Oh God! Oh God!" over and
over as I turned from slashed limbs, contorted bodies,
gaping wounds and from the faces that wore death masks
of surprise, terror and pain.

Behind me Gill stumbled and cursed. "What the
devil—?"

He jerked his hand from my grasp as he fell to one
knee, groping in front of him.

"I kicked something: a flagon of wine, a bladder of
lard?"

This time I was sick, though there was little save bitter
water to spit out. The thing he had stumbled over was
a severed head.

"Let's get outta here," said Growch. "Nothin' left but
stink o' death."

True enough. The assassins had stripped the caravan of
everything: clothes, goods, weapons, valuables, harness,
horses and mules, even all food and drink. There was no
reason to believe they would return, and they were probably miles away by now, but I still felt uneasy. They had
said three others had run off, but if it were true about
the bogs they were probably drowned by now.

As if to echo the dread and fear that still lingered
among the corpses, a thick miasma of mist started to rise
from the ground around us, curling round my ankles with
cold fingers.

I took Gill's arm. "We must move. There is nothing
we can do for these poor souls save give them our prayers." And we bowed our heads, the muttered prayers
sounding loud in that unnatural stillness. There was only
one way to go; that was down the road we had come by,
for none of us wanted to linger near the slaughter longer
than we could help. Even a mile or two would make a
difference, for who knew what ghosts might not rise from

those poor unshriven souls, to harry us through the night?

Growch slipped off ahead, and I extinguished the lantern: I could not risk the murderers seeing a light, though common sense told me we would never see them again. I knew the dog's and horse's ears were sharp enough to pick up any danger, but we walked forward cautiously, a step at a time. Growch came running back.

"No sign of anyone for miles, but there's a bundle what they musta dropped just ahead. Over to the right . . ."

Two new blankets, still smelling of sheep oil and practically waterproof. I strapped them on Mistral's back. They had been someone else's property, but that person was now dead: no point in leaving them there to rot. There was also a small sack of various broken foods: no point in wasting that either.

We stumbled forward for another mile or so, then Growch had found the rocks we were now sheltering beneath. I shared out the broken pies and bread and cheese and covered us with the new blankets, and then tried to sleep for a few hours.

And was still trying.

But the sights and sounds of the carnage we had left behind were still sharp and shrill in my imagination, too clamorous for sleep. Why did it have to end like that, the journey I was becoming so used to, was even beginning to enjoy? I had become accustomed to walking all day, to spending the occasional night huddled under the stars, to cleaning and mending and patching and gathering wood and cooking. I had met more people in the last few weeks than I had come across in the whole of my life before, seen more villages, towns, hills, rivers, forests and fields than any lord could own in one holding. Of course I had been bone-weary at times, hungry, cold and burdened with responsibility but, given the choice, I would not have retraced one step. Had not my father traveled the world, and Mama been one of the Travelers?

No, I would not have gone back—until now.

Right now I would give almost anything to be back in my own village, under any conditions—even working in the tavern, or as kitchen maid to the sharp-tongued miller's wife. I wanted desperately for life to be ordinary again, safe and predictable. I didn't want responsibility for anyone or anything but myself; I didn't want to think, to plan, to *lead*. I wanted to have all the decisions made for me. No more choices, please God! I couldn't cope, I couldn't, especially if they were going to turn out like this.

I snuggled into the scratchy, uncomfortable-because-new blanket, more awake than ever. Gill was now snoring loudly, Growch smelt like a dung heap and I was sure I was starting a miserable cold. . . .

I awoke with the sun full on my face.

"What time is it? Why didn't you wake me?"

"I thought you needed the sleep," said Gill gently, putting out a tentative hand till he found my shoulder, then patting it. "You do so much for us: you deserve a lie-in once in a while. We couldn't manage without you, you know. . . ."

And suddenly, somehow, it all seemed worth it.

CHAPTER
ELEVEN

We regained the crossroads at midday. It was empty. The road north by which we had originally come stretched back into the distance, a straight arrow. The turnoff that had proved so disastrous, we left thankfully. There remained two ways: southeast and southwest. I sent the turd expert down first one then the other.

He came trotting back triumphantly. "Not thataway," he said, indicating southeast. "They went along some twelve hours back, then camped for the night and struck off 'cross the moor."

I turned to Mistral and the pigeon. "Does this southwest road seem all right to you?"

Unfortunately I had used human speech, and Gill stared towards me irritably. "Do we have to consult—pretend to consult—the impedimenta every time anything is to be decided? Or can't you make a decision on your own?"

"Animals have a much better sense of direction than we humans have," I said stiffly. "And I *do* communicate with them, whatever you may think!" And I explained about Growch's foray down the roads. "If you still aren't convinced, we can waste time going down the southeast road till we find the relevant horse droppings and you can feel and smell them for yourself!"

He shook his head and sighed. "No. I believe you somehow manage to tell them what you want, better than most. Now, can we go?"

I turned to Mistral and the pigeon once more. "What do you say?"

She snuffed the air. "We go the right way, for me."

"It will do," said the pigeon. "If only I could fly up and take a look . . ."

"Patience," I said, "you are healing nicely."

"I know . . . Not fast enough." He paused, and preened himself shyly. "They—the others—have names. I should like a name too. If you wouldn't mind. If it's not too much bother . . ."

"But of course!" I suddenly realized that the name had been there all the time. "I have been thinking of you as 'Traveler' all this while. Will that do?"

He crooned to himself. " 'Traveler' . . . Thank you."

We camped off the road that night, and made reasonable progress the next day, without seeing another soul. The same the day after, though by midday we were down to a handful of flour and two wrinkled apples, so it was with relief that I saw the outline of roofs and a church tower some distance ahead. The land around us became cultivated, there were sheep in a fold guarded by two dogs and I could hear wood being chopped in a wood to the west. Small tracks came to join the highway from left and right: it all pointed to a fair-sized town.

Indeed it was so prosperous that on the outskirts were two or three large houses standing in their own walled grounds, which must mean this was a peaceful area too. We were passing the last of these mansions when I stopped abruptly. My ring was tingling and I thought I heard something—no, not heard, rather felt.

"What was that?"

"Bells ringing for afternoon Mass," said Gill, as indeed they were.

"No. Something else. Listen. . . ." There it was again: a sad, cold, dying call.

"Came from over the wall," said Growch, ear pricked. "Somethin' shufflin' about."

"Anyone there?" I called and thought, "Answer me!"

There was a longish pause. "Help. . . ." The sound was faint, drawn out like a thread. "Sooo . . . cooold . . ."

I had to find out what It was, what It wanted. I looked about, but the pebble-dash walls surrounding the house were some ten feet high. No way could Gill lift me up—besides he'd discover just how fat I was—and there were no handy trees to climb. I followed the wall till I came to a small gate, but it was firmly bolted. Still—

I called Mistral and explained what I wanted. We managed it on the third attempt as she bucked me up high enough to grab the top of the gate, climb over and drop to the other side. The first thing I did was to draw back the bolts to ensure a swift exit, just in case. Then I looked about me.

I was in a small formal garden, with apple and pear trees, leafless now, graveled paths, boxed alleys, square and diamond-shaped plots edged with rosemary, a scummy pond and the remains of a camomile lawn. All winter-dead and desolate. The house beyond was shuttered and quiet too.

I peered around in the gathering gloom. Nothing moved. And yet—I started back. Over there, at the edge of the shriveled lawn a rock moved. Rocks don't move, I told myself firmly. But It did it again and I backed away.

"Heeelp . . ."

Talking, moving rocks? If it hadn't been for the positive feeling in the ring on my finger I think I would have fled, but instead I approached It cautiously, ready however to run if It jumped up and tried to bite. Seen closer It was a sort of rough oval, almost black, with orangey-brown patches. I stretched out my hands to pick It up and It suddenly sprouted a smooth head, four scrabbling claws and a stumpy tail. I sprang back: perhaps It did bite!

"Caaarefuuul," came the mournful, slow voice again. "Faairly fraaagile. Chiiip eaaasily . . ."

I squatted down to look more closely. "What are you?"

"*Reeeptillia-cheeelonia-testuuudo-maaarginaaata . . .*"

It was talking Latin, and that was not my best subject. I understood Church Latin and some market Latin—both understood wherever one went in a Christian country of course, whatever local language the native people spoke—but classical and scientific Latin were beyond me. "Er . . . How can I help you?"

"Coooold . . . Fooorgotten. Neeeeeed fooooood. Sleeeeeep . . ."

It was getting more and more difficult to understand. Obviously as the house was shut up It could expect no help from there. At least I could see It-whatever-it-was-in-Latin got some warmth. "You'd better come with me." I bent to lift It, my hands closing round a cool, horny shell. "Don't stick your claws in . . ." but I was brought up short by a sharp tug. I put It down again. "What's this?"

"Chaaain. Caan't escaaape. Caaan't buuurrow . . ."

Looking more carefully I could see that a thin chain was looped through a hole pierced in the rear of the shell and then went to an iron staple driven into the ground some eighteen inches away. It was an easy matter for me to lift the chain over the staple and release It, but I could see how constricting it had been, for the creature's walking round had worn a deep circular trench, the limit of the chain.

I looked around, but there was nowhere I could put It that wasn't just as exposed, and no food that I could see.

"What do you eat?"

"Greeeeeens. Fruuuit . . ."

I sighed. "And where do you come from originally?" but even as I asked I knew what the answer would be.

"Sooouth . . ."

Another one! Whatever would Gill say? I stooped to wrap the chain around Its shell and started to lift It, but was arrested by a hiss of pain. "Tooooo faaast . . . Huuurts heeead."

Slow and steady then. I wrapped him in my shawl and left by the side gate; I couldn't bar it again. There was nothing to steal in the garden, and anyone wanting to rob the house was perfectly capable of climbing the wall.

"What you got?" asked Growch. I showed him. "Hmmm. Smells like dried grass and shit."

Gill asked the same question and I placed It in his hands. He ran his hands over the shell and his face lit up. "Ah! A tortoise! Had one when I was a boy. . . . Laid eggs, but never came to anything. Ran off one August and we never found it again. . . ."

I was delighted. He had not only identified the strange creature, but it had also touched off another piece of memory, however irrelevant. And I had heard of tortoises, but never seen one before.

I hesitated. "Do you mind if we take it with us? I believe its kind live farther south. . . ."

"Of course. Tortoises can't stand winter here. Ours used to bury itself in cold weather. Where did you find it?"

I explained. "It feels as though . . . I think it's hungry. I believe they eat greens, but there aren't many to be found right now. . . ."

He was delighted to be consulted. "Some sops of bread in milk. Ours used to love that."

So that was one problem solved: bread and milk as soon as we reached a decent inn. I wrapped the tortoise in a piece of sacking and tucked him up on Mistral's saddle.

"Food soon. You may find your perch a bit rocky, but you'll get used to it. What do we call you?" I wasn't going to make the same mistake as I had with Traveler, the pigeon.

Now he was warmer his speech wasn't (quite) so slurred or slow. "Back at hooome," he said, shuffling around a little as if he were embarrassed, "the ladies called me Basher. Could hear me for miles," and he gave a little sound, which, if he had been human, I would have interpreted as nothing more or less than a snigger.

By the time we reached the town proper it was near dark and we were lucky to knock up an inn with reasonable stable accommodation, which we shared with the animals, snug enough on fresh hay. I was lucky also with chicken stew, bread and mugs of milk for Gill and myself, and Basher the tortoise had his first meal "for three or four mooonths," he said. He didn't eat much, but as he said: "Little and oooften. The shell is a bit cooonstricting on the stomach." Like armor must be, I thought.

"How did they come to forget you?" I asked.

"Neeews came. Someboooody ill. All left. Forgooot me."

I fingered the chain wrapped around him. "Shall I take this off?"

"Please. Dooon't want to be reeeminded."

I found there was a catch, easy enough to unfasten, and it now looked just like a gold necklet, something used as an expedient rather than something permanent.

"Who put this on you?"

"Maaan drilled hole. Huuurt. Lady put on chain. Laaaughed . . ."

"Do you want it? It looks as if it might be gold, enough to buy us more food and lodging."

"It's yours. Paaay for my travel . . ."

In the morning we found the town full of people, and the landlord told us many had come from roundabout for the feast day of the Eve of St. Martin, the last chance of fresh meat before the spring. There was a traditional fair to be held on a piece of common land and dancing on the green in front of the church. "Be glad when it's all over," he grumbled. "House is full of the wife's relations. We'll dine early tonight, if you don't mind. Everyone'll be at the fair later."

I didn't know whether to stay another night or no: it rather depended on whether the tortoise's necklet was indeed gold. I remembered Mama's strictures on trading and bargaining, and went to three different coin and metal traders. It was indeed gold and the middle one offered the best price but was too inquisitive: "Who gave it to you? Where are you from? Where are you bound for?" and in the end the last man, an elderly Jew, exchanged it for enough moneys to keep us in food and lodgings for many a day, and without too much haggling.

So much money, in fact, that I decided to sleep another night in the town and also visit the fair. I had never been to a fair before. I had been partly persuaded to find in my travels round the town that our acquaintances of a few weeks earlier, the jugglers, were to perform that night.

When told of the disaster that had overtaken us at the hands of Captain Adelbert and his men, the juggler's eyebrows rose into his thatch of fair hair, and his mouth made a great "O" of surprise. He crossed himself several times in thanks for his deliverance and promised us a free show that evening. I left him going into the church to give a donation for his lucky escape, for I was reminded to report the caravan master's perfidy to the authorities.

This took longer than I had expected, as everything had to be written down, and as it was a holiday the town clerk was nowhere to be found and I had to be content with his deputy, who was mighty slow with pen and ink. I could have done better myself. Then they had to have Gill's corroboration, for what it was worth, so we were only just in time for our midday meal—rabbit and mushroom stew, dumplings, bread, cheese and ale—and the fair was already in full swing by the time Gill and I arrived. I had wanted to leave Growch behind, but he had promised he would sneak out and follow us anyway.

"Like a couple of unweaned pups, you two! Not fit to let out on your own . . ." So he trailed a few yards behind us.

I took hold of Gill's hand, and because this was a leisure time, not leading him to relieve himself or across obstacles, the touch of his skin sent little shivers of excitement rolling up and down my spine. Routine flesh to flesh contact became, in my case, imbued with all sorts of undertones and overtones that had my palm sweaty in a minute, and I had to wipe it a couple of times and apologize.

It was difficult in any case to thread our way through the crowds that milled more or less aimlessly among the stalls, tents, platforms and stages that filled the common ground. Like me, I suppose, they wanted to see everything before making up their minds what to spend their money on. As it was afternoon, over half the crowd consisted of children: tonight husbands would bring their wives, young men their sweethearts and the singles would seek a partner.

We found our friends the jugglers easily enough and, as promised, had our free show, though I could tell Gill was bored, his blindness making a mockery of the tumbling balls, daggers and clubs. I found some musicians and we listened to those for a while, then I bought some bonbons which we shared. I described a couple of wrestling falls for him, as best I could, also the greasy pole contest, which to me was hilarious, but again irritated Gill because he could not watch the humor.

The further we went, the more I realized how much these entertainments relied on visual enjoyment—morris dancers, animal freaks, the strong man, a woman as hairy as a monkey, a "living corpse," and all the throwing, catching, running and contests of strength. The only real interest he showed was when I found a stall selling rabbit-skin mitts, and I treated him to the biggest pair I could find.

I was reluctantly leading him back, when I came across a treat I could not resist. Outside a tent hung a sign saying: THE WINGED PYGGE. To reinforce the words (for most could not read) there was a lurid poster depicting something that looked like cross between a huge bat and a plum pudding with a curly tail. Perhaps I would have lingered for a moment, yearned for a while and then walked on, but at the very moment we stopped, the showman flung aside the flaps of his tent and strode forward, ready to capture the passing trade with his spiel.

"My friends, lads and lassies, youngsters: I invite you

all to come in and see the marvel of the age!" His restless little eyes darted amongst us, noting those who had paused, those who would listen, those who were customers. "Here we have a magic such as I dare swear you never have seen! A horse may swim, an eel walk the land, but have you ever seen a pig fly? No, of course you have not! But here, fresh from the lands of the East—the fabled lands of myth and mystery—at great expense I have managed to purchase from the Great Sultan Abracadabra himself, the only, original, once-in-a-lifetime Flying Pig!"

The crowd around us was growing, their eyes and mouths round with speculation and awe. The showman knew when he was on to a good thing.

"Here is your chance to see something that you can tell your children, your grandchildren, your great-grandchildren, knowing they will never see the same! And how much is this marvel of the senses, this delectation of the eyes, this feast of the consciousness?" He had captured them as much with his long words as with his subject, I realized. "I am not asking the gold I have received from crowned heads, nor the silver showered on me by bishops and knights. . . . No, for you, my friends, I have brought down my price, out of my respect and fellow feeling, to the ridiculous, the paltry, the infinitesimal sum of two copper coins!"

The crowd hesitated, those at the fringe began to break away, but immediately the showman drew them back into his embrace with a dramatic reduction.

"Of course this ridiculous price includes all children in the family. And for the elderly, half price!" Some people who had been leaving turned back, but others remained irresolute. Down came the price again.

"All right, all right!" He spread his arms in supplication. "But this price is just for you: you must not tell your neighbor how little you paid, else will I starve. . . . My final offer: one copper coin, just one, for the treat of a lifetime! Come on, now: who will be first?"

Should we, shouldn't we? After all, I would have to

pay for Gill and he would see nothing. I nudged Growch with my foot.

"There's supposed to be a pig with wings in there," I nodded towards the tent. "Be a dear and check up for me. I don't want to waste money if it's a con."

He slipped away towards the back, presumably to squeeze under the canvas unseen. A steady trickle of people were now paying their coin: soon the tent would be full. Growch nudged my ankle.

"Well?"

"Dunno. Honest I don'. There's summat in there. . . ."

"Is it a pig?"

"Could be . . ."

"What do you mean 'could be'? It either is or it isn't. Which?"

"Looks like one, but don' smell like one. Don' smell o' nuffin, really. Nuffin as I recognizes."

"Perhaps somebody washed him. Unlike some I could mention," I added sarcastically. "Does it have wings?"

He scratched. "Sort of. Bits o' leathery stuff comin' out o' its shoulders. Like bat wings . . ."

That decided me. I bargained for Gill's blindness but got a "takes-up-the-same-space-don't-he" answer. Inside it was dark and stuffy, lit only by tallow dips. Tiptoeing, I could see a small stage hung with almost transparent netting that stretched from floor to ceiling and was nailed to the floor. To stop the creature flying away, I thought.

There was a rustle of anticipation. The showman reappeared, on the stage this time. He was carrying a large cage which he set down before him, and then started another harangue.

"You've got your money," I thought. "Why prolong it?"

"Once in a lifetime . . . marvel of the age . . . far lands of the East . . ." It went on and on, and the thirty or so people in the tent started to grow restive, shuffle their feet, mutter to one another. A baby began to cry and was irritably hushed.

"Get on with it," somebody shouted from the back.

The showman changed his tack. "And now, here is the

moment you have all been waiting for! Come close, my
friends—not too close—and wonder at this miracle I
have procured solely for your mystification and delight!"
And with this he opened the cage, groped around in the
interior and finally hauled forth, by one leathery wing, a
small disreputable object that could have been almost
anything.

It could have been a large rat, a mangy cat, a small,
hairless dog or, I suppose, a pig. A very small, tatty pig.
Pinkish, greyish, whitish, blackish, it certainly had four
legs, two ears, a snout and a curly tail, but even from
where I stood I could understand Growch's earlier
confusion.

There was a murmur of astonishment from the audience, which quickly grew to ooh's and aah's of apprecia-
tion as the showman plucked at first one stubby little
wing and then the other, extending them until the creature gave very pig-like squeals of protest.

"There now, what did I tell you? Never seen anything
like this before, I'll be bound! Worth every penny, isn't
it?" He brought the creature nearer to the front of the
stage and the crowd pressed forward, making the tallow
dips flare and the net curtains bulge inwards.

I held on tight to Gill, explaining what I had seen as
best I could.

"Sounds like some sort of freak to me.... Are you
sure those wings aren't sewn on?"

He wasn't the only one to express doubts. Once the
first wonder had worn off there was muttering and whispering all about us, one man going so far as to suggest
that there was a manikin sewn up inside a pig's skin.

"Let's see it fly, then," shouted one stalwart, encouraged by his wife. "You promised us a flying pig, so let's
see a flying pig!"

His cry was taken up by the others, and for the first
time I saw the showman discomfited.

"Well now, the creature does fly, I can certify to that,
but it strained its wings last week, and—" but the rest
of his words were drowned in a howl of protest.

"You promised ... we paid good money ... cash back ..."

It was probably the last that decided him. Retreating to the back of the stage, he held the creature high above his head.

"Right, then!" He seemed to have recovered his equilibrium. "A flying pig you shall see! Stand back!" and he threw the creature as high as he could, as you would toss a pigeon into the air. For a moment it reached the top of the tent and seemed to hang there, desperately fluttering its vestigial wings. Then, abruptly, they folded and it spiraled to the floor, to land with a sickening thump and a heart-rending squeal.

Quite suddenly it was over. The creature was stuffed back in its cage and we found ourselves out in the sunshine. For no reason that I could think of I found my eyes were full of indignant tears. It was so *small*! I told Gill what had happened. He shrugged his shoulders.

"They would have done better to wire it up and suspend it in the air," was his comment. "I'm getting hungry: shall we go?"

I took Gill to Mass and then we ate a rather scrappy supper, everyone in the inn eager to be off to the evening's festivities. There was to be a bullock roasted in the churchyard, maybe two, and all you could eat for two pence. I was in two minds what to do. Part of me couldn't get the images of that pathetic little pig out of my mind and wanted to see him again, the other part knew that Gill would be bored and unhappy if I dragged him round the fair again.

My dilemma was solved in the most satisfactory way. One of the landlord's cronies came dashing into the inn for a quick ale before the festivities started, grumbling that their best tenor had dropped out of the part-singing with a sore throat.

"We'll just have to cut out 'Autumn leaves like a young girl's hair' and 'See the silver moon.' Pity: they're very popular...."

From the corner by the fire came a soft humming,

then a very pleasant tenor voice started to sing the descant from "Autumn Leaves." It was Gill; I had never heard him sing before and my heart gave a sudden bump! of unalloyed pleasure.

Everyone turned to listen.

"Can you do 'Silver Moon'? 'The bells ring out'? 'Take my heart'?" and a half-dozen more I had never heard of. Gill reassured the landlord's friend he knew all but two.

"Then you've saved us all! You come alonga me, we'll slip into the church for a quick practice, then you're part of our singers for tonight. No arguments: there'll be plenty to drink and eat. Blind, are you? Pity, pity . . . Don't worry, we'll look after you!" and he took Gill's arm and whisked him away before one could say "knife." At first I was dubious, but one look at Gill's face reassured me. It was full of animation: at last he had found something he could do for himself, I realized, and wondered for a moment whether I was coddling him too much. No man likes to be smothered, Mama used to say. . . .

Which left me free for an hour or so. At first I pretended to myself that I was just going to have a general look around, perhaps buy a ribbon or two, arrive at the barbecue in time for some roast beef and then stay to listen to Gill sing, but my feet knew a different route. Before long I found myself once more outside the "Flying Pygge" tent listening to the showman's spiel. This time I pushed my way to the front, determined to be near the stage. And the silly thing was that I didn't know why, though there was a prickling in my ring that told me that somehow it was important.

I stopped the speech in mid-flow. "My penny, sir!"

He stopped and glared at me, and I realized he had not yet reached his "special reduction" bit. Blushing, I prepared to step back into the crowd, but he recognized me, and seized on his opportunity.

"See how eager this—this young lady is to see the show! Don't I remember you from this morning?"

I nodded.

"And you have come back because you marveled at the show, never having seen its like before? And you told all your friends about it, so I have had two more performances than usual?"

I nodded again. Anything, but let's get a move on!

He beamed. "There's your proof, then," he said to the rest. "Can't wait to see the performance again ... The young lady perhaps forgets that the price is *two* copper coins, but I think that this time, as a special treat—and don't tell your neighbors—I shall do as she suggests and reduce the entrance to just one penny. . . ."

Once inside I rushed to the front as if blown by a gale and clutched at the curtains. The showman brought out the cage and far away in its depths I could see two sad little eyes staring out, and a great shudder shake the small frame. "It's not fair, it's not fair!" I thought angrily and, impelled by I knew not what, I bent down while the showman had his back turned and ripped up a section of the curtain nearest the bottom of the stage. Looking at the pig as he hung in the showman's hands I willed him to see what I had done. All the while the ring on my finger was pulsing like mad.

The pig was held on high, then hurled towards the ceiling. Once more it appeared to rise a little, then hover, but it was only an illusion, for down it came to land with a crash and a whimper right in front of me—

I ripped up the rest of the curtain, snatched the pig into my arms and, using surprise and my considerable weight, carved my way through the astonished crowd and out into the darkness. I could hear the howl of the showman behind and ran until there were a couple of stalls between us. Then I set down the pig and gave it a little shove.

"Now's your chance to escape! Run, run away as fast as you can!"

But the stupid creature wouldn't move. . . .

CHAPTER
TWELVE

I took a quick glance behind. The crowd were still pouring out of the tent, getting tangled up with the tent flaps, guy ropes and each other. I hesitated, then darted back and picked up the creature from under the noses of our nearest pursuers and set off once more. If the silly animal hadn't the sense it was born with—!

I ran in the direction of the town, dodging between strollers, around trees and bushes, tents, wagons and stalls until my heart was banging in my ears. I was wheezing like an old woman and could hardly draw a breath. My feet felt like balls of fire and the salty sweat was stinging my eyes till I could hardly see. Behind me I could hear the thud of pursuing feet and cries of "Thief! Stop thief!"

Twice I tried to rid myself of my burden but each time part of it became entangled with my clothing some way or another, and I was scared to pull too hard lest I damage its fragile wings. At one moment it felt as heavy as lead, at another as light as a farthing loaf; it seemed to change shape with every step I took: now long and thin, now short and fat; round, square, oblong—

"What the 'ell you *doin*'?" Growch was dancing alongside. "Got the 'ole town after you . . ."

"Don't—ask—questions," I panted. "Help me get away!"

He swerved off to one side and a moment later I heard a loud crash. Risking a backward glance I saw he had cannoned into a stall selling cooking pots; those that survived the fall were rolling about on the grass, bringing some of my pursuers down. But not the showman: he was in the van of about twelve yelling, shouting villagers. I then saw a blackish blur run between his legs and bring him crashing to the ground, also bringing down another who upturned a stall of fruit and vegetables in his wake. The rest of the pursuers lost interest in the chase and began to fill pockets and aprons with the spoils.

Slowing down I gained the outer streets of the town and sought the temporary refuge of a deserted doorway, panting, disheveled and exhausted, the pig-creature still clutched beneath my arm. Growch came trotting down the alley, tail jaunty.

"Well, that stirred 'em up! What was you doin' anyway?"

"Tell you later . . . Thanks, anyway. Let's get back to the inn."

I crept into the stable, looking fearfully behind, and deposited the creature in the manger.

There was a long moment of silence.

"W - e - l - l," said Growch. "Don't look any better close to. What you want to pinch that for?"

Mistral blew down her nostrils then sniffed, trying to catch its scent. "Strange . . ."

"Those supposed to be wings?" asked Traveler.

"Claaaws like mine . . ." mused Basher, awake for once.

Indeed, its cloven hooves did have tiny hooks embedded in the horn. Those must have been what caught in my clothes when I tried to put it down earlier.

"What *are* you?" I whispered, as if the whole world were asleep and the answer was a secret.

Was it a pig? The snout seemed too long, the bum too high, the skin hairless. The backbone was knobbed as though it hadn't eaten for ages and the tail had a little spade-like tip. The ears were small, and then there were the wings. . . . Scarcely stretching beyond the span of my hand, they were leathery like those of a bat, but without the claw-like tips. He was stretching them out tentatively right now—there was no doubt it was a he—but when folded they tucked away in a couple of pouches on either side of his shoulders. It was a freak—

"I am a pig. At least I think I am. . . . When I came out of the egg—"

"Egg?"

He looked at me. "Yes. Does not everything come from an egg?"

I didn't think so. As far as I knew horses, cows, sheep, dogs, cats, rats, mice, people and—yes—pigs were born bloody and whole from their dams. But on the other hand hens, ducks, birds, snakes, lizards, fish, frogs and toads laid eggs. But he wasn't one of the latter. It was all very puzzling. Perhaps he was a new species.

"Some creatures come from eggs," I said cautiously. "Are you absolutely sure you did?"

"I remember being in a tight place and fighting my way out with my nose. Then there was my mother and my brothers and sisters; they were all pigs. But they picked me out and sold me because of these things," and he nodded along his back to where his wings were folded away. "A man said pigs do not have wings. Said I was a freak. Called me not a pigling but a wimperling, because I cried so much when they tried to stretch my wings. So I suppose that is what I am."

"A Wimperling?" I shook my head. "I'm afraid I've never heard of one of those." It looked sadder than ever, its big brown eyes with the long lashes seeming ready to shed tears any minute. "But I'm sure you're not on your own," I added hastily.

"Thank you anyway for rescuing me. I hope I shall not get you into trouble?"

I hope not, too, I thought. Pig stealing was punishable by hanging. "Of course not. Er . . . Now you are here is there anywhere I can take you? Drop you off?" I waited for the dreaded word "south," like Mistral, Traveler, Basher and Gill, but it didn't come.

Instead: "I do not know where I belong. Nowhere I suppose. Perhaps I might travel with you a while? I shall be no bother. And I eat anything and take up but little space. . . ."

What could I say? After all, I had stolen him from his owner, and so I was now responsible for his well-being. But what about Gill? What would his reaction be when he learned I had burdened us with yet another responsibility? And another thought: how long would it be before they traced the stolen pig to me? After all, I was scarcely invisible and there were plenty of people to remember.

First things first. I must hide the little thing securely—from both the villagers and Gill. I made a space under the manger behind our baggage.

"Just for tonight. We'll be away early in the morning. Are you hungry?"

The Wimperling shook his head, but Growch muttered: "Starving, I am. What about all that roast beef?" and my stomach gave a growl of sympathy. I decided that my best cover was to go out again, in my hooded cloak this time instead of the shawl, and try and look as though I had been listening to Gill's singing all the time. Trying to be insignificant was easier than I thought; everyone was so busy enjoying themselves that no one gave me a second glance. Growch and I chewed the rather tough meat—the roasted ox was down to skin and bone by the time we got there—and I was able to listen to the last couple of songs, in which Gill comported himself very creditably.

Afterwards Gill's newfound friends escorted us back to the inn, roistering noisily. On the way I heard a strange tale of a long-haired witch who, accompanied by a pack of fierce hounds, had stolen a flying pig and rode up into the sky on him. . . .

"Wake me an hour before dawn," I said to Mistral.

In any event I was awake long before, spending most of the night tossing and turning, my snatched dreams full of visions of the hooded hangman. We were away long before anyone else was stirring. Gill, of course, had no idea it was still dark. Unfortunately it was a damp, misty morning, threatening rain. The dropleted air smelled of wood smoke, night soil, last night's bad ale and wet wool as we groped our way out of the town, but once on the road again it was wet leaves, damp earth, the complicated decay of December.

A fine, hazy rain started to fall, too light yet to do anything but lie on top of everything like an extra skin. Growch, as usual, grumbled like mad, but Mistral was easy, plodding forward at walking pace, her load balanced so the tortoise and pigeon were basketed on one side, the pig in a pannier on the other. I made sure Gill walked on the former side.

I had bethought myself the day before to renew our dry goods and buy more cheese, so we breakfasted by a quick, small fire on gruel, oatcakes and honey. I dowsed the fire as soon as the food was cooked, pleasant though it was, because I was still afeared of pursuit. I had made extra oatcakes for our midday meal, to be eaten with the cheese, and without thinking I handed them to Gill to tuck away under Mistral's blankets while I finished scouring the cooking pot. There was a sudden sharp squeal and a shout of anger.

"Summer! Come here. . . ."

Oh *no*! I had thought to get away with it a while longer. "Coming . . ."

"What is *this*?"

"What's what?"

"You know perfectly well what I'm talking about—"

"Oh, that . . ."

"Yes, that!"

"Um. It's a pig. Sort of. A very little pig. It'll be no trouble. . . ."

"And where did it come from?"

"Er . . . the town. Last night. It's come along for the ride."

"That's a ridiculous thing to say, and you know it!" He frowned in my direction.

"As you're determined on being flippant, I suppose

you are now going to suggest to me that it's another of your talking animals and that it stood by the roadside and begged a lift? Tchaa!" he snorted. "Well, it can come right out of there and—What's *this*?"

Damnation, hell and perdition! He had been fumbling inside the pannier and he must have found—

"*Where did you get this animal*?"

"I told you—"

"You stole it! This is the creature we went to see yesterday afternoon, the one you told me had wings! You were the 'witch' they were all talking about last night!"

I wanted to giggle: he looked so—so *silly*, when he was angry, not at all like his usual handsome self. More like a cross little boy.

"I didn't exactly *steal* him; it was more of a rescue."

"Don't play with words! Don't you realize this could be a hanging matter?" Suddenly he looked scared. "And they might say I was aiding and abetting you—"

"Nonsense!" but my heart began to beat a little faster. I had never thought my deed might involve anyone else.

The pig's head popped out of the pannier like a puppet on cue. "I told you I don't want to be any bother. Let me out and I'll—I'll just disappear. No bother . . ."

"You just stay right where you are!" All this was beginning to make me quite angry. "I said you could come with us and I meant it." I turned to Gill. "This animal was being badly mistreated. If I had left it where it was it would have died. After that stupid story about a witch, no one is going to come after us. And as for anyone recognizing the animal, I'll—I'll make it a little leather coat so you can't see the wings. Satisfied?"

He looked dumbfounded. I had never shouted at him before. Growch sniggered. "All right, whatever you say. But don't blame me if we get caught."

"I won't." I shouldn't get the chance: everyone would be too busy blaming me.

We made damp progress during the rest of the morning and ate our midday meal on the move. Only a few weeks ago I hadn't been able to walk more than an hour without having to rest for another; strange how easily one became accustomed to a different life-style. Besides, it helped that I had lost at least a little weight; my clothes no longer fitted as tightly as before and I didn't have to lever myself up from the ground by hanging on to something. A small victory, perhaps, but it did me the world of good.

Around three in the afternoon it began to rain in earnest, the sort of rain that states its intention of continuing for some time. We pulled off the road to shelter while we donned our cloaks and I adjusted Mistral's load to give the animals maximum protection; it also gave Growch the opportunity to shake himself all over us.

It was lucky we were off the road, for Mistral pricked her ears and gave us warning of horsemen approaching. We crowded back farther into the trees as six horsemen rode by, looking neither to left nor right, mud splashing up from the horses' hooves to mire the fluttering cloaks of the riders. They went by too fast for me to recognize anyone and they were probably not seeking us at all, but their appearance gave us all a nasty jolt.

Besides, even innocent travelers were wary of sudden strangers, especially when they were as unprotected as we were. Bandits, brigands, mercenaries were none of them averse to slitting a quick throat and making off with the spoils and even opposing armies had been known to break off the conflict for long enough to plunder a caravan and share the spoils, then happily rejoin the conflict.

We waited for half an hour before rejoining the road, just in case, and the downpour grew steadily worse. We found we were plodding, head down, the freshening wind driving into our faces and under our clothes till we were all as blind as Gill and soaked through. There was little shelter to either side and I couldn't have lighted a fire, so we just struggled forward, hoping against hope for a deserted hut, a byre, anything at all we could use to get out of the wet.

To add to our misery there came an unseasonal thunderstorm, lightning crackling down the sky with a noise like ripped cloth and thunder bouncing along the road ahead of us. We even seemed to be walking through the

fires of hell, for the road by now was a shallow lake with
the rain, and the sheets and daggers of lightning were
reflected off it like a burnished shield, till I was almost
blinded.

A bolt of lightning split a tree off to our right and as
I instinctively started back I thought I could see a building just beyond the smoldering tree. Another flash lit up
the sky and yes! there was definitely something there.
Grabbing Mistral's bridle with one hand and Gill with
the other I started to follow a narrow path that seemed
to lead in the right direction. As we drew nearer the
building the storm revealed it as a small castle built of
stone, but there was no sign of life.

We ended up in front of a massive oaken door studded
with iron and with a huge ring set in one side. I thumped
on the wood and shouted: "Anyone there?" two or three
times, but there was no answer. I tried again with the
same result, and at last, greatly daring, twisted the iron
ring. At first it was so stiff it would not yield an inch,
but when Gill lent a hand it slowly turned and the door,
with our weights behind it, juddered open a fraction.

"Once more," I panted, and suddenly it swung wide
with a loud groan. As I stepped forward into the stuffy
darkness I became aware of two things: my ring was
burning like fire and the pig was crying: "No, no, no!
It's *bad*!"

CHAPTER
THIRTEEN

Too late for any warnings: we were in. The relief was so great that any trepidation I might have had was canceled by the luxury of four walls and a roof. The place was dusty, fusty, stuffy, but it was sheer heaven contrasted with outside. Obviously old and untenanted, except probably by rats, mice and cockroaches, it nevertheless must have once been a place of some consequence.

It was fashioned on the old lines; a great hall on the ground floor with a fire in the center that would have found its way through a hole in the roof, a raised dais at one end for the lord and his guests to dine, and presumably outhouses for cooking and stabling. There were turret stairs leading to two round towers I had noticed from outside, but the stairs had collapsed and there was no way up. There was a stairway at the back, but this led only to the chaos of storm-ridden battlements.

Our priorities were warmth and food. There were plenty of crumbling sticks of furniture—tables, stools, benches—so I soon had a brisk fire burning in the central fireplace, unpacked Mistral and rubbed her down, plonked Gill down on a rickety stool near enough the fire for his clothes to steam and hung our sodden cloaks to dry. Deciding to feed the animals first, I gave the pigeon some grain and dashed out in the rain again to pull up some grass for Mistral and the tortoise. I set out some corn for the Wimperling, but he cowered under Mistral's belly, still moaning about things being "Bad, bad!"

Growch, stretched out beside the fire steaming gently and beginning to smell quite high in the warmth, told him quite rudely to shut his trap.

I rummaged in our packs for food, wishing I had had time to stock up better. There must be something. . . . In the end I decided on an experiment. I had plenty of beans and grain, but no time to soak the former. Perhaps the latter would yield to drastic treatment. I put some pork fat in the cooking pot, heated it till it smoked, then dropped in a handful of grain. The results were quite dramatic.

There was a moment's pause and then the pot crackled, spat, popped, and grain cascaded everywhere, all puffed up to three times its size or more. A lot sprang back into the fire, more over the floor and I caught some in my apron. Too late I slammed the lid on the pot. In the end I had a large bowlful of something crunchy and very tasty. I devoured a handful then gave the rest to Gill, under protest from Growch.

"Mmmm," said Gill. "Any more?"

The second and third lot was much better because I remembered the lid. Not entirely filling, but certainly better than nothing. I offered some to the Wimperling, hoping to tempt him out of his terrors, but he wasn't having any.

"No, no, not here! This place is bad. . . ."

"Suit yourself," I snapped, by now quite cross, more so because my ring was still tingling and yet my sight and common sense told me there was nothing wrong. The place was old, but it was empty of threat, I was convinced.

"Seems to be getting colder, Summer," said Gill. He was actually shivering. Suddenly it seemed also several degrees darker in the hall. Of course it would, I told myself: it must be well after the set of a sun we had

never seen; time to make up the fire and settle down to
a night's rest. I made up the fire, fetched out the blankets, luckily only slightly damp, and wrapped myself up
tight. I fell into an uneasy sleep, waking every now and
again almost choking with the smoke that no longer
found its exit in the roof, but was wreathing the hall with
bands and ribbons of greyish mist.

Growch and Gill were snoring, but Mistral was restless,
twitching her tail; the pigeon was still awake, and so was
the tortoise. There was no sign of the pig. I got up to
replenish the fire yet again, but it was no longer throwing
out any heat. It sulked and spat and burned yellow and
blue around the wood, which smoldered but would not
catch. I lay down again but sharp cold rose from the
flagstones beneath me, making my bones ache. Flinging
the blanket aside I grabbed Gill's stool and hunched as
near as I could to the fire, till my toes were almost in
the embers and the wool of my skirt smelled as though
it were scorching, though it was cool to the touch.

"May I join you?"

I must be dreaming, I thought. I could have sworn
somebody spoke. I glanced around: nothing but wreaths
of smoke crowding the shadows. No one there except
the animals, Gill and myself. I kicked the fire, hoping
for flame, but there was none. It must be well after
midnight—

"Greetings! May I join you?"

I whirled around, my heart beating like a drum.
"Who—who's there?" It didn't sound like my voice, all
high and squeaky. In spite of the cold I could feel myself
beginning to sweat. Cautiously I slid my hand towards
the bundles and luckily found a candle almost at once.
Lighting it in a stubbornly flameless fire was more difficult, but the melting wax encouraged a quick flare. Holding the candle high I stood up.

"I said: 'Who's there?' "

"Only me. Sorry if I gave you a fright." Whoever it
was gave a little laugh as though he was perfectly at
home.

"Where are you?"

"Here . . ."

The voice came from the shadows on the other side of the fire, and now I thought I could see an indistinct shape among the clouds of smoke that made me cough and squint.

"Do I have your permission to join you?" From what I could make out the figure was small and slight, not much taller than I was. What a strange question though: presumably the place was as much his as ours; we were all trespassers.

"Are you alone?" I asked.

"Alone? I am always alone." Again that light, sneering laugh. "No one has visited this place for a very long time. You must be the first for . . . oh, I suppose at least fifteen years. Before that—Nice to see fresh faces. The last people here were a band of robbers. Not very nice people. No *culture* . . ." The figure came nearer, but the smoke made it seem blurred at the edges. "I ask again: may I join you?"

Why this insistence upon invitation? It was the fourth time. From the way he spoke—

"Is this your place? Do you live here?"

He paused for a moment, then laughed again. "This is my family home, yes. But I don't *live* here. Not exactly. More visitor's rights, you might say."

"Then we are the intruders. Please—" "make yourself at home" I was about to say, but there was an agonized squeal from the shadows.

"No, no, no!" cried the Wimperling. "Don't ask it in! Part of the spell! Bad, bad, bad!"

I felt him creep against my skirts, and nudged him with my foot. "What spell? You're being stupid. He has more right than us to be here. Just be quiet."

"Don't invite him to join you—"

But this time I kicked him quite hard, my irritation getting the better of me, and he scuttled away into the shadows again, with a pitiful cry like a child's. I was instantly sorry, of course, but turned my pity into a welcome for our visitor.

"You are most welcome. Please come and join us."

"Us?"

Couldn't he see? "My—my brother and our animals. They are all asleep. Except for the pig."

I could have sworn he hissed between his teeth. He moved forward, however, and now I could see him more clearly.

To my surprise our visitor was little more than a youth, perhaps a year younger than myself, with the beginnings of a fluff of beard. He was fair, with unfashionably long hair curling down to his thin shoulders, and likewise his clothes were unfamiliar. A long tabard reaching to below his knees, complemented with old-fashioned cross-gartered hose and set off with a short, dark cloak, fastened to one shoulder with a gold pin. In his left ear he sported a gold earring, and there were rings on his fingers and a twisted bracelet on his right arm. He carried, of all things, a tasseled fly-whisk, which he waved in one languid hand.

I vacated my stool. "Please . . ."

He smiled and sat down, showing small, pointed teeth. "I thank you, fair damsel."

Unaccountably flurried, I found a backless chair and joined him by the fire. We stared at one another across the cold flames. I was shivering, but he seemed perfectly comfortable.

"You said this was your family's home? Do you live nearby?"

"I regard this as my home. Do you know any stories?"

I blinked at the change of subject. "Why, yes, I suppose so. My mother was a great storyteller. But first—"

"Nothing like a good story to pass the time." He wriggled on the stool like an expectant child. "I hope you have a *great* story to tell me." He stroked his almost nonexistent beard. "A story is almost my *favorite* thing in the world. . . ." Close to he was very, very pale, almost chalk-like, the skin near transparent. Obviously he didn't get out much. Contrasted with him, Gill and I looked disgustingly tanned and healthy. So far he made me feel uneasy, uncomfortable: I couldn't say I liked him at all, but we were intruding in his home, and I thought I should try and make myself agreeable.

"Would you like something to eat? There isn't much, but—"

He turned on me a look of fury. "What makes you think I am hungry for your disgusting comestibles? Of what use are they save to make you better able to— Never mind. . . ." With a visible effort, it seemed, he settled back on the stool and gave another of those rather unpleasant sniggers. "Don't mind me; I am my own company much of the time, and it makes me forget the social niceties." He waved that absurd fly-whisk in front of his face. "Quite warm for the time of year isn't it?"

As I was practically freezing and it seemed to be getting colder and colder, I didn't know what to say to this. I changed the subject.

"You said this was your home?"

"I have lived here all my life." He leaned forward and quite deliberately passed his thin, white hands through the blue flicker of flame in the fireplace. I reached forward to snatch at him, but the fingers were white and unmarked as before. Suddenly I wanted to wake Gill, Growch, all of them. "Very fond of this place I am," he mused.

"I am sorry we intruded. I did call out. . . ."

"I heard you, but—but I was some way away at the time. Don't apologize. You are more welcome than you know. It is rare that I can welcome strangers these days. . . ." He stroked his beard once more, once more came that disconcerting giggle. "Of course in the old days this place was quite, quite, different. . . ."

A story was coming, I was sure of it. *His* story. I leaned forward on the chair, my chin in my hands, as I used to do when Mama had conjured up a fresh tale for my delight.

The stranger smiled, showing those pointy teeth again. "The story starts many years ago—I *am* enjoying this: it is many years also since I had the chance to tell it—when the country was wilder and less civilized than it is now. It all began when a great chief who had fought in many wars and gathered much plunder decided to build for himself and his new wife (part of his booty) a home in which to settle down and raise a family. He was now well into middle age and wearied of battle." The stranger almost absent-mindedly passed his hands through the flames again, and this time it seemed for a moment as though his thin, white fingers were lapped in fire. "He chose this site, near the highway, topping a small rise, surrounded by forest and near enough a stream for water. He annexed a thousand acres of the forest for his hunting and set those slaves he had captured to building this castle. By the time it was completed his eldest son was nineteen, the second seventeen, the youngest . . ." For a moment he hesitated. "The youngest near sixteen."

There was a movement at my side: Gill had woken and was propped on his elbow, listening. Quickly I explained what had happened. The stranger frowned petulantly: obviously he did not care for interruptions.

"To continue . . . The finished castle was furnished in the most exquisite way possible. The Lord had brought with him hangings, gold, silver, silk, wool, carved chests of sandalwood, pelts of wolf and bear, timber and pottery, all part of his conquests, and his wife, children—even his servants—were dressed in the finest of materials."

My eyes half-closed, I could see it all: the splendor, the comfort, the ease of living . . .

"It seemed nothing could ever mar this idyllic existence: a united family, devoted servants, a fine home, but all was not as it seemed." He shifted on his stool, stroked his wispy beard, flicked the fly-whisk, toyed with his earring. "From an outsider's point of view the three sons were all their father could have wished for. The eldest, tall and fair-haired like his father, was skilled at arms, a womanizer and a prodigious quaffer of ale; the second son was dark like his mother, merry and careless, with a fine singing voice. It was the third son who was different. Outwardly unlike either parent, except for his father's fairness and his mother's eyes, he was slighter, more refined in manner, a great reader and penman. His ideas were in advance of his time; he wanted his father to annex more land, build onto the castle, expand a common holding into a kingdom! But his parents were not interested." He frowned. "They should have known better...."

I glanced around. All the animals were awake too.

"His father's hairs were grey now, and when he wasn't in the saddle with his falcons he was dozing by the fire. The mother died of a low fever and the two eldest boys ran wild, promising each other how they would enjoy life after their father's death, filling the castle with wine, women and song! They laughed at the youngest son, gibed at his bookish ways, his ineptitude at the hunt, his miserable showing with the two-handed sword, his distaste for wenching, his lack of prospects as the youngest. By law the estate should be divided between all three equally on their father's demise, but he knew he had little chance of a fair deal with two such brothers."

The stranger was still scowling, now biting at his nails between sentences. He really was absorbed in his story, I thought. The ring on my finger was now colder than I was. Biting cold ...

"The youngest son smoldered with anger, with frustration, with contempt for his weak father, fear of what would happen when his brothers inherited. It was as he feared. His father was scarcely in his grave when the two eldest brothers filled the castle with whores and roisterers. Week-long, month-long, they caroused and capered till the air was thick with the stench of scorched meats, sour wine and stale sex!" He rose to his feet and paced back and forth, the smoke from the fire swirling round his fingers like an extra cloak. "Driven to near madness, the youngest son consulted a witch, then sought certain plants in the forest. Taking them up to the turret room where he spent his days he brewed and distilled them until he had a vial of liquid the color of blood and clear as wine. He tasted—Ach! Bitter! Too bitter to mix with anything. He added more water, cloves, honey; much better.

"Waiting for another night of feasting the youngest son

crept down with the vial beneath his cloak to join the revelry. He watched until the servants had been dismissed and the eldest brothers were too drunk to notice his actions. He then proposed a toast to a long life and a happy one, taking care to open a new bottle and add his poison to the brew. It did not take long: within five minutes they were slumped at the table, no longer breathing. The young man then went out to the kitchens and stables and threw out the servants, not caring where they went. Coming back into the hall he gloated over the bodies at the table, then remembered his two young sisters, asleep in the other turret. Taking a knife he crept up the stairs and cut their throats as they slept. It was like slaughtering two suckling pigs. . . ."

I shivered, not from the cold this time. I saw out of the corner of my eye that Gill had made a grimace of distaste; he liked the story no better than I did. I liked even less the way it was being told—there was a sort of gloating about the stranger that I found scary.

"Coming back to the hall the young man noticed with horror that one of the brothers was groaning. Obviously diluting the poison had weakened it, so he took his brother by the hair, tilted back his head and slit his throat. Then he did the same to the other, just in case, and the bright blood spurted onto the linen cloth, quite ruining it." He sounded more regretful of the spoiled napery than the murders—I shivered again. I could swear that a fine mist was stealing through the high slit windows of the hall and under the door, to thicken the smoke that already seethed around us.

The young man reseated himself, rubbing his hands together with a dry, whispery sound like the shuffle of dead leaves. "A good story, don't you think?"

Gill sat up and rubbed the sleep from his eyes. "And all this happened right here? Then I am surprised it has not been pulled down long since! Such places are accursed! If we had known . . ."

"But we didn't and it has done us no harm," I said briskly, as much to convince myself as him. "I presume the young man was taken and hanged for his crimes?"

"No, it was not at all like that," said the stranger. "No one came near the place—the servants were all gone, if you remember, and this place is very isolated—so the young man's crimes went undiscovered. At first he delighted in the solitude, the peace, but after a while the silence began to oppress him and he found he was talking to himself, just to hear another voice. He even invented conversations with the corpses at the table. . . ."

"They were still there?" I queried, aghast. Something too terrible to name was nagging at the back of my mind, but as yet I couldn't put a name to it. But when I did—

"Oh, yes. He left them as they were, a reminder of his victory. As time went on and no one came to investigate, he loosed the horses, hounds and falcons and the corpses were chewed by rats till nothing but the lolling bones, strands of hair and scraps of clothing were left." He sighed. "After a while even talking to the dead began to pall, so the young man traveled to the nearest town, seeking company. He had not eaten for weeks and he thought perhaps the lack of food had made him transparent, for all passed him by as though he did not exist and none answered his pleas for help. In the end he went back to his dead family, for that was all he had left. After many years, at infrequent intervals, travelers—like yourselves—sought shelter. Then the young man was happy, for he persuaded them to tell him stories, tales to remember that he could hug to himself during the long years when no one visited." And he hugged his arms around his knees, much as that other young man must have done all those years ago.

"And the bodies?" I asked, glancing about me fearfully.

"Oh, they eventually crumbled into dust," said the stranger indifferently. "It all happened over two hundred years ago. Even the bodies of the last travelers are dust. . . ."

"The last travelers?" said Gill sharply, while a rising panic threatened to choke me. "Why did they not leave?"

"They didn't know any stories," said the stranger discontentedly. "The young man wove his spell about them, but still they didn't understand. He even offered to break the chain that held them, let them out one by one, but they still wouldn't play fair. So . . ." He fell silent.

"And so?" prompted Gill, and in his voice I heard an echo of all the horrors that were threatening to envelop me entirely.

"Eh? Oh, the usual thing happened. When they found they couldn't escape they went mad. Killed each other. The only exciting thing was betting on the survivor. Not that he ever lasted long on his own . . ."

Gill rose to his feet. "Then, with all these bloody murders, I'm surprised the place isn't haunted!"

"Oh, but it is," said the stranger. "It is haunted by the ghost of the youngest son. He still waits here for those who have a tale to tell."

I could feel the hair rising on my scalp. "Then—then why aren't you afraid?" I backed away, my chair overturning with a crash.

"Afraid? Why should I be afraid?" He smiled at us sweetly. "You see—I *am* the ghost!"

CHAPTER
FOURTEEN

It is impossible to describe what happened in the next few moments. For one thing, I was too frightened to do anything except open my mouth and yell; for another, everything happened on top of itself.

I screamed, Gill fell over something and brought me down with him, the animals panicked and yelled as well and the stranger rushed round and round bleating trivialities like a demented sheep. That made it worse. My expectant terror had anticipated that he—It—would turn into something shrieking and gibbering, wearing a linen sheet, dragging Its chains and blowing like the east wind through a fleshless mouth—

Instead he—It—seemed to flow around us like the smoke from the fire, never touching us but making little patting, placatory gestures, tut-tutting in that high, mellifluous voice, soothing as if the terror I felt had an origin other than Itself. Apart from Its outlandish dress, It looked disturbingly normal, capering around us with Its senseless blandishments.

"No need to panic ... didn't mean to alarm you ... all a joke really. Want to be *friends* ... you must stay awhile ... don't run away ..." It went on and on till the whisperings were as thick in my ears and nose and mouth as the air I breathed and I would have promised anything if it would just stop for a minute and let me *think*. . . .

So this—this creature—purported to be a two-hundred-year-old fratricide! This pale, frail youth walking and talking like anyone else . . . No, it just wasn't believable. It was a joke: in bad taste, to be sure, but still a joke. Well, I would call Its bluff.

"That's a—" My voice was coming out like a bat's squeak. I tried again. "That's a good act of yours. . . ." Better. "I congratulate you. But perhaps if you dressed differently, tried a few screams and howls, colored lights . . ."

It stopped rushing about and looked at me doubtfully. "What do you mean? I can't change myself. It's how I was—am! You don't like the story? I can't change that either." It seemed really put out. "You want special effects? Well, perhaps I can arrange some of those. Wait just a minute or two. . . ." and It turned and walked up to the other end of the hall.

There was a violent nudge at my ankle.

"Get away, quick!" whispered the Wimperling. "Now's our chance!"

"What for? I want to see what he's doing—"

"No, you don't!" and this time he gave me a sharp nip. "If he weaves a strong enough spell he can keep us here forever! Didn't you listen to his story?"

"Of course I did! But he's not a *real* ghost; ghosts don't look like that. He's just a storyteller, playing a game—"

"Game, my arse!" growled Growch, shivering so hard his teeth clattered. "You've lost yer senses of a sudden; let's go!"

I looked round at the others. Mistral had backed away into a corner and the pigeon and the tortoise had hidden their heads. I suddenly felt betrayed by them all. Even Gill looked disturbed, afraid, but I knew there was no harm in the youth: how could there be? All I wanted was to see what It would do next. Even my accursed ring was hurting so much I wanted to tear it off.

All right: if I couldn't have my fun, then I would teach them all a lesson! Striding over to the horse with the blankets over my arm, I rolled and stowed them, snapped shut the cages that held Basher and Traveler and fetched the cooking pot and slung it over the other goods. Lucky I hadn't unpacked all our gear. If I'd had to start at the beginning my temper would have gotten even worse.

Running over to the door I flung it open with a crash, letting in a howling gale and lashing rain.

"You are scared shitless? You want to go out in that? Then go, and good riddance! Me, I'm staying here."

They cowered away from me as though I had struck them, all save the Wimperling. He stood his ground.

"We're not going without you," he insisted. "But don't you *see* what danger you're in? There is no more substance to that—that *Thing* than the shadows which surround him!"

"Rubbish!" I snapped, and went back over to Gill, still standing by the cold fire, moving his blind head from side to side like a wounded animal.

"Summer? Is that you? What's going on?"

"I'm here. . . ." I took his hand, if possible even colder than mine and clammy with fear. "Don't worry; there's nothing to be scared of. The stranger has promised us some magic. Special effects, he said. Ah, it looks as though they are starting now."

Beyond us, on the dais where once the high table had stood, came a reddish glow. I moved down the room, dragging the reluctant knight with me, and out of the incandescence I could hear the high, mannered voice of the stranger.

"Come nearer, nearer! That's it, right at the front. No, you won't need that candle. . . . Now, watch!" It sounded just like a showman at a fair.

As I stared at the red light, which shifted and swayed like smoke, now brighter, now dimmer, I thought I could discern the outlines of a table, a bench, shadowy figures seated in front of dishes and goblets.

"Closer . . ." urged the voice, now almost in my ears. The smoky dimness swirled back like a curtain and everything became clearer. There was no sound and the outlines wavered now and again like wind on a tapestry, but I could see distinctly two men seated at the table, obviously enjoying the remnants of a feast. A silent carousal, I nevertheless added imagined sounds to myself. They chewed at lumps of meat, quaffed their wine, tossed back their heads and laughed, clapped one another on the shoulder. They both seemed to be dressed in the same quaint way as the stranger, but their outlines were so changeable it was difficult to be sure.

"Not perfect," said the languid voice in my ear, "but memory is not infallible. Watch this: enter the villain!"

Behind the two men I saw the stranger, a flagon of wine in one hand, a vial in the other. He was as insubstantial as the others but I saw part of the story he had told enacted before my credulous eyes. The vial was tipped into the flagon, the men drank a toast and then their heads sank to the table as though they were asleep, and the stranger tiptoed away with a silent giggle. The wavering picture remained thus for a minute or two and I explained to Gill what I had seen.

"It's very clever," I said. "I don't know how he does it!"

"I don't like it," muttered Gill. "Please can we go?"

"It's pitch-black, blowing a gale and raining torrents outside," I said. "Besides, I want to watch. . . ."

The men in the illusion were very still, but then one of them moved a little, choked, flung out an arm. The figure of the stranger appeared again, but this time he carried a knife, a knife that already dripped blood. A hand came out, plucked at the hair of the man who had moved, jerked back his head until the throat was stretched tight, and then slit it from ear to ear. At first a thin beaded seam where the knife had entered and then a great gush of blood that fountained across the table—The stranger turned to the second man—

"No, no!" I screamed. "I believe you, I believe you!"

I pulled at Gill's hand, my heart thumping, and turned to run, but now, between us and the open door at the other end of the hall, stood the grinning figure of the stranger, the murderous ghost, knife still in hand, and now he seemed of a sudden more substantial than anything else around us. Even the animals huddled by the

door were assuming a dim and cloudy aspect, seeming
to have lost their colors like well-leached cloth.

It smiled that sickly-sweet smile at us again. "Well, I
gave you your special effects: did you like them? You
must admit I have played *my* part: now it is *your* turn
to entertain *me*." The last words were as sharp and
threatening as the knife he carried.

"Let us go, we haven't harmed you. . . ." Why, oh why,
hadn't I listened to the Wimperling?

"You haven't done me any good, either! That illusion-
making takes it out of me." The tone was as sulky and
whining as a child's. "Tell me a story, you promised me
a story. Lots of stories! I'll let you go when you have
told me a story—if I like it, that is. If I haven't heard it
before." He moved closer, tossing the knife in the air
and catching it. "Come on, we haven't got all night. . . ."

I backed away, still clutching Gill's arm, looking desperately for a way to escape, but the ghost was still
between us and safety, and now he seemed to be taller,
broader than before. I fetched up against the wall, side-
stepped and seemed to find another I couldn't see, only
feel—like cushioned stone. I moved the other way and
there was another barrier. It seemed as though we were
surrounded—was this what the Wimperling had warned
me against? Was this the invisible "chain" that had
trapped all others who visited the hellish place? There
was only one thing for it.

"Just one story and you will let us go?"

"If I like it well enough."

"What—what kind of story?"

"Oh, knights and ladies, witches and dragons, giants
and ogres, shipwrecks and sea monsters, spells and
counter-spells—Heaven and Hell and the Four Winds!"

Up until that very moment I had known dozens of
tales; ones my mother had told me, stories from the Bible
the priest told us, tales we had heard on our travels, ones
I made up for myself (the largest amount). I could have
sworn that with a minute or two's thought I could spin
a yarn to satisfy any critic, but all of a sudden my mind
was completely empty. I couldn't even summon up the

magic formula that started all stories, that first thread drawn from the spinning wheel that has all else following without thought.

"Well? Why haven't you begun?"

"I—I . . ."

"Get on with it! I warn you, I'm beginning to lose my patience! You're just like all the others: no fun. . . ." The voice managed at the same time to be both petulant and menacing. " 'Once upon a time . . .' "

That was it! I looked once more at the ghost, who had stretched and expanded until his head nearly touched the beams overhead, a thin wraith like a plume of colored smoke, a genie escaping its lamp. I opened my mouth to start, hoping now that the rest would follow. My ring throbbed mercilessly.

"Once—"

"No!" It was another voice, a small voice but one made sharp and decisive by some sudden determination. It didn't sound like the Wimperling at all. "He'll have you if you do! Don't say another word. Just get ready to run. . . ." And with that I saw the most extraordinary sight.

A roundish object suddenly launched itself like a boulder from a catapult. As it reached a height of a couple of feet from the ground it seemed to waver for a moment, then there was a snap! and a crack! like a pennon flapping in a gale, and wings sprouted on either side, a nose pointed forward, a tail balanced back, and the pig rose to ten, twelve feet in the air and then, yelling like a banshee, swooped down and passed right *through* the ghost's body, just where its stomach would be!

The ghost-thing wavered and twisted and began to thicken and shrink back to its normal size, but where the Wimperling had flown through there was a great gaping hole, a sudden window through which everything once more looked clear and sharp. But the hole was beginning to close up again, to heal itself even as I dragged Gill forward. Then was a buzzing above our heads like a thousand bluebottles and the Wimperling zoomed above our heads, yelling: "I'm going to try it again, but my strength is failing. . . . As I go through, run for your lives!"

He arrowed down once more on the now normal-sized figure and as his flailing wings beat aside the trails and tatters of vapor that made up the creature, Gill and I ran hand-in-hand right through what remained. For one heart-stopping moment there was resistance, a sudden darkness, a frightful stench, then we were near the open door. Now the darkness was only that of night; the resistance, the wind; the smell that of rain. Never had I been so glad to face a storm before!

I grabbed Mistral's bridle with my free hand and we all ran down the path away from the castle, unheeding of dark and wind and rain. Some fifty yards away I stopped and counted heads.

"Oh, God! Where's the Wimperling? He must be . . . Wait there, the rest of you!" and I ran back to the castle door, my heart thumping with renewed terror. Growch, to do him credit, was right at my heels. I stepped into the hall and there was the ghost, still gathering pieces of itself together, gibbering and mouthing threats; there, too, was the little pig, trying vainly to drag its battered body towards the door. Growch hesitated only a moment then rushed forward, barking and snapping hysterically. Seizing my chance I dashed forwards, snatched up the pig, tucked him under my arm and, shouting to Growch to follow, escaped down the path once more.

As we moved off into the storm we could hear a wailing cry behind us, full of reproach and self-pity.

"Come back, come back! I wouldn't have hurt you. . . . all I wanted was a *story*!"

After that it was hard going, for all of us. The weather cleared for a while after that dreadful night, but the Wimperling lay for days in his pannier in a sort of coma, hardly eating anything. Tenderly I greased his sore wings and saved the choicest pieces of food, and gradually he started to pick up. Gill, however, caught a chill and could not shake it off; night after night I heard his cough get worse. Mistral, too, coughed and shivered; Basher the tortoise retreated into his shell and refused to eat, and Traveler's wing wouldn't heal. As for me, my stomach and bowels churned for days and I had to keep dashing off the road to find a convenient bush.

The weather grew steadily colder, with a biting east wind that snapped at our faces, bit at our heels, snatched at our clothes and blew a scud of leaves and grit into the food. The fires wouldn't light and if they did the hot embers scattered and threatened to set fire to everything. To add to our miseries, we seemed to have lost our way. All the roads were mere tracks between villages, and however much we asked for directions south and followed the road indicated, we still twisted and turned until, as often as not, we ended up facing north again.

The lodgings and food we found were poor and mean, and we were charged far too much: they knew, of course, that we had no choice but to pay what they asked. I began to think we were accursed, except that the ring on my finger was quiet—never again would I ignore its warning—and that of course Gill and I had made confession as soon as we could and been absolved. But the days themselves ceased to have individual meaning, apart from the labels of the Saint's days as we passed through various villages: Barbara, Nicholas, Andrew, Lucy, Thomas . . .

After a particularly hard day—we hadn't seen a village for forty-eight hours and were on short rations—and five hours walking without rest, it started to snow. Just the odd flake floating prettily down, but the sky above held a grey cloak that was gradually spreading from the north-east and the air smelled of cold iron. I shuddered to think what might happen if we were caught without cover; we had escaped any heavy falls so far south, but that searing east wind canceled any advantage of distance.

But it seemed our luck had at last turned, for the next twist in the road revealed below us what seemed like a fair-sized town, with at least five or six streets, a large square and two churches. For the first time in days I could feel my cold face stretching into a smile.

"Warm lodgings and a fair supper tonight, for a change! Come on, it's downhill all the way. . . ."

By the time we reached the outskirts the snow was falling with that unhurrying steadiness that meant that, like an uninvited relation, it was here to stay. Because of the weather there were few folk around; those that were were engaged on last-minute precautions: putting up shutters, stabling beasts, hurrying home with a bundle of kindling or a couple of pies. We enquired for an inn, but the first we found was closed for the winter, as we were informed by the slatternly girl who answered my knock, slamming the door in my face before I could ask for further directions.

The snow was now so thick that we found the square by luck only; I caught at the sleeve of a man hurrying past with a capon under his arm and a sack over his head for protection.

"An inn, good sir?"

He paused for a moment, blinking the snow from his eyelashes, then pointed to the other side of the square, gave us a left and a right and a left. "Martlet and Swan," he said and was gone, swallowed by the swirling snow.

Now we were the only ones moving in a world of white. We found the first turning right enough, but I had a feeling we had missed the second. I could scarce see more than a few yards; the snow was clogging our footsteps and weighting our clothes. I took a last left turn, but it seemed as though we were right on the outskirts of town again. I was just about to turn and retrace our steps, knock at the first door that would open to us, when I caught sight of the inn sign swinging above my head. Snow had already obliterated most of the sign, but I could make out the "M-A" of the Martlet and the "S" of Swan, so I knew we were on the right road.

It was larger than the inns we had frequented so far. Double-fronted, the door was locked and barred and there were no lights to be seen. I knocked twice, but there was no answer. On the right, however, the gates were open onto a cobbled yard. We passed under the archway into lights, bustle, activity. On the far side a wagon had just been unloaded and was now being tipped against the snow, while its cargo of sacks was being hurried into shelter. Two steaming draft horses were being led into stables on the right, and buckets of water were sluicing down the cobbles. To our left the door was open onto firelight and the enticing smells of food.

Everyone was too busy to notice us, until I spied out the man who seemed to be directing operations, a well-fed man with a long, furred cloak and red hair, on which the snow melted as soon as it touched. I went over and tugged at his sleeve.

"Sir! Sir? You have lodgings and stabling for the night? For myself, my brother and the animals . . ."

The face he turned towards me had a pleasant, lived-in look, but he seemed to be puzzled.

"Lodgings?"

"Why, yes." Quickly I explained how I had been directed here. "And I saw the sign outside—only a couple of letters, but it was obviously the right place. You aren't full up, are you? I'm afraid my brother is not at all well, and we are cold and hungry. . . . If you are, perhaps you could direct us somewhere else, but . . ." Then I am afraid I started to cry. I couldn't help it. It had been a long, hard, frustrating time since we had fled the castle and the ghost.

He looked at me for a moment longer, then he smiled, a full, heartwarming smile. "Never let it be said . . . Come on, let's look at that sign of mine." Hurrying me out into the street, he gazed up at the nearly covered letters. " 'Martlet and Swan' . . . Dear me: I must get that cleared. No matter, little lady: you found me." And he smiled again, and I knew we were home.

Before I knew what was happening, and with the minimum of direction from the landlord, Gill, his blindness noted, was being led away towards that enticing open door, and I, having insisted, was bedding down the animals with the help of the young stable boy. A rubdown and unloading for Mistral, followed by bran-mash; sleeping Basher tucked away in his box under the manger. Grain for Traveler and the run of the stall. Chopped

vegetables and gruel for the Wimperling and a large bone
for Growch: everything I asked for, diffidently enough,
appeared as if by magic. But then the inn was obviously
not full: Mistral had a commodious closed stall to herself,
and there were only the draft horses and a brown palfrey
to occupy the rest of the large stables.

The stable boy lighted me over to the side door, now
closed, after fastening the yard gates and bolting them.
He was obviously glad to be back in the inn, and after
a dazzled look around the large kitchen in which I found
myself I agreed with him wholeheartedly.

It was the largest kitchen I had ever seen, stretching
the length of the stables which matched it across the
yard. And there were *two* fires; one obviously incorporat-
ing some kind of oven, the other a large spit. Two long
tables, one for preparation of food, the other for serving.
Cupboards and shelves full of pots and crockery, long
sinks for scouring and cleaning, wood stacked waist-high,
clothes drying on racks, herbs, onions and garlic swinging
gently from strings, hams and bacon hanging from hooks
in the smoke-blackened ceiling, baskets of eggs and vegetables, jars of pickles, preserves and dried fruits ...

And everyone merry and busy, not a long face or lag-
gard step among them. And the nose-tickling smells ...
My mouth was watering as I followed a beckoning finger
and found, behind a hastily slung screen, Gill immersed
in a large tub of hot water.

"You all right?"

He couldn't answer, for at that moment one of the
giggling maids who were scrubbing him put a cloth across
his mouth, but he looked happy enough. The landlord
poked his head behind the curtain.

"I thought it was the quickest way to warm him up.
He'll feel better with the grime of the road away, too.
You're next."

No arguments, I noticed. A moment later my clothes
were taken away to be washed and I was relaxing in the
hot, herb-scented water, my hair combed and rinsed. A
brisk rubbing in warmed towels and someone handed me

a clean shift and wrapped me in a blanket, shoving my feet into felt slippers a size too large.

I looked around for Gill, but he had evidently preceded me, for by the time one of the servants had ushered me into a parlor at the front of the house, he was already tucking into a bowl of thick vegetable soup. A small round table in front of a blazing fire was laid with linen, bread platters, spoons and knives. I sat down and was instantly served. As I supped I gazed around the comfortable room. Red tiles on the floor, shuttered window, tapestry, huge sideboard decked with pewter and silver, linen chest, a rack of wine . . . What a strange inn!

Hot baths, clothes washed, expensive surroundings—I hoped to God my purse would cover the cost! And where were the other guests? True, there was a third place laid at the table: we should have to wait and see. I must discuss terms with the cheerful landlord as soon as possible. I finished my broth and the bowl was whipped away, to be replaced by steaming venison-and-hare pasties, the juice soaking into the bread platter beneath. A pewter goblet of wine appeared at my elbow as I leaned over to cut Gill's pasty and guide his fingers.

"May I join you?" It was our host, changed into a crimson wool robe and a white undershirt, his feet in rabbit's-wool slippers. He should *never* wear that shade of red with his color hair, I thought abstractedly, even as I welcomed and thanked him for his excellent hospitality. I had better tackle him straightaway, I thought, even as fruit tarts and cheese were placed on the table. He gave me the opening I needed. "I trust everything is to your satisfaction?"

"Everything is just fine, sir, and we are most grateful, but I am afraid we cannot afford—"

He frowned, then smiled. "I had forgot. Perhaps I had better explain. That notice, so helpfully cloaked by the snow, does not read 'Martlet and Swan', but rather 'Matthew Spicer, Merchant.' The inn is two roads away, I'm afraid, but the natural mistake has given me the opportunity to enjoy your company. As my guests, naturally, so no more talk of money, little lady!"

CHAPTER
FIFTEEN

Those weeks we spent in Matthew's house were like another world to me. Not only were we cosseted, fed, warm, entertained and cared for—we were *safe*. We had only been on the road some seven weeks or so, and yet it seemed to me that I had spent an eternity footsore, usually hungry and cold and always anxious. Not anxious for myself so much as the others. And to have that burden of responsibility taken, however temporarily, from my shoulders was like shucking off a load of wood I had carried, and immediately feeling I could bounce as high as the trees.

My mother had taught me a trick when I was little; lean hard against a wall, pressing one arm and shoulder as tight as I could. Count to a hundred then stand away from the wall. Your arm rises up of its own accord, like magic! I felt like that released arm.

Of course on that first evening there was a lot of explaining to do. At first I had felt like grabbing Gill's arm and rushing out into the night, so embarrassed was I at mistaking a rich merchant's house for an inn, but our host soon made us feel at home.

"A natural mistake, little lady, in all that confusing snow! And what would you have done in my place?

Confronted by a damsel in distress, what could any
Christian do but take her and her brother in?" He chuckled. "Besides, the servants tell me it is getting thicker by
the moment out there. Six inches settled already, and by
morning it will be two or three feet. No, it was Provi-
dence that brought you to my door, I'm convinced, and
Preference will keep you here! But of course," he added
hastily, "if after a while you tire of my hospitality, you
are perfectly free to go elsewhere."

"But we cannot impose on you like this! You must
allow me to—"

"Now you're not going to spoil our new acquaintance-
ship by talking about money, I hope! Money is one thing
I don't need. Companionship I do. As a widower without
family I find I do not make friends easily, and strangers
such as yourselves will give me an interest to take me
out of my usual dull routine. So, you will be doing *me*
the favor by staying for a while. . . . Ah, mulled ale! Just
what we need."

It was piping hot, redolent with cloves, cinnamon and
ginger. I stretched out towards the fire, dazed with heat
and food and drink. I hadn't felt as good as far back as
I could remember—in fact since before my mother died,
when we had stoked up the fire, told stories and eaten
honey cakes, while the wolf wind of winter had howled
down the chimney and keened under the door, making
the sparks at the back of the chimney glow into patterns
among the soot.

"Perhaps for a day or two, then . . ." I said weakly. He
had sounded as though he meant it.

Gill was seized with a fit of coughing and clenched his
fist against his chest with a look of pain. I leaned over
and rubbed his back but the merchant went into action
at once.

"Time we got your brother to bed. That cough sounds
bad. Tomorrow we shall engage a doctor, snow or no
snow."

He led us up a winding stair to the next floor and
pointed to the left. "That is the solar. And here . . ." to
the right: "the bedroom."

It was a long, commodious chamber, strewn with
rushes, hung with tapestries, dominated by a huge bed
that would have slept six with ease. A huge fire burned
in the hearth; candles were glimmering on a table by the
fire and on two blanket chests against the walls. Two
heavily carved chairs stood on either side of the fireplace
and a series of hooks on one wall provided hanging space
for clothes. Between the two shuttered windows was a
small *prie-dieu*. A low archway at the far end was protected by a curtain.

"For washing and the usual offices," said the merchant, following my gaze. "I shall show your brother.
Come, sir," and he led him away.

I moved over to the bed but let out a stifled gasp as
I saw the covers move, and a moment or two afterwards
a naked man and woman slipped from beneath the covers
and unselfconsciously donned the clothes they had left
on the floor. The woman bobbed a curtsy.

"I believe the chill is off the sheets now, mistress, but
a maid will be up in a minute or two to renew the hot
bricks. . . ." and with that the pair of them disappeared
downstairs, leaving me open-mouthed. What luxury! Was
this the way it was done among the rich? Come to think
of it, many times at night my mother had insisted I retire
first "to warm up the bed for my old bones. . . ." A maid
scurried in with hot bricks wrapped with flannel, which
she exchanged for those that must have already cooled.
The bed looked very inviting, piled high as it was with
furs.

The merchant came back with Gill, now shivering.
"Into bed at once. Shall we put him on this side? No, I
think it better if he is in the middle, then with you and
me on either side he will keep warmer." He helped Gill
under the covers and slipped into bed beside him. He
nodded at the curtained recess. "Take a candle with you,
little lady," and I headed for the *garde-robe*.

When I returned another maid was handing Gill a
posset; she waited till he drank it then snuffed all the
candles but two slow burners, in case we needed to
relieve ourselves during the night. She bobbed away, but

I hesitated. I knew it was the custom for a host and his lady to share their bed with guests, but even in the ill-assorted places in which Gill and I had slept we had never shared a pallet. In the open we had slept with more intimacy, but the animals had been there too. . . .

Matthew Spicer propped himself on his elbow. "Something the matter?"

"Er . . . No. That is . . . I think I'll just stay here by the fire for a while. I—I'm really not tired—"

"Nonsense, young lady! You've been yawning and blinking for the past two hours!" He scrambled out of bed and came over to me, the long night-shift flapping round his ankles. "It's something I've done, isn't it? Or not done . . . Tell me." For a successful merchant, he had the least self-confidence I had ever seen. But perhaps women made him nervous. Mama had always said that men like that were a pain to begin with but sometimes made the best lovers. Eventually.

"No, no! You've been kindness itself. It's just that—" I glanced over to the bed: Gill was snoring softly. "You see, even at home I never shared a bed with my brother, and on our travels I slept separately also. I have never shared sleeping space with a man. Perhaps I'm being silly, but—"

He struck his forehead with the palm of his hand. "Of course, of course! Being a widower I don't have someone to remind me of the niceties. Come to think of it, if we had people staying overnight they were always married couples who shared. Since then all my guests have been men. Do forgive me! I shall have a pallet made up for you immediately. I— Whatever in the world is *that*?"

"That" was Growch.

He must have escaped from the stables and somehow infiltrated into the kitchen, for in his mouth was a large piece of pastry. He was soaking wet and smelled like a midden, but he rushed to my side and sat on my feet, growling softly through the pasty, his eyes swiveling from me to the merchant, the servants who were in pursuit, and back again.

He "spoke" through his full mouth. "Found you! What's goin' on then?"

"Nothing is 'going on'! You've no right up here! Why couldn't you stay where you were put?" To Master Spicer: "I'm sorry. It's my—our dog. I left him in the stables, but he's been spoiled, I'm afraid, and is not used to being on his own." To Growch I added furiously: "Just get back to the stables right now, and behave yourself!"

"No way! Needs lookin' after, you does. . . ." He belched, having swallowed the pastry whole. "My place is with you." I could see him eyeing the fire greedily. "Never tell what mischief you'll get into without me. No, here I am, and here I'll stay." He looked up at me through his tangle of hair. "Send me back down there again and I'll howl all night, full strength. Keep yer all awake . . . Promise!"

I turned to the merchant apologetically—my exchange with Growch had taken no more than a couple of silent seconds. "I'm sorry if he has been a nuisance. May he stay up here for tonight? I'll—I'll make some other arrangement tomorrow."

He considered. "I have no objection, though in the morning he might reconsider his decision. I happen to share the house with a rather large cat. . . ." He smiled. "Saffron will sort him out. In the meantime he could do with a bath. While they make up your bed."

No sooner said than done. Up came a large tub, in went Growch, and by the time his outraged grumbles had subsided, the bed was made up and he was clean and combed—probably for the first time in his short life. In the meanwhile Matthew Spicer sent for more wine and little spiced biscuits and we sat by the fire together. He didn't ask any questions, but I decided I had better tell him our names and our story. Not the real one of course: I used the one I had told everyone so far, but this time I killed off our parents and for some reason didn't mention my "affianced," or the dowry.

"You have had a hard time, Mistress Somerdai. That *is* a pretty name, by the way: most unusual. If I may say so, it suits you. . . . I see your bed is made up. We shall talk further in the morning."

Shyly I knelt before the *prie-dieu* to give hearty thanks for the temporary haven we had found, then cuddled down in the pallet by the fire. I lay awake for a while, tired though I was, listening to the gentle contrapuntal snores from the bed, and the occasional stifled cough from Gill. There was a soft *flumph!* from outside as a load of snow slid off the roof to the yard below. The fire crackled pleasantly but there was another, less endearing sound: Growch was scratching his ears, flap-flap-flap, and snorting into his coat as he chased fleas made lively by the heat. It seemed a bath wasn't enough.

I raised myself on one elbow, my head swimming with the need for sleep. By the light from the night-candle and the fire I could see that my scrawny little black dog was black no longer. He looked half as big again, now his cleaned coat had fluffed out—though nothing could lengthen those diminutive legs—and he was not only black, but tan and brown and grey and ginger and white also.

He sneezed six times.

"Can't you stop that?"

He glared at me from under a fuzzy fringe. "Sneeze or scratch?"

"Both."

"Listen 'ere . . . Never mind. All I can say is, if'n you 'ad these little buggers chasin' around, you'd scratch."

"You wanted to be beside the fire! And don't pretend it was all concern for my welfare, 'cos it wasn't! Anyway, why the sneezing? Caught a chill from the unexpected bath?"

"Nar . . . Stuff they washed me in: smell like an effin' whore, I do."

In the morning Gill was definitely worse, tossing and turning in a fever, his cough hard and painful. Matthew Spicer shook his head. "He needs treatment right away." He flung open the shutters: snow was still falling. He closed them again, and shook his head. "Don't worry; one of the servants will get through."

Up and dressed—my clothes returned clean, mended, pressed—I slipped across the cleared yard to the stables. The others were fine; Mistral had been given fresh hay, Basher was still asleep, and I found grain in the bins for Traveler. The Wimperling's nose peeped out from a nest he had made for himself.

"Everything all right?"

I told him about Gill, and the merchant sending for treatment.

"Don't let him bleed the knight; he needs all his blood." I wondered what on earth he knew of doctoring, but let it pass. After all, he had been right before.

"Are you hungry?"

"A little grain will do. I've had a nibble of hay already."

The "apothecary" arrived an hour or so later, in a litter. I don't know what I had expected, but it was certainly not the small, scrunched-up man with the brown skin, hooked nose and black eyes whose candle-lit shadow on the stairs was the first I saw of him. The stooping silhouette with the grotesque reaping-hook nose at first made me cross myself in superstitious fear, but face to face there was nothing to alarm, quite the reverse. The black eyes sparkled with a keen intelligence, the mouth curved easily into a smile and the thin, hunched shoulders and long, clever fingers emphasised everything he said: a shrug of the body, a wave of the hands more expressive than mere words. These he spoke with a heavily accented touch, at first a little difficult to follow.

Matthew Spicer introduced him with pride. "My friend Suleiman, who comes from the East and specializes in many things, including medicine. We have worked together for many years. He has for a long time been my agent in Araby, but now he has been caught by the weather, providentially for us, I might add! I know of his healing powers and salves of old, and he has consented to treat your brother, Mistress Somerdai." He noted my expression of doubt—so did the visitor. "You couldn't do better, I assure you!"

This was soon evident, at least in Suleiman's meticulous examination of Gill. The Arab first questioned his patient thoroughly, asking for all the symptoms, their duration and severity, before he even touched his body. Then he felt his forehead, looked in his eyes and ears with a little glass, put a spatula in his mouth and peered down his throat, then counted the pulse at his wrist.

He glanced up at me. "Your brother has a high fever; to bring this down is our first priority, but first we must find the seat of it. I believe it is in the chest, and I shall now listen to this."

"How?" I was by now too interested for politeness.

"Watch." From the folds of his capacious red robes he brought forth a metal object shaped like a Madonna lily with a hollow, twisted stem. He held it out to me. "Copied from the horn of a rare antelope in the sands of the desert." He held a silver cup to Gill's mouth and asked him to cough, looking gravely at the sputum. "Too thick . . ." Then he placed the wide end of the metal object on Gill's chest, the thin end in his own ear, and listened intently. Repeating this on various parts of the knight's chest, he asked him to sit up and repeated the process on his back. He then beckoned to me. "Do as I did and listen; make sure the instrument is firmly against his chest."

At first all I could hear was a shush-beat, shush-beat which I realized must be the heart, then as Gill breathed in there was a gurgling wheezy noise, as he breathed out a whistling bubble. Incredible!

Master Suleiman took the instrument from me and held it to his own chest. "Listen to the difference. . . ." The steady heartbeat, somewhat slower, but no wheezing, no whistling. "You understand? Your brother has a deep infection in the lungs, hampering his breathing: it is almost as though he drowns in the ill humours that have gathered. So, we can only cure the fever by eradicating its cause: the lung infection. I shall return to my rooms and prepare certain medicines—"

"You're not going to bleed him, then?" I blurted out, remembering what the Wimperling had said.

He shot me a sharp glance from under dark brows. "Sounds as though you are no friend to leeches?"

"A—a friend of mine ... He says it takes away your strength."

"Perfectly correct. I sometimes wish we had a method to pump blood *in* instead of taking it *out*." He looked over at Gill, manfully trying to stifle another bout of coughing. "We'll soon ease that.... Keep my patient warm, no solid food, plenty of drinks. I shall prepare herbs to be steamed over water on a low boil, to soften the air he breathes in here. Please see the fire does not smoke too much. I shall also prepare an expectorant, a potion to reduce the fever and a sleeping draught."

For once I didn't think of cost: whatever he needed, Gill must have. "Will ... will he be all right?" I asked, hesitantly, fearfully.

Suleiman glanced at me sympathetically. "I tell the truth. He is very ill, your brother. I have seen men die in his condition and I have seen them live. His advantages are his youth and strength—and, I hope, my medicines. And a prayer or two wouldn't come amiss."

For three days my knight seemed to hover between life and death, but gradually the fever abated, his breathing grew easier and the coughing less painful. I did not leave his side save to tend the animals, relieve myself and wash. I even ate my meals by the bedside, though I have no memory of their content.

Suleiman called twice a day, Master Spicer fussed and cosseted, the maids washed and dried the patient, gave him fresh linen and night clothes daily. I dozed in fits and starts on a stool by the bed, trying always to be ready for the turn of the sand-glass for the regular dosings, to see the fire was kept topped up, to be ready with cooling drinks and a damp sponge to wipe away the sweat.

On the morning of the sixth day from our arrival Suleiman came in, examined his patient, then crossed the room and flung the shutters wide.

"The sun is shining, the wind has dropped, the temperature is rising and my patient is recovering! Some fresh air will do us all good." He glanced at me, dazed by sudden sun and ready to drop. "I have the very thing for you, Mistress Somerdai. . . ." and he handed me a vial of thick, greenish liquid. "Half of this in a glass of wine—now!—and I guarantee you will be a new young woman before you know where you are!"

I hadn't the strength to resist and downed the bitter-tasting liquid without a murmur. I don't know about feeling like a new woman, I thought, but if I just lie down for a moment or two and close my eyes I'm sure I will. . . .

"Time to wake up," said Matthew Spicer, gently pinching my earlobe. "I'll bet you are hungry. Hot milk and honey has been recommended. Sit up and take a sip."

I did as I was told, opening gummy eyelids, considering how I felt. Apart from an unpleasant taste in my mouth, soon dispelled by a sip or two of the milk, remarkably fit.

"What time is it?"

"A little after two in the afternoon."

"I must have slept over four hours! Sorry . . ."

"Four? More like twenty-eight. You took that draught yesterday morning."

"Yesterday? But I can't have. . . ."

"You did!" said another voice, and there, sitting in one of the large chairs by the fire, wrapped in blankets, sat Gill. A pale, thin Gill, but the hectic flush was gone from his cheeks. He smiled in my direction. "Sleepy-head Summer!"

My heart turned over with love and longing. It was a long time since I had had the chance to study him at leisure. Being on the road had been such a struggle just to survive, especially latterly, that I had grown accustomed to an unshaven, grumbling, blind man who needed all my spare attention. Now he was washed, shaved, fed and at ease, and I found once more I was seeing him as I had that first day, and all the old adoration rushed to the surface, so that I had to hide my face lest Matthew Spicer saw my confusion.

"And in case you are worrying about your menagerie,"

said the merchant, chuckling: "Don't! The horse and the pig—that one will never fatten—have been given mash, the pigeon grain and the reptile left to sleep. When we have some time you must tell me how you acquired such a motley collection! As for your dog—" he nudged a recumbent form lying in the hearth: "—he has been bathed again and near eaten his weight in leftovers. . . ."

Growch was stretched out in a nose-twitching, leg-paddling dream. His curly coat of black and tan, ginger and grey, his white chest and paws, all gleamed in the fire and candlelight, and his stomach was so full it was stretched as tight as the skin on a tabour, the thinner hair on his belly showing the pied skin underneath.

"He met Saffron, my ginger cat, on the stairs," continued the merchant. "And he retreated at once, as I knew he would: Saffron makes two of most dogs, especially in his winter coat. However, I think you will find they have come to some agreement. Your dog is allowed inside as long as he recognizes who is boss. . . . And now, Mistress Somerdai, when you are dressed and have broken your fast, perhaps I may show you something of my house?"

Through the archway at the top of the stairs was the solar, a pleasant room with a deep hearth, set with benches on either side. The floor was polished oak, partly covered with two large rugs the merchant told me had come from a place called Persher; these were pleasant underfoot and partially muffled the creak of the floorboards. Two carved chairs stood by the window, and leather-topped stools provided further seating. On one side of the curtained doorway were hooks for cloaks; there were two chests, one containing cushions for extra comfort, the other a set of games: chess, draughts, backgammon and dice.

In the center of the room was a table, the top inlaid in marble to represent a chess or draughts board; a hanging cupboard contained three precious books: a psalter, a breviary, and a delightful Boke of Beestes. Eventually I read this from cover to cover more than once, carefully examining the delightfully illustrated initials, head- and tail-pieces, marveling all the while at the strange creatures—spotted, dotted, patched, striped; furred, feathered, scaled; toothed, beaked, tusked, clawed—that curled, writhed, marched and snaked across the pages. There were creatures I had never heard of, others I couldn't believe in—gryphons, mermen, crocodiles, elephants—and yet, amongst them all were tortoises! Very strange . . .

The walls of the solar were part paneled, part painted, these latter in patterns of yellow suns, moons and stars on a pale blue background. Just as the bedroom windows overlooked the yard, the window in the solar looked out over the street in front, and it was this window that was the most curious item in the room. There were the usual shutters, of course, but now no one need freeze to death to look out on the busy street below, for the merchant had installed proper windows that opened outwards for summer and remained closed in winter—all of glass! Not just plain glass, either: he knew a man who restored stained-glass in churches, and the window was filled with a higgle-piggle of colors, all small pieces like a patched cloak—red, blue, yellow, green, purple and even some that had been part of trees, creatures, faces—so that one looked out on the street through colors that discolored the folk below, and yet when the sun shone these same pieces threw a rainbow of light onto the polished floor. Like a spring lawn sown with wildflowers . . .

Down the stairs and there were the long kitchens at the back where the staff lived, ate and slept. At the front was the room where we had dined on that first night: "Near the kitchens so the food doesn't get cold," my host explained, and, next to it, with a separate entrance and shuttered counter to the street, the shop where the merchant did his day-to-day business.

A long counter held weighing scales, paper, wax and string. Behind this were piles of small sacks, neatly tied and labeled and above them shelves reaching to the ceiling, filled with bottles, jars, pouches, boxes of all shapes and sizes and parcels. Behind the counter was the merchant's assistant, a small, pocked man called Jacob. But it was the smell of the place one remembered. All through

Matthew Spicer's house little teasing scents met one on
the stairs, hid in chests, fled down nooks and crannies,
popped up in the linen, but here was the source, the
heart of it all.

There were herbs in plenty—rosemary, thyme, dill,
fennel, sage, rue, peppermint, balm, bay, basil, but it was
the scent of the exotic spices that overlay all. Cloves,
ginger, cinnamon, cardamom, nutmeg, mace, saffron,
pepper, cumin, all combining to tickle the nose with their
pungency and invite their flavors to match their aromas.

Matthew Spicer was a member of the Guild, and he
explained that most of his goods came from the East to
a place called Vennis, a magical town that floated on the
sea like an anchored island. From there the goods traveled overland to the nearest western port and again took
ship across the Mediterranean to a southern port. From
there it came by road to the merchant's house, the bulk
being stored in the large sheds at the back of the yard,
to be packed into smaller containers ready for distribution to various large towns and cities throughout the
country, and even farther north.

It sounded like a long and complicated business, and
I said so.

"Certainly it is," he said. "Sometimes it can take up to
three years between ordering something and its delivery."

"And what if one of the ships founders, or your wagons
are attacked? Or the spices spoil in transit?"

"Luckily that doesn't happen very often. God is good."
He crossed himself. "Also, there is a very good profit
margin. I am not poor." He sighed. "But money isn't
everything. I lost my wife seven years ago, God rest her
soul, and I have no family to carry on the business."

"You could marry again. . . ."

"I could, yes, but if I found a woman who pleased me,
who knows but that she might refuse me?" He attempted
a smile. "I am not very good at understanding the fair
sex, I'm afraid, and I am no longer a young man."

I presumed him to be in his early forties. Not stout,
but not slim either; not handsome, but not ugly: he had
a pleasant, lived-in sort of face. His reddish hair was

thinning slightly but his teeth were still good. I spoke to him as I thought Mama would have done.

"I am sure any woman you chose would be only too pleased to accept your offer. Youth is only an attitude of mind, after all, and you are the kindest man I know."

His face brightened. "You really think so? You have cheered me more than I would have thought possible!"

What with Gill's illness we had missed any Christmas festivities, but with Suleiman as another guest we four celebrated the New Year in style: the rooms decorated with sprays of evergreen, sprinkled with rose water, alive with candles; Mass (except for Suleiman), then back to a veritable feast. Chicken stuffed with dates and olives— two fruits I had never tasted before—a baked ham stuck with cloves and glazed with honey, root vegetables in butter with a touch of ginger, small pastry cases full of meat and spices, the latter so hot they made you feel you breathed fire, roast chestnuts, rice with apple, apricot and other dried fruit and a soft, sheep's-milk cheese.

And to drink a toast to the rebirth of the year, an ice-cold sweet white wine that came, like the silken hangings, from a place called Sissilia . . .

I had anticipated taking our journey up again within days, but the visit to church had not done Gill any good—except spiritually, of course. He started to cough again, and Suleiman insisted that he stay quiet and within doors for a week or more at least. This meant that we fell into a certain routine. After breaking our fast we would, Gill and I, go into the solar, where I would take up sewing and mending, which our clothes sorely needed.

I was surprised to find just how much thinner I had become, and the chore of sewing was mixed with a secret delight in being able to take in my clothes as well as patch and repair them. I regretted that my things were so shabby and worn, but they still covered me well enough and I could not afford to indulge in non-necessities. Gill was a different matter. He had been used to so much better, whether he remembered it or not, and

as I had taken to exercising Mistral and Growch if the
weather was fine, I took the opportunity of buying some
rough woolen cloth, burel, and fitting my knight for
longer braies and a new surcoat. The town was a pleasant
place and obviously Matthew Spicer was held in high
regard, for once folk knew we were staying with him—
and news travels faster than a grass fire in a place like
that—we were welcomed with smiles and cheerful greetings. I suspect, too, that I was given a special price for
my cloth, and for the repair of our shoes which was also
essential.

One morning Matthew—he had asked us to dispense
with the more formal address—came into the solar looking helpless, a length of fine green wool over his arm.
He hesitated for a moment, then asked if I had much
sewing in hand.

"Why, no. I have only to finish attaching the ties to
these braies. Is there something you would like me to
do?"

"Er . . . yes. There is, actually. If you're sure you don't
mind? I have a sister, married to a Dutchman, and she
writes in her letters that she finds it difficult to buy wool
in this particular color." He held the soft wool against
my shoulder. "Yes, the shade is just right! Her coloring
is near yours, and I wonder . . ."

"Yes?" I encouraged, indulgent of this successful man
who could yet be so diffident.

"If you could make her a surcoat," he said, all in a
rush. "Something simple and serviceable, nothing fancy?
You and she are much of a height and size, and if you
make generous seams and hems . . . But perhaps I ask
too much?"

"Of course not! I only hope I can do this beautiful
material justice." I fingered it: strong and hard-wearing,
it was still fine enough to hang practically creaseless. "A
lovely color: like fresh mint."

He was obviously pleased. "Again, if it's not too much
trouble, she would need two undercottes; I have some
fine linen dyed a soft brown which would go nicely. . . ."

It was the least I could do. He had been so kind to us both: a man in a thousand.

During the time I sewed, Gill would be practicing on a small lute Matthew had found, or on my pipes, although he soon became bored and restless; sighing deeply, drumming his fingers on the furniture, yawning. Then I would coax him to sing: "Winter's weary winds," "Silk for my sweetheart," or, if Matthew joined us, tenor, baritone and soprano would essay a round: "The beggars now have come to town," or something similar.

Afternoons I would read while Gill rested, though if there were a hint of warmth and sunshine I would take a stroll with Growch—who had become so used to Matthew's majestic cat, Saffron, that they would now share the solar hearth together. In the evenings we played chess or draughts or backgammon, Matthew against Gill and me. Not surprisingly, Gill was familiar with all the games, and once recalled a chess set he had had, each piece carved in relief, birds for red, animals for white. If Suleiman joined us the men would swap rhymes and riddles while I stayed quiet and listened, for it was not proper for women to assume an equality with men in this sort of area.

If enough wine had been consumed after Suleiman went home, then Gill and Matthew would sing again, each trying to outdo the other. First Gill might chant the "Gaudeamus igitur," Matthew follow this with the drinking song: "Meum est propositum in taberna more" and both finish with the sentimental "My mistress she hath other loves."

We had further snow in mid-January, but by the end of the month Suleiman pronounced Gill fit enough to travel. He had been taking more exercise each day and almost looked as good as new. But Matthew was a puzzle: the nearer the time came for us to leave, the more restless he became. Then one night it all became clear. Gill had just retired and Matthew roamed around the solar, then abruptly followed Gill. I stretched and yawned, enjoying a few more moments before the fire, when suddenly the curtain was flung back and Matthew appeared, looking thoroughly upset. Had something happened to Gill? I rose to my feet in alarm.

"Whatever's the matter?"

He hesitated, then came towards me. His face was all red. "I'm not sure. . . . Perhaps you can explain?"

"I don't understand. . . ."

"I—I approached the man you call your brother upon—upon a certain matter, only to be told that you and he were not related at all." He really did look most upset. "I think I deserve an explanation!"

CHAPTER SIXTEEN

So I gave him one.

Not the real, entire, whole truth. He wouldn't have believed me. He heard about the knight passing through our village one day, being ambushed the next and wandering about blinded until I found him by chance and had promised to try and find his home, when it was obvious no one else either believed his story, such as it was, or was willing to help.

I told Matthew how Gill couldn't even remember his name, that all I could recall was an impression of his standard. I even brought out the scrap of cloth I had kept, but he shook his head. No help there. From there it was an easy progression to explaining away the "menagerie" as he called them. My dog, fair enough, a horse to carry our gear, no trouble there. The pigeon? Found wounded, a carrier, unusual color, might breed from him. Satisfactory. The tortoise? Abandoned, feed him up and sell him off. Fine.

The pig was more difficult. Runt of the litter, got him for next to nothing. Foraged off the land as we passed, always a useful standby for barter. He accepted that, too, and I breathed a sigh of relief. No need for him to know we "talked" among ourselves: animals didn't in Matthew's

167

circle, in spite of all the folk tales of talking foxes, mice, bears and fish. People should pay more attention to stories: they didn't make themselves up.

I thought I had gotten away with it beautifully, but there was obviously something still bothering our host. He umm'd and aah'd and then came to the point.

"And you had no hesitation in—in helping this man, Sir Gilman?"

"Of course not! I had nothing to keep me in the village, I had some money put by, and thought I would like to see a little of the world before I settled down. Besides, if you had seen him that first time, all handsome and elegant, just like a prince in a fairy tale! He was so utterly unattainable, that when I saw him again, all threatened, maimed and desolate, it was like being given a present! Even beaten up and dirty as he was, he was still the handsomest man I had ever seen in my life! And with him being blind, it was like an extra bonus, because—" I stopped. I had given myself away well and truly this time.

He looked at me in a way I couldn't fathom. "Because what?"

So I told the truth. What did it matter, now? "Because he couldn't see me; he couldn't see how fat and ugly I was. And, please God, he never will. I don't ever want him to know what I look like: I couldn't bear it!" I paused: he was looking most odd. "There, now I've told you. I would be obliged if you don't disillusion him." I looked down at my feet—yes, I could just about see them now—feeling very uncomfortable; I hated remembering my ugliness, my obesity.

But he didn't give me time to feel sorry for myself. "Fat?" he said. "Ugly? Whatever in the world gave you that idea? A little on the plump side, perhaps, a comfortable armful for any man, but ugly? Not at all! You have lovely greeny-grey eyes, a straight nose and—"

"Please don't!" I cried. "You're only making it worse!" I lost all discretion: kindness and tact could go too far. I *knew* what I looked like: hadn't I seen my reflection in the river often enough? Piggy eyes, squabby nose, double chins and all? And Mama had sighed, but added that my superior education and dowry would "go a long way towards overcoming" my other deficiencies. "You know perfectly well that in a million million years I could never attract a man like Gill, that the only time I will ever be able to hold his hand, care for him, gaze unhindered on his beautiful face, is now, when he's blind!"

"You—you love him, then?"

"Of course I do! How could I not? He is the sort of man every woman dreams about, and I am lucky, *lucky*, that even part of that dream has come true! I don't *want* to find his home, I don't *want* him ever to see again, may God forgive me!" Suleiman had examined his eyes and could find no obvious cause for the sudden blindness and loss of memory, except the blow to the head. He had advised him that memory might return gradually and he could even regain his sight one day as quickly as it had gone, if the circumstances were right—what circumstances he wasn't prepared to say. "I shouldn't have said that, I know I shouldn't, but each day I have him as he is, is one day snatched from heaven!"

Matthew looked completely different: older, greyer, sort of crumpled. "I did not realize. . . ."

"And neither does he!" I said quickly. "He treats me like a sister since we decided on the story we told you earlier: it is easier to travel that way."

He gathered his robes tightly around him as if he were suddenly cold. "Don't worry: your secret is safe with me. . . ."

The next time we were on our own I asked Gill how he had come to betray our true relationship.

He laughed. "You won't believe this, Summer, but he actually came and asked me, as your brother and next of kin, if he had my permission to pay court to you! Of course I couldn't say yea or nay, could I? So I had to tell him we weren't related. Anyway, I gather you must have talked your way out of it. Pity: you could have done worse, I imagine, and he seemed very taken. . . ."

Just imagine what my mother would have said! She would have considered him the perfect catch. "You should have had more sense!" I could hear her scolding. "What future is there traipsing around the countryside with a blind and helpless knight, handsome though he may be, when there is absolutely no future in it? Here is a comfortable home, a good-natured husband who is bound to die before you and leave you with his wealth; you just haven't the sense you were born with!" and then she would have given me a good beating, and it would have been no use pointing out that I had no idea Matthew felt that way.

Too late now, and it wouldn't have made any difference if I had known: my heart, for however short the time, was given to Gill. I was truly sorry if I had hurt Matthew, but I hoped it wouldn't spoil our last few days with him.

I needn't have worried; he was quieter than usual perhaps, and spent more time at his work, but there were no sulks, no reproaches, although I sensed he was under strain and would be glad when we were gone. Suleiman was going to supervise a consignment of spices further north and it had been agreed we would accompany him as far as the crossroads on the main north-south highway, for we had indeed come much too far east for our purpose.

So we set off at Candlemas, in a fine drizzle, all save Mistral safe under cover of one of the wagons, with Matthew out to see us go. I watched him dwindle on the road and then vanish as we turned the corner towards the countryside. I said a short prayer for his future well-being: I felt sorry for him, but had no regrets as to my decision.

"Nice to be on the road again," said Gill. "Perhaps this time I can get nearer home. . . ."

I think the animals felt the same way. The rest and food had benefited them all: Mistral had filled out and her coat shone with regular brushing; Basher was eating a little and still sleeping a lot, but Traveler's wing was almost healed and he was taking short flights with increasing regularity. The biggest change of all was in the Wimperling. He had grown almost out of recognition;

he was three times as big as before, easily, and tubby with it. No more lifts in the pannier for him: he would have to walk with the rest of us. There seemed to be changes in his shape as well. His nose was longer, the claws on his hooves were bigger, his rump was higher than his head and the vestigial wings were vestigial no longer, in fact they looked definitely uncomfortable. In fact he looked so odd that the first thing I did that first night on the road was to fashion him a sacking coat that at least hid the worst of his strangeness. Funnily enough, though, other people didn't seem to notice he was any different from a normal pig. Very strange . . .

Too soon our journey in comfort came to an end. At the crossroads, the third day after we had set out, I loaded up Mistral once more, checked and double-checked that everything was where it should be, then turned to say good-bye and thanks to Suleiman. He handed me a parcel.

"You'll have to find room for this," he said. "It's from Matthew."

Inside were the green woolen dress and undershifts I had made for Matthew's sister. "He must have made a mistake. . . ."

Suleiman smiled. "No mistake. He has no sister, never had." He handed me a small leather purse. "He said this was for the extra care of your knight." Inside were five gold coins. "He asked me to remind you that love cannot feed on thin air, and that the rain and wind are no discriminators. . . ."

Less than an hour later we were lucky enough to catch up with a small caravan of pilgrims and journeymen; the weather fined up, the road was easy, other travelers joined us. We became friendly with our companions of the road, swapping experiences and comparing dogs and horses: I even remember boasting that Growch was the cleverest dog for miles and that our pig could count to twenty—and this last idiocy got us into real trouble.

It all started about two weeks after we had left the crossroads. It was around midday, the sun was shining, a soft breeze came from the south, the grass was looking greener than it had for months, little shoots were pricking up through the earth, buds were starting to uncurl on bush and shrub, birds were becoming much more urgent in their courting and I was planning ahead for the next two days' meals. Someone ahead was singing a catchy little tune, behind us a baby was being hushed; Gill was whistling the same tune as the singer, the pigeon was giving his wings a tryout on Mistral's back and—

—and they came out of the woods on our left with a clatter of arms and thud of hooves. A dozen or so men, mounted and in half-armor, all in burgundy livery. They clattered to a halt and their leader drew his sword.

"Halt! Halt, I say! Stay right where you are, or it will be the worse for you!"

Panic does all sorts of strange things to people. Some freeze in their tracks, others run, it doesn't matter where; others scream and scream; some faint, others wet themselves. Remembering the last attack in which I was involved, I was about to run to the shelter of the tree— we were at the back, and I could probably have made it—but was brought up short remembering Gill and the others.

At least they weren't killing anybody yet, but a couple of the soldiers cantered down to our end and rounded up the stragglers.

"Move along there, now: not got all day . . ."

Now we were circled by restive, sweating horses, stamping their hooves, tossing their heads till the harness jingled. Behind me someone was moaning in terror. I reached for Gill's hand, whispered what was happening, conscious of Growch's unease, of the Wimperling rock-steady at my other side. My ring wasn't sending out signals, either.

The leader of the troupe stood in his stirrups and addressed us.

"Just shut up, the lot of you, and listen to me! I mean you, you miserable worms! I am Captain Portall from the Castle of the White Rock—look, if you aren't quiet I shall be forced to make you. . . ." and he raised his sword threateningly. "That's better. . . ." He gazed around us, his expression adequately conveying just what a sorry lot we were, how far below his normal consideration, and just how wearisome he found the whole business. "Now, as I said, I am from White Rock Castle, and my lady Aleinor is bored—even more bored than I am in talking to you peasants." He brushed at his drooping mustache with a mailed fist. "And when the lady is bored we all suffer! And her husband and four sons being off on some crusade or other doesn't help; she wants cheering up, does the lady, and that's what I'm here for." He looked at us all once more, even more despondently. "Now, what I want to know is, which of you likely lot has the skills to entertain a lady? And you can drop that sort of thought," he said threateningly at a ribald snigger from somewhere at the back. "I mean singing, dancing, tumbling, juggling, minstrelsy, tricks, that sort of rubbish. Trifles to amuse, tales to entertain, ballads to hearten—something to make her *laugh*, dammit! Come now, half-a-dozen volunteers . . ."

Such was my relief at realizing that we were not about to be hacked to death, robbed or raped that I paid little attention to the captain's speech. Everyone else began to relax also, picking up whatever they had dropped, gathering their scattered belongings, chattering among themselves.

"Well, that's that!" I said to Gill confidently. "We should be on our way—"

"I meant what I said!" suddenly shouted the captain. "Unless I find volunteers to accompany me back to the castle to entertain the Lady Aleinor, there will be . . . trouble! And I mean trouble! I want half-a-dozen right now: if not, I shall start stringing you all up, one by one!" He leaned from his horse and grabbed a man by his ear. "And we'll start with this one!"

A woman and girl started wailing, and everyone seemed to shrink into little family and friends groups. The circle grew smaller as the horses closed in. Fear became something you could touch and smell.

"Well? I'm waiting. I shall count to ten. One, two, three . . ."

"I've done a bit of juggling in my time." A man pushed forward. "Nothing fancy, mind . . ."

"You'll do." Captain Portall released the ear he was holding and rose in his stirrups once more. "Who else? You'll get a meal and a handful of silver if you please the lady. Come on, now. . . ."

"Should have mentioned that earlier," muttered a man to my left. He raised his hand. "I know a ballad or two might suit her."

One by one we got a tumbler and his son, a teller of tales, a man who could twist himself into impossible positions.

"Is that all? I'm disappointed, very disappointed! Singers, tumblers, a juggler, contortionist, story-teller: can't any of you do something *different*?"

To my horror one of our fellow travelers piped up with: "That girl over there, the one with the blind brother, she's got a dog what does tricks and a pig that counts. . . ."

I could have sunk straight into the ground! What a fool, what an utter idiot I had been to boast in such a way the other night! And it was lies, all lies—

But the captain on his horse was towering over us. "A counting pig? Now that *is* different. Never come across one of those before. Right, that's enough! Get them all organized, men! This the pig? I'll take him, then." And before I knew it he was down, had heaved up the Wimperling onto his saddle bow and remounted. "Heavy, isn't he?" and he turned and trotted off.

What could we do but follow? We couldn't desert the pig.

Our anxious way took us down a broad ride of the wood for perhaps a half mile, the fallen leaves of the autumn before muffling the thud of the escort's hooves, the chinking of the harness echoed by the chattering of a jay as it jinked away to the left. About twenty minutes later we came through thinning trees into the afternoon

February sunshine and saw a picture that might have graced a Book of Hours.

Perhaps a couple of miles away, girdled by the neatest fields I had ever seen, rose the towers of faery. Perched on a grey-white outcrop of rock, from where we stood it looked insubstantial, a building from the edges of dream. There were four towers of unequal height, one much taller than the others. The castle itself was built from white stone, just whiter than the rock from which it rose; silhouetted against the clear, blue winter sky it looked like something one could cut from card.

As we drew nearer we could see the crenellations along the walls and even small figures patrolling the perimeters, and the road along which we traveled curving up towards a drawbridge and portcullis, over what looked like a moat of some kind. On our travels we had glimpsed other castles in the distance, most of them squat and frowning, with solid grey foundations and the hunched look of a sick animal, but this was quite different. Apart from its coloring, the way it seemed to spring upwards out of the rock, there were colored flags fluttering from the gateway, and the thin sound of a trumpet announcing our arrival.

We were traveling through fields plowed or already sown, through orchards of fruit trees beneath which not a single weed could be seen—unlike the unfamiliar orange groves outside the last town we had visited, the goat's-foot trefoil beneath their trunks a yellow so bright it seared the eye—and past the twisted, bare branches of dead-looking vines, that later would cluster with heavy grapes. There was also an avenue of pollarded oaks, their knobbed branches giving no hint of the summer lushness to come. Everything neat, everything tidy, not a wavy line in the plowing, not a weed in the fields, not a dead leaf on the paths. Perhaps I had an untidy mind, but I would have welcomed a little disarray, a hint that outside belonged to nature as well as man.

Small houses were clustered at the foot of the White Rock, all as spic and span as the rest, and these we passed, together with the huge communal bread ovens, as we trudged up the sudden steep ascent to the castle proper and clattered over the short drawbridge. I peered over the edge as I passed: as I thought, a dry moat, and judging by the stench and the brown streaks down the walls that had not been evident from a distance, showing that refuse from the kitchens and garde-robes was allowed to flow unchecked, it was evident that there was no constant source of water. The creaking of the portcullis preceded us, but it needed only to be drawn halfway for us all to squeeze beneath.

We found ourselves in a large, cobbled courtyard, full of noise and bustle. Horses were being curried and exercised, wagons loaded and unloaded, soldiers were practicing with short swords, others examining armor and mail newly come from the sand barrels that were rolling up and down a short slope. A bowyer was stringing bows, a fletcher feathering arrows, an armorer busy at his anvil. Stable boys were shoveling ordure into an empty cart and a couple of cooks were gutting and jointing venison. The noise was indescribable.

Captain Portall dismounted his troop and started issuing orders as to our disposition. He lifted the Wimperling from his saddle with a look of distaste: the pig had just let loose a series of little popping farts.

Once down, the Wimperling nudged me. "We must be together. . . ."

"Right!" Captain Portall turned to me. "You and you—" he pointed to Gill: "—over there in one of those huts. Animals in the stables. Gerrout, you mangy hound!" and he aimed a kick at Growch, who was trying to christen his boots. "Whose is this?"

"Mine," I said firmly. "Just like the horse and the pig. All part of our act. And if you want a decent performance for your—your lady tonight, you'll see we are kept together. To rehearse," I added. "It is a couple of months since we have performed together. I presume you want us to be at our best?"

It worked. Ten minutes later we were snug in a stall at the end of the stables nearest the entrance, and a sullen stable boy was bringing hay, oats, mash and buckets of water.

"Two more buckets," I said firmly, twisting the ring on my finger to give courage. "This time of hot water. And towels. Hurry, boy."

Then I had to explain everything to Gill: where we were, what we were supposed to be doing.

"But we are performing nothing until we are clean and presentable: it's obvious the Lady Aleinor places great store on everything being just so. She also wants entertainment, so we've got to prepare something to please her. Besides, we could do with the silver she is offering."

"Have you ever done anything like this before?" asked poor, bewildered Gill.

"There's always a first time. . . ."

"And a last," muttered Growch. "Glad I'm not part of this farce."

"Oh, but you are," said the Wimperling unexpectedly. "We all are. That's why we couldn't be separated."

"Well, what we goin' to do, then? *She* said you could count, whatever that means: I heard her. What about me? The 'orse, the tortoise, the pigeon? Them," indicating Gill and me.

"Be patient," said the Wimperling. "And listen. . . ."

CHAPTER SEVENTEEN

It was both hot and smoky in the hall. Although there was a huge modern hearth, tall and wide enough for half a dozen to stand upright, there seemed to be something amiss with the chimney, or perhaps the wind was in the wrong direction, for as much smoke came down and out as went up. The torches smoked in their holders on the walls, the candles on the tables smoked; an erratic wind would seem to have taken possession of the kitchens as well, for the bread was burned, the meat tasted half-cured, the fowls were charred on one side and nearly raw on the other and the underdone chickpeas, lentils and onions sulked in a sauce that reeked of too much garlic and was definitely full of smuts.

But we were too hungry to care much. The ale was good, the smoked herring and eels very tasty and the cheeses of excellent quality. We were seated at the very bottom of the left-hand table, and it was a good place from which to see everything. The edge off my hunger, and Gill well provided for, I had time to gaze around, and a word or two with our neighbors identified who was who.

There must have been upwards of a hundred and fifty people in the hall, counting servitors. The level of conversation was deafening, and this, coupled with the hysterical yelping and snarling of hounds fighting for bones and scraps in the rushes, the roar of flame from the fireplace, the clatter of knives, the thump of mugs impatient for refill and the intermittent screeching of a cagefull of exotic multicolored birds, made hearing a sense to endure rather than enjoy.

So I used my eyes instead. At the top table, raised some two hands high from the rest of us, sat the Lady Aleinor with a neighbor, Sir Bevin, and his wife on her right, and on her left her sister and her husband on a visit. Also on the top table were her daughter, a pudding-faced girl of twelve or thirteen, her chaplain, steward and Captain Portall. Below the salt ran the two long tables, seating about thirty on each side, crammed elbow to elbow on benches with scarce room to lift hand to mouth. At the ends nearest the top table were accommodated the more important members of the household: reeve, almoner, chief usher, head falconer, armorer, apothecary, head groom and verdurers; between them and us were the middle to lower orders: smiths, farriers, bowyers, fletchers, coopers, dyers, gardeners, soldiers, hedgers, cobbler, tinder-maker, trumpeter, clerk, wine-storekeeper and all my Lady's maids, her housekeeper, tirewoman, sewing ladies and her daughter's nurse-companion.

The table manners of those nearest us left much to be desired. Those sharing two to a trencher were using their hands rather than their knives, and even those who had their own place were tearing at the bread and meat instead of cutting it neatly. There was much munching with open mouth and unseemly belching, and few were using cloths to wipe their fingers and mouths: it appeared sleeves were more convenient for the men, hems of skirt or shift for the women. Not that the manners on the top table were much better, though the Lady Aleinor did at least lick her fingers one by one before applying them and her mouth to the linen tablecloth.

We had not yet seen the lady close to and were bowing respectfully when she entered the hall, so I had only had

a quick impression of a tall, slim woman in rich red robes
and an elaborate headdress of linen, lawn and ribbons.
Now I could see her more clearly I saw she was handsome enough, but her face was marred by a discontented
expression—much as my mother used to wear if bad
weather kept her customers away too long. The lady was
obviously bored.

The hall grew hotter, noisier, smokier, but at last the
tables were cleared, the hounds kicked into silence, a
cover put over the squawking birds and water brought
for finger-washing. The steward rose to his feet, banged
on the top table for silence, and announced that the
entertainment would begin. A young varlet, one of the
two cadet-squires who had been serving at the top
table—much more palatable food than we had been
served with, I noticed—walked down the room and
picked out the first of our "volunteers."

After a whispered conversation he walked back
between the two lower tables, bowed to the lady, and
announced that Master Peter Bowe would sing a couple
of ballads: "Travel the Broad Highway" and "Lips Like
Cherries." He had a pleasant enough voice, but it was
suited to a smaller place than this vast hall, whose tim-
bers reached up into a ribbed darkness like leafless trees.
However the Lady spoke to her steward and he was
rewarded with a couple of silver coins.

Next it was the turn of the juggler, who was reasonably
dextrous. He was certainly good at improvisation, for he
had only what lay around to toss and catch; eventually,
one by one, he had two shriveled apples, a goblet, a large
bone and a trencher all in the air at once. He, too,
received two silver coins.

The teller of tales was found to be hopelessly drunk
and was thrown out, so it was the turn of the tumbler
and his boy. Once the man had obviously been very good,
but he was well into middle age and I could tell by the
grimaces that he suffered from rheumatism, and both his
spring and balance were faulty. The boy did his best to
cover for his father's deficiencies—one day he, too,
would be very good—but in the end he was dropped

heavily; judging by his resigned expression as he rose to his feet, rubbing his elbow, it wasn't the first time and wouldn't be the last. They were given three coins.

Now it was the turn of the contortionist, but I had to miss his performance to slip outside and collect Mistral and the others, for we were next—and last. I brought them in by the kitchen ramp, for the steps up to the main door would not have done: too steep. Leaving them just outside, I rejoined Gill for the applause and coin for the contortionist. The varlet walked up to us, I whispered to him, he went back and announced us.

"My lady . . ." a deep bow: "for your entertainment I present travelers from the north, the south, the east, the west: fresh from their successful performances all over the country, I crave your indulgence for brother and sister, Gill and Summer, and their troupe of performing animals!" Another deep bow, a ripple of interest.

Smoothing down the dress Matthew had given me with nervous fingers I led Mistral towards the top table, Gill on her other side, flanked on either side by a sedate dog and a sedater pig. Traveler was perched on Mistral's back. We all looked our best, I had seen to that, and the animals wore colored ribbons—a sad good-bye to my special ones, I thought. (We had had to leave Basher behind, for there isn't much lively capering to be got from a hibernating tortoise.)

Reaching the dais we performed the only trick we had rehearsed together: we all knelt—man, girl, horse, pig, dog. Traveler bowed his head.

Applause. Encouraged, I rose and addressed the lady. "First we shall show you a roundelay. . . ." and pulling my pipe from my pocket I gave Gill the note and he began singing the "Bluebell Hey." For a dreadful moment I thought it wasn't going to work, then my dear animals obeyed my unspoken instructions. Mistral and the pig revolved slowly, majestically, and Growch began to chase his tail. No matter they were not in time with the music: we were receiving applause already. Traveler rose into the air and gracefully circled the top table. . . . Then it happened.

It is well-nigh impossible to house-train birds, and
Traveler was no exception. On his last circuit, obviously
full of grain, he let loose and an enormous chunk of
pigeon-dropping landed unerringly on the bald pate of
the lady's chaplain. There was a long drawing in of breath
and then total silence. I stopped playing, Gill stopped
singing, Growch stopped chasing his tail. Mistral and the
Wimperling stood like statues.

We all gazed at the Lady Aleinor. She rose to her feet,
her face suffused with color. If she had said: "Off with
their heads!" I would not have been surprised. I twisted
the ring on my finger, still cool and calm. The lady's eyes
seemed ready to pop out of her head, and the silence
was something palpable, a thing you could touch and
weigh. She opened her mouth—

And laughed.

And she went on laughing. Not a genteel titter behind
her hand, as I had been taught, but a gut-wrenching
belly laugh, the sort my mother had produced one day
when the butcher had risen from her bed in a temper,
tripped and landed bare-arsed and bum-high with his
nose in the dirt.

What's more, she went on laughing. She laughed until
the tears spurted from her eyes, she laughed till her ribs
ached and she had to double up to stop the ache, till
she had to cover her ears for the pain behind. And the
more indignant the lugubrious chaplain became, trying
to wipe the yellow mess from his bald head with the
tablecloth, the more she laughed.

Her sycophantic household took its cue from her, and
soon the whole place was rocking with guffaws and the
very flames of the torches and candles were threatened
by the shouts and table-thumpings. The most relieved
face in the hall, apart from mine, was that of Captain
Portall, who had promised amusement for his lady.

The noise, however was upsetting Mistral, however I
tried to calm her, and Traveler was no better. Growch,
too, was starting to growl at the lymers, brachs and mas-
tiffs who had started up again with their baying and yelping, so I grabbed the horse's bridle and led them back

to the courtyard. Growch, of course, took advantage of this to snatch a rib bone from a distracted greyhound on his way out.

Picking up a leathern bucket I had appropriated earlier I rejoined Gill and the Wimperling, the latter of whom seemed totally unmoved by the hullabaloo around him. In fact his snout was working happily above exposed teeth, almost as though he were laughing too. As I re-entered the merriment was dying down, and the lady leaned forward and addressed us.

"I hope the rest of your act is as stimulating: I declare I have not been as diverted for months! Of course—" she waved her hand dismissively: "I realize it was but a fortuitous accident. Presumably the rest of your performance owes more to skill?"

I bowed. "My lady ... First my brother will sing a ballad dedicated especially to yourself. An old tune, but new words." I gave Gill his note, and he began to sing:

> "When I hunger, there is meat;
> When I tire, there is sleep;
> I am cold, there is fire;
> I am thirsty, there is wine.
> But when I love, unless you care,
> I am poorer than the poor.
> Hungry, thirsty, sleepless, cold.
> But smile, lady, and I am full;
> Touch me and I am warm;
> Kiss me once and I
> Need never sleep again. . . ."

It was a touching song, and Gill sang it as if he held a picture of a secret love tight behind his blind lids. So heartfelt was the throb in his voice that it gave me goose bumps. The lady seemed to like it too.

Now for the culmination of our act: I crossed my fingers and went down to the Wimperling.

"Ready?"

"If you are . . ."

I upended the bucket and lifted his front hooves onto the top, catching one of my fingers on the funny claws that circled them. "We will have to clip those. . . ."

"I think they are meant to be there . . ."

Gill finished his song to sentimental applause from Lady Aleinor, which everyone copied. So, the lady decided what amused and what did not. In that case, the Wimperling and I would play to her alone.

"And now, my lady, we present to you the wonder of this or any other age: a pig who counts. As good as any human, and better than most. Would you please give me two simple numbers for the pig to add together?" I saw her hesitate, and gathered that tallying was not her strong point. She would probably be furious if we exposed her weakness so I played it safe. "Perhaps we could start more simply: if you would place some manchets of bread in front of you in a line, so that your guests may see the number, then I will ask the pig to guess correctly. He cannot, of course, see what is on the table."

She looked more pleased and lined up five pieces of bread. I thought the number to the Wimperling, then made a great fuss and to-do with waving of arms and incantations.

Obediently the Wimperling tapped with his right hoof on the top of the bucket: one, two, three, four . . . There was a hesitation, a ghastly moment when I thought everything was going to go wrong, then I saw from the gleam in his eye that he was enjoying himself . . . five.

Applause, again, and from then on in it was easy. Shouts from those on the top table who could count: "Three and two . . . Six and one . . . two and four . . ." The lady was counting frantically on her fingers to keep up with her guests, then nodding and beaming as though she had known the answer all the time. Her daughter intervened in an affected lisp.

"Does the creature subtract as well?"

It could, if my mental counting was swift enough.

We finished, by prior agreement with the Wimperling, by me asking him a leading question: "You are a pig of perspicacity: tell me now, O Wise One, who is the fairest,

the most generous, the most beloved lady in this castle?"
I went along the tables, touching each woman on the
shoulder as I passed, and each time the Wimperling
shook his head—a pity, for some of the ladies were really
far prettier than our hostess. At last, and last, I came to
the Lady Aleinor. At once the pig drummed both hooves
on the bucket, squealed enthusiastically and nodded his
head.

Everyone clapped, as they knew that had to, and the
lady was so pleased she snatched the purse of silver from
her steward and threw it to me. As I shepherded Gill
back outside, the Wimperling trotting behind, I counted
the coins: twelve!

"Told you it would be all right," said the Wimperling
happily.

We had almost reached the stables when there were
running footsteps behind us. It was the varlet who had
introduced us earlier.

"You are invited to dine with the rest of the household
at dawn," he panted, "and the lady requests that you and
your brother—and the wondrous pig—attend her at noon
in the solar. I am to come and fetch you at the appointed
hour."

Back at the stables I requested more hay and made
comfortable resting places for Gill and myself, then went
to say goodnight and congratulate the animals.

"You were absolutely marvelous, all of you! The lady
liked our performance, and we have a purseful of silver
to prove it! She wants to see Gill and me and the Wimperling again tomorrow morning, but we shall be on the
road again just after noon, I expect."

"Tonight was one thing," said the Wimperling, "but
tomorrow might be different again. . . ."

"Oh, stop being such an old pessimist!" I cried. "You
were the star of the show, remember?" and in my eupho-
ria I raised his front hooves, bent down, and kissed him
fair and square on his pink snout.

Bam! I felt as though I had been struck by a thunderbolt. Once when combing my hair at home by the fire,
I had leaned forward to sip at a metal dipper of water

and had the same sharp prickling, but this was a thousand
times worse. I must have jumped, or been thrown, back
about six feet, my lips numb and feeling twice their size,
my hair standing up from my head. But this was as nothing to the effect it had on the pig. He leapt up at the
same distance I had back, his wings creaked into action
as well and bore him still further until he cracked his
head against the rafters and came plummeting back down
to the floor.

We stared at one another in horror. The feeling was
coming back to my lips, but I still had to put up a hand
to convince myself they weren't swollen. They tingled
like pins and needles, only far worse.

"What *happened*?"

He shook his head as though his ears were full of ticks.
"I don't know. . . . I feel as if all my insides have turned
over. Most peculiar. I'm not the same as I was, I know
that!"

"I won't do it again, I promise!"

"No, don't. It's just that . . . I don't know. Very
strange. . . ."

I had never seen or heard him so confused. After a
moment or two he slunk off into a corner under the
manger and hunched up. I thought he would sleep, but
when I settled down on my bed of hay he was still awake,
his eyes bright and watchful in the light of the lantern
that swung overhead.

When we entered the solar a little after noon, the
Lady Aleinor was seated in a high-backed chair by a
roaring fire; like all the chimneys in the castle, this one
smoked. The lady's daughter was on a stool at her feet,
the nurse and two tirewomen stood behind the chair.

Though the room was sumptuously furnished, it did
not have the cozy, lived-in look of Matthew's solar: it was
a room to be seen in, rather than used. Candles were lit
because the shutters on the one window at the back were
tight closed.

The lady received us graciously. We were invited to
move into the center of the room—though not asked to

sit down—and she started to question us: where we trained the animals, where we were bound, etc. From anyone except a fine lady like herself it might have seemed an impertinence, but we had been long enough together for the brother/sister story to come out like truth. It was more difficult to answer questions about the animals, but I did emphasize (in order that our performances were worthy of reward) the years of training, the bonds of familiarity that had to be forged, the difficulty of communication—and here I mentally crossed myself and touched my ring.

"But surely the whip speaks louder than words?"

I was shocked—would I have been before I wore the ring of the Unicorn? I wondered—but did my best to hide it. Her ways were obviously not ours.

"You may use a whip when breaking in a horse, my lady, or beat a dog, but how can you use punishment to train a pigeon? Our training is accomplished by treating the animals as if they were part of our family and rewarding their tricks, not punishing their mistakes. It has worked well, so far."

Her eyes flashed as though she would argue, then once more she was sweetness itself. "Would you let me see what else your pig can do? I am sure there were tricks you did not show us last night. . . ." I almost looked for the honey dripping from her tongue.

I was deceived, I admit it, even as a warning message came from the Wimperling. "Don't intrigue her too much. . . ."

"Hush!" I thought to him. And to the lady: "I am sure we can find something to divert you. . . ." Back to the Wimperling, quick as a flash: "Can you keep time to a song? Find hidden objects if I tell you where they are?"

He answered reluctantly that he thought he could: "But *don't* overdo it!" Why? More tricks, more money, and we should be away from here in an hour or two with enough to keep us going for weeks.

I asked Gill to sing "Come away to the woods today" which was a song with a regular, impelling beat, and my pig trod first one way and then the other in perfect time, to polite applause from the lady and her daughter.

"Now the pig on his own," demanded Lady Aleinor, dismissing Gill's song, which privately I thought wonderful, as a mere trifle. "Come on girl: show us what else he can do!"

"Very well. Perhaps, my lady, if you would hide some trifling object—yes, that needle case would do fine—while the pig's back is turned—so, then I will ask him to discover it."

And behind a cushion, under a chair, beneath the sideboard, in the wood-basket—he found it every time. After I had told him where to look, of course.

The lady watched him perform with a gleam in her eyes. "Very good, very good indeed! Anything else he can do?"

I was about to open my mouth and rashly volunteer his flying abilities, when his thoughts struck into my mind like a string of sharp pebbles to the head. "No, no, *no*! Don't tell her that! Tell her I am tired, anything! Let's get out of here!"

Confused, I stammered out an excuse. She looked at me coldly. "Very well, you may go now and rest. But I shall expect another performance tonight. I have sent out messengers to others of my neighbors and I look forward to an even better exposition of the pig's power." She saw my face. "What's the matter, girl? A few coins? Here you are, then. . . ." and she tossed a handful of silver at my feet.

Automatically I bent to retrieve it, then straightened my back. "It is not a matter of money, my lady, thank you all the same. Last night you were more than generous, and we had not planned to stay longer than midday today. We must be on our way as soon as possible."

Another flash of—what?—from those hooded eyes, then the pleasantness was back again, on her mouth at least. "Of course, of course, but I couldn't possibly let you go without one more of your marvelous performances! You can't let me down after I have invited extra

guests! Please say you will do this last favor? One more
treat for us all and then you may go on your way. . . ."

It would have been more than churlish of me to refuse,
in spite of the warning signs I was getting from the
Wimperling. Gill, poor dear, had no idea of the conflict
that was going on and added his voice to the lady's plea.

"Of course we must oblige the Lady Aleinor, Summer:
it will be no hardship to stay one more night, surely?"

I could hear the Wimperling almost screaming at him
to stop, stop, stop! but of course he couldn't hear the
pig's thoughts as I could, and he went on with a few
more complimentary sentences until I could have
screamed also. There was no doubt as to the outcome
now, and I picked up the coins and we made our way
down the winding stone stairs to the courtyard. Up had
been much easier for all of us, and the Wimperling
nearly ended by rolling down the last few twists. Once
in the courtyard he started to say something, but I
hushed him, using our midday meal in the hall as an
excuse. Right at that moment I didn't want any prognos-
tications of doom and disaster, so I saw him back to the
stable before hurrying back for what was left of the meal.

I purposely lingered over the last night's leftovers, plus
a thick broth, a blancmange of brawn and custards of
potted meats, but I couldn't put off the reproaches forever. Even so, it was a little past two by the time Gill and
I regained the stable, whereupon I immediately found a
stool for him out in the sunshine, and returned alone to
face the agitation I had sensed at once.

They all had something to say, but it was Growch who
was noisiest. "What's all this, then? 'E tells me—" he
nodded towards the pig: "—that we're all in danger!
Danger from what, I'd like to know? Last night you was
full of how well we done, and now 'e tells us the Lady-
of-the-'Ouse is poison! In that case, why don't we all go,
right now? O' course, if I was just to nip into the kitchens
and fetch a bone first . . ."

"I think we should go," said Mistral restlessly. "But our
companion tells us we we must perform again tonight."

Traveler flapped his wings. "Listen to the pig: he is a wise one."

Thank the Lord the tortoise was still asleep! "What's all this, then?" I asked the Wimperling. "We have a purse full of money and will get more tonight. All we have to do is one more performance and we can leave in the morning. What's one more day? The more money the better."

"*If* it is only one more day ... I do not trust her. I can read her heart a little way and it is full of wickedness, guile and greed. I cannot see what she intends, for I believe she does not yet know herself, but it is not good for any of us, of that I am sure."

"You have no proof—"

"No, Summer, but in this you must trust me. Tonight when the performance ends we must be ready to leave, all packed up. If we don't, tomorrow may bring disaster to us all."

I shook my head. I just couldn't believe she meant us harm. And yet—I recalled those flashes of spite from her eyes. Perhaps ... "It would be too dark to see. Besides, the porticullis will be down."

"Stays up for them as was guests and isn't stayin' over," said Growch. " 'Sides, we've traveled at night before. Moon's near full."

"I shall have to ask Gill," I said weakly.

"Consult 'im? When've you ever consulted 'im? You tells 'im what to do an' 'e does it! Couldn't 'ave got this far without you, an' 'e knows it!" Whenever he got particularly agitated Growch's speech went to pieces. "Consult 'im indeed!" And he emphasized his annoyance by kicking up a shower of hay with his back legs.

"You've all had your say: why shouldn't he?" I was angry, largely because I wasn't sure that they weren't right.

"Becoz-'e-don'-know-nuffin!" said Growch. "Not-nuffin!'

"That's only because he's blind," I said quickly. "You try going around for a while with your eyes tight shut and see how you get on! Anyway, I shall ask him just the same. We're all in this together."

And before I could change my mind I went outside and suggested to a dozy Gill that we leave that night. Of course I couldn't give the true reason, and, understandably, he couldn't see why we didn't postpone it till morning. I decided to wait and see what the evening brought, but packed everything ready, just in case.

We made a good job of our performance that night, repeating much of what we had done the evening before, but adding a couple more tricks to the Wimperling's repertoire. Led by the lady, we received prolonged applause, a purse from her and another from one of her guests. When we returned to the stable there was disappointment: none of the guests was leaving that night and the portcullis remained down.

Right, first thing in the morning then, when the first wagons came up with provisions. If we were ready in the shadow of the wall, we would sneak out as soon as the portcullis was raised. . . . I willed myself to wake up an hour before dawn.

I woke on time, loaded up our gear and we were ready in the darkest part of the courtyard a good quarter-hour before we heard the first wagon rumble across the drawbridge. The driver called out; two yawning soldiers ran across and started to wind up the portcullis with enough creaks and groans to awaken the dead. I shivered: my teeth were chattering both with the early morning chill and with dread.

Three wagons passed through, steam rising from the horses' and the drivers' mouths. I grabbed Gill's hand and Mistral's bridle, and we had almost reached the first plank of the drawbridge when two sentries I hadn't seen stepped out and barred our progress, their spears crossed in front of us.

"Sorry girl, sir," said one of them peremptorily. "None of you is to leave the castle. Orders of the Lady Aleinor . . ."

CHAPTER
EIGHTEEN

I stared at them in horror. "But why?"

They looked at one another and then the spokesman said: "We don't ask questions of the lady. All we know is, orders were sent down yesterday midday as you weren't to be let go."

"Doesn't pay to disobey," said the other soldier. "We just does as we're told. Sorry an' all that ... Enjoyed your performance, by the way: that pig's a good 'un. Would he do a trick for me?"

"No, no," I said distractedly. "Only for me ..." Which was the best answer I could have given, although I didn't realize it at the time. "Er ... Under the circumstances, perhaps it would be better if—if the lady didn't think we were trying to leave." Scrabbling in my now full purse I handed out a couple of coins. "I think she might be annoyed if she thought we didn't appreciate her hospitality."

On our dispirited way back to the stables I noticed a boy from the village unloading his wagon and eyeing us speculatively: he had obviously seen the exchange of coin. I clutched my purse tighter and hurried past.

I was all for requesting an instant audience with Lady Aleinor, demanding to know the reason for our confinement and insisting on instant release, but Gill urged caution.

"I reckon that might make her more determined to keep us a while. She seems to be a very contrary lady. . . . After all, where's the harm of a few more days? Personally I'm growing a bit tired of singing love ballads to a woman I can't see, but at least it means more money, and we are fed and housed. Not that the food is all that good, but—"

"The most important thing is to be very, very careful," said the Wimperling. "We must find out what she has in mind. Don't force the issue: corner any vicious animal and you relinquish the initiative."

"I want to go," said Mistral impatiently. "This place is bad, and—"

There was a rustling noise from farther down the stable and silhouetted against the open door was the figure of the boy I had noticed earlier. "Hullo . . ." he called out tentatively.

I was in no mood to be polite. "What do you want?"

He hesitated for a moment then moved towards us, twisting a piece of straw between his fingers. He was dressed in a rough, patched jerkin, trousers tied beneath the knee with twine, and was barefoot. He was also filthy dirty—I could smell him from where I stood—and his thatch of hair could well have been fair if it had ever been washed. He could have been any age from twelve onwards.

"To see if I can help. I heard what was going on. Gather you want out of here?" His speech was country-thick but in the lantern light I could see a bright intelligence in those grey eyes.

I temporized: who knew where his real interest lay? "Maybe we do—but why should you help?"

"No love for the Lady 'Ell-an'-All," he muttered. "Killed my father she did," and he glanced over his shoulder as if he, too, was afraid of being overheard.

"Killed him?" and once he started telling us, I thought his story to the animals at the same time as he told it.

"We live in the hamlet beneath the castle. Two rooms,

patch of ground behind. Lived there happy, father, mother, self and three young sisters. Father was a forester for the lady, mother helped in the fields with the girls, weeding and picking stones. I was a crow-scarer, then a shit-shoveler. Still am. Bad winter last year, after the lord and his sons went off. Not much food. Pa helped himself to a hare—"

"A poacher?"

"First time he ever done it. We needed the food, and there were a glut of 'em. Kept helping theirselves to our vegetable clamps. Pa caught this one with the dog, on our patch at the back. Someone saw him, told the Lady 'Ell-an'-All. No excuses, no trial. Hanged the dog, old Blackie, castrated my father—"

"Oh, my God!" It was Gill. "How barbaric! My father—My father . . ." He put his hands to his head. "I don't remember. . . ."

"And then she had his eyes put out," continued the boy, stony-faced. "My father stood it for six month. Last August we came in late, found he'd cut his throat. With the trimming knife. They let him keep that."

I put my hand on his arm, but he shook it off.

"Don't want no sympathy. Understand why he did it. Less than half a man . . . Anyway, if you means harm to the lady, then I'm your man."

I didn't know what to say. We still didn't know if our position was serious. It might just be that all the lady wanted was a couple more performances. Even as I tried to persuade myself that the situation didn't warrant any panic, I got a strong signal from the Wimperling to enlist this boy on our side.

"Thank you," I said formally. "We don't wish personal harm to the lady, but we do wish to leave here as soon as possible."

"If she's taken a fancy to you, here you stay."

"We've given her what she asked—"

"Obviously not."

"Look," I said. "First we have to find out exactly what is going on. I don't quite know how you can help, but—"

"You'd be surprised. Bet I can get you all out of here

in twenty-four hours." He hesitated. " 'Course, there'd be a price. . . ."

I thought rapidly of what we could afford. "Ten silver pieces. If we need you, that is . . ."

His eyes gleamed. "Done! I'm getting out myself, soon as I can, but can't leave Ma and the sisters without. See you later. . . ."

"But I don't understand," I said.

Gill and I were in the lady's solar again, having requested an audience after the midday meal. She had us standing in the center of the room as before while she reclined by the fire. There was more light in the room today, for the shutters at the window had been flung back on a sunny sky. The room must face south, for low bars of February sunshine slanted through the window and across the floor, specks of dust dancing like midges in the beams. Outside I could see a forest of leafless trees stretching to the horizon, while black specks rose and fell lazily above the branches, a soft breeze carrying the quarreling cries of nest-building rooks.

I had come straight to the point and asked why we had been refused permission to leave. She had gazed at us through half-closed lids.

"I should have thought that would be perfectly obvious."

But when I said I didn't understand, she seemed to come to life and sat up, arms gripping the sides of her chair. "You are not an idiot, girl. If I say you are not to leave, it is because I wish you to stay. And why? Because, for the moment, I find you and your animals—diverting. Life can be *so* boring. . . ." Leaning back in her chair she closed her eyes. "And now I shall rest for a while. I expect more entertainment this evening. Some new tricks, please. . . ." And she let her voice die away, as if indeed it was too tiring to try and explain further to peasants such as ourselves.

"But I don't want—*we* don't wish to stay," I said. "You told us we might leave if we gave an extra performance, which we did. We do have a life of our own to lead, you know, and—"

She rose to her feet in a sudden swirl of skirts, the cone-shaped headdress she wore wobbling dangerously.

"How dare you! How *dare* you! What matter *your* wishes, *your* little lives? All that matters here is what *I* want! This is *my* castle, *my* demesne! Within its bounds I have jurisdiction of life and death over everyone— *everyone*, do you hear?" She was almost hysterical, red blotches on her neck and face, her eyes snapping sparks like fresh pine bark on a fire. She rushed forward and struck first me and then Gill hard across the face. My eyes smarted with the sudden pain, for one of her thumb rings had caught my lip and I could taste the salt of blood. Gill swayed on his feet and would have fallen had I not caught at his arm and steadied him.

"God's teeth! What was that for, lady?"

"Impertinence, blind man! And there's more where that came from if you do not both watch your tongues. I will not be disagreed with, do you hear?"

I was so angry with the way she was treating us that given a pinch of pepper I would have sprung forward and given her a dose of her own treatment, but the presence of Gill gave me pause. That, plus the possible danger to the animals. God knew what she could do if further provoked.

"We have no wish to cross you," I said, as meekly as I could. "But we would like to know when we can leave. If you could let us know how many more performances you require? And if you have any special tricks in mind . . . Of course, it will take time to teach them all—"

"There is no need to teach them all fresh tricks: I am only interested in the pig! Any fool can make a horse turn, a dog obey, a bird fly in circles. You combine them cleverly, I agree, but it is only the pig that has real intelligence. Your brother has a pleasant enough voice, I dare say, but singers are a dozen a week, and you know it! No, the rest of you may leave as and when you wish, but the pig stays!"

"But—but he can't!"

"What do you mean 'can't'? If I say he stays, he stays."
She looked at us for a moment, then changed her tactics.
Sitting down once more, she smoothed her skirts, turned
the rings on her fingers. "Of course you will be recom-
pensed. I realize your pig is a means of livelihood and
that you are seeking a cure for your brother's blindness,
which will need special donations. I will give you what I
reckon it will cost for a further three months' travel.
Now, I cannot say fairer than that, can I?"

"You don't understand! It's not just—just what he
could earn us, he is *part* of us: I couldn't leave him
behind. Besides, he won't do tricks for anyone else, only
me."

"Well, you can stay for a while, too. Just till you have
taught me how he works."

The woman was mad! "But I can't teach you—"

"Can't? Or won't?" She rose from her chair again, as
angry as before. She narrowed her eyes. "Everything can
be taught—unless it's some form of magic.... Magic?
Yes, I suppose that could be the answer. If so," and now
her voice was full of menace: "I could have you
denounced as a witch! And you know what that means:
trial by fire, earth and water and lastly, being burned at
the stake...."

"I'm no witch!" I felt the ring of the unicorn cold,
cold on my finger. Was that a form of witchcraft? It had
never occurred to me, being as it was a gift from my
dead father which helped me understand the speech of
animals and also warned me of danger, gave me courage—yet perhaps to the lady, to the gullible majority, it
would seem like a form of magic—

Suddenly I was terrified. Death came in many forms:
illness, accident, war, pestilence, age, famine—but to be
burned at the stake! God, please God, sweet Jesus, Mary,
Mother of Sorrows, No! I was trembling; the lady saw
it, and smiled gleefully.

"Then if it is not magic, it is trickery, and that can be
taught. Right? And if you do not wish to teach me, and
your—companions—are so precious to you, then perhaps
they can be persuaded to persuade you.... Pigeons'

necks can be wrung, a horse can be hamstrung, a dog hung by its tail, a man—"

"Stop it, stop it!" I had my hands over my ears. "Leave them alone! They have no part in all this! You said they could all go. . . ."

I should not have been so vehement. I realized from the gleam in her eye that she now knew I was vulnerable to the threat of harm to the others.

"Certainly not! I have changed my mind. They can all be hostages to your good behavior. And just so as there will be no mistake, we can start the lessons right now! Go fetch the pig!"

There was nothing I could do but obey. As I led the Wimperling back I told him what had happened. "What are we going to do?"

He looked worried, as worried as I felt, the loose skin over his snout all wrinkled up in perplexity. "The only thing we can do is go along with what she wants for the moment and trust to luck. You had better make plans with that boy to escape if you can. In the meantime give me something simple to do—count to five, perhaps—give her some gibberish to learn, then say I can only adapt to a new mistress slowly and tomorrow she will learn more."

So it was decided, but unfortunately it didn't turn out quite as we had planned. . . .

At first it was all right. I gave the Lady Aleinor some rhyming words to repeat—taking great pleasure in correcting her twice—and obediently the Wimperling tapped his hoof five times. She practiced it half a dozen times, but in the middle of the nonsense the pig sent me an urgent message.

"Take a look out of that window. Remember everything you see."

I wandered over and did as I was bid. A sheer drop of some forty feet to the dry moat below; beyond that the forests, with a stretch of greensward in front of the trees.

"What are you doing, girl?"

I walked back. "Turning my back on the pig, lady, just to prove I am not influencing him. I just thought—"

"You do not think! You do as you are told. Come back here and teach me some more."

"The pig is tired, it will take time for him to get used to—"

"Rubbish! We have been at this less than an hour! Do as you are told!"

"He won't—"

"He *will*! You can make him." She paused, and her next words came honey-sweet and loaded with sting. "Unless, of course, you would rather I summoned my soldiers to give your brother here a painful lesson. They are experts, I assure you. . . ."

The Wimperling flashed me a warning. "Do as she says! Simple addition: two and one, two and two. She can't count."

And so it went on, until the Wimperling himself took a hand, sinking to the ground with a groan and puffing and panting, rolling his eyes round and around.

"There! I told you so!" For a heart-stopping moment I believed he was indeed ill, but as I rushed forward and knelt distractedly at his side, I saw him wink.

"Tell me, quickly, what you saw from the window. . . ."

So, as I fussed over him, I described the scene outside.

"Mmm . . . Doesn't sound too promising. Don't look so worried! We'll find a way out of this."

The Lady Aleinor at last seemed persuaded she could go no further today. She sank back in her chair, still repeating to herself the rubbish I had taught her.

"Very well," she said after a moment. "What does it eat?"

"*He* eats most things," I said. "When I get back to the stables I can ask for—"

"The stables? The creature stays here. It's mine now, and I shall look after it."

I was devastated. How in the world could we all escape together when we were down there and he was up here? Together we had a chance: apart, none.

"But—but he needs exercise, grooming, companionship, light. . . ."

"All of which he will get. My soldiers will escort him out twice a day—the exercise will do them good as well. A nice trot around the castle grounds . . . Now, you can go. Attend me tomorrow at the same hour."

"But—but I . . ."

"Do you want a beating? No? Then get out! The creature will soon adapt to its new surroundings. As soon as you have taught me all I need to know you may leave. But if there is any more argument or backsliding I shall have to reconsider. Just remember what I said about the expendability of your other animals. . . ."

Back in the stables I sobbed in despair, trying to explain to the others the mess we—I—had gotten us into. Gill patted me awkwardly on the shoulder, Growch whined in sympathy and Mistral and Traveler shifted from foot to foot in anxiety. I felt terribly alone. I had not realized before how much I had relied on the simple common sense of the Wimperling, his stoicism, his comfortable, fat, ugly little body. Not that he was so small anymore . . . Only a few weeks ago I had been able to tuck him under my arm, and now he seemed near full-grown. One of the nicest things about him was that he never grumbled, and now he had been taken from us I felt utterly helpless: I couldn't even think straight.

"There's the boy," said Gill. "He said he could get us out of here, remember?"

"But that was before she took the Wimperling," I wept.

"Let's see what he got to say, anyways," said Growch. "Ain't nuffin more than we can do today: gettin' dark already."

So it was, and we had missed the midday meal. I found, too, that no one was going to rush to feed the animals, and in the gathering gloom I had to find my own oats and hay, and fill the buckets with water from the well in the courtyard.

It was even more obvious that we didn't exist when

we went into the hall for the evening meal. Word had obviously got around of the lady's displeasure, for we were elbowed away from the table, were not offered a trencher, nor any ale. In the end I snatched what I could for both of us and we ate standing; rye bread, stale cheese and a couple of bones with a little meat left on them.

Worse was to come. The Lady Aleinor brought in the Wimperling, an animal so bedecked with ribbons and bunting as to be practically unrecognizable. She made him go through what I had taught her in front of the whole assembly, mouthing the rubbish she had learned; she had a little whip in her hand with which she stroked his flanks: if she had actually struck him I don't know what I would have done.

The applause was loud and sychophantic, and as soon as she had done I rushed forward to give him a reassuring hug before they dragged me away. He managed some quick words: "See the boy! If the rest of you can get away, I think I can manage as well. . . ."

Slightly reassured, we all spent a better night, and in the morning, after feeding and watering the animals and snatching some bread and cheese from the hall for Gill and myself, we settled down to await the boy and his wagon. He brought winter cabbage, some turnips, a barrel of smoked fish and some firewood for the kitchens. Once he had unloaded he picked up a shovel and started to clear the far end of the stable.

"Down here as well, please!" I called out, as if I had never seen him before. He walked down the aisle, trailing a barrow behind him, and bent to shovel out Mistral's stall.

"Well? Thought about it, then?" All the while he spoke to us he never stopped his steady shoveling. "Still want out?"

"Yes, yes; we do. Are you willing to help us?"

"I said so, didn't I? Ten silver pieces you said? Good. How many are there of you?"

I pointed to the others. "And our packages." I mustn't forget the tortoise, either. "The—the pig has been taken into the castle."

He shook his head. "Can't help you there. There's no getting it out now. One of them out there—" he jerked his thumb over his shoulder: "—told me as how you had taught the lady some magic words?"

"Not really," I said hurriedly. "Just the words I always use to direct his act. She's a slow learner. . . . What about the rest of us, then?"

He carried on shoveling. "Dog can slip through the portcullis any time: bars are wide enough. Pigeon can fly over, right?"

"And my brother? He's blind."

"Him and your packages can go in the back of the wagon. I'll back it up to the door at the end of the stables tonight. He'll have to sit under a load o'shit, though, but I got a cover."

"And me?"

"Got a cloak? Right, then. Pin up your skirt and I'll bring a pair of my pa's braies. Be a tight fit, but . . . At dusk, won't matter as much. Get you a hat as well. Find a sack of something to put over your back, walk out t'other side from the soldiers. Dirty your face a bit, too."

"What about the horse?"

"Swap her for mine. Blanket over her, bit of muck on her quarters and head, sack on her back. I'll let on mine's lame and I'm borrowing."

"Tonight?"

"Quicker the better. We'll all meet behind the castle, in the forest. Follow the wood trail. Clearing about quarter-mile in."

"But . . . will it work?"

He stopped shoveling and grinned. "Got to. Else I don't get my money, do I?"

There was much to do. Everything, including the tortoise, to be parceled as small as possible, Traveler and Growch to be briefed as to our meeting place, Mistral to be dirtied up, Gill to be encouraged—

"Hidden in a manure cart? I couldn't possibly. . . ."

—and in between as much food as possible to be filched from the hall and kitchens.

Promptly at midday I was summoned once more to

the Lady Hell-and-All (as I now thought of her). More instruction included the Wimperling "finding" lost objects. He was deliberately slow, earning one sharp reprimand and a slash with her jeweled girdle at me for not teaching her properly. In between I managed to convey to him what we had planned and where we were to meet.

"But what about you?"

"Have you forgotten? I can fly. . . ."

I thought he was joking, trying to make me feel better.

The afternoon seemed interminable, though there was only now some three hours till dusk. I checked and re-checked that all was packed and prepared; noted that the sky was clear and remembered there would be a helpful moon; worried lest we didn't get away quick enough, for the lady's soldiers and her scent-working lymers and brachs could pick up a trail easily enough if she discovered us missing too soon; I also prayed: hard.

In between I paced the courtyard restlessly, watching people come and go, all busy, all employed on some task or another. Soldiers drilling, squires practicing with wooden swords, wood being stacked, slops emptied, weapons being cleaned and sharpened, horses groomed and exercised, dogs fighting, chickens being plucked for the evening meal . . .

I felt terribly conspicuous, as if everyone could read my mind, knew what I was planning, but in fact no one took the slightest notice of me. Most were too busy, but as for the others, all knew I had incurred the lady's displeasure, so it was as if I didn't exist at all. If there had been any dungeons in the castle, I should have been shut away in those; being denied the gates, the courtyard was as good a prison as any.

At long last the sun started to sink behind the castle walls. The boy's was one of the last wagons to enter through the gate, and to my dismay he was directed, not to the stables, but to picking up empty water casks. This meant he was half-loaded. He then backed the wagon as near as he could to the stable door and muttered: "Can you get your dog to start a fight?"

Get Growch to fight? It had been with the greatest

difficulty I had restrained him during the last few days, and now he needed no further bidding. He chose a pack of hounds near the gateway, slipped on his short legs beneath their bellies, and with a couple of sharp nips here and there and a heap of shouted insults had them in a trice snapping and barking and snarling and biting at one another, in an unavailing attempt to catch him. As soon as the pace got too hot, even for him, he careered through the open gates and across the draw-bridge, yelling the dog equivalent of "can't-catch-me!" Half-a-dozen hounds tore off in immediate pursuit, which meant at least the same number of servitors went in pursuit, to ensure the lady's precious dogs came to no harm.

The chase was enlivening an otherwise boring after-noon, and more and more people were breaking off what they were doing to cheer, laugh or shake their heads disapprovingly. A couple of the horses who were being groomed chose that moment to display temper, snapping and kicking out at their handlers, scattering the rest of the dogs and some hens and ducks, whose squawks added to the commotion.

"Load up now!" hissed the boy, and in a fumblingly long moment I had Gill and our packages up and into the back of the wagon, and a tarpaulin hastily thrown over the whole. I threw Traveler up, and after a couple of abortive flutters he took wing and wheeled out of the gate, heading west. "Bring out the horse!" and in a moment he had exchanged her in the traces for his own animal, stooping to fiddle for a minute with his horse's off-hind hoof. He then thrust a bundle into my hand: "Change into these!" And a moment later was noncha-lantly loading up a couple more casks and roping them down. All this had taken perhaps three minutes. "See you in the forest," he muttered, and led Mistral and the wagon towards the gateway, his own horse limping behind.

I watched them, my heart in my mouth, but no one took the slightest notice, and in a minute they were trundling across the drawbridge and away, just as the last of the protesting hounds were being led back to the courtyard. I heard a derisive bark from the far side of the moat and knew Growch was safe.

But I was wasting precious time. Ducking back into the stables I opened the package the boy had given me, tucked up my skirt as best I could and struggled into the braies, a very tight fit. I shoved my hair up under the broad-brimmed straw hat—why the hell hadn't I thought to braid it up! —and wrapped my cloak around me. Picking up the sack I had earlier filled with hay I flung it over my shoulder and stooped over as though I was carrying a much heavier burden.

It was perhaps twenty yards from the stable to the gateway, but it seemed like a million miles. I had to walk slowly, I had to hunch up to keep my face hidden, and with the broad brim of the hat I could only see a couple of paces in front of me. At last I could see the penultimate wagon ahead trundling through the gateway, and hurried a little to pass through in its wake. I had my hand out ready to hang on to the tailgate when everything went horribly wrong.

I had hurried too much in changing and hadn't fastened my skirt up securely. It started to drop down and, bending to retrieve it, I felt my hat fall off and my hair cascade down round my face. There was a shout off to my left and I dropped the sack and was panicked into running, my heart thumping like a drum. A soldier slipped from the shadows, stuck out a foot and I landed flat on my face in the dust, winded and bruised.

I was hauled to my feet, none too gently.

"What's all this, then? Trying it on again, are we? We'll just see what the lady has to say about all this. . . ."

CHAPTER
NINETEEN

The lady had a great deal to say, or rather scream, the words punctuated with slaps, punches and pinches which I was helpless to avoid, being held firmly by the two soldiers who had brought me upstairs. I was almost blinded by tears of rage and pain and at first I only half heard the little voice in my head. There it was again: "Courage; we'll soon be out of this. . . ." Then I realized the Wimperling must be in the solar as well.

The lady eventually ran out of breath and went back to her chair, her face crimson with rage and exertion. "After all I've done for you, you ungrateful little whore! Oh, I see I shall have to teach you a real lesson this time? Misbegotten little tart! You can't say I didn't warn you. . . ." She turned to the soldiers. "Go and wring the neck of that pigeon of hers, then take it to the kitchens and bid them make a little pie of it: I shall start my meal with it tonight. Then bring her brother here: we'll see how he likes losing his tongue was well as his eyes. . . ."

"Oh, *no!*" The words were out before I realized that the others had gone, were hopefully safe for a while, but she enjoyed my reaction, clapping as if she had just performed a clever trick and was applauding herself. Her tongue flickered back and forth between her teeth, a snake tasting the air for my terror.

"I'll show you just who is in charge here! If you don't want your brother to lose other parts as well—a hand, his ears, his balls perhaps—you will swear on God's Body not to dare cross me again!"

We were alone now—where *was* the Wimperling? The fire smoked abominably, my face hurt and the soft flesh on my upper arms throbbed where she had pinched and nipped with unmerciful nails. My loosened hair was plastered across my face, and I lifted my hands to braid it back, but she half-rose from her chair on an instant.

"No tricks, now, or I'll call the guard!" I let my hands drop again and she subsided. Just then the Wimperling appeared from behind her chair, festooned as before with ridiculous ribbons and bows. He gave me a reassuring wink; I could see his ears were cocked, listening to something I could not hear.

"Not on their way back yet," he said to me. "On my count of three run across to the window and open the shutters as wide as you can!" He started to take deep breaths. The lady's expression changed; she bent down to caress him.

"But you can't—"

"Don't argue!" he said. "Just go. Trust me. . . . One, two, three!"

I should perhaps have rushed to the window without risking a glance back. As it was I nearly knocked myself senseless on the corner of the ornate sideboard just to glimpse the lady rise from her chair and call out, the Wimperling circling her warily with exposed teeth—he had real tusks I noticed—all the while hissing gently.

I reached the window without further mishap and looked round wildly for the fastening. Of course! There was a heavy bar that dropped into slots on either side. I tried to lift it, but it wouldn't budge. Swearing under my breath, I heaved and heaved again. One side started to move, the other was stuck. Helplessly I shoved and pulled, then realized that one shutter hadn't been closed properly and was catching against the bar. I slammed it shut with the heel of my hand then hefted the bar once more. It came loose so easily it flew up in the air and narrowly missed my feet as it crashed onto the floor. I tugged the shutters open as hard as I could till they crashed back against the wall and suddenly the room was flooded with dusk-light and there was a great gust of welcome fresh air.

"Right!" I yelled, and turned back to an incredible sight. The Wimperling appeared to have grown to twice or three times is normal size: he was blowing himself up as one would inflate a bladder, and looked in imminent danger of bursting. I could hardly see his eyes, his tail stuck straight out like an arrow and his wings were unfolding away from his shoulders, because there was no room to tuck them away.

The lady's eyes were almost popping out of her head, but she was still making valiant attempts to reach me, thwarted by the pig's circling motions. I took a quick peep out of the window; we couldn't possibly escape that way. It was a sheer drop down to the dry moat and I didn't fancy suicide.

The Wimperling took a last, deep, deep breath, adding yet more inches all over, until his tightly stretched skin looked as if it were cracking all over onto tiny, fine lines like unoiled leather.

I could hear footsteps on the spiral stair.

"Bolt the door!" cried the Wimperling. "Then watch out!"

As I ran to the door I saw him charge the Lady Hell-and-All, knocking her flying into the hearth, shrieking and cursing. I threw both bolts and dashed back, the lady being occupied in trying to extinguish the smoldering sparks that had caught her purple woolen dress, doing less than well because the bright-edged specks were widening into holes and then crawling like maggots this way and that in the close weave.

Somehow the Wimperling had managed to heave himself up onto the windowsill, and was now balanced precariously on the edge. He was so fat he could barely squeeze his bulk through the frame.

"Hurry up, Summer!"

"What? Where?"

"On my back," he said impatiently. "Hurry!"

"You can't—"

"I *can!*"

I tried to scramble up, but whereas the windowsill had been on a level with my waist, with the pig's bulk on top his back was at chin-height and I kept slipping off. Now behind us we could hear a hammering on the door, the lady was still screeching and any minute she would rush over and snatch me back—

I grabbed a stool, climbed on that and found myself lying flat on the pig's back.

"Arms round my neck and hang on tight! Here we go-o-ooo!" and before I could take a breath there was a sudden sickening plunge and we were away. I felt a shriek of pure terror wind its way up from my stomach and escape through my mouth, the sound mingling with the screech of disturbed rooks and the rush of air past my ears. There was a sudden Whoosh! of sound and then a Crack! as of flags snapping in a sharp breeze, and we were flying!

A steady rush of air came from the Wimperling's backside and his wings spread out from his shoulders, balancing us on our downward path away from the castle. The moat slid away from beneath my frightened eyes; there were the trees of the forest, the patch of greensward rising gently to meet us. . . .

It was a terrifying, wonderful few moments. The wind blew my hair all over my face, I felt utterly insecure, my teeth were chattering with fear, yet there was enough in me left to appreciate just what I was experiencing. The world was spinning, I was a bird, I was going to the moon, I would live forever, I was immortal, omnipotent—

The hiss of escaping air behind us stopped suddenly, started again, then deteriorated into a series of popping little farts, and in an instant we were wobbling all over the sky. The world turned upside down and a moment later we landed on the strip of grass in front of the trees with an almighty crash that rattled my teeth and knocked all the breath from my body.

For a moment—a minute? longer?—I lay fighting to regain my breath, then sat up and felt myself all over. Plenty of bruises and bumps, but nothing broken. Where was I, what was I—?

The Wimperling! Oh, God, where was he?

I gazed around wildly, saw what looked like a shrunken sack lying a few yards away. "Wimperling? Are you all right?" I crawled over and poked the heap.

"Yes," said a muffled voice. "No thanks to you. I was underneath when we landed. . . ."

He sat up slowly, shook each leg in turn, then his tail and ears and took a deep breath. Immediately he looked less like a sack and more like a pig.

I shook my head admiringly. "How did you *do* it? The flying, I mean?"

"Improvisation. I don't think I'd try it again, though: not easy enough to control emission. Without it, though, I couldn't have managed you as well—my wings aren't strong enough yet."

There was a sudden shout from the direction of the castle. I looked back and could see the lady hanging out of the window we had just left, waving her arms and shouting, and around the corner of the castle came a party of foot soldiers, trotting purposefully our way. I scrambled to my feet.

"Quick! We've got to find the others. Something about a firewood trail . . ."

"I saw it on the way down, as well as I could for mouthfuls of your hair," said the pig tranquilly. "Off to the left." And he set out at a fast trot, with me stumbling behind. We swerved into the undergrowth and it was hard going, for the bushes were thick and overhead branches became tangled in my hair while roots tripped my feet. But the Wimperling kept going and soon we burst out into a twig-strewn ride.

Behind us we could hear shouts, the lady's fading screams, and we ran as fast as we could down the ride into the forest, me fearful lest we had missed the others.

The trees swung away on either side and there were stacks of part-chopped wood, two charcoal-burner's huts and—yes, they were all there, Mistral already loaded.

Growch came bouncing to meet us. "Hullo! Got away all right, I see. Didn't I do well? Saw that lot off, I did."

Gill fumbled for my arm. "You all right? That cart . . . I smell terrible." He did.

I mind-checked the others: all well. Even Basher was awake, and grumbling. "A-a-all that bouncing . . . Chap ca-a-an't sleep. . . ."

The boy was dancing about impatiently. "Hurry! I must be away before they come. Wind's from the east— them to you, which'll help you with the dogs. I'll try and head 'em off. . . ." and he swung a smelly sack from his hand.

"Thanks!" I panted. I had a stitch in my side from running. "Why the extra help?"

"Catch you and they catch me," he answered succinctly. "If they screwed your arms out of their sockets you'd tell. Have to."

I pulled out my purse from under my skirt and poured coins into my hand. "Ten silver pieces: one, two— Hey! What are you doing?" To my consternation a dirty brown hand had snatched the purse and scooped the coins from my hand.

The boy stepped back well out of reach. He pulled a knife from his belt, and I bent down to restrain a growling Growch.

"Why?"

"For my Mam and sisters, remember? Reckon they need the money more'n you. You got the pig: reckon he can earn for you. Better get going: the lady has a long arm. Take the path to your right, then first left to the stream. Walk in the water to confuse the hounds till you come to a grove of oaks. After that take the path either to the east or south. Lady's demesne finishes at the road you'll find either way. Twenty miles or so. Get going, will you?"

"Wait!" I called, as he made for the shelter of the trees. "What's your name?"

"Dickon. Why?"

I should have been furious with him, risked setting Growch on him, fought him myself for the money, but in a queer way I knew he needed it more. It was a shame, but I still had some of Matthew's money left: we'd manage. "When are you leaving?"

"Soon as the weather brings the first leaves on the beech. Go and get myself 'prenticed. Come back for the family once I'm earning."

"If you go north, seek out ..." and I gave him Matthew's name and direction. "Say we sent you. He's a kind man but a canny merchant. He might fix you up with something. Treat him fair and he'll do the same."

"Thanks. I—" But there came a flurry of shouts and barking behind us and we fled one way, he the other.

At first it was easy, in spite of the deepening dusk. Behind us we could hear the hounds and then a sudden whooping, hollering sound and gathered they had picked up a scent. I only hoped it wasn't ours, but the sounds seemed to be away to our left, no nearer. We nearly missed the path to the stream, it was so overgrown, but at last we found ourselves splashing ankle-deep in freezing water, and by the time we managed to identify the grove of oaks the icy chill of my feet had crept up to my stomach and chest. It was near full dark; Mistral, the pigeon and the tortoise were fine, but Gill, Growch and I were so cold that all we wanted to do was light a fire and roast ourselves by it, forgetting bruised feet, turned ankles and scratched faces and hands.

But there was no way we could risk that. Far away I could still hear the mournful belling of the hounds, though the distance between us seemed to be increasing. I hoped Dickon was safe back home. Even if he had laid a trail, eventually when it came to an end they would cast back, though they would probably wait now until morning: the lady would not thank them for losing any of the hounds, even to catch us. And I knew she would be even keener to do that now she knew the pig could fly. . . .

We stumbled on as best we could through the long

night, halting only for a quick snack of the bits and pieces I had managed to bring with me. We had the advantage of clear skies, a near-full moon and the prickle of stars, but it was still hard going. There were no rides here and the undergrowth hadn't been cleared for years. Fallen trees, hidden roots, sudden dips and hollows, the tangle of briars, an occasionally stagnant pond—all contrived to hinder our halting passage.

The noise of our progress effectively drove away most of the wildlife, though tawny owl hunted relentlessly. There was the intermittent scurrying in the undergrowth as some small animal was disturbed, and we almost fell over a grunting badger, turning the fallen leaves for early grubs. Towards dawn I called a halt under some pines and we hunkered down in an uneasy doze. There was nothing much to eat for break-fast but the rest of what I had brought from the castle, and that was little enough: the bread stale, the cheese hard, the pie so high only the Wimperling and Growch would touch it. Luckily there was grazing for Mistral, some seeds for Traveler; Basher had dozed off again.

It was a long day. Once or twice we heard the far-off sounds of men, dogs and even horses, but even these receded after a while. At the midday halt Mistral and the Wimperling foraged as best they could, the pigeon found some thistle heads, and Basher, thankfully, had decided to hibernate again. Gill and I just had to tighten our belts and trudge on. Luckily that afternoon I found some Judas' Ear growing on elder: it was a tough fungus with little taste, but after dusk I risked a small fire— during the light I reckoned smoke could be still seen from the turrets of the castle, but a tiny red glow in a hollow was more difficult to spot at night—and chopped the fungus into the pot with oil, salt, a pinch of herbs and a little flour and water and it made a filling enough mess. I also made some oatcakes to eat in the morning. Of course we were still hungry, but at least our stomachs didn't grumble all night.

And this was the pattern of the next two days. Luckily the sun shone and we took whatever promising trail we

could, though very often these animal tracks started
going east or south, and then wandered all over the place,
sometimes even circling right back, and the undergrowth
was too thick for us to wade through, unless we found
bare ground beneath pine or fir. Twenty miles straight
it might be, crooked it was not. I wondered how far we
had really come: probably halfway only.

I looked for more fungi and found a few Scarlet Cups,
better for color than taste, some Blisters, and a few
Sandys. This time I boiled them up with a dozen or so
chicory and dandelion leaves and the last of the flour.
Growch dug up a couple of truffles and I added these
and the result was quite tasty. Gill and I were down to
one thin meal a day, though the animals fared better
with their foraging, and the Wimperling it was who found
us both some shriveled haws and the handful or so of
hazelnuts the next day. But we were all weakened and
weary by the evening of the fifth day when the trees
started to thin out and at last we could walk straight with
the setting sun to our right.

I don't think any of us quite believed it at first when
we found ourselves actually stepping on a proper road,
able to see in all directions and with no pushing and
shoving along a trail. I looked back. Nothing save anony-
mous trees: it could have been anyone's demesne. I felt
like putting up a great notice by the side of the road
saying: "Beware! The Lady Aleinora is an evil Bitch!"
But what good would it do? Most who passed here would
not be able to read, and for those who did the castle was
twenty miles away from this side.

I hadn't realized how tired I was: we were on a road,
pointing in the right direction, but we had no food and
no shelter: I didn't feel I could go a step further. Growch
nuzzled my knee sympathetically, but it was Traveler who
called to be let out of his cage.

"I'll fly a little way and see what I can see. . . ."

He was back in ten minutes, to report a hamlet some
two miles ahead. I don't know how we made it but we
did, just before dark. We had to knock them up, the
food was poor, the shelter minimal, but at that stage we

couldn't be choosers. We ate, we slept, and the next day we did the same. On the second day we were on our way again, wending from hamlet to hamlet. The weather remained dry, the village folk were hospitable, the food adequate, but I was worried at how far east we were veering, although there was no alternative except the occasional track. Even Traveler, who was a definite bonus, could see no alternative way, fly as high as he could.

The countryside was changing, too. It was becoming more rocky and the road more undulating, and we passed through scrub and pine as the land gradually rose. On either side mountains rose in sympathy, at first blue and distant, then nearer and sharper each day, till we could clearly see the tall escarpments, the towering crags, the black holes of faraway caves, the skirts of pine that clothed their waists. Above our heads we could hear the complaint of flocks of crows and sometimes see the mighty soar of eagles, their great wings fingering the winds we could not feel.

Understandably Traveler became wary of flying too far with so many predators about, but one day he came winging back to report a "town of sorts" off to our left. Three or four flights away, he said, but a pigeon's flight was variable, relying as it did day by day on weather conditions: wind, rain, cloud, sun and the type of flight needed to suit each variation.

"Can we reach it before nightfall?"

"Up the hill, down the hill, round the next hill, turn east, twisting road between high escarpments, down to the valley . . . Yes."

"And what's it like, this town?" A town meant proper shelter, a full replenishment of our stores, mending of shoes, a warm wash—everything we had sorely needed for the past two weeks.

"Difficult to say. Never seen anything like it. Lots of tents, few buildings. Many people and animals. No castle, no church. Big road leading off to the south."

And that is what decided me. This was the road we needed, and if it meant going through the "town"

Traveler had described, then that was the way we had
to go, although many times during that long day I cursed
the pigeon's directions. Birds fly, they don't walk, and
their "up" and "down" meant little to them, but a hell
of a lot to those on foot. The narrow path we followed
that crawled and looped what seemed a million miles
towards the valley floor nearly finished us all off: it was
so frustrating being able to see our goal one moment,
and then having to turn away from it. That, plus the
falling rocks, the blocked paths we had to climb
around, the streams that poured on our heads or mean-
dered across the track . . .

I had already lit the lantern and fixed it to Mistral's
crupper by the time we reached the valley floor. Ahead
was a short walk through well-trodden scrub to the
perimeter of the "town," marked by a regular series of
posts set into the ground, a very shallow artificial moat
and a couple of temporary bridges. Beyond we could see
a score of small stone buildings, a mass of tents, a half-
ruined amphitheater and a slender temple, the broken
columns throwing exquisite shadows in the moonlight.
Obviously once this had been the site of an earlier civilization. And now?

We were stopped at the nearest bridge. Not by a soldier, but by a fussy little civilian with a mass of papers
in his hand, a quill behind his ear and an ink pot in his
pocket. His very officiousness calmed any fears I might
have had, and before long I was trying not to smile at
his earnestness. Here was normalcy: no shrinking houses,
ghosts or wicked ladies.

"What have we here, then? There are only two weeks
left, you know: you're late!" He consulted his lists. "Do
you know just how many models we have had this year?
Nearly two hundred! And of course now accommodation
is at a premium. . . . Do you have a sponsor? No? Still,
there is always Mordecai, the Jew, or Bartholomew. . . .
I believe they are both short this year. Now, how many
are there of you? A man, a lady and a horse . . . And
what's this? A pig? and do I see a dog? Well, I don't
think I've seen a pig, this year, but of course dogs are

two a farthing. You have a pigeon? And a tortoise? Now that *is* a novelty! This might make all the difference. Quite a call for exotic creatures like that, especially for breviaries. Haven't by any chance got a coney or a hedge-pig, I suppose? Pity; both in short supply this year. Seven of you, then: lucky number, seven ... Come far? Now, that will be nine of copper: two each for the humans, one for the animals."

I was completely confused. "Models," "sponsors," a tortoise to make all the difference? Instead of the expected normalcy, this place sounded like a madhouse. But the word "models" gave me a clue: perhaps this place contained artists who wanted various creatures to draw and paint, human and animal?

"How many artists here this year?" I asked diffidently, to make sure I was on the right track.

"Artists? A few more than last year ..." So now I was right. "Now, let's have your names. ..." He took them down.

"What—what are the rates?"

"Depends on your sponsor. You haven't been before? No, well if you follow me I will try and find someone to take you on."

He led us across the wooden bridge to a squalid huddle of temporary huts, a line of tethered horses, mules and donkeys. Small cooking fires burned in the deepening gloom and people scurried back and forth carrying washing, water, pots and pans, babes in arms.

"This is the poorer end," said our guide, wrinkling his nose. "Not organized at all, this lot ... Farther in are the stores, stables, cooking and washing areas. Plus of course the hiring place, market and artists supplies ... Stay here: I won't be long." And off he strode with a purposeful air, papers flapping.

"What *have* you got us into this time, Summer?" said poor Gill.

He might well ask!

Our guide, Master Fettiplace, returned, and led us a few hundred yards to a row of orderly tents. "Let me introduce you to Master Bumbo—" a small, bustling,

bald-headed man, with a snub nose red from wine and
a potbelly to match. "He is willing to take you on, providing terms can be agreed."

"No reason why not!" cried our new sponsor. He
beamed at us all, but the smile did not reach a pair of
small, black, calculating eyes. He would drive a hard bargain but we had no option. He had a large black mole
on his left cheek, from which sprouted three bristly hairs:
this should not have made him any less likable, but somehow it did.

"Come along, come along, all of you!" said Master
Bumbo. "Let's get you settled in. You'll be hungry and
tired, I have no doubt.... Er, you did say you had a
tortoise ...?"

I sized up Master Bumbo, and decided it would be a
battle. But we needed the money....

"Of course," I said. "A trained one. As are the horse,
the pigeon, the pig and the dog. Very expensive animals.
They will do exactly as I say: stand, sit, walk, fly, or be
perfectly still. But they only obey me. We do not come
cheap, my brother and I...."

"Of course, of course! My commission is small, very
small—and in return you will have bountiful accommodation, free, and one good meal a day. And of course your
fees for posing ..." He walked along the row of tents,
disappeared into one; there was the sound of an altera-
tion and a moment or two later a tawdry female came
flying out, followed by half a dozen cushions, a blanket
and various pots and pans. Master Bumbo returned with
an ingratiating smile and a bruised lip. "As soon as you
like ..." The tent smelled like a whorehouse, and showed
signs of the hasty eviction of its former occupant: underwear, pots of perfume, a torn night dress. I handed these
gravely to our sponsor.

"You mentioned a meal.... I think we will take today's
now. And if I may accompany you to the cooking lines,
I believe we shall have better service when we need it.
Precooked meals, or will they cook our own?"

"Er ... Either. They are not cheap, but who is these
days?"

I decided to build our own fire. Hanging our lantern on a hook, I saw there was rush matting on the floor and a few rather tatty cushions. We had our own bedding, so that was all right. "Is there a bathhouse?"

"Over there." He pointed. "Again, not cheap . . ."

Right. We would pay for hot water once, and I would wash the clothes, myself; there must be a stream nearby.

He tried again. "Fodder for the animals a hundred yards to your right—"

"Not cheap," I said gravely.

"Er . . . No. Your horse can join the lines down—"

"My horse," I said, "stays here, behind the tent. She's trained, remember?"

And so the first small victory was mine, but it didn't remain that way for long. Every day it swung first one way then the other, as first Master Bumbo then I gained advantage. Of course he tried to cheat us, and I retorted by snatching the odd freelance for any of us I could.

The "town" was as I had suspected: a winter retreat for artists where they could paint, draw or sketch in peace with everything provided—from the latest tube or pot of Italian Brown to the row of whores' tents behind the temple. They had all the scenery they needed—a river, mountains, forests, romantic ruins—and all the models imaginable; black, white, brown; tall, short, wide, thin; dwarfs and giants, men, women and children; the beautiful, the ugly and those in between. They had animals of all shapes and sizes (but ours was the only tortoise), the flowers of the field carefully painted on wood and cut out to be placed where they wished and all the impedimenta of indoor life—pots, pans, candlesticks, stools, chairs, tables, hangings, goblets, knives etc. There were costumes and armor, swords and spears, in fact everything an artist could need. At a price.

Why in this hidden valley? I had thought we were miles from anywhere, but in fact the road Traveler had seen led straight to an important crossroads, and was only ten miles from the nearest town. The whole venture was run by an Italian, who had another such project in his own country, held in the autumn. Signor Cavalotti, whose brainchild this was, believed that exchanges of ideas and techniques were essential to the development of art; indeed, I was told there had been significant advances in perspective and the mixing of paints in the ten years the two "towns" had existed.

Well, Signor Cavalotti may have had high ideals and thought he was a philanthropist, but the consortium who ran this caper was very far from being either. Everything was very highly priced, but those who came off worst were probably the models like us. It went like this: the artist paid the model, who then relinquished some seventy percent to the sponsor; he in turn paid ten percent for food, five percent to pitch the tents, and then perhaps twenty percent to the consortium for the privilege of sponsorship. Probably the artists spent more than everyone else—space, canvas, paints, props, costumes, models, food, accommodation—but then they had the money to start with.

Most of them were sponsored by rich families or the church—I counted at least a dozen altar pieces and triptychs in various stages of completion—and many had private means. There was a handful of students and apprentices, but most of these were under the patronage of the artists themselves. Useful to be able to take credit for the important bits and have an unpaid lackey to fill in the background!

Master Bumbo had very little idea how to promote his models—he had ten others besides ourselves—but in spite of his laziness, incompetence and avariciousness Gill's good looks provided us with two St. Sebastians and a disciple; I got two crowd scenes, very background, and Basher was fully occupied with two young monks composing a bestiary and an artist creating a series of panels on popular legends. One artist was interested exclusively in birds and their plumage and anatomy and was very pleased with the (private) sittings with Traveler.

And what of the Wimperling in all this? All in all, he earned more than the rest of us put together. Master Bimbo gave up on him after the first day: he was, after all, a rather ugly pig—but I had better ideas. A German artist who had used poor Mistral in an allegory for famine recommended a Dutchman who was looking for "odd" creatures, and I saw why when I peeped round the corner of his screened off area. He was painting the pains of Hell on a large canvas, and very frightening they were, too. Fires, flames, smoke; imps, demons, devils, trolls, dragons: all delighting in torturing, beheading, raping and disemboweling the hapless sinners who cascaded down from the top of the canvas in a never-ending stream. And everywhere there was an inch or so of space capered creatures from a wildly demented imagination, gleefully cheering on the destruction.

These creatures could never have existed: birds with fish heads, lizards with horses' hooves, cats with six arms and two heads, mouths with thin spindly legs, spiders with human faces, torsos with heads in their stomachs, a pair of legs with wings—It was this last that gave me the idea. Withdrawing quietly before the artist noticed me, I returned later with a fully briefed Wimperling.

The artist was a thoroughly unpleasant little man, hunched and smelly, so much I had already heard, but I wasn't prepared for the brusque way he dismissed me before I had opened my mouth.

"Unless you've got an extra pair of tits or balls I don't want to know: bugger off!"

But I wasn't going to be thrown out just like that. Instead I dared his wrath and looked critically at the lizard-like thing with wings he was trying to draw.

"You've got the wings wrong," I said. "They should be more leathery and the tips less scooped. . . ."

"What? What do you mean? How do you know anything about Wyrm-wings?"

"Look," I said, and the Wimperling carefully extended one wing. "And if it's claws and hooves you are after, just look at these. . . ." The pig lifted one hoof. "And as for fangs—" Obligingly the Wimperling bared his teeth. I hadn't realized just how sharp they were till now. The pig folded himself away again. "What do you say?"

"Christ-on-the-Cross!" breathed the artist. "Do that again!"

The Wimperling obliged.

"How much do you want for it?" snapped the artist, his eyes even piggier than the pig. "I'll give you what you want. Within reason . . . Ten gold pieces?" His fingers were crawling towards the pig with desire, his sleeve smudging the charcoal sketch I had criticized.

"He's not for sale," I replied firmly. "But I am offering him to you as a model: exclusive rights, of course. At a reasonable price."

"For the rest of the time here? Nine days? One gold coin."

"Two. He's worth far more, and you know it. *Exclusive* rights, remember: you'd better keep him hidden away." I was calculating on his artistic greed in this: I didn't want anyone else to know about the wings. I needn't have worried: the artist's "find" was far too precious to share, and at the end of our two weeks the artist had dozens of sketches of every part of the pig's anatomy, from the tip of his fanged snout to the end of his spade-tipped tail and everything in between.

I supposed this was the way to assure immortality, I thought, looking at the sketches, remembering the other drawings and paintings of all of us, even my crowd scenes. Some day, many years hence perhaps, people would look at a pigeon's wing, a horse's flanks, a scruffy dog, a tortoise in a bestiary, the wings on a creature from hell, a woman bending over a basket, a saint's agony, and maybe wonder at the originals they were created from. But only we would know, and we wouldn't be there to tell them. It was a shivery thought.

But once more on the road, with the warm wind lifting the hair from my forehead and the prickly-sweet perfume of the gorse on the hillsides tickling our noses, all such somber thoughts were chased away.

"I can smell spring," said Gill, lifting his blind eyes to the sun. "And after spring comes Summer!" and he smiled at his own little joke, a smile to lift my heart and renew my love.

CHAPTER TWENTY

It was true, Spring had arrived, and with it came an uplifting of the spirit, a healthy optimism that had nothing to do with reality. I would wake in the mornings, stretch the creaks from my bones (for the nights were still cold), sniff the crisp dawn air and feel as though I had drunk a bucketful of chilled white wine.

As we traveled further and further south, I delighted in plants, trees and herbiage that were strange to my northern eyes. All seemed brighter, bigger, pricklier; citrus trees with evergreen leaves sprouted little dots of white bud; bushy grey-green cacti and succulents were tipped with barbs like daggers; a yellow cascade of mimosa poured over stone walls, and miniature iris and crocus speared up through the scrub under olive and carob. Of course I had to ask the names of all these, but there were plants I recognized, though their flowering was at least a month ahead of ours at home.

I found the pale tremble of pink-white-purple wood anemones, petals ready to fly on the slightest breeze; heart-shaped leaves of deepest green hiding the thick, soft scent of violets; the perfumed cream of wild jonquil; shaggy coltsfoot and tender celandine, days-eye, lions-tooth—the last two demanded daily by an awakening

Basher, together with the tender young leaves of chicory and clover.

As we passed through villages and hamlets the pink smoke of almond blossom clothed the slopes of the hillsides, though the knobbed vines were still bare. I experimented with the new-grown herbs: wild mint (good with lamb and goat), young and bitter shoots of asparagus, pale among its prickly adult cage, the tasty tips of nettle, and thyme and rosemary (excellent with all meats and fish).

And the birds and animals echoed this burgeoning promise. Sparrows, thrushes, blackbirds, green- and goldfinch, tits, siskin, flycatchers, brambling, all were busy picking and pecking for insects, snails and young shoots, twigs, hair, moss and mud for nests. Wrens scuttled along old walls, tree-creepers sidled up the bark, and against the eaves of buildings the house martins were already building new nests or repairing last year's, dark mud against pale. In the trees the russet squirrels were dashing about with their usual indetermination, all mouth and ruffed tails; shy roe deer leapt among the ground elder and sweet cicely, the hinds already heavy with young; the jaunty scuts of coney were glimpsed flashing through the undergrowth, we could hear the crash and grunt of swine, the faraway howl of wolf and scream of vixen; the shepherds who walked their sheep and goats along the slope often carried new-dropped lambs, their wool still sticky with pale birth blood, the ewes reaching up anxiously to nuzzle their young, the dogs chewing at strings of afterbirth as they followed the flock. Above our heads came the first sweet babble of the ascending larks, and if you searched carefully you could find in nests soft with down and moss the incredible promise of eggs blue as the sky, or scrambled with speckles and blotches, like a child's scribbles.

The first flies came to torment us, yolk-yellow butterflies quivered on the scarcely less bright gorse and broom, mornings showed the sliver-slime trail of snails, clouds of midges danced about our heads, bees buzzed from flower to bush; from the groves of pines crept processions of striped caterpillars: I picked up a couple, disturbing the caravan of their passage, and was well rewarded with a crop of white blebs which itched intolerably till an old crone in one of the hamlets took pity on me and threw a jug of sour wine over me: I stank for days, but the irritation was gone.

In the ponds and ditches humps and strings of spawn showed where frog and toad had been: some had already hatched into flickering life and sun-warmed lizards ran along the stones. Fish began to spawn, a flurry among the stones of streams, three or four males to every female, or so it seemed.

The farther south we went, the more the countryside changed: arid, mountainous, yet conversely in the valleys, more fertile. The air was clearer, colors brighter, contours sharper; the people wore more colorful clothes, too: patterned skirt, red scarf, purple jacket although the elderly were still in a contrast of black, for mourning: who at their age had not lost a member of the family? We passed repainted shrines and gaily clad processions for St. Joseph's day, disregarding the rigors of Lent, and then the hearty celebrations for the new Year of Grace on March 25, a fiesta full of green branches, embroidered shawls and colored ribbons.

The going became easier the farther south we went, perhaps because our feet had become accustomed to the rubs, bumps, flints, pebbles and stones of the highways. More and more we traveled in company, too many for ambush or treachery. Many languages were distributed among the mighty campfires each evening; men spoke of ice, fog and snow in islands to the north and west, even in summer; of sand, sun and people black as ink to the southlands, of great temples of stone and creatures as tall as a house and with horns of ivory; when they spoke of the east they told of beasts of burden who never drank, yet carried houses upon their backs, of heathens who sang to their gods from tall towers, of men as yellow as a canary bird who fought like devils. The west was full of great grey seas, ships with bird's wings that skimmed the waves to deliver their cargoes of cloth and wine, spices and silk, of great sea monsters who devoured a ship in one mouthful, and of the sea maidens with long hair and fishes' tails who sang the mariners to destruction on the rocks.

All this talk was heady stuff: it whetted my appetite to see more of the world before I finally found a husband and settled down. If men could travel around the world, why not a woman?

Travel seemed to improve the health and well-being of us all. Gill became tan-skinned, his step was bolder, he lost his gauntness. Mistral grew rounder and sleeker, her tail and mane longer, her hide lightened to a creamy color. Basher ate till he filled his shell and developed an extra ridge on his carapace, demanding a short walk each day to exercise off the excess. Traveler declared himself fit and wing-whole again, taking longer and longer flights and dancing back in brightened browny-pink feathers to wheel and dive above our heads. The Wimperling grew stouter and stronger by the day, until he was fast becoming the largest pig I had ever seen, and I felt lighter and fitter every day.

But it was Growch who took full advantage of all spring had to offer. One day the caravan in which we currently traveled was joined by an abbess and her servants, bound to take healing waters. She rode in a litter with silk curtains and was too superior to mix with the rest of us. Not so, apparently, her dogs. With her in the litter, fed on a diet of chicken and milk and sleeping on silk cushions, were two small, long-haired bitches, silky hair trimmed, curled, plaited and beribboned; they were exercised four times a day by the lady's attendants, waddling around like small brown sausages, their long black claws clip-clipping on the road, their plumed tails cleaned every time they excreted, their hair combed free of tangles by their mistress herself, using the same comb she used on her own hair, it was rumored. Growch's inquisitive nose and eyes found them the first time they set paws to ground, although his first essay was beaten back by the lady's attendants.

"Stripe me like a badger! What little chunks of

sweetness! Plump and petted and just ready for it! You've no idea—"

"Now just you keep away from them," I said severely. "We don't want any trouble. The lady's servants will chop you in half if you—"

"Garn! Got to catch me first! 'Sides, I can have 'em away any time I choose. They fancies me, I can tell. . . ."

And apparently they did, to my amazement, for first one and then the other managed to escape from the servants and disappear from sight in the undergrowth, hotly pursued by a dog I promptly disowned. The abbess was distraught and insisted on staying behind until her "darlings" turned up again. . . .

Growch rejoined us two days later, some fifteen miles further on, absolutely shattered, his belly dragging on the ground. He was even filthier than usual, and declared himself starved.

"You don't deserve a thing!" I said, giving him a hunk of cheese and some stale bread. "You're absolutely disgusting! Er—what happened to the bitches? Did their owner get them back?"

" 'Ventually. Servants caught one, t'other went back when she was hungry. Not before we'd had a coupla nights of it . . . I can recommend a threesome. Never enjoyed one before," and he smacked his lips, whether from the cheese or fond memory I wasn't sure.

"I'd never seen dogs like them before," I said, remembering their snub noses, plumed tails and flouncy way of walking.

"Come from a place east, long-a-ways," said Growch, scratching furiously. He smelled like a midden, and I determined to dump him in the next stretch of water we came to and scrub him, hard. "Nice manners—none of this nonsense of equality between the sexes—just the right height with them little bow legs, and virgins as well . . . Not that that made much difference once they got goin'—"

"Shut up!" I said automatically. "I don't want to know!" I wondered whether the pups would look like him: probably a mixture. The abbess would have a shock. "They had nice faces...."

"Faces? *Faces*?" He leered. " 'Oo the 'ell was looking at their faces?"

We were holed up for five days by howling winds and driving rain, which Basher assured us were normal at this time of year. "Good for the young heather shoots," he said. Traveler took advantage of the downpour to sit in puddles and air his wing-pits to the rain.

"Gets rid of the ticks," he explained.

I decided to take the opportunity of tidying us all up. We had taken a large loft above the stable in a hospitable farmhouse and there were a couple of rain butts in the yard below, now overflowing, so we were allowed unlimited bucketfuls and paid for two cauldrons of water heated over the kitchen fires.

First I scrubbed Growch—who immediately went out and found something disgusting to roll in—then the Wimperling and Mistral, combing out the tangles in the latter's mane and tail. With fresh water I washed our winter clothes, hoping that now we could wear our lighter things. With the hot water I found an old tub and first submitted Gill and then myself to a thorough going over. I remembered thinking it was a good job he was blind, else he would have seen my blushes as I washed those parts difficult for him to reach....

I felt wonderfully fresh myself after I had bathed and washed my hair, changing into a clean shift and my thinner bliaut, surprised to see how winter storage had stretched the material: it was far roomier than I remembered, and I had to take it in an inch or two down the side seams.

I finally caught Growch and washed him again, threatening permanent exile in the rain if he did it again.

Being a stock farm we were staying in, there was no lack of leather and I bought some and busied myself stitching fresh boots for Gill. I used my mother's simple recipe: triple leather soles turned up at the sides and hemmed for a lace that fastened at the front, the whole stuffed with discarded sheep's wool for comfort and warmth. While I was about it I also made us sandals for the warmer weather: thick soles, a single band across the instep, a toe thong to go between the big toe and its brother, and a loop at the back to thread with a lace that tied round the ankle.

When we took to the road again we found that the wind and rain had washed the world as clean and fresh and new as we were. The grass was greener and taller, all the trees were in leaf, the woods were full of birds shouting, singing, quarreling, wildflowers and weeds had sprung up overnight and the stones and rocks sparkled and glinted like jewels in the sun.

Now many roads joined the highway and wandered off again and the houses were whitewashed against the summer sun. People were smaller, darker and spoke with a harsher patois and used their shoulders, hands and their faces to express themselves, like actors in a play.

Our little group was just one of many traveling the roads, but I could see that while we were nothing out of the ordinary, the Wimperling did attract attention. He was so large that I could see by the speculation in many an eye that they were measuring him for chops, sausages, brawn, roasts and bones for soup. I was careful to keep him by my side at night, though I believe he was more than capable of taking care of himself.

By now I was content with our little group, used to all their idiosyncrasies and fond of them all, but I knew it couldn't last. One by one the animals would leave us when they found whatever haven they were seeking, and each departure would diminish me. Once I had been alone except for my beloved Mama; now it seemed I was friends with all the world via a dog, a horse, a pigeon, a tortoise and a pig. I couldn't bear the thought of losing any of them, and when the time suddenly came for the first of them to leave us, I was unprepared.

One fine morning Traveler ate a handful of grain, pecked digesting grit from the roadside, drank from a puddle and rose in the air to scan our road southward as usual. But this time he was gone longer than usual, so long in fact that I began to gaze anxiously up in the sky for eagles or falcons but could see none. I was beginning to get really fidgety when I saw him skimming back across the trees as he slowed his wings, starting to curve down at the tips, and waver a little as he gauged the wind. He skidded down in front of us, trembling from both excitement and exhaustion.

"I've found it! It's there! I had begun to think it wasn't—I hadn't—"

"Calm down!" He was so elated his beak was gaping and I was afraid his heart would stop. "Here, take a sip of this," and I poured some water from my flask into my horn mug. "That's better.... Now, tell us!"

It seemed he had flown higher than usual to surmount a range of hills to the southeast and had seen through the haze a large town and a ribbon of river, much like others on our journey, but as the mist cleared and he flew closer the sun touched the towers and pinnacles with gold, and he knew he had found his home town.

"I flew on and on, just to make sure, but there was no need. The knowing in my body, the thing that tells me where to go, it was pointing right at the city...."

"What's going on?" asked Gill. "Why have we stopped? Don't tell me you are talking to your animals again...."

"Hush! Let him finish. What then? You're sure it's the right place?"

"Sure as eggs become squabs ..."

"Did you go near enough to find your home?"

"Not enough wing-time. Tomorrow, perhaps."

"Summer—"

I turned back to the pigeon. "Just a *minute*, Gill! Will you ... Will you go on your own, then?" I was suddenly scared that the time had come to say goodbye, and I wasn't ready, not yet.

"No, of course not! I need you to tell the lady about the broken wing so she understands why I was so long."

"Very well ... The message on your leg is for her, if I remember?"

"Yes, I told you. From her lover."

"Then she will forgive the delay, I'm sure. How far away is this town of yours?"

He considered. "For you, three, four days," and began to nibble at the tender shoots of grass by the roadside, tired of talking.

I knew Gill still didn't believe I had any real communication with the animals, but I reported exactly what the bird had said. There was a silence.

"I'd like to say I'll believe it when I see it," he said carefully. "But you know that's impossible. I'll say this, though; if we find this town, *and* his home, *and* the lady he speaks of, then I will ask your forgiveness for doubting you. If . . ." He suddenly grinned. "Ask him if the lady is pretty." And he grinned again, not really expecting an answer.

"He says he doesn't know the meaning of the word 'pretty' as applied to humans," I translated after a moment or two. "He says she is smaller than me and that her hair is straight and pale. He says she has a quiet voice and gentle hands."

He thought about it. "Well . . . Tell you what, as long as there's a town ahead, she can be tall or small, fat or thin, dark or fair, just so long as we have a day or two in comfort again. No reflections on your cooking, Summer, but it will feel good to have my feet under a table again, eat a great chunk of game pie and drink a quart of ale."

"Well in that case," I said stiffly, "the sooner we get going the better!"

We arrived at our destination mid-afternoon of the fourth day, guided all the way by an ever more excited pigeon. After a couple of his disastrous "shortcuts," we kept to the roads; the flight of a bird takes no account of hills, rivers, stones or forest.

Once we had entered the town by the west gate and paid our toll, Traveler disappeared. He had obviously flown straight on, but like all the towns we had been in, there was no straight way anywhere; side roads, crooked lanes, blind alleys, and everywhere choked with traffic:

horses, mules, carts, wagons, litters, pedestrians laden and unladen, children, cattle, sheep, pigs, dogs and cats.

He eventually returned and tried to guide us, soaring above us one minute, on a ledge the next, but several times we lost sight of him altogether. I became more and more conscious of the curious glances we were attracting: a blind man holding on to a horse's tail, and a scruffy dog, large pig and fat girl all scanning the rooftops like stargazers.

It seemed to take hours, but at last Traveler led us, fluttering just above our heads now, down a quiet street near the river, with high-walled houses on either side and a tall church at the end just striking the office for three hours after noon, echoed by others near and far.

Traveler came to rest atop a large double gate and fluffed his feathers. "It's here. . . ." I could feel his anticipation and anxiety as if it were my own and shivered in sympathy. Lifting my hand I knocked firmly: no answer. Somewhere down the road a dog, awakened from his siesta, barked for a moment. I knocked again, and there was a limping step, a creaking bolt and a face peered out at us, the chain still prudently fastened. Traveler hopped down to my shoulder.

"Yes?" said the door porter. He was almost bald and nearly toothless but had fierce, bushy eyebrows.

"I wish to—to see the lady of the house," I said, conscious that a name would have been better, but of course names meant nothing to a bird. "About a pigeon. This one," and I touched Traveler with my finger. "I believe he is one of hers. He has a message to deliver."

The porter stared out at us, at our travel-stained clothes, our generally tatty appearance, and I didn't blame him for his next remark.

"My mistress don't entertain rogues and vagabonds. Why, you don't even know her name, do you? Besides, how do I know it ain't all a trick to get in and rob us all? Could be anyone's pigeon you got."

"This color?" and I stroked Traveler's wing. "Pink pigeons don't come in dozens. Besides, only your mistress has the key to the message strapped to his leg. . . ."

He thought about it. Finally: "I'll go and see," and he shut the gate again.

We waited for what seemed an age. I urged Traveler to fly over the gate and find his mistress, but he refused.

"We go in together," he said firmly.

Once more the shuffling steps approached the gate, but this time one half was flung open. "Mistress Rowena is in the garden at the back. Leave the beasts here." I took Gill's hand and followed the way that was pointed out to me, across the cobbles and down a narrow alleyway at the side of the house to a garden full of sun and sleepy afternoon scents.

Square beds were planted centrally with bay or evergreen, fancifully trimmed, and edged with box or rosemary. In the beds themselves were the long runners and green tips of miniature strawberries, the soft faces of violet and pansy, the tight buds of clove carnations. Beside each bed ran a little canal of water, probably fed from the river I could see glinting at the foot of the garden, beyond a lawn starred with daisies, camomile and buttercups. Against one wall were trellises for the climbing roses, on the other were tall clumps of dark Bear's Braies and pale fennel, and behind was a thick hedge of oleander.

At the top end of the garden fat, lazy carp swam in a pond plated with water-lily pads and there, tossing pinches of manchet into their hungry mouths, was Traveler's owner, who turned to meet us with a smile. She was as the bird had described: small, slim, with icy blond hair hanging straight down her back with a blue and gold fillet binding her brow, to match her deep-sleeved dress. Her face was pale, as were her lashes, brows and blue eyes.

Her smile revealed white teeth as small as a child's, with tiny points. A cat's smile, I thought. She held out her hands and reached for Traveler, fluttering nervously on my shoulder, and pinioned him in her soft white hands.

"My servant, Pauncefoot, told me you had found one of my birds, but I never expected it to be my Beauty!

Where did you find him?" and she put her cheek against his head, crooning softly.

I started to explain how I had rescued him, about the broken wing and how long it had taken to heal, but as soon as I mentioned the message on his leg I could see the rest didn't matter. Still nursing the bird she fumbled in her purse pocket and drew out a tiny key, as fine as a needle and in a moment the leg ring was open and she was unrolling a thin strip of paper between finger and thumb. For the first time I saw a tinge of color in her cheeks as she read the few words it contained. She looked at us, smiling that cat smile.

"He comes at the end of this month, as he promised. . . ." Her eyes were dreamy. "I knew he could not stay away. He was my father's apprentice. When he asked for my hand, my father stipulated that we spend a year apart and he sent Lorenzo north on business, with the added proviso that we should not communicate with each other. He still thinks Lorenzo is after my money. . . ." She cuddled Traveler closer. "I thought of a scheme to circumvent my father's dictum. Lorenzo took two of my pigeons with him: a grey, and Beauty here. The grey arrived back in October confirming his love, and he must have sent Beauty soon after. My father will know nothing of the message. He had bribed the servants to intercept any letters, but he never thought of the pigeons." She turned to me. "I cannot thank you enough: with my father ill I cannot ask you to stay overnight, but perhaps with these—" She handed me some coins, one gold, I noticed "—I can combine my thanks with assurance you may find good lodgings."

At first I was shy of accepting, but looking at the well-cared-for garden, her clothes, the tall house behind, I realized she could well afford it. "Thank you . . . The pigeon: his wing has healed, but he may not be able to manage such long flights as before. You will . . . ?"

"Still care for him?" she supplied. "Of course. Somehow he guided you here with my message—I can always breed from him. I have a couple of females the same shade. . . ."

I turned to go but suddenly Traveler—I couldn't think of him as "Beauty"—flew from her arms onto my shoulder. I turned my head to see his ruby eyes regarding me steadily. "Thanks," he crooned. "I shall always remember you, all of you. . . ." And he leaned forward and pretend-fed me, as an adult pigeon would a squab, then sprang from my shoulder and flew to the pigeon loft against the house wall.

I heard his owner draw her breath in sharply as she watched his flight, but my eyes were suddenly too blurred to see the expression on her face. She called out peremptorily to a gardener's boy raking the gravel between the flower beds. "Shut the loft door! Hurry . . ."

Out in the street again, the doors shut behind us, the coins jingling satisfactorily in my pocket, I should have felt satisfaction at a task well completed, a wanderer having found his home, but I didn't. I felt uneasy, depressed, somehow all *wrong*. I opened my mouth to say something and the ring on my finger, dormant so long, gave me such a sudden painful jolt that I cried out instead. At the same time a voice full of terror rang in my mind: "Help me! Help me. . . ." It was Traveler. What in the world had gone wrong?

Obeying an instinct stronger than thought or caution I turned and began to beat on the closed gate: "Let me in!" but there was no answer, and all the while I could sense the feather-flutter of Traveler's fear in my mind. I threw myself against the gate, but it wouldn't yield; by now the others, with the exception of course of Gill, had also "heard" the pigeon's panic. They needed no urging to help my assault on the gate. Growch barked hysteri-cally, setting off other dogs down the road, the Wimper-ling added a shoulder-charge to my efforts and Basher even battered his head against his basket, but it was Mis-tral who got us in.

Turning, she aimed two vicious kicks at the gate panels, which gave on the second blow, allowing me to reach in and slip the bolts. As I reached the garden again at a run, I saw the gardener's boy hand a feebly fluttering bird to his mistress. Grabbing his wings cruelly with one hand she put the other hand around his neck, the tendons on her wrist already tightened to twist his head off.

"Stop!" I cried. "In the name of God, stop!"

CHAPTER
TWENTY-ONE

She paused, her fingers still cruelly tight on Traveler's wings and neck. "Get out! What business is it of yours?"

"But you promised. . . ." I was bewildered. "You said you would care for him. . . .I don't understand!"

"It doesn't matter whether you understand or not!" she hissed. "It is *my* bird, to do with as I will! If I wish to wring the wretched thing's neck because it has betrayed me—"

"Betrayed you? How?"

She showed her small, pointed teeth in a grimace. "He is *my* bird, he does as *I* say, he owes *me* all his devotion! I saw what he did to you: he has never done that to me!"

She was jealous! Jealous of an affectionate gesture the poor bird had given me. . . . She must be mad. Feeling in my pocket I tossed her coins to the ground in front of her.

"Take your money: I don't want it! Instead, I'll take back a bird you obviously don't want either."

White lids came down over pale blue eyes, but not before I had seen the sudden gleam of cunning, so quickly veiled. "Very well," she said slowly, but her fingers were almost imperceptibly tightening round the bird's neck. At the same moment the ring on my finger gave me another sharp shock and my hand jerked forward, the ring now pointing at the Lady Rowena.

She screamed as though she had been stung and dropped Traveler, who lay at her feet, fluttering feebly, scrabbling round in the dirt in helpless circles. I picked him up gently and held him close. "It's all right now. . . ."

His owner backed away from me, crossing herself, her eyes wide with an emotion I couldn't fathom. "Witch! What have you done?" I moved towards her and she crossed herself again: I realized now the emotion she felt was fear. "All right, all right, take him! I wouldn't have kept him anyway: there is a knot in his wing, and I never keep anything that isn't perfect. . . ." And she spat at me, the phlegm landing in a yellow gobbet at my feet. "Now get out, before I call the servants to have you thrown out, or summon the soldiery and have you all arrested for theft and witchcraft!"

We went.

When I told Gill what had happened he actually put out a finger and stroked the still-trembling bird. "Poor little thing," he said. It was the first time I had seen him ever evince any interest in any of the animals: his usual stance was indifference. "What will you do with him now?"

"The first thing to do," said the Wimperling, "is to get out of this town right now, before she pulls herself together and does get us all thrown into jail. A woman like that cannot bear to be bested."

We took the southern gate from the city, not stopping even to eat. A trembling Traveler sat on my shoulder, looking back at the towers and pinnacles from which he had hoped so much, now bathed in the magical light of a yellow-orange sunset. I smoothed his feathers.

"Don't worry," I said. "We'll find you somewhere better. . . ."

"But that was my home," he said with sad, unassailable logic.

The Wimperling looked up. "A home is not one place," he said slowly. "A home can be a place where you are born and brought up, a place you like better than any other; it can be a dwelling where your loved one lives, a house in which your children are raised, or somewhere you have to live because there is no other. A home is made by you, it does not create itself. It can be large or small, beautiful or ugly, grand or mean. But in the end it is only one thing: the place where your heart is. And you don't have to be there in your bodily self; you can carry it with you in spirit wherever you go. . . . Like love," he added.

I thought about what he had said later that night when we had found a farmhouse and paid a couple of coins for well-water and a share of the undercroft with their other animals—goats and chickens. What did "home" mean to the bird, the tortoise, the horse, the knight? For them it was where they were born, where their own kind lived, simple as that. Growch and I were on the lookout for comfort and security, in my case a husband, and in his case I suspected he would settle wherever I did—and wherever it was, and with whom, there we would call "home."

But what about the Wimperling? He was the philosopher, but he had never indicated where he wanted to go, where his heart lay. Born from an egg (if his memory was to be believed), raised as the runt of a litter of piglets and sold into a life of performing slavery—where did *he* want to go? South, he had said, but I believed he had no clear direction. I must ask him. If he went on growing at his present rate he would have to go and live with the hellephunts, which I understood were as big as houses, or live by himself in a cave, for no sty would hold him.

We traveled south and west for six days and the terrain grew gradually wilder; the roads more tortuous. Now the hills were of limestone, striped by tumbling streams fed by the snow water that still lingered on the high peaks. Pockets of reddish earth were starred with the scalding yellow of gorse and broom, pink-plumed spears of valerian and blossom from wild cherry. The pines and fir were showing a new, tender green at their tips, and the air was full of the scribble-song of siskins; orioles

swung above our heads, gold and blue; flycatchers, wag-
tails and bee-eaters chittered and bobbed ahead of us on
the road, and from far away I could hear the strange call
of the hoopoe. Bees droned on the bushes, all on the
same soporific note, ants marched in lines across our
path, wasps were after anything we ate and the dusk
was full of the piping of pipistrelles—the airy-mouses of
legend.

And above and beyond all this there was a teasing,
ephemeral scent that came and went with the southern
breeze: a smell that could have been wet rocks, a drying
lake, salted fish, dried blood but was none of these.

"It is the ocean," said Traveler, soaring high above
us.

"It's the Great Water," said Basher, now stuffing himself from dawn to dusk with heather shoots, clover and
young grass till his scales shone and his voice no longer
was drawn out, thin and feeble.

"It's the sea," said Mistral, her pink nostrils flaring as
she snuffed the wind. "But not my sea. This is a little
sea; mine is endless and comes crashing in from the far
corners of the world and the foam is like the manes of
my people as they outrun the waves. . . ."

"Can you see this Great Water from your home?" I
asked Basher curiously.

"It is a glint in the sun, far, far away, but you can
taste it in the breeze and the salt sometimes touches the
air like seasoning." He scurried away among the undergrowth, his long black claws clicking on the stones.
"Thirsty-making . . ."

Southward still we went, leaving the great snow-tipped
mountains behind. The land was gentler, there were
farms, orchards, tilled fields, small towns. The midday
sun burned Gill's and my faces, arms and legs and we
shed clothes till he only wore a pair of shortened braies
and an open shirt, and I kilted my skirt between my legs,
glad that he could not see my bare legs.

One night, when sudden warm rain and a gusting wind
that chased up and down like a boisterous child made
us seek shelter, we found a ruined chapel on a little hill.

Once there had been a settlement of houses nearby, but these were deserted and had fallen into disrepair, like the chapel. There was no clue as to what had happened to the previous inhabitants, but beneath the chapel walls were more than the usual number of untended graves. Perhaps one of the sudden pestilences had decimated the villagers and they had abandoned their homes; perhaps marauders had carried off the women and children: who knows?

It was near dusk when we sought shelter under the crumbling tower of the chapel, and I found enough broken sticks of furniture in the deserted houses to build a good blaze. There were no church vessels to be seen, nor any crosses, and the once-colorful murals had faded to blisters of pale brown and yellow—an arm, a leg, part of a flowing robe—so the place had obviously been de-consecrated, and I had no hesitation in building a fire to cook our strips of dried meat and vegetables.

The smoke rose upwards and then wavered as the gusts of wind from the round-arched windows caught it and blew it like a rag. Soon enough the pot was bubbling and the seductive smell of herby stew set my—and Growch's—stomach rumbling. I pulled the pot to one side and lidded it, to simmer till the ingredients were softer, and set about cutting up the two-day-old bread to warm through.

Suddenly there was a wild flutter and commotion above our heads and debris showered down amongst us. I was glad the lid was on the pot: I didn't fancy stewed pigeon shit.

"What in the world . . . ?"

Traveler took wing and circled our heads. "I'll go and see. . . ."

He was gone some time, and there were more flutterings, scrapings and dried excreta, which luckily burned well. The noise subsided, the were a couple of coos and soft hoots and he rejoined us, feathers ruffled and disheveled, but he looked brighter, less despairful, than he had since we left his hometown.

"There are couple of dozen of my kind up there—wild

ones, with little civility, but they are thriving. They have been in the tower since any can remember, and manage well enough foraging off the land. I have promised we will douse the fire as soon as possible, for the smoke is choking the young squabs who cannot leave their nests. I shall talk to them again in the morning."

With the morning came the sun again, and I built a fire in the open for oatmeal porridge and cheese and toasted bread. At dawn Traveler had disappeared up into the chapel tower again, and I saw him perched on a ledge with some of the other grey pigeons, or flying around the tower in formation, his pinky-brown color the only dissonance in the otherwise perfect unison of their wheeling and turning.

I scrubbed out the cooking pot with grass and sand from the nearby stream, filled the water bottle, packed everything up, washed my hands, feet and face, and helped Gill to do the same, but Traveler still did not reappear. I went into the chapel again and called him, and eventually he came fluttering down to land on my shoulder, his feathers a little disarranged.

"Time to go," I said, stroking the soft feathers on his neck and scratching him under his chin. He shuffled about on my shoulder.

"Do you mind . . . Do you mind if I stay?"

I looked up at the tower above; little heads peeped down, there was a ruffling of neck feathers, a warning "hoof!", a croon or two, the pleading cheep of a squab. "Are you sure? They don't look very friendly to me."

"They know I am different: it will take time. But there are more hens than cocks and rats got at the eggs last year. The ropes the rodents used to climb with have rotted and gone, but the flock needs building up. I think it will be all right. . . ." He sighed. "I hope so."

"But you don't know how to forage the countryside as they do," I objected. "You will go hungry."

He straightened up and preened himself. "Then I shall just have to learn, won't I? I have all the summer to learn, and by winter I will be no different from the others."

"This wasn't what I meant for you. . . ."

"I know that, but you cannot decide my life for me: only I have the right to do that, now that you have freed me. Do not worry, I shall be fine. It is better that I take this chance while I can for I may not find a better. Living is better than not-living, whatever it brings. . . ."

"Good-bye," I said and kissed the top of his head. He sprang away and flew up to the rafters.

We had not gone far down the road, however, when there was a rush of wings and he was circling above us. "May you all find what you seek. Remember me!" And he was gone, leaving me feeling as empty as though I had had no breakfast.

"We have a dovecote at home," said Gill unexpectedly. "Their cooing was the first thing I used to hear when . . ." He trailed off. "I don't remember any more."

But at least he was recalling more and more; inconsequential little fragments maybe, but one day they might all fit together like a tapestry. And if I was missing the pigeon so much, what would it be like when my beloved knight finally found his home?

It was about a week later that we came to a place on the road where the land sloped sharply down to the south and there, a glittering shield that stretched away as far as the eye could see, was Basher's Great Water. I sniffed the air and there it was again, that tantalizing salt smell that was like no other, even mixed as it was with pine, heather, wild garlic and gorse. I started to point it out to Gill, before I remembered he couldn't see.

Mistral was also snuffing the air, as was Growch, and Basher stopped chewing the chicory leaves I had put for him in his basket.

"It's here," he said. "Here, or hereabouts. We've found it. . . ."

"You're sure this is the place?"

"Smells right. There should be land sloping to the sea, way off in the distance. Lots of heather, sandy soil for the eggs and hibernation. Pools or a stream, trees for shade. Rocks to keep the claws strong. No people. Lots of lady tortoises."

"From what I can see—"

"Oh, let meee doooown," he said impatiently. "Let meee see ..."

Holding him to my chest, I scrambled down the steep slope to level ground, Growch beside me. I stood and looked about me for Basher's specifications. The sea was about three miles distant and there was no sign of human habitation. The soil was sandyish, rocky, there was the sound of a stream off to the right and there were both pines and heather in abundance. Gorse, broom, wild garlic, oleander, fan palms, Creeping Jesus, the huge leaves of asphodel, thyme and rosemary—"Looks all right," I said cautiously. "But I can't see any other tortoises."

"I can!" helped Growch, who had christened every bush in sight and was now foraging farther down. "There's more movin' rocks down here: 'ow the 'ell do you tell if'n they're male or female? Looks all the effin' same to me. . . ."

"Females larger, flat shells underneath," said Basher succinctly. "Males undershells curved concave. Makes sense. Think about it . . ."

But I was about to get a demonstration. Growch came panting back.

"Two females down there. Tell you what, don't like bein' up-ended! Cursin' like 'Ell, they is!"

By the time we got there they had righted themselves again, their pale brown patched shells disappearing into the undergrowth at speed. I put Basher down and immediately he was off, pausing only to eye the disappearing females with an experienced eye and turn in scurrying pursuit of the larger. A moment later there was a resonant tap-tapping noise, a pause, then a sort of triumphant mewing. Cats? No, just a tortoise enjoying himself; as I came nearer I could see him reared up at the back of the female, his mouth open on pointed pink tongue. "M-e-e-w! Oh, what bliss! How I've missed thiiiis! Hey—"

With several violent jerks from side to side, the female

disengaged herself and charged off once again, Basher in pursuit. Then once again the tap-tapping, pause, and "M-e-w! Bliss . . ."

"Basher! Are you all right?"

"Couldn't be better! Thanks for eeeeverything . . ."

"Basher, wait . . ." There was something wrong, something about him, about the female . . . Oh, God! They were a different species! He was black and gold with a shell that frilled out at the back, they were pale brown shaped in a perfect hump. . . . I ran after him. "Wait! They're a different species! Come back, and we'll go on further. . . ."

"No fear!" His voice was rapidly diminishing. "This'll do me. Color isn't everything. . . . Their parts are in the right place!" Tap-tap. "This is far better than freezing to death! May you all find what you seeeeek. . . ."

When I rejoined the others, my heart heavy, Gill was listening, his ears cocked. "That tapping noise: reminds me of the cobbler mending my boots. . . . Is he all right?"

"Yes," I said. "He has—what he wants." What he thinks he wants, I added to myself. But there would be no eggs to hatch into little black and gold tortoises: his would be sterile couplings. Why couldn't he have waited till we found the right place? And yet, like Traveler, he seemed to be content with a substitute, and they had both said it was better than being dead. . . .

Were none of us to find what we really sought, I wondered?

"Half a loaf is better than none," said the Wimperling unexpectedly. "Especially when you're hungry."

"Talkin' of bein' hungry," said Growch: "Ain't we stoppin' for lunch today?"

CHAPTER
TWENTY-TWO

We had come as far south as we could, without crossing into another country. As one accomodating monk explained when next we sought food and lodging (overnight stay in the guesthouse, sleeping on straw; stew and ale for supper, bread and ale for breakfast and please leave a donation, however small), our country was a rough square, bounded to the northeast by one kingdom, the southeast by another and the south by a third. The other boundaries were sea, but there was still a lot of the square to explore. He drew everything in the dirt with a stick so I could understand.

Because he was a monk I told him a bit more of the truth than I had anyone else, and once he understood I was looking for Gill's home he worked out roughly for me the way we had come, like the right-hand side of a tall triangle. He suggested that I travel along the ways that led from east to west till I came to the sea, then either completed the triangle by going northeast, or bisected it by going straight up the middle.

That seemed good advice, but there was not only Gill to consider. The Wimperling contemplated for a moment, then said he had felt no tuggings of place so far, and was content to continue as I suggested. Growch scratched a lot—warmer weather—and said that as long as there was food and company he wasn't bothered. But it was Mistral who was keenest on the idea. She said that the distance south seemed about right, and if there was a real sea to the west of us, that would be right too.

Not having told Gill about consulting the others, of course, he was happy enough to fall in with the idea, so we walked the many miles west during those spring days in a sort of dreamy vacuum. Mistral became more and more convinced we were heading in the right direction and I knew I wasn't about to lose Gill, for he had suddenly recalled that he couldn't see any mountains from his home—which was comforting to me, as we were leaving the highest ones I had ever seen to our left as we traveled. The range seemed endless, rearing purple, snow-fanged tips so high that the sun hid his face early behind them, the shadows stretching cold in our path.

But even the biggest mountains come to an end, and gradually they sank away the farther west we traveled. By now we looked like a band of gypsies, brown and weatherbeaten, our clothes comfortably ragged, although I tried to keep Gill as smart as possible by trimming his hair and beard regularly, and I kept my hair in its plaits. Mistral was shedding her winter coat, and I could have stuffed a mattress with the brown hair that came out in handfuls when I tried to brush her. Growch evaded all attempts to wash, brush or trim anything.

But it was the Wimperling that was changing faster than anyone else—so much so that his name seemed too childish to fit the long-as-me-and-growing-longer animal that trotted away the miles beside us. He was taller, too, near up to my waist, and his knobs and protruberances were growing more pronounced as well. The claws on his hooves were real claws, the tip of his tail more like a spade than ever and his wings were bigger as well.

He was shy of showing them off, preferring to flex them behind a tree or large rock or in a dell, but I saw them once or twice. They resembled bat's wings more than anything else, but they were proper wings, not extended hands and fingers like the night-flyers. I began to

feel embarrassed in villages or with our fellow travelers, for
fear they would think him some sort of monster and
stone him to death, but for some peculiar reason they
seemed to see him as just another rather largish pig: they
even looked at him as if he were much smaller, their
eyes seeming to span him from halfway down and halfway across. It was most peculiar, but the Wimperling
merely said: "They see what they expect to see. . . ."

"But why don't I see you like that?"

"You wear the Ring." And quiet it was now, almost
transparent, with tiny flecks of gold in its depths.

As he had no objection, every now and again the pig
gave a simple performance in a village square, to aug-
ment our dwindling moneys—nothing fancy, just a bit of
tapping out numbers, no flying, and Gill and I would
sometimes literally sing for our suppers.

Growch disappeared a couple of times—I caught a
glimpse of him once on the skyline at the very tail end
of a procession of dogs (five hounds, two terriers, three
other mongrels), following some bitch in season, but he
had little success, I gathered, spending more time fighting for a place in the queue than actually performing.
Being so small, he was a master of infighting, but he
would have needed a pair of steps to most of the females
he coveted. He remembered with nostalgia the two little
bitches with plumed tails he had successfully seduced
way back.

"Don't make them like that round here. Some day,
p'raps . . ."

I hoped so. Fervently. Then perhaps we would all get
some peace.

The terrain became flatter, more wooded, and every
day I peered ahead to try for my first glimpse of the sea.
Now and again I thought I caught a teasing reminder of
that evocative sea smell, and Mistral was forever throwing
up her head and snuffing the breeze. Now she had shed
her winter coat she was a different creature. Her coat
was creamy white, her mane and tail long and flowing,
and the sharp bones of haunch and rib were now covered
with flesh. Her step was jauntier, her chest deeper, her

head held high and proud; she was no longer just a beast of burden, and sometimes in the mornings when I loaded her up I felt a little guilty, as though I were asking a lady to do the tasks of a servant.

At last one morning she sniffed the air for a full five minutes, and she was trembling. "It is here," she said. "Over the next ridge, you will see . . ."

And there, glittering in the morning light, some five miles or so distant across flat, marshy land, was her ocean.

"You are sure?"

"I am certain. This is the place. This is where I came from."

I looked more carefully and there, sure enough, some two miles away, were other horses, mostly white, some with half-grown brown colts, grazing almost belly-deep in grass. Perhaps because we were not as high as when we had seen Basher's Great Water, this sea seemed different: steely, clear, sharp against the horizon. And the smell was subtly different, too; colder and saltier.

"Right," I said, my heart strangely heavy. "Let's go and find your people, Princess." And taking Gill's hand I followed the sure-footed Mistral towards the shore. As we drew nearer the sands, I could see that the grassy stretches I had taken for meadows were in fact only wide strips of green, full also of daisies, dent-de-lions, butter-cups and sedge, bisected by narrow channels of water, so that the ground was sometimes treacherous underfoot and we had to take a circuitous path.

Growch took a flying leap into the first channel we came to, after what looked like a bank vole, which disap-peared long before we hit the water, and we had to spend the next five minutes or so fishing him out, as the banks were too high for a scramble. When he finally landed he was soaking wet and, choking and hawking and spitting, he managed to let us know that the water was: "salty as dried 'erring, and twice as nasty!"

Now we were in a marshy bit—it didn't seem to bother Mistral, and for the first time I noted that her hooves were wider than usual in a horse—and Gill and I took off our shoes and boots, squelching with every step. The Wimperling and Growch were even worse off, and when the horse noticed our difficulty she led us off to the right and firmer ground, through a thicket of bamboo twice as tall as Gill.

At last we emerged on a firm stretch of sand and there in front of us was the sea, stretching on right and left as far as the eye could see. From here I could see white-capped waves that looked like the fancy smocking on a shirt, but moving towards us all the time, like never-ending sewing. A cool breeze lifted the hair from my hot forehead and flared Mistral's tail and mane.

I lifted the packs from her back, undid the straps and took off the bridle, laying them down on the sand. Strange: I had never thought how we were to manage our burdens when she was gone; share them out, I supposed now. I looked at the pile with growing dismay—we had taken her bearing of our goods so much for granted.

"There you are," I said. "You're free now. . . ."

In a moment she was flying across the ribbed sand away from us and towards the foam-fringed edges of the sea, then turning and galloping along the shoreline, her hooves sending up great gouts of water until she was soaked and streaming. Then she came thundering back and wheeled round us, her hooves whitening the sand as they drove out the water, the prints hesitating before they darkened again into hoof-shaped pools.

"This is wonderful," she neighed. "It's been so long, so long. . . . And now I'm free, free, free!" and away she galloped again, until she was only a speck on the horizon.

I sighed. Was that the last we would see of her?

"Let's walk down to the sea," I said to the others. "I have a fancy to paddle. And I want to taste it, too. I've never done either."

It was farther than I thought, nearer a mile than a half, but the long walk was worth it once I got there, for it entranced all my senses. The regular shush, shush, shush as the waves broke on the shore like a slow-beating heart, the faraway scream of a sea bird; the limitless horizon seeming to curve down at either side as if the

world were round; the unutterably strange and pleasurable feeling of walking along the water's edge, the yielding sand spurting up between my toes, the sharp taste
of salt on my tongue, the smell of water and mud and
weed . . .

I stepped into the water and it lapped around my
ankles like the warm tongue of a calf or pup. I had been
so certain it would be cold that I threw away all caution
and kilted up my skirt till my behind was bare and waded
further in, until the water was round my knees, up to
my thighs. I lifted my skirts higher, and now it was round
my waist, but also noticeably colder, too.

Suddenly I began to feel the power of the sea. What
at first had been a gentle push against my knees, my
thighs, now became a more insistent thrust against the
whole of my body. At first the sensation was pleasurable,
then a stronger wave actually lifted me from my feet,
knocked me off balance, and I tipped back into the
water.

Help! I was drowning! There was a roaring in my ears,
my hair was floating round my face, I swallowed a
mouthful of water, I couldn't breathe, I didn't know
which way was up. Desperately I flailed with my arms,
paddled with my legs and, perhaps five seconds later,
though it felt like forever, I was once more standing
upright. I coughed and choked, dribble running from my
mouth and nose, my eyes stinging, my ears still bubbling
and popping.

As soon as I had pulled myself together I turned to
wade back to the others—but they were miles away!
Surely they had been nearer than that? Now I could see
Gill waving, apparently calling my name, saw Growch
shaking with barks, the Wimperling running up and down
the shoreline anxiously, but I could hear nothing for the
freshening breeze, which was whistling in my ears and
making the waves angry, so that they swished past me
with foam on their tips.

I set off towards the others as fast as I could, but I
was now hampered with the drag of wet clothes, and fast
as I tried to go the sea seemed to beat me, and I could

see the others retreating even as I watched. The water was definitely pushing hard at me now, even when I was only thigh and knee deep, and twice I nearly stumbled and fell, but at last it was only round my calves, and I thought I was safe. But then came another hazard; as I reached the shoreline the waves no longer pushed, they pulled, scooping back from where they broke and drawing the sand with them so that I almost lost my feet again.

At last I stood on firm sand, chilled to the bone and shivering violently.

Gill groped towards the sound of my heavy breathing. "Are you all right? You were gone such a long time. . . ."

"Look just like a drowned rat," said Growch, with relish.

"I can't swim," said the Wimperling, "else I would have come in after you. Come on, we'd better get going: the tide's coming in fast."

"What's that?" I asked, wringing the water from my hair and skirt as best I could.

"The very thing that means you were on dry sand a moment ago and now are standing in water again," he said, retreating as the water washed over his hooves. "Twice a day the sea comes in, twice a day it goes out. That is a tide. Hurry, there's a way to go till we're safe."

We set off at a brisk walk, the sun and breeze soon drying my exposed skin, though my bodice was damp and my skirt flapped in dismal, wet folds, irritating skin already chapped by salt and sand. The latter had even got between my teeth, making them grind unpleasantly together.

The Wimperling was right: the tide was coming in very fast, and the haven of the fields ahead was still a long way away. We trudged on through sand that seemed to drag at our feet like mud, till my legs were aching and Growch was whimpering away to himself, lifting his feet more and more reluctantly. At last I picked him up and tucked him under my arm, only to have him grumble about my wet clothes.

"Shut up, or I'll put you down!" I threatened. Turning

round I glanced back at the sea, to comfort myself that it was at least as far behind us as the fields were ahead, meaning we had come at least half way. To my horror the creeping water was only some twenty yards behind us, creaming forward inexorably like a brown flood. Surely we had not stood still? Even as I watched the next wave spread within a few yards of us. The tide . . .

"Run!" I yelled. "Run!" and I grabbed Gill with my free hand. As we stumbled along I saw we were at last keeping pace with the sea, it was no longer gaining on us, thank God! But now, on either side of us I could see arms of water creeping to surround us; with relief I realized the fields were much nearer, I could see the shrubs tossing in the wind, the heap of our belongings. . . . I slackened speed nearly there.

The Wimperling and Growch had galloped ahead as Gill and I caught our breath, but now I saw them come to a sudden stop, Growch running from side to side and barking hysterically. I pulled Gill forward again and my heart gave a sudden lurch of fear: ahead of us, cutting us off from safety, a swirling mass of water frothed and bubbled and roiled, growing wider and deeper by the second. To either side the arms of water encircled us and behind the tide raced to catch us up.

We were trapped!

CHAPTER
TWENTY-THREE

I was riveted with fear and panic, terrified of coming into contact with that suffocating water again.

"Gill, we're cut off by the tide: can you swim?" I was unable to keep the panic from my voice.

He shook his head. "I don't think so. . . . Is it that bad?"

"Yes, and getting worse every minute!" I glanced back: the water was flooding towards us, and now we had to retreat a step or two from the flood in front as it bubbled and frothed. Without being asked Growch and the Wimperling dashed off in different directions to see if there was any escape to left or right, but returned within a few moments to report we were entirely cut off.

Now we were marooned on a strip of sand some hundred yards long and twenty wide, and it was getting smaller by the second.

"We shall have to try and wade across," I said firmly, twisting the ring on my finger to give me courage: strangely enough it was not emitting any warning signals; a little bit warmer than usual, with a light throbbing, that was all. We must be all right: we *would* be all right, please God! "The water can't be all that deep. Dogs can swim, Growch, so you'll be all right. Now's the time to

find if you can paddle as well as you can fly, pig dear."
I tried to smile, but it was difficult. "Right, Gill: keep
tight hold. Off we go!"

The animals plunged in ahead of us gamely enough,
Growch's legs going like a centipede, but the swirling
currents were making a nonsense of him swimming in
anything but circles, until I saw the Wimperling, who
had floundered a couple of times, suddenly spread his
wings and float like a raft. He came up alongside the dog,
who grabbed his tail in its teeth and then they headed in
the right direction.

I pulled Gill into the water, but as soon I did so I
knew we had no chance. The water deepened after less
than a couple of steps and the swirling water clutched
at our legs, so that we had to lean sideways as if in a
great subterranean wind. We couldn't swim and we
couldn't float, and as soon as we took another step we
were immersed up to our shoulders, our legs flailing
helplessly in the water. I lost hold of Gill and we were
were swept apart, choking and gasping. I grasped his
tunic and we were swept together again and somehow
we managed to scramble back to our "island" again, now
half its size.

I clutched the ring on my finger, shaking so hard it
nearly slipped from my fingers. "Help us, please help
us. . . ."

Across the widening stretch of water I saw the dog
and the pig struggle out of the water and flop down on
the sand, completely exhausted. Thank God, they at least
were safe. Gill was muttering a prayer, but prayers were
a last resort: surely there must be something we could
do? If only there was something we could cling to and
paddle across, if only the tide would suddenly turn—

I gazed around wildly, and suddenly saw what seemed
like an apparition racing through the water towards us
from our left, throwing up great clouds of spray as it
came.

"Mistral! Gill, it's all right, it's all right! Mistral's
coming!"

She arrived with a snort and a skid of hooves, her body flowing with water.

"I heard your call. . . ." The ring on my finger gave a sudden throb. "I should have warned you about the tides. Quick, follow me: it's shallower this way." She led us at a trot to a place where the water was wider, but I could see none of the eddies and swirls of deep currents. "It will only be a short swim this way; wade out as far as you can, one on either side of me, and then hold fast to my mane when I tell you." I told Gill what we were going to do, guided his hand to her neck, and after that it was easy, taking only a few minutes to cross what had once seemed impossible, her warmth and steadiness against me giving me back all my confidence, so that once we were safe I flung my arms about her neck and gave her a big hug.

"Thanks, Princess Mistral, thanks a million times!" Once the word "princess" applied to the tatty, broken-down horse I had first known was nothing more than a joke, but now it was nothing more or less than the truth. She was utterly changed from the swaybacked skinny creature who had trudged the roads with us, head down: now she was white as the foam of the sea, sleek as the waves; her eyes were bright, her neck arched, her long mane and tail like curtains of mist. "You are so beautiful now. . . ."

"Thanks to you."

"I did nothing, . . ."

"You rescued me, healed my hurts, fed me, talked to me and burdened me but lightly. I am grateful to you. And now . . ."

"And now you must go and join your kin. We shall miss you." I had seen out of the corner of my eye a mixed herd of horses, colts and foals, led by a great white stallion, moving across the fields to the reeds and shallows. She neighed once and the stallion flung up his head. She turned to me. "Make for that clump of trees; keep to the higher ground. You will be safe now. Remember me: and may you all find what you seek!"

And she was gone, cantering up to the other horses and wheeling into the middle of the herd.

She was full-grown now, but I saw with a stab of pity how much smaller she was than the other mares. Her hard life had stunted her growth. Would the great stallion consider mating with one so undersized? Could she carry a foal to full term and deliver it successfully? To me she was the most beautiful of all those beautiful horses, but would they see it that way?

My eyes filled with tears. It was the tortoise and the pigeon repeated again. Why could not their lives be as perfect as they deserved? One robbed of his home and forced to fight a wilder existence, another living in the wrong place, and now one handicapped among her peers by the life she had been forced to lead. If these were to be the precedents, then what in the world would happen to Growch, the Wimperling, Gill and me?

"We keep thirty horses in the stables," said Gill suddenly. "My stallion is called Fleetfoot, but I take Dainty when I go falconing. My tiercel kills rooks and we ..." He trailed off. "I forget...."

I opened my mouth but was interrupted by Growch's salt-roughened bark. "Better get 'ere quick! The blankets is soaked and yer pots and pans is floating out to sea...."

Midsummer's Day, and we were no nearer finding Gill's home. Yet there seemed no hurry. Deceived by a summer dreaminess we drifted down tiny lanes and dusty highways, the former further drowsing us with the honey-sweet scent of hawthorn and showering us in the pale petals of the hedge rose, the latter a patchwork of blinding white road and the black shadow of forest.

Everywhere color brightened the eye; scarlet poppies shaking out their crumpled petals, gold-hearted daisy and camomile, creamy elder and sweet cecily, sky-blue lungwort, vinca and chicory, pink mallow and bindweed, white asphodel, purple vetches. And all the greens in the world: willow, beech, oak, ash, pine, fir, reed, duckweed, grass, ground elder, horsetail, clover, moss, nettle, sorrel, ivy, bracken—grey-green, red-green, blue-green, yellow-green, shock-green and baby green: both a stimulus and a soothing to the eyes. There was color, too, in the myriads of butterflies, in the dragon- and damsel-flies and even in the barbaric stripes of wasp and hornet.

The spring shrillness of the birds had abated somewhat; at one end of their scales was the brisk morning chirping of sparrows scavenging hay and straw for seeds and the faraway bubble of ascending larks; in the middle, hot afternoons held the sleepy croon of wood pigeons and the evening sky rang with the high scream of swifts scything the sky. We passed lakes and ponds where frogs barked like terriers and sudden splashes marked the recklessness of mating fish; whirring grasshoppers sprang from beneath our feet, bees and hummingbird hawk moths droned like bagpipes, cicadas sawed away incessantly and great June bugs racketed clumsily by.

We were surrounded, too, by the particular scents of summer; not just the dried dung and dust of the highways, the pungent smells of grass and leaves after rain, the thin, evocative perfume of wildflowers, but sudden surprises: a pinch of fresh mint, crush of thyme and rosemary underfoot, warm river water, salty smells of fresh sweat, the clean smell of drying linen, the oily smell of resin from fresh-cut logs stacked to dry for winter and the gentle, fading scent of drying hay.

Different tastes, too. Salads instead of stew, fresh meat instead of salted, plenty of eggs and milk, newly brewed ale. Fish and eel and shellfish from the rivers, butter and cheese so light they had practically no taste at all. A deal of vegetables I could collect myself from the fields and woods: hop tips, ground elder, chickweed, dent-de-lion, nettle, wood sorrel, broom buds, ash keys, young bracken fronds and the leaves of wild strawberry and violet. Chopped up with a little oil and salt and eaten with a hunk of cheese and fresh rye bread it made a feast.

Not that we were short of food. If there was a fair, a saint's day or a local fiesta, out would come my pipe and tabor and Gill would sing, Growch would "dance for the lady," answer yes or no and "die for his country." My instructions to him were simple enough; the "dance" consisted of him chasing his tail, yes and no barking once or twice, nodding or shaking his head—"bend your head down as if you had fleas under your chin, shake your head as if you had mites in your ears—you haven't, have you?"—and dying was merely lying down and pretending to go to sleep. But he had a short attention span, and if we really wanted to bring in more than a few coppers then the Wimperling would do some of his tricks.

He was still growing—which was just as well, for he was needed to share with Gill and me the carrying of our bundles—but still people saw him as smaller than he was: in fact one traveler accused us of overloading him! But he was looking at a pig he expected to see, as the Wimperling reminded me, not the giant he had become.

June became a warm, thundery July. Once I had decided that Gill's home must lie farther north—for he had not recognized many of the plants I had described to him, nor the terrain this far south—I led them first east northeast then west northwest as best my judgment and the countryside would allow, trying to cover both the left-hand side of the triangle the monk had described and the bisection of the whole at one and the same time.

Gill was recalling more and more as the days went by; little inconsequential things for the most part, like a favorite tapestry; the pool where they bred carp for the table, the time he was scraped by a boar's tusk—sure enough, there was a crescent scar on his thigh. Once or twice he did remember facts relevant to our search. I already knew there were no mountains, I realized that if he went falconing for rooks his home was probably surrounded by fields of grain crops and there must be woodland or forest for both the birds and wild boar; now he talked of the Great Forest half a day's ride across the plain where once the king had hunted. Which king? He shook his head. He also spoke of the wide and lazy river that curved round the estate, but again a name meant nothing.

So we were looking for a province of plains, rivers and forests, and as he never spoke of the sea we didn't travel too far west and kept the mountains to a distance. I continued to question people we met and showed them the sketch I had made of Gill's escutcheon, also the scrap of silk I had kept, but they all shrugged their shoulders and shook their heads.

The breakthrough, when it came, was entirely unexpected.

We had lodged on the outskirts of a largish town overnight, on the promise of celebrations for St. Swithin on the following day. There was to be a fair in the marketplace and dancing in the church yard, plus the usual roasts. I groomed both Growch and the Wimperling thoroughly, a ribbon round the neck of one, the tail of the other. The skies remained clear and as long as the prayers at Mass that morning were efficacious, it would remain that way until harvest, so the superstition went.

We did well in the marketplace, for folk were happy at the prospect of a good harvest, and wished to relax and enjoy themselves. There were other attractions of course, but a counting pig was still a novelty, and I collected enough coins that afternoon and early evening to keep us going for a week or two.

As it grew dusk, great torches were stuck in the ground and lanterns hung from the branches of the trees, and the people gathered to dance away an hour or so as the lamb carcasses turned slowly on the spits set in a corner of the square. A traveling band—bagpipes, two shawm, a fiddle, trumpet, pipe and tabor and a girl singer with a tambourine—performed for the dancers. Round followed reel and back again, until the dust was soon rising from the ground with the pounding and stamping of feet, jumps and twirls. When they paused for breath jugs of ale were brought out from the nearest tavern, and enterprising bakers sent their assistants round with trays of pies and sweetmeats.

As Gill couldn't see to dance I had not joined in, though my feet were tapping impatiently to the music. During one of the intervals I brought out the Wimperling again for a few more coins, then went and joined the line for slices of roast lamb and bread. Afterwards we sat for a while longer, watching and listening. As the evening wore on and it became quite dark, one by one the dancers dropped out, exhausted; couples snuggled up to one another in the shadows, children fell asleep in their parents' laps, babies were suckled, dogs snapped and snarled over the scraps, the church bells sounded for nine o'clock and some went in to pray. Somewhere a nightingale provided a soft background for the girl with the tambourine to sing simple, sad songs of love, of longing, of childhood.

She sang without other accompaniment than her tambourine, just an occasional tap or shake to emphasize a word, a phrase. She sang as if to herself and to listen seemed almost like eavesdropping. It was so soothing that I found myself nodding off, and was just about to gather us all together and find our lodgings, when Gill suddenly gave a great start as though he had been bitten.

"That song . . . !"

Song? A sentimental song of swallows, eternal summer, of home. One I had never heard before, with a plaintive descending refrain.

"What about it?"

But he wasn't listening to me, and when she started on the second verse, to my amazement he joined in, at first hesitantly, as though he had difficulty remembering the words, then more confidently. At first they sang in unison, then he took the harmony in the last verse.

> "The sun is warm, the wind is soft,
> O'er wood and plain, house and croft;
> I long to wake again at dawn,
> In the land where I was born. . . ."

Gill looked as though he had awakened from a dream and to my embarrassment I saw that tears were pouring down his cheeks. He rose to his feet.

"The singer . . . Take me to her!"

But she had come over to us. "Congratulations, stranger: you sing well. But where did you learn that song?" Close to she was no girl. The paint on her cheeks,

eyes and mouth had disguised at a flattering torchlit distance that she must be at least thirty. "I had thought no
one outside my own province knew it. Do you come
from there?"

Gill stretched out his hand to her, and it was shaking.
Quickly I explained his condition and that we sought his
home, and this was the first real clue we had had.

"Tell me, are there great plains, a big river, forests,
much grain growing?" I was trying to remember all Gill
had recalled.

"Assuredly the land is flat. There are cattle, many
fields of grain, great orchards—"

"Apples," said Gill. "And plum and cherry."

She glanced at him. "You are right. And there are wide
rivers, and forests stretching as far as the eye can see.
Can you not remember your name, now?"

He shook his head. "But I know that is where I come
from," and his voice was strong with a confidence I had
never heard in him before. "My nurse taught me that
song when I scarce out of the cradle." He turned to me.
"That is the way we must go, don't you see? Oh, Summer, take me there, take me there!" And now his tears
were spilling down onto the skin of my arm, warm as
summer rain.

"Of course we will!" I turned to the singer. "Thank
you so much, you don't know how much this means! We
have been searching for nine months, so far. . . . Here,
do you recognize this emblem?" and I pulled the scrap
of silk from my purse.

She peered at it, listened to what else I could recall
of it, but shook her head regretfully. "No, but it is a
large country. I come from the southeast, but your—your
friend may well live to the north and west. But you can
ask again when you get there."

"How far away is it?" asked Gill eagerly. "How long
will it take us?"

She shook her head again. "Straight, I do not know.
Many days. You will have to ask my husband. We travel
as the will and the weather take us, following as best we
can fairs and feast days, the larger towns." She turned

and beckoned, and the short, dark man who had been playing the fiddle joined us.

Once she had explained he, too, shook his head. "It lies to the northwest of here, but I can give you no direct route. If you head that way, and take the better roads, it might take a month, perhaps two. It depends on the roads, the weather, your pace, as you must know. If you are lucky, you will reach there in time for harvest—"

"The best time of the year," murmured Gill. "Great feasts, hunting songs, dancing ... We must start at dawn."

"Yes, yes, of course," I said. "But now we must sleep. In this weather it's better to travel early and late and rest at midday—"

"But not for long! I could walk a hundred miles without rest if I knew home was at the end of it!" Gone was the often sad, sometimes complaining man I had known: here was an impatient young man with hope in his face, as eager for tomorrow as any eighteen-year-old.

The singer and her husband wished us luck, and I emptied the day's takings into her hand. "Pray that this time we were heading in the right direction. . . ."

Gill fell asleep as soon as he lay down in the straw of the stable we occupied that night; all the way back he had been humming the song that had awakened his memory, but I could not sleep. I tossed and turned restlessly. Outside a full moon shone through the gaps in the planking of the walls, its pale light seeming to touch my closed lids whichever way I turned on the rustling straw. I told myself I was relieved we knew the way at last, how happy I was for Gill; in a month, two at most, he would be restored to his family, and my responsibility towards him would end. Then I would be free to pursue my original objective and find a safe, respectable husband and a comfortable home.

And at that happy prospect, I cried myself to sleep.

CHAPTER
TWENTY-FOUR

It took us exactly six weeks.

We departed at dawn on the day after St. Swithin's and arrived on the feast day of Saints Cosmos and Damien. It was a long, hard trek, with a hotter August and early September than I could remember. At home with Mama, of course, I was not exposed to the merciless heat of an open road; I had been able to take my ease under the trees in the forest, once my chores were done, and perhaps cool my feet in the river. Even at night we sometimes slept with the door open, the goat tethered nearby to challenge any intruder and give us time to bolt the door.

But now I was walking all day—at least the hours between dawn and two in the afternoon, and then again for a couple of hours in the evenings. Often there were no trees to shade our path, no streams or rivers to cool our feet or to bathe in. In fact water became scarcer the farther we traveled, and often they had none to spare in the villages we passed through. I bought another flask and filled it when I could, sometimes walking a good way cross-country to find a river, after spying out the land to find the telltale signs of willow, shrub and reed which marked its course.

I think the flies were the biggest nuisance. Somehow they always managed to find us, great tickling, annoying things, alighting on any part of our exposed bodies to suck the salty moisture from our skins. They buzzed, they clustered, they crawled; other insects, midges, mosquitos, horseflies and wasps stung also, and unless one flailed ones arms like a windmill all day long, or waved a switch cut from the hedgerows, one was irritated to say the least and, more usually, infuriated and exhausted by nightfall, for they wouldn't even let us alone during the afternoon rest.

No food could be left uncovered for more than a moment because it was immediately attacked. I had never particularly disliked any insect before, except perhaps for the ugly black cockroaches that scuttled and tapped around fireplaces at night, but now I had a personal vendetta against any fly, wasp, hornet, midge, mosquito, horsefly or ant in the country. Gill was not as badly affected as I was—perhaps he didn't taste as good—and Growch's thick coat protected most of him, although he was regularly infested with sheep ticks, which were as difficult to dislodge as body lice.

Strangely enough, they all left the Wimperling well alone.

All around us the country was getting ready for harvest. In the south the grapes were swelling and coloring, often on land that looked too arid to support anything, and we passed olive and orange trees that looked ready for picking, but as we headed north it was the grain that caught the eye and the orchards of apple and espaliered pears that promised delights to come. It was a bounteous time in the woods and wayside, too, and many a skirt of raspberries and blackberries I gathered. Hips, haws and hazelnuts had a month or so to go, but the autumn mushrooms and fungi were coming to their best.

The drought dried many of the ponds and streams that would have provided fish, and sheep and cattle were being fattened for the winter salting, poultry were wilting in the heat and there was little milk, but we managed, though I could feel the lighter clothes I wore were hanging looser by the day, and Gill and Growch looked leaner and fitter. Not so the Wimperling.

He still appeared to eat anything and everything with gusto and to my eyes was bigger than a small pony and no longer as pig-like as before, though it was difficult to say exactly what he did resemble. One day I took a piece of the rope we used for tying our bundles and surreptitiously measured him as he lay snoozing. From stem to stern he was as long as Gill was tall, and, if my calculations were right, near as much around the middle.

"No, you're not imagining things," he said, opening one eye. "I'm growing. A lot of it is the wings, though."

I was so startled I dropped the piece of rope. "Wings?"

"Round the middle. Look." And he rose to his hooves and slowly, lazily, extended his left wing. What I had taken for fat was in fact a combination of the wing itself and the disguising pouch he hid it under, grown larger with its contents. The wing itself now extended some five feet away from his body, a warm, living extension of himself, lifting in the slight breeze of evening. "See?"

"I still don't understand how everyone else sees you as small," I said helplessly, more shocked by the revelation than I cared to say. "When—when will you stop growing?"

"I told you: people see what they expect, and to help that I think pig." He didn't answer the second question, I noticed. Perhaps he didn't know.

This was a silly conversation, and I decided to be silly, too. "So if I wanted people to believe me beautiful, all I would have to do was think it?"

"Matthew the merchant thought you were beautiful. . . ."

"But I didn't try and make him think so!"

"So perhaps you are anyway."

"Rubbish! My mother always said—"

"You shouldn't believe all she said. Many mothers tell their daughters they are plain in order to steal their beauty for themselves. Think yourself ugly and unattractive and you will be."

"My mother wouldn't have done a thing like that!" Would she? No, of course she wouldn't. That would have been cruel. Besides I must have been ugly: I was never considered as her replacement when she died. Then had I thought myself ugly, as he was suggesting? No, I remembered my reflection in the river: fat, double-treble-chinned, mouthless, eye-less, disgusting. "Anyway, I'm fat, gross, obese." These at least were true.

"Was."

"Was what?"

"Fat. Didn't you boast once to your knight about how well you were fed by your imaginary family?" How did he know I hadn't been telling the truth? "You said your mother fed you with all the greatest delicacies; it sounded more like force-feeding, and you were the Michaelmas goose. That was another way to make you less attractive than she was. No competition."

"Nonsense! She wouldn't have done a thing like that! It would be wicked!" Why, she had loved me so much she had had me educated for the best in the land, and could not then bear for me to leave her to seek a husband!

Apparently the Wimperling could read my mind. "Most men don't choose their spouses for their education. A pretty face goes further than being able to construe Latin. Child-bearing hips and a still tongue go even farther. And a dowry, of course . . ."

"I have that!" I said, stung with anger. "My father left it for me."

"All of it? Or was some of it gone? And did your mother show you it?"

"No, but—"

"Exactly. Another five years as her slave and there would have been no dowry left, only a grossly fat woman tied irrevocably to her mother's side, a useless human being who could hold a pen, add two and two, sew a seam, cook a meal—and eat most of it—and who would have had ideas far above her station. When your mother died you would have been released from your bondage only to starve, or become a kitchen slut. You would have been the pig, not I!"

"But she didn't know she was going to die!" I flung

back at him. "She—she thought she would live a long, long time, and ... and ..."

"I know that, don't get angry. I don't suppose for a moment she realized how selfish she was: she just didn't want to lose you. But she went about it all the wrong way. There are people like that, so scared of losing the ones they love that they cling to them like ivy on a wall, not realizing that you have to let go to retain."

I thought about it: poor Mama, she should have realized I would never leave her. If she had found me a husband I would have been happy for her to live with us, or at least have a house nearby.

"But I'm not like that now," I said, subdued. "Life is very different on the road. . . ."

"Yes, and thank the gods for that! But mostly you have your father and the ring he left you to be grateful for."

"My father? The ring?"

"He bequeathed a ring to the child he would never see, a ring he knew he could no longer wear because he did not deserve it. It probably served him well in earlier years, but his life must have been such that the ring shed itself from his finger. The ring on your finger—diluted by age and wearing—is part of a Unicorn, and as such cannot be worn by anyone undeserving of its protection."

How did he know all this?

Again he seemed to read my mind. "Because your tumbled thoughts spill out into the wind sometimes, and before you have a chance to catch them back I can pattern them in my mind. Better than you, sometimes. Besides, I can sense the power. Unicorns—and witches and warlocks, wizards and dragons, fairies and elves, trolls and ogres—are become unfashionable in this modern world of ours. Yet all are still there, if you look for them or need them, although their power is greatly diminished by man's indifference and disbelief. One day they will disappear altogether, and the world will be a sadder place."

I looked down at the ring on the middle finger of my right hand. A sliver of horn, almost transparent, nearly indistinguishable from the flesh it clung to. And yet it had served me well. How else would I have been able to communicate with the others, the animals? I should have rejected Growch, probably misused Mistral, would not have been able to mend Traveler, never heard Basher in his cold misery. And what of the Wimperling himself? Would he not still be a showman's toy if the ring had not sharpened my pity when I heard his cry for help? Or dead?

One way or another, the ring had given them all another chance: me too.

The farther north we traveled, the more soldiery we came across. Not fighting, just minding their own business: wars were things that happened all the time. Some soldiers were quartered in the villages we went through, and there food was scarce: for whatever king, lord or seigneur they served made it a practice to utilize their subjects to supply their troops. Cheaper than having them loll around the castles idle, and out on the borders they were nearer the action, if and when it came.

Apparently no one had fought any battles for at least three years but rumors were rife of imminent attacks here, there and everywhere and hostilities were expected any time. I began to wonder if we should find Gill's home under siege or razed to the ground, but said nothing of my fears, for each day he grew more and more tense, fuller of longing to see his home again—for he was sure, too, that once back his sight would return also.

"It is a fine place, Summer: not a fortress, more a fortified manor house, as I recall. . . . I seem to remember my nurse's name was Brigitte. I think my mother was as tall as my father, but very thin. . . . We have lots of hounds. I seem to remember a friend called Pierre. I don't think I enjoyed my lessons. . . ." And so on.

I tried to keep him as clean, shaved and smart as I could, just in case we suddenly came across someone who recognized him, for I remembered only too well how magnificently he was dressed and accoutered that never-to-be-forgotten day when he had asked me the way to the High Road. Now I doubted even his mother would recognize him, in spite of my care. I bought a length of linen and made him a tunic that reached mid-calf, as befitted his station, but kept it hidden till the time was right. When the light lingered in the evenings I would take it out, to complete the key pattern I was edging the hem and side slits with, in a blue to match his beautiful, blind eyes. . . .

One August morning, around ten of the clock, we came to a confused halt, we and the dozen or so we were traveling with, for ahead of us the highway, which had broadened out considerably during the last few days, was now blocked by a formidable line of the military. A caravan ahead of us had also been halted, for beasts were already tethered for foraging by the side of the road, carts and wagons were drawn up in orderly rows, their occupants either resting or arguing with the captain of the troops, with much gesticulating and nodding and shaking of heads.

Whatever it was, it obviously meant delay. Seating Gill in the shade, I pushed my way forward, asking first one and then the other the reason for the delay, but got only confused replies. "It's the war. . . . Road ahead is blocked. . . . Plague . . . Robbers and brigands . . ." In the end I approached one of the ordinary soldiers, relieving himself in a ditch some way away from the others, a bored expression on his face. I remembered what the Wimperling had said about thinking oneself into what people expected to see, so I tried to project myself as pretty.

"Excuse me, captain. . . ." He turned, shook off the drops and tucked himself in again. I saw the boredom on his face replaced with interested speculation. Perhaps it was working!

"Yes, missy? How can I help you?" His gambeson was food- and sweat-stained, he hadn't shaved for days, his iron cap was missing and his hose full of holes. Most of his teeth were rotting or gone, and he spoke with a thick, clipped lisp.

I smiled sweetly. "I can make neither head nor tail of what is going on, sir, so bethought me to seek out one who surely would." Mama had taught me how to flatter. "One can tell at a glance those worth talking to." I smiled again. "A man of experience such as yourself must surely know *everything*. . . ."

It worked. He grinned self-consciously, then with a quick look over his shoulder to where his captain was still waving his arms about and shouting, he settled the dagger at his belt and took my arm, drawing me away behind a clump of elder bushes, strutting like the dung-heap cockerel he was.

"Well, look here, pretty missy, it's like this. . . ." The Wimperling had spoke true! He had called me "pretty"! "You knows of course we is at war, has been for as long as I can remember. . . ."

"But there haven't been any battles for years. . . ."

"That don't matter round here. 'Readiness is all,' as the captain says, and we can't afford to relax for a moment." He spat on the ground. "Arrogant bastard! Thinks he knows it all because he fought in a couple of campaigns abroad! Still, no use crossing him. Worth a flogging, that is." He peered at me. "What's a nice-spoken lass like you doing here, anyways?"

But I was ready for that. "Traveling north with my father, a spice merchant," I said quickly, conscious that he had moved closer. "He's over there," and I pointed in the direction of the still-arguing captain. "He's also trying to find out what is going on—but I think I am having a better success! Er . . . I heard somebody say something about a renewal of war?" And that was the last thing we needed, I thought.

"Not exactly, but there have been a couple of skir-mishes on the border last few days. Still it puts us on alert, and means the border's closed for a while. Usually it's open twice a day for trade and barter: they likes the wine and fruits from the south, we likes their grain, cider and cheese. Everyone gets searched, 'cos that's enemy territory over there, there's a small toll, and everyone's happy. Not strictly official, mind . . ." He sucked his teeth. "Still, none o' that for a week or so." He looked disconsolate: I could imagine in whose pockets the "tolls" went.

Oh, no! Gill, I was sure, could not bear to be patient for so long now he was near his home. Our money was running out, there'd be little food nearby and as for entertaining, with only the soldier's pay to depend on, we should soon starve.

"Is there no other way across?"

He turned me round to face north, taking the opportunity to put his grimy hands round my waist. My mind shuddered at his touch, my nose wrinkled up at the stinking breath whistling past my left ear, but I kept my body still. He pointed over my shoulder.

"See there, that line o' trees? That's the border between *here*, what belongs to our king, and *there*, what belongs to the king over-water, Steady Eddie, they calls him. Got quite a bit o' land over here: that's what the battles are about. Road across goes through the trees. Left there's thick forest for miles, fifty or so, and their patrols go up and down there day and night." He swiveled me towards the right. "There's the village. T'other side o' that's the river what runs into enemy territory. They got their camp on the banks; we patrols this side, they patrols the other. No way through . . ."

But there had to be: somehow we must cross that border. From the other travelers I had confirmed that what lay ahead was indeed Gill's part of this divided country, so for his sake it was imperative we lingered no longer than was necessary. But how to evade the patrols? Alone, I might have tried to creep through their lines at night, especially with Growch to spy ahead, but a blind man was clumsy at the best of times and the Wimperling's bulk precluded any attempt for the four of us together.

Successfully evading the importunate soldier we ate what little we had left and lazed the day away, but in the evening, to quiet Gill's restlessness, I took him to the tavern in the village for an indifferent stew and a mug or two of thin ale, together with half-a-dozen or so other disconsolate travelers.

And there, in that stuffy, malodorous little ale house, came the answer to our prayers. . . .

five in two of the back has that with sull
at last down close provider

And there, on that stuff, amid thence little skymast
come this way to the prayer.

CHAPTER
TWENTY-FIVE

"Hullo, Walter! How many this time? A dozen? Good. Welcome to our side, gents—and lady. . . ."

A trap, a stupid, miserable trap! All we had thought of was crossing the border, too eager to question the ease with which our "safe" passage had been procured. If I had had half the sense I credited myself with we should have been suspicious from the start and never joined this sorry enterprise.

Thinking back, Walter the ferryman had been a shifty-looking individual from the start, but his suggestion of slipping through enemy lines on his raft—at a price—had seemed like the answer to a prayer to all of us. He said that if we set off around three in the morning we could drift past the sentries on both sides, and assured us he had done it many times. Twelve of us had paid the silver coin demanded, and rushed back to gather up our belongings. The Wimperling said that nothing in the world would get him on a raft, he would spread his wings and float past, and Growch said that if he couldn't slip past a sentry or two we could chuck him in the river. Next time . . .

The raft nearly tipped twice, although the river was low and sluggish, for most of the other passengers were

PIGS DON'T FLY 275

frightened of the water and didn't heed instructions to keep to the center and be still, but rushed from side to side, imperiling us all. The boatmen poled us out from the bank with a suck and a slurp and a pungent smell of mud, and once all was settled we drifted downstream through the oily water.

There was a quarter moon, few stars and an absence of sound: no wind, no birds. It was warm and still, the heat of the day still lingering in the heavy air. I trailed my fingers in the river: water warm as my skin. The banks on either side seemed deserted.

All at once the sneaky Walter started to pole us in towards the bank—surely we couldn't be beyond the enemy lines yet?—and I could see a makeshift landing stage through the gloom. The raft slapped against the pilings with a jolt that nearly had us all in the water, sudden torches flared, a dozen hands pulled us from the craft and hauled us up on the bank. By the flickering light I could see we were surrounded by soldiers. Different ones.

"Welcome," said their leader again, snickering. "Line 'em up, lads, and let's see what they got. . . ."

They relieved us of our packs and bundles, chuckling and commenting to themselves all the while. "Sorry-lookin' set o' buggers . . . Which pack belongs to the Jew? Pity they don' close the border more often. . . . Got a blind 'un here, with 'is girl. . . ." One of them gave a couple of coins to Walter, our betrayer.

"Bringin' more tomorrow?"

"If'n I can con 'em. Two lots if possible. Twenty-four hours'll make 'em keener. Don' let any o' these slip back to give a warnin'. . . ."

A moment or two later the Jew broke away from the rest of us and fled into the darkness and another of our companions jumped into the river, where he foundered and gasped and was twirled away on the current, flowing faster here, his mouth open on a yell drowned by a gurgle of water. A moment later he was swept out of sight.

They brought the Jew back five minutes later. He was unconscious and had obviously been beaten. He was thrown to the ground and disregarded, while the soldiery enjoyed themselves opening the packs and sharing out the contents, including our blankets, which they declared "a fine weave—good against the winter," and promptly confiscated. Luckily they could find no use for Gill's new tunic, and by the time they had emptied the other pack they were so surfeited with some golden spices, oils and unguents, jewelry, embroidered cloth, carved bone figures, some fine daggers and a silver crucifix that they tossed my pots and pans to one side. They were momentarily puzzled by my precious Boke, ripped off its cover looking for a hiding place, then tossed the loose pages into a bush.

Anyone who protested was beaten quiet. My pens and inks were scattered on the ground but they took what little food we had, chomping noisily on hastily divided cheese. The ten of us who could still stand were then searched. Rings were pulled from fingers (mine went suddenly invisible), brooches unfastened, earrings torn from ears, embroidered clothes ripped from the owner's back, leather boots pulled off. Ours were too tatty to bother with. Luckily Gill and I looked so poor that our search was perfunctory, and they didn't discover the dowry, or the few coins I had left of ordinary money.

Some of our compatriots were weeping and wringing their hands, but I held Gill's hand and preserved a stoical silence. What else could I do? I was worrying about Growch and the Wimperling, but at least we no longer had Mistral, Traveler and Basher with us: I could well imagine what would have happened to them if we did.

Searching and scavenging done, one of the soldiers ran off in the darkness to return a moment or two later with a man on a horse, obviously in command. There followed what was a well-rehearsed interchange between the captain and his troops. I don't think it fooled anyone.

Captain: "What have we here, then?"

Soldiers: (One, two, three or seven, it didn't matter which: sometimes they answered singly, sometimes together, like a ragged chorus. Suffice it to say they all knew their parts off pat). "Infiltrators, sir! Crossing the border without permission, sir!"

Captain: "Have you examined them and their belongings?"

Soldiers: "Yes, sir!"

Captain: "And?"

Soldiers: "All guilty, sir! Carrying contraband, some of 'em . . ."

Captain: "Let me see the goods."

Here some of our fellow travelers tried to protest, but a stave round the legs, a buffet to the jaw soon silenced them. The captain dismounted and pawed through the heap of spoils, finally selecting the silver crucifix, one of the more ornamental daggers, a ring set with a ruby and the gold coins. "Mmmm . . ." He shook his head. "Obviously stolen goods. I shall have to confiscate these while further enquiries are made." He carried a big enough pouch to hold them all. "Now then, men: what is the punishment for spies and thieves?"

Chorus: "Death!"

I gripped Gill's hand so tightly I could feel my ring biting into flesh. One of the other travelers broke away and flung himself at the captain's knees, scrabbling at his ankles, sobbing pitifully.

"Mercy, kind sir, mercy! I have a wife, three children. . . ."

The captain kicked him away. "So have I, so have the rest of us! You should have thought of that before you entered a war zone." He rubbed his chin. "Mind you . . ."

I think we all took an anxious step forward, for the soldier's voice held a considering tone.

"Mind you . . ." he repeated: "If they were willing to pledge themselves against a little ransom, as an earnest of their repentance, men, I think we might reconsider, don't you?"

Immediately the man still on his knees was joined by three others, all well-dressed, pledging house, money, jewels, coin or livestock as bribes. The four were led aside into the darkness, their faces now expressing a hope none of the remainder could hope to match. The captain gestured at the unconscious Jew. "And him?"

"Caught trying to run off, sir . . ."

"His baggage?"

"Nothing of consequence. Papers mostly, sir." The soldier pointed to a scatter of vellum.

"Cunning bastard; not worth the investigation. Get rid of him!"

To my horror two of the soldiers came forward, picked him up and flung him into the river. A couple of large bubbles broke the surface and that was all.

The captain surveyed the rest of us. "Send the rest of them back: let their own side deal with them." My heart leapt, but I might have known it was just a cruel jest. "No, wait: they can either enlist with us or work as slaves: give them the choice." He turned away to remount but one of the soldiers who had been eyeing me with a leer went over and whispered in his ear. The captain turned back, beckoned us nearer. "And what have you to say for yourselves?" He addressed himself to me.

I kept my gaze modestly lowered, my voice meek. "My blind brother and I are returning home, sir. We traveled south in a vain attempt to find a cure for him. We live in this province, we are not spies, and we have spent all our money in doctor's bills. We are only here because war does not take account of innocent travelers. . . ."

He stared at me in a calculating manner. "What was in their baggage?"

One of the soldiers indicated the scattered pots and pans, the flasks, odd bits of clothing. "Just these, sir."

"Whereabouts do you come from? What does your father do?"

I had dreaded such questioning. "Our—our father is a carpenter. We were sent—" I twisted the ring on my finger in my agitation and out of nowhere came a name I must have heard somewhere, sometime I could not recall. "We were sent south with the recommendation and blessing of Bishop Sigismund of the Abbey of St. Evroult," I said firmly, and raised my head to look at him straight.

He raised his eyebrows. "I see. . . . Let them continue their journey." He crossed himself. "I have no quarrel with the church." He turned away again, but once more the soldier whispered to him. He turned and looked at me again. "Very well: I am sure she will cooperate. But no rough stuff, mind." And with that he remounted and clattered off into the darkness.

The importunate soldier came over and took my arm, not unkindly. "You come along o' me, you and your brother."

"Our things . . ." I pointed to the pots and pans.

"Well, pack 'em up, then," he said impatiently. "Coupla minutes, no more . . ."

Well within that time I had retrieved everything, even my torn Boke, and tied it into two bundles. The pans were dented, one of the horn mugs was cracked and one of the flask stoppers had disappeared, but at least we were alive. The soldier plucked up one of the torches stuck in the ground and nodded to us to follow, winking at his fellows as he led us off.

"She'll keep till later!" one of them yelled, and suddenly I realized the implication of the captain's words: "I am sure she will cooperate. . . ." and a cold finger of fear and revulsion touched my spine.

He led us to a broken-down hut that must once have housed sheep or goats, for the earthen floor was covered with their coney-like droppings and the place smelled of fusty, damp wool. There was no place to sit so we huddled against a wall, and he took the torch with him so we were left in darkness. As we became more used to our surroundings, however, I could see, through the gaps in the wattle and daub walls and the rents in the reed thatch, a certain lightening outside: false dawn preceding the real one.

I tiptoed over to the flap of skin that served as a door and peeked out. To my right, about ten yards away, two soldiers sat cross-legged by a small fire, playing dice. No escape that way. Coming back into the darkness I felt my way round the wall seeking for a weakness, but apart

from a few fist-sized holes there was nothing. If only we
had been able to reach the roof, now, there was—

I nearly leapt out of my clothes as something damp
and cold touched my bare ankle.

"For 'Eaven's sake! It's only me. . . ."

I knelt down and hugged him, tacky though he was.
"Where've you been? Are you all right? Where's the
Wimperling?"

" 'Ush, now! We're all right. More'n I can say for you
. . . Now, listen! I gotta message for you from the pig."
And he told me what they planned to do, but when I
started to question, he shut me up. "No time to argue:
we gotta get goin'. Be light soon," and he slipped out of
the door as I felt my way back to Gill and explained,
slinging our packs ready as I spoke.

This time he didn't argue about talking to animals but
shrugged his shoulders fatalistically. "Just carry on: we
couldn't be in a worse position, I suppose."

I felt like saying that it was me, not him, that was
liable to be raped, but thought better of it. "It'll be all
right, I'm sure: just a couple of minutes more. . . ."

It felt like an eternity, and I kept wiping my hands
nervously on my skirt because they were sweating so
much. I pulled Gill over to the doorway with a fast-
beating heart so that we were ready—ready for the shout
that came moments later from over to our left. Peering
through a gap in the hide covering I could see a tongue
of flame shoot upwards at the fringes of the forest, some
quarter-mile away, then heard the drumming of hooves
from a couple of panicking horses. The two guards outside leapt to their feet, undecided what to do, but when
a second tongue of flame started to run merrily towards
the tents of the soldiery and there were more galloping
hooves, ours abandoned fire and dice and started running
towards the confusion.

Now was our chance. Grabbing Gill's hand I led him,
stumbling, out of the hut and to our right, where the
river should be. It was much closer than I thought and
in fact we nearly fell in, because at the wrong moment
I risked a glance behind us, to see a merry blaze had

caught the summer-dry grasses at the fringe of the forest and, fanned by the dawn breeze, the flames were creeping towards the encampment. Luckily Gill fell full length as we reached the riverbank, just before we both plunged down the slope into the water, and a moment later Growch appeared to lead us further downstream to where a small rowing boat was tethered in the reeds. Untying the rope I helped Gill aboard, instructed Growch to jump in, and—

"Where's the Wimperling?"

"Right here," grunted a hoarse, cindery voice and he rolled up, panting and covered with smuts. "Don't wait: I'll float. Need to get rid of the smoke . . ."

"You're sure?"

"Just get going! Push off from the bank, keep your heads down and the boat trimmed."

"Trimmed?"

"Both of you in the middle. No looking over the side. The current will carry us away from all this."

It was as he said. I kicked off from the bank and collapsed in an ungraceful heap at Gill's feet, as the boat nudged out into the center and found the current. It seemed my knight had been in boats before, for he told me much the same as the pig: "Sit down in the middle, Summer, hands on both thwarts—"(thwarts? I presumed he meant the sides) "—and don't lean over the side, either. That's it. . . ."

Slowly and surely we gained speed to almost a walking pace. Over to our left fires were still burning, accompanied by shouts and curses, but everyone was too busy to have noticed our defection, and a moment later we swung round a bend in the river, shaded by trees, and the fire and commotion died away behind us. Gill seemed calm and content, but I was still terrified of rocking the boat, and desperately needed to relieve myself. The Wimperling was floating just behind us, so when I told him he gave the boat a nudge out of the current and I scrambled ashore, and thankfully ran behind some bushes, while Growch christened the nearest tree.

"Do we have to go back?" I asked the pig, gesturing

towards the boat, where Gill was happily trailing his fingers in the water. "I—I feel safer on land."

"Not safe yet. Besides, we can travel faster by boat."

"We're not going very fast now," I objected.

"We will, just wait and see. Back you go. . . ."

We swung out into the channel again, and I gripped the sides as tight as I could, till my knuckles turned white with the strain. The Wimperling swam up behind us once more.

"Move towards the bow—the *front*—both of you." I told Gill and we both shuffled forward and it was just as well we did, for a moment later the rear of the boat tipped down as the pig hooked his useful claws into the broad bit. I thought for a moment he was going to try and clamber in, but a moment later there was a flapping noise and his wings lifted out of the water and spread until they caught the now freshening breeze behind us, and we were bowling along in a moment at twice the speed, and the banks of the river were fairly whizzing by.

We traveled this way for the rest of the day, with a couple of stops for me to forage for berries, for we had nothing to eat. We saw no one, and I became used to the rocking motion of the boat eventually. The only creatures we disturbed were water fowl, a couple of graceful swans with their grey cygnets and an occasional water vole. At dusk the Wimperling steered us to the bank again.

"There's a village ahead—you can see the smoke. You can find a buyer for the boat. It'll provide you with enough for some days' food."

"Thank the gods for that!" said Growch. "The sides of me stummick is stuck together like broken bellows. . . ."

And the thought of dry land, food, and perhaps a mug or so of ale, rather than the risk of river water, so filled my mind that I quite forgot the question that had been tickling at the back of my mind since our escape: how on earth had the Wimperling managed to light those fires?

No one questioned where we had come from, where we were going, and there were no soldiers. I got a reasonable price for the boat, even without oars, and that night we slept in comparative luxury in a barn attached to the alehouse. It was fish pie for supper with baked apple and cheese, but everything was fresh and tasty. There was no talk of war and battles, only of the approaching harvest. I tried once more to describe Gill's home and showed them the piece of silk, but they shook their heads.

"Further north's best place for grain and orchards. . . ."

My hopes were momentarily dashed, but Gill's enthusiasm was unabated. He declared he could hear in the villager's voices the echo of the patois they used near his home, and the more ale he drank the more details he seemed to remember. Wooden toys, servants, fishing, a boat, a blue silk surcoat, a flood . . . After he had downed his third flagon of ale I tried to dissuade him from more, but he declared petulantly that I was spoiling his evening and was worse than a nursemaid, so I mentally shrugged my shoulders and ordered a fourth.

Halfway through he fell asleep with his head on the trestle table, and I had to enlist the help of a couple of the locals to carry him back to the barn and lay him down on the straw, face down in case he vomited during his sleep. I stayed awake for a while, for sometimes when he had drunk too much he woke and the liquor excited that ache between the loins that all men have, so Mama used to say, and he would toss and turn and groan until his hands had accomplished relief; at times like that I couldn't bear to listen, and would tiptoe away till he had finished.

Tonight, however, everything was quiet and peaceful, so I wriggled myself about till I was comfortable and fell asleep at peace with the world—

To awake in the dark with a hand on my bosom and a voice in my ear.

"My dearest one . . . I've waited so long for this moment! I've been thinking of you night and day. Don't turn me away, I beg you, I implore you! I need you, oh, so much. . . ."

My heart was thumping, my breath caught in my

throat with a hiccuping sob, and I reached up in wonderment to hold Gill's head with my hands, ruffling the familiar curly hair with my fingers. I had waited so long for a sign, anything to prove he cared for me, and now my whole body was filled with an aching, melting tenderness, a yielding that left me trembling and helpless. His hand left my breast and slipped beneath my skirt, his hand warm on my thigh, and his seeking mouth found mine in our first kiss. . . .

So that was what it was like to be kissed by the man you loved! A little, distracting voice from somewhere was whispering: "Not yet, not yet! He's drunk too much, you only lose your virginity once. . . ." But if he was drunk, then so was I: drunk with desire for this man I had secretly loved so long.

Already he was fumbling with the ties of his braies and I felt him gently part my thighs.

"My sweet Rosamund, my Rose of the World . . ."

CHAPTER
TWENTY-SIX

I froze, like a rabbit faced by a stoat. Rosamund? Who the hell was Rosamund? Not me, anyway. But perhaps I had misheard. . . .

I hadn't.

He nuzzled my neck. "I have waited for this so long, my Rosamund of the white skin, the golden hair! At last you are mine. . . ." and he thrust up between my legs, still murmuring her name.

That did it. In a sudden spurt of anger, disappointment and frustration I kneed him as hard as I could then rolled away from beneath him, got to my feet and ran out into the night. He yelled with pain, then groaned, but I didn't look back: I couldn't. My fist stuffed into my mouth to stifle the sobs, I let the stupid tears run down my cheeks like a salty waterfall till my eyes were swollen and my throat felt all closed up.

I didn't know whether I hated him or myself the most.

Hating him was irrational, I knew that in my mind, but my heart and stomach couldn't forgive. He was drunk, and in his dreams had turned to a suddenly recalled love; he had found a female body and mistaken me for her.

But I was worse, I told myself. Without thought I

had surrendered to my feelings and immediate emotions, forgetting all Mama had impressed upon me about staying chaste for one's husband, not succumbing to temptation, etc. All I wanted was to indulge myself with a man I had fantasized about for months—husband, future, possible pregnancy, all had been disregarded in the urgency of desire. And if I thought about it for even one moment, I would have realized that it could never lead to anything else once he returned home, for he was a knight and I was nothing. I cursed myself for my stupidity.

But at the back of my mind was something else, something worse: hurt pride. He had preferred his dreams, his memories, his vision, to me. In reality I hadn't even been there. Summer was a companion, his guide, his crutch, his eyes: if he had known it was me he wouldn't have bothered, drunk or no. The tears came so fast now they hadn't time to cool and ran down into my mouth as warm as when they left my eyes. They tasted like the sea.

There was a shuffling and a grunt behind me and the Wimperling lumbered out of the barn and looked up at the lightening sky, sniffing. "Another fine day . . . Did I ever tell you about the story of the pig with one wish?"

"Er . . . No." I couldn't see what he was getting at. Surreptitiously I wiped my eyes on the hem of my skirt. "What—what pig?"

"It was a tale my mother pig used to tell us when we were little. Once there was a pig who had done a magician some service, and in return he was granted one wish. He was a greedy thing, so immediately without thinking he wished that all food he touched would turn into truffles, because that was what he liked most. His wish was granted, and for days he stuffed himself so full he nearly burst. Then as he grew surfeited, he wished once more for plainer fare, and he cursed the day he had wished without thought. . . ."

"And then what happened?" I was interested in spite of my misery.

"Well, first he tried to punish himself by trying to starve to death, but that didn't work, so, because he was basically a kind and caring pig, he decided to turn his misfortune into a treat for others, going around touching other pigs' food so they had the treat of truffles. And it did his sad heart good to see them enjoying themselves. . . ." He stopped. "What's for breakfast?"

I smiled in spite of everything. "Not truffles, anyway! And then what?"

"Then what what?"

"The pig."

"Oh, the pig . . . I disremember."

"You can't just leave it like that! All stories have a proper ending. They start 'Once upon a time . . .' and end '. . . and so they lived happily ever after,' with an exciting story in between."

"Life's not like that."

"I don't see why it can't be. . . ."

"That is what man has been saying for thousands of years and look where it's got him! Without hope and a God the human race would have died out eons ago."

"You say that as if animals were superior!"

"So they are, in many ways. They don't think and puzzle and wonder and theorize, look back and look forward. What matters is only what they feel right now, this minute, and if they can fill their bellies and mate and keep clear of danger. And when they dream, and twitch and paddle in their sleep, then they are either the hunters or the hunted, nothing more. No grand visions, no romance—and no tears, either."

So he *had* noticed. I felt embarrassed and went back to his tale. "But the story was a story, so it must have an ending. . . ."

"Well, then, you give it one, just to satisfy your romantic leanings."

I thought. "Because the pig turned out to be so unselfish after all, helping his friends to enjoy the truffles when he could no longer, the wizard reconsidered his spell and then lifted it. And—and the pig was properly grateful to have been shown the error of his ways and never again yearned after something unsuitable. He married his sweetheart pig, who had stayed loyal to him through good times and bad, and they had lots of little piglets and lived happily ever afterwards. There!" I stopped, pleased with myself, then had another thought. "Oh, yes: The strange thing about it all was, that the piglets and their children and their children's children couldn't *stand* truffles!"

The Wimperling made polite applause noises with his tongue. "A predictable tale—redeemed, I think, by the last line. I liked that. And the moral of the story is?"

"Does it have to have one?"

"All the best ones have. Disguised sometimes, but still there."

"Er ... Don't make hasty decisions; think before you open your mouth?"

"Or your legs," said the Wimperling. "Exactly!" And off he trotted.

Over a breakfast of oatcakes, fish baked in leaves and ale, Gill told me he had had a wonderful dream during the night. "And Summer, it seems my memory is really coming back!"

It was lucky for him he could not see my face, and did not sense the desolate churning in my stomach that made me push aside the fish with a sickness I could not disguise.

"In this dream I was wandering through a building that seemed familiar yet wasn't, if you know what I mean. Then I realized I was in the household where I had served my time as first page, then squire. But I was no longer a boy, I was as I am now, but without the blindness—you know how illogical dreams can be."

I nodded, then remembered. "Yes." In *my* dreams I was slim. And beautiful ... How illogical could you get?

"Then suddenly I was in a barn—a barn in the middle of a castle, Summer!—and there, lying in the straw, was my affianced, my beloved, my Rosamund!"

"Rosamund?"

"Yes—I told you my memory was coming back. Any more ale?"

I handed him mine. "Tell me more about—about this Rosamund."

"Ah, what can I say? No mere words could do her adequate justice! I met her when I was a squire and with my parents' consent we became affianced. Her father was a rich merchant and his daughter Rosamund the middle one of three, with a handsome dowry. She is two years older than I, but as sweet and chaste and demure as a nun. We plighted our troth five years ago, but I was determined to earn my knighthood before I claimed her as my bride. I journeyed north to bring her gifts from my parents and say we were ready to receive her, and on my way back I think I . . . That bit still isn't clear. I don't remember."

On that journey back he had been ambushed, and he wouldn't be here if I hadn't rescued him, I thought bitterly. "Is your bride-to-be as pretty as she is chaste?" I asked between my teeth.

"Pretty? Nay, beautiful! Tall, slim, perfectly proportioned. Her skin is white as milk, her cheeks like the wild rose, her hair like ripened corn—"

"And her teeth as white as a new-peeled withy," I muttered sulkily.

"How did you know? I was going to say pearls. . . . A straight nose, a small mouth—" He sighed. "Truly is she named the Rose of the World. . . ."

I rubbed my smallish nose and practiced pursing my not-so-small mouth.

He sighed again. "As I said, she is as chaste as a nun, and has never permitted me more than a kiss or two, a quick embrace. . . . But in this dream I had my impatience got the better of me and I threw aside her objections and embraced her long and heartily. It was just getting interesting when—when . . ."

"Yes?" I said sweetly.

"When all of a sudden I was in a tournament and my opponent unhorsed me, to the detriment of my manhood, if you will excuse the expression. . . ." He scowled. "Very painful."

"You got kicked in the balls," I said succinctly. "And woke up. Are you sure it wasn't the fair Rosamund defending her chastity?"

He looked shocked. "Really, Summer! Even in dreams she wouldn't be so—so unladylike! And she was never coarse in her language . . ."

Of course not. "Seeing how much your memory had improved, was there anything else you recalled that we might find useful in our search for your home and family? Such as a name, or a location?"

He looked surprised. "Oh, didn't I say? How remiss of me. I meant to. I remembered my father's name a few days ago, just before we came to the border. But then there was so much to think about, with escaping and all. . . ."

I could have throttled him. "Well?"

"My father's name is Sir Robert de Faucon and our nearest big town is Evreux; we live some thirty miles to the west. My mother's name is Jeanne, and—"

"Why in the world didn't you tell me before!" Of course: the bird on his pennant was a falcon; I remembered it now. And the name was the same. Simple.

"We were trying to cross the border—"

"But your name might have meant something—"

"Yes! A ransom. And we'd still be there."

Very reasonable, but I was sure it had never crossed his mind till now. I simmered down. We would make our way to Evreux, the place that had come so providentially to mind when we were questioned at the border, and from there on it should be easy.

Not as easy as I had hoped. There were fewer travelers on the road and fewer itinerants as well, for these latter were hoping for jobs with the imminent harvest. It was the wrong time and the wrong place for pilgrimages also, so we had to keep to the high roads in daylight and not chance evening walking. We also found these people of the north stingier with their money and their handouts, more suspicious of strangers: maybe it was the war that had been going on for so long, maybe their northern blood ran colder, I just do not know.

We took some money with a performance or two in the cathedral town of Evreux, and confirmed the westerly road towards Gill's home. Now we were so near our objective I would have expected him to be far more impatient to press on than he actually was. Instead he walked slower than usual, complained of blisters, said his back hurt, had an in-growing toe-nail. I pricked and dressed his blisters with salve, rubbed his back and examined a perfectly normal toe. Next day he felt dizzy, had stomach pains, nausea, vomiting and cramps. I treated all these, difficult to confirm or deny, but on the third day, when we were less than five miles from the turn-off that we had been told led straight to his estates, and he said his legs were too weak to hold him, I knew something was seriously wrong.

I sat him down under the shade of a large oak tree, dumped our parcels and asked him straight out what was the matter.

"For something is, of that I am sure. And it has nothing to do with bad backs, blisters or your belly!" I remembered how he had "forgotten" his father's name so conveniently, until I had jolted his memory. "For all your talk of your beautiful lady, you are behaving like a very reluctant bridegroom! One would almost think you didn't *want* to go home!" I was joking, trying to bring an air of ease to a puzzling situation, but to my amazement he took me seriously.

"Perhaps I don't."

"What do you mean? Ever since I first met you we have been trying to find out where you live, and no one has been more insistent than you! We have traveled hundreds of miles—never mind your blisters, you should see mine!—and have gone through great dangers, faced starvation, scraped and scrounged for every penny, crossed innumerable provinces, just so that we can bring you to the bosom of your family once more! You can't mean at this late stage that you don't want to go home, you just can't!"

His blind eyes were fixed unseeingly on his boots. He muttered something I couldn't catch, so I asked him to repeat it.

"I said: what use to anyone is a blind knight?"

Dear Christ, I had never thought of that. How terrible!

When first I had rescued him I had thought of nothing
but helping him to recover, largely, now I admitted, for
my own gratification. His blindness had been an inconve-
nience for him, but a bonus for me. It had meant I could
worship him unseen; feed him, clothe him, wash him,
cut his hair and beard, touch him, hold his hand. . . . And
all without him realizing how fat and ugly I was. Facing
it now, I could see that all I had wanted was his depen-
dence, in a false conviction that that would bring me
love. And also boost my own self-importance: was that
why I had also taken on a hungry tortoise, a broken
pigeon, a decrepit horse? Just so that they would pander
to my ego by being grateful to me? Dear God, I hoped
not: I hoped it was the gentler emotion of compassion,
but how could I be sure? I had had little choice with
Growch, and the Wimperling was almost forced on me,
but the others? It didn't bear thinking of.

And now my beloved Gill had faced me with an impossible question: what, indeed, was there for a blind knight?
Knights fought in battles, competed in tourneys, hunted,
went on Crusades—what did a knight know save of arms?
Would his overlord, the king from oversea, want a man
incapable of warring?

Quick, Summer, think of something. . . .

"There are plenty of things you can do," I said briskly.
"People will still obey your commands, won't they? A blind
man can still ride a horse, play an instrument, sing a song,
run an estate, make wise judgments, and . . . and . . ." I
had to think of something else. "Remember what that
wise physician, Suleiman, said? He foretold you would
regain your memory, as you have, and he also said there
was nothing wrong with your eyes that time also couldn't
cure. He said you could regain your sight suddenly, any
day!"

I don't think he was listening. There was something
even more pressing at the back of his mind. "Of what
use is a blind husband?"

I was about to observe that most lovemaking took
place in the dark anyway, but suddenly realized just how
much he must be fearing rejection: some women

wouldn't consider allying themselves to a blind man, never mind that to me it would be an advantage. But then, I wasn't beautiful. . . . I remembered that Mama had told me that a man's pride was his greatest emotion. Let's give him a boost and a get-out, however frivolous the latter.

I put my arms about him and hugged him. "Any woman would be crazy to look elsewhere!" I said comfortingly. "A handsome man such as you? Why, if she won't have you, I will!" I added in a lighthearted, teasing way. "We shall take to the road again, you and I, and have many more adventures, until your sight is returned. We'll go back and stay with Matthew the merchant for a start, and—" I stopped, because his hands had sought the source of my voice, and now they cupped my face.

"You know, you are the kindest and most warmhearted woman I have ever known," he said, then leaned forward and kissed me. "And I don't think I shall ever forget you. Tell me, Summer, are you as pretty as your voice? If so, I might even take you up on your offer," and now his voice was as light and teasing as mine had been.

I leapt to my feet, my stomach churning, my face red as a ripe apple, my mind all topsy-turvy. It was the first time he had ever offered me a gesture of affection. Why now? I screamed inside, why now when you are so near home and in a few hours I am going to lose you? If he had told me before of his fears, if he had once shown me any love, then I would have ensured it took twice as long to reach here. And now how I regretted refusing his love-making attempt: what would it have mattered if he had thought me someone else? What would have been simpler than to take what he offered and enjoy it, then perhaps confess to him afterwards?

But all I said was: "You can judge of that when you can see again. But the offer's open. . . ." in my gruffest voice, adding: "Enough of all this nonsense! Let's get you cleaned up, bathed and properly dressed, so you will not disgrace us all. And I must do the animals as well. . . ." and I grabbed Growch, who had gathered the main import of what I had been talking of in human speech, and was about to disappear down the road.

Luckily there was a meandering stream not far away through the trees, and though it was summer-low I managed to dunk the dog and comb out the worst of the fleas, and freshen up the pig. Then I gave Gill an all-over, my eyes and hands perhaps lingering too long on those special parts that would soon belong to another. I trimmed his beard and mustache as close as I could and cut his hair, then gave him a fresh shirt and the new blue-embroidered surcoat.

There was little I could do for myself except bathe, plaiting my hair, donning a fresh shift and the woolen dress Matthew had given me, but I felt clean and more comfortable. One bonus was to find some watercress to supplement our bread and cheese.

We still had several miles to walk before we reached Gill's home. Once we found the left-hand turning we were bounded by forest on both sides, and the road narrowed to a wheel-rutted track, but after a mile or so we came to a pair of gates that seemed to be permanently fastened back, and through them the road wound among orchard trees and harvested fields towards a fortified manor house some half-mile away. There were few people about, and no one challenged us as I led Gill slowly towards his home.

It was now late afternoon, but the sun had lost little of its heat and we finished off the water in the flask and I picked three apples from those near-ripe. Then another and another for the Wimperling, who had suddenly decided they were his favorite food. I picked them quite openly, for there were none to see, save a boy coaxing some swine back from acorns in the forest, and a girl with her geese picking at the stubble. Besides, I thought, these are Gill's orchards, or will be some day.

I started to describe our surroundings to him, but I had no need. Now his memory was nearly complete once more, he could smell, hear, taste and touch his own land; at first tentatively, then more assured as he described what lay on either side of us as we passed. Here a copse, there a stream, crabapples on one side, late pears on the other, and he even anticipated the flags flying from the gateway.

As he drew nearer I could see that his memory of the grandness of the manor house was a little exaggerated, like most fond memories. It was nothing special; we had passed much grander on our travels. The original structure was of wood, in two stories, but a high stone wall now surrounded it, embracing also the courtyard, stables, kitchens and stores; outside, small hovels housed the workers, though everything seemed empty and deserted.

"Entertainers?" said the porter at the side gate. "Everyone's welcome today, even your beasts. Round to your right you'll find the kitchens. Tonight's the Grain Supper: always held on this day, come rain or shine." And he went back to gnawing at what was left of a large mutton bone.

"This is ridiculous!" protested Gill, as we started off again across the courtyard, also deserted. "I belong here: this is my home! What in God's name are we doing creeping round like a couple of thieves? Just lead me over to the main door—no, I can find my own way!"

"Wait!" I said, catching hold of his arm. "Let's not rush it. You don't want to give them all heart failure! Let's surprise them gently. Listen a moment, and I'll tell you what we'll do. . . ."

Leaving Gill and the animals outside, I went to the kitchens and was given a large bowl of mutton stew and a loaf of the "poor-bread" I remembered as a child, before Mama could afford better: the grain was mixed with beans, peas and pulses, and this was fresh as an hour ago and very filling. We ate hungrily, sitting in the courtyard with our backs to a sunny wall, then I went back and asked to see the steward, asking permission to perform in the Great Hall later. As it happened there were a juggler and a minstrel already waiting, but we were added to the list.

All that remained was to keep out of the way of anyone who might recognize Gill, and a couple of hours later I was waiting nervously at the side door, Gill tucked away

in the shadows with the hood of his cloak pulled well
down over his face, Growch and the Wimperling at his
side. As the minstrel sang the song of Roland, I peeped
into the hall; so thick with smoke, I could barely see the
top table, but obviously the thick-set, bearded man must
be Gill's father, the thin woman with the tall headdress
his mother. And there, sitting beside Gill's father, was a
slim woman with long blond hair fastened back with a
fillet: the fair Rosamund, if I wasn't mistaken. I wished
I could see her more clearly.

Beside me the kitchen servants brushed past, ducking
their heads automatically as they passed under the low
lintel, laden with dishes and jugs, though this was the
last course: fruits in aspic, nuts and cheese, so there was
more clearing away than replenishing.

The juggler had passed back to the kitchens a half-
hour ago, jingling coins in his hand, and now the minstrel
was coming to the end of his recital. There was polite
applause, the tinkle of thrown coins, and a hum of conversation as the singer made his way back to the kitchens.
Our turn next: I don't think I had ever felt so nervous
in my life.

One of the varlets announced us. "Entertainers from the
south, with a song or two and some tricks to divert . . ."

Growch "danced" to my piping, somersaulted, rolled
over and over, nodded or shook his head as required and
"died" for his king, then the Wimperling did some very
simple counting; a) because I was nervous to the point
of nearly wetting myself and b) wanting to get it all over
and done with, at the same time fearing the outcome—a
little like having severe toothache and knowing the tooth-
puller was just around the corner; it was the last few
steps to his door that were the worst.

I finished the tricks to a good deal of applause and
dismissed the animals, picking up the coins that were
thrown and putting them in my pocket. "Thank you
ladies, knights, and gentle-persons all. If I may crave
your indulgence, my partner and I will conclude with a
song," and taking a candle branch boldly from one of

the side tables I walked back to the doorway where Gill
was waiting, his hood hiding his face.

"When I come to the right words," I whispered, "throw
back your hood, hold the candles high and march through
the doorway, straight ahead. I'll come and meet you."

Walking back to the space in front of the high table I
started to sing, beating a soft accompaniment on my
tabor. It was an old favorite, the one where the knight
rides away to seek his fortune.

> *A knight rode away.*
> *In the month of May,*
> *All on a summer's day;*
> *"I shall not stray,*
> *Nor lose my way,*
> *But return this way,*
> *On St. Valentine's Day. . . ."*

It had several verses, with lots of to-ra-lays in between,
and I had to sing quickly to turn "Valentine" to "Cosmos
and Damien." The ballad tells of how news came to the
knight's fiancée that he was dead; she visits a witch and
sells her soul to the Devil in order that her beloved will
return. And, of course, he returns, the rumor of his
death having been exaggerated, right on the day he foretold. Just as she calls on the Devil to redeem his promise
she hears the voice of the knight. This was Gill's cue,
and his clear tenor rang out through the hall.

> *"I have returned as I said,*
> *I am not dead,*
> *But astray was led. . . ."*

I answered his words with the words of the song:

> *"Knave, knight or pelf:*
> *Come show yourself!"*

Gill threw back the hood of his cloak, held the candles
high and stepped firmly forward. There was a hush from

the audience, then a muffled scream as his face was
illuminated. He hesitated for a moment on the threshold,
then threw back his head and marched briskly forward.

And then it happened.

There was a crack! that echoed all around as his head
came into contact with the low lintel of the doorway. He
teetered for a moment, rocking back and forth on his
heels, then dropped like a stone to the rushes.

I ran forward with my heart full of terror and reached
his side, kneeling to take his poor head in my arms,
looking with horror at the red mark across his forehead
where he had struck.

"Gill! Gill . . . Are you all right?"

He opened his eyes, thank God! and stared straight
up at me.

"That bloody door was always too low. . . . And who
the hell are you?"

CHAPTER
TWENTY-SEVEN

After that everything became confused.

I got up, was knocked down, rose again and tripped over the Wimperling and Growch, was overwhelmed by a great rush of bodies, flung this way and that, buffetted and elbowed. I saw Gill embraced, hugged, kissed, slapped on the back, borne off, brought back, cried over. Women fainted, men wept, dogs howled; trenchers, mugs, jugs, cups, food, drink littered the rushes. Trestles and small tables were overturned, candles burned dangerously and the clamor of voices threatened to bring down the roof.

Little by little the animals and I found ourselves, from being at the center of the fuss, to being on the fringes of the activity. Behind us was the door to the kitchens. I looked at them, they looked at me, and with one accord we marched off. The kitchens had been abandoned as the staff heard the commotion in the Great Hall, and we found ourselves alone, surrounded by the detritus of the Grain Supper in all its sordidness. Unwashed dishes, greasy pans, empty jugs; bread crusts, bones, fish heads, chicken wings littered the tables and floor, and half-eaten mutton and beef showed where kitchen supper had been left for the excitement elsewhere.

"Well . . ." I said, and sat down suddenly on a convenient stool. There didn't seem anything else to say.

Growch was sniffing round. "Pity to waste all this," he said, helping himself to a rib of beef almost as big as he was.

The Wimperling rested his chin on my lap. "Give it all time to settle down," he said. "He'll remember about us later. In the meantime, why not stock up on a bit of food and drink and find a stable or something to settle in for the night?"

I scratched his chin affectionately. "Why not?"

There were some boiling cloths drying on a rack, so I wrapped up a whole chicken, slightly charred, three black puddings, a cheese and onion pasty and a half-empty flagon of wine, and crept away guiltily to the courtyard. The stables were all full, but I found a small room that must have been used for stores, but was now empty except for a heap of sacks in one corner and a pile of rush baskets. The whole place smelled pleasantly of apples.

We could still hear sounds of revelry and carousing from the direction of the Great Hall, but it was full dark outside by now, so I closed the door and lit my lanthorn and we shared out the food. I had half the chicken and all the crispy skin, and the pasty, and I shared the rest of the chicken and the black puddings among the other two, though the Wimperling said the latter could be cannibalism.

"I thought you said you didn't know whether you were a pig or not," I said sleepily, for it had been a long day and the unaccustomed wine was making me feel soporific. I arranged the sacks to make a comfortable bed for us.

"True," said the Wimperling. "And I'm still not sure. . . ."

"Then pretend you're something else. A prince in disguise . . ."

Growch snorted.

We were wakened at dawn by an almighty hullabaloo. I was grabbed from the pile of sacks and held, struggling, between two surly men; another had hold of the Wimp-

erling's tail and was hauling him towards the door and
two others were trying to corner a snapping, snarling
Growch. The storeroom seemed to be full of people all
jabbering away, pointing at me, the animals. What had
we done? Then I remembered the food I had filched
from the kitchens the night before: was I about to lose
a hand for thieving?

"Is this the one?" shouted one of the men who was
holding me.

The steward stood in the doorway, consulting a piece
of vellum. "A girl, named of Summer; a pig and a small
dog. Seems we've got 'em. Well done, lads." And,
addressing me: "Is your name Summer?"

What point in denying it? "Let the animals alone:
they've done nothing!" I suddenly remembered. "I
demand to see Gill—Sir Gilman, immediately! There's
been some mistake. . . ."

He thrust the piece of vellum back in his pocket.
"You're all wanted, girl, pig and dog. Do you realize just
how long we've been looking for you?" He seemed in a
very bad temper, and my heart sank. "Why, not a half-
hour ago I sent mounted men out to chase you up. . . .
Have to send more to recall them. All this fuss and
pother, never a moment's peace. . . . Well, come on then!
They're waiting. . . ." and without giving me time to tidy
my hair or smooth down my dress I was hauled across
the courtyard, in through the main doorway, across the
Great Hall—still full of last night's somnolent revelers,
the smoldering ashes of the fire and a stink of stale food
and wine, dogs, guttered candles and torches, vomit and
sweat—closely followed by a man carrying the Wimperling, who seemed to have shrunk of a sudden, and three
others still trying to catch Growch.

Up a winding stone staircase hidden by an arras behind
the top table and we were thrust, carried or chased into
a large solar wherein were seated four people: the lord
of the manor, Sir Robert, his wife, the golden-haired
Rosamund and—and Gill. A Gill close-shaven, handsomer than ever, clad in fine linen and silks. He looked

now just as he had when I first saw him: beautiful, haughty and unattainable.

As we were shoved into the room he rose from the settle where he had been holding hands with his affianced, a look of bewilderment on his face as he gazed first at me, then the animals, and back to me again.

"Can it be . . . ?"

The steward gave me a shove in the back that had me down on my knees and addressed Sir Robert. "Is this them, then?"

Sir Robert glanced at his son. "Gilman?" but Gill had started forward, a look of anger on his face as he helped me to my feet.

"Whether it is or no, you have no right to treat a girl like that! Leave us, I will deal with this!" The steward and his men bowed and retreated and Gill looked searchingly into my face. "Is it really you, Summer?"

Of course he had never seen me, except for that time he had asked the way, and he didn't know it was the same girl. I blushed to the roots of my hair that now he should see me in all my ugliness.

"Yes," admitted finally. "I am Summer. And this is the Wimperling and that is Growch," hoping he would stop staring at me.

"But I had no idea. . . ." He plucked a dried leaf from my hair abstractedly, then took my hands in his again. "I thought—I had thought you were quite different. . . ."

"Blind men have all sorts of strange fancies," I said, then forgot myself to ask anxiously: "You are all right, then? You can see properly again?"

"Apart from a slight headache, yes. You and Suleiman were right. I reckon it was the knock on the head that did it. It all happened so quickly I still feel confused—"

"And so you should!" came a cool voice from behind him and there stood the fair Rosamund, who pulled his hands from mine and tucked them round her arm, all so gently done that it seemed the initiative had come from him. She gazed at me, a faint sneer on her lips. "I'm not surprised you feel confused! Used as you are to the best, it must have been hell for you to traipse around the countryside with this tatterdemalion crew!" Her cold blue eyes raked me from head to foot. "Still, I suppose the girl needs some recompense, before she and her— menagerie—take to the road again." She paused. "I may well have a dress I need no more, though I doubt it would fit. . . ."

"Enough of this!" It was Gill's tall, thin mother Jeanne who spoke. I had the impression that nothing short of a catastrophe gave her the courage to speak normally, though now of course her beloved Gill's return must have sparked her into fresh resolution. "The girl brought our son back to us safe and sound, and she deserves the very best we can give her. As long as she wishes to stay, she is our honored guest. As—as are her pets! See that they are accommodated in the hall tonight: I myself will find a length of cloth so she is decently clad."

"The hall?" said Gill. "Father, Mother, nothing less than a good bed will do! Why, I am sure my betrothed would be only too glad to share her room with Mistress Summer?"

She looked at me as if I had the plague, then turned to Gill as sweet as honey. "My dearest, whatever you wish. But—" and she flashed me a glance that would have split stone as neatly as any mason's chisel and hammer: "—perhaps we should ask the young person herself? She may have other ideas. . . ."

Meaning I had better. She needn't have worried. The last person in the world I wished to share a bed with was her. Now, if it had been Gill . . . I pulled myself together and addressed Sir Robert and his wife.

"I thank you Sir, Lady, for your kind offer," I said, and curtsied. "The length of cloth would be most welcome, and I can make it up myself. As for accommodation, however, if I might be allowed to sleep in the storeroom where I spent last night, then I can be with our traveling companions, who are used to being with us and have been of great assistance in our travels, as no doubt Sir Gilman has told you." I curtsied again. "I should also be grateful for hot water for washing and some extra thread: I used the last to make Sir Gilman a surcoat."

There! I thought: that should give them something to
think about. Polite, accommodating, clean, thrifty and yet
independent, with a couple of reminders of the life we
had led and how I had cared for Gill ... I smiled at
him. Never mind my ugliness: he still seemed to care
about my welfare.

Sir Robert inclined his head. "As you wish. I shall see
to it that the room you prefer is made more comfortable.
And now, I think it is time to break our fast. ..."

And while we ate—just below the top table this time:
on it would have been too much to ask—the storeroom
was transformed. Swept out, sacks and baskets removed,
a table, stool and truckle bed installed, hooks for our
packages knocked into the wall, two large lanthorns and
a pile of straw for the animals—luxury indeed!

After breakfast servants brought hot water, soap, linen
towels, and from Gill's mother came a length of fine
woolen cloth in blue, needles and thread, a new comb
and ribbons for my hair, and even a new shift: too long,
of course, but surprisingly, none too tight. I took it up,
cut out my new surcoat, mended my old one, washed
and indulged recklessly in the bottle of rosemary oil that
came with the soap and towels, washed my other two
shifts and stitched my shoes where they were coming
undone.

The midday meal was at noon, the evening meal at
six, and by that evening I had my new surcoat finished,
so for the first time I felt comfortable enough to survey
my hosts at my leisure. My position just below the top
table gave me ample opportunity to look at both Gill's
parents and his affianced.

Sir Robert was stout rather than tall; he had fierce
mustaches and a rather dictatorial manner, but he always
treated me with kindness. His wife was normally silent,
looked older than her husband, and her usually careworn
expression only lightened when she talked to her beloved
son. I scarcely recognized him that evening, for he had
had his curly hair cropped short like his father's, to facili-
tate the wearing of the close-fitting helmet they affected
in these parts. I liked him better with it long.

It was the fair Rosamund however who intrigued me most. "Fair" once I judged, but whatever she may have told Gill about her age, she must be at least four or five years older. Already fine lines radiated from the corners of her eyes when she smiled, which was seldom enough, and her mouth had a discontented droop. She was also missing two teeth; perhaps that was why she didn't smile much, that and the fear of deepening her lines.

She had pretty manners however, using her table napkin often to dab away grease from mouth or fingers. Her voice was pleasant enough, her figure good and her walk swaying and graceful and her hands were white and beautifully shaped. Her hair was rather thin—or mine was too thick—but it was her pale complexion I envied most of all; but, come to think of it, if she tramped the roads as we had, it would have reddened and blotched it a most unsightly way.

In all this I was fully aware that I was being over-critical, but I knew she didn't like me, and I hated the way she monopolized Gill, snatching his attention if ever he glanced over at me, and giving exaggerated little "oohs" and "aahs" as he told of our adventures. And it didn't do any good for me to remind myself she had a perfect right to do so.

Several times during the next few days he tried to speak to me alone, and each time he was foiled, usually by her, sometimes by other interruptions. Sometimes I would catch him gazing at me, and if I smiled at him he would smile back, but it was always an uncertain, puzzled smile. It got to the stage when I started worrying whether I had two noses or was covered in some disfiguring rash.

But life drifted by for a week in this lazy fashion, eating, sleeping, and I let it, for I was in no hurry to leave. A golden September would all too soon give way to October. The mornings even now held a hint of the chill to come, dew heavy on the millions of spiderwebs that carpeted the stubble till it glinted in the rising sun like diamonds; the swifts were long gone, but a few swallows still gathered on the tower tops, and martins on the slopes of the roofs like a scattering of pearls. The leaves of the willow were already yellowing, and across in the forest the trees were a patchwork of color.

Noons were still warm and heavy, the sparse birdsong drowsed by heat, only the robins still disputing their territory in fierce red breastplates. Nights were colder and it was nice to snuggle under a blanket once more and listen to the tawny owls practicing their "hoo-hoos" across the empty fields.

I thought of Mistral; at this time of year, she had told us, the tide sometimes raced in and overwhelmed the fields till even the horses ran from it, their coats flecked with foam from the waves that roared in over the ribbed sands from the other side of the world. I thought of Traveler, safe I hoped in the ruined chapel tower; at this time of year there were still seeds and fruits in plenty, but soon would come the harsh winter, when the weakest would die. I thought of Basher: about now he would be looking for a soft, sandy place to dig himself in for the winter, till that funny shelled body of his was safe for the long sleep. . . .

I thought of them all, I missed them all, I prayed for them all.

And what of the fourth of the travelers to find his "home"? The others had accepted less than they deserved: would Gill, too, be cruelly rewarded? I hoped not, but I sensed there was something amiss, in spite of the fact that he had regained his sight, his home, his beloved.

One night after supper he caught at my sleeve and murmured urgently, "At the back of the room you sleep in there is a stairway up to the walkway on the wall: meet me there in an hour. I need to talk to you."

My heart gave a great thump of apprehension: what was so important we couldn't discuss it openly?

I found the doorway he described, behind some stacked hurdles, but it was so small I could only just manage to squeeze my way up the dusty, cobwebbed spiral. Obviously it hadn't been used in years and there was a stout wooden door at the top, luckily bolted on my side, but it took all my strength to slide back the rusty iron.

Once out on the guarded walkway I felt a deal better; I had never liked confined spaces, and now I took deep breaths of the welcome fresh air. Not that it was all that invigorating: the night was cloudy, the atmosphere oppressive, as though we waited for a storm. Down in the courtyard the little chapel bell rang for nine of night and I could see one or two going for prayers. An owl hooted, far away in the forest; a dog barked from the cluster of huts beneath the wall. Somewhere a child wailed briefly, then all was quiet once more.

I leaned against the low parapet and rested my eyes on the darkness. I heard quick footsteps mounting the outside stair to my right but didn't turn; for a moment longer I felt I didn't want to know what Gill had to say, didn't want to become involved once more. Whatever it was, I had the feeling it would mean more heartache, one way or the other.

"Summer?"

"Here . . ." I turned and was immediately taken into an urgent, awkward embrace that had my nose squashed against his shoulder and the breath knocked out of me. I pushed him away as hard as I could.

"Are you mad—?"

He stepped back, but regained possession of my hands. "I'm sorry, I didn't mean . . . Look here, Summer, I can't stand this much longer, not being able to see you and speak to you! There is so much we must talk about, and I—"

"Hush!" I pulled my hands from his grasp. "If you yell like that you'll have everyone up here!" for his voice had risen with his anxiety. I looked down into the courtyard but all was quiet. "Now, just tell me—quietly—what on earth's the matter?"

"Everything."

"Don't be so dramatic! You are back home, safe and comfortable, you have your sight back, and are reunited with your betrothed—so what could possibly be wrong?"

He hesitated. "I don't know. . . . It's just that—that

everything, everybody's changed. It's not what I expected...."

My breathing slowed down a little. Silly fellow! "You've been away for over a year, you know! But they haven't done anything drastic like moving the house or burning down the forest, have they? Perhaps there are some new faces, old ones gone, different fields plowed, but—"

"It's not that. How can I explain it?" He ran his hand through his close-cropped hair. "Everything looks somehow smaller, shabbier, meaner!" he burst out.

"Shhh ... That's easily explained. While you were away you'd built up a picture in your mind, that's all—like a dream. Things always look larger in dreams."

"But what about the people? My mother looks older, sort of—defeated. And I don't remember my father's beard having so much grey in it."

"But they are older: over a year older. So are you.... Life didn't just stand still, waiting for you to come home. They probably feel the same about you. You are thinner, browner, more restless, and have had enough adventures and mishaps to change anyone. You've got to have patience, time to settle in once again." I patted his arm. "There: lots of good advice! I'm afraid there's no other way I can help...."

He turned away, gripped the parapet, stared out into the darkness. "Yes. Yes, there is."

"How? Do you want me to talk to them? I don't think they would take much notice of me."

"It's not that.... It's Rosamund." He exhaled heavily, as though he had been holding his breath, and turned back to me. "You see, I just don't love her anymore."

I was speechless. Of all the things I had expected him to say, this was the last.

"It happened as soon as I saw her again," he hurried on, as if now eager to tell everything as fast as possible. "Perhaps, as you say, I had built up an idealized picture of things in my mind, and especially her. It wasn't only that she looked—looked older, harder; it seemed she had changed in other ways, too. I hadn't remembered her as so overpowering and at the same time sickly-sweet. And

I had forgotten her little mannerisms; things that I found once so enchanting now did nothing but irritate me. You must have noticed them, too."

Of course I had. But let him tell it in his own way.

"You know the sort of thing: the little cough to get attention, the way she keeps smoothing her throat to draw notice to its whiteness, how she holds her head to one side when she listens to you and opens her eyes wide like an owl's, the way she sucks her teeth. . . . She's stiff, unreal, mannered, like one of those jointed wooden puppets you can buy. . . . I can't explain it any better."

What could I say? I tried the same arguments I had used before, how it took everyone time to adjust, that he had changed too and there were probably things about him that annoyed her too, and all the while I had the horrible feeling that I knew just what he was going to say next, and I hadn't the slightest idea how to deal with it.

"But you are not like that, Summer! You are young, younger than I, and so full of life! If I had had the slightest idea what you were really like, if I hadn't been blind in more ways than one, then—then I should never have come back! Not unless and until I could have brought you back with me as my wife!"

He couldn't mean it! Not now; it was too cruel a twist of fate! For how many months had I worshiped him in secret, never once letting him know how I felt? If only . . . He couldn't see the tears on my cheek but I tried to keep them from my voice.

"You know it wouldn't have worked. I'm not your kind, would never fit into this kind of life. No, wait!" For he had moved forward to embrace me. "Besides, you could never have broken your betrothal vows. They are sacred things, as sacred as marriage itself, and you know it. The dowry has been paid, she has been accepted into your family, there is no going back now. In the eyes of God you are already wed."

"God could not be so cruel, not now when I have found my one, my true and only love! To hell with the dowry, that can be paid back. . . ." He took me in his

arms, and I could smell the acrid sweat of emotion and
anxiety. "The contract can be canceled. Come away with
me, Summer! We can go back on the road, we managed
before. Now I can see again I can find work somewhere
farther south where no one will follow us." He tipped
up my chin with one hand. "And don't tell me you have
no fondness for me: I know you have!" and he bent
his head and kissed me, at first soft and then hard and
hungry.

It was my first real kiss; I had always wondered where
the noses went, how the faces would fit, what it felt like
to taste someone else. Now I knew, but even as my
whole body seemed to melt against him, part of me knew
it was wrong, wrong!

"Stop it, Gill! Let me breathe, let me think....
Please!"

He released me and I had to cling to the parapet, I
was shaking so much. He took my hand. "I know it's
sudden, my dearest one, but don't you see? It's the only
way. Please say you will at least consider it. I have some
moneys, not a lot, but enough to find us a safe haven
for the winter. I swear to you that I will make it worth
your while. Why shouldn't we both be happy instead of
both miserable?"

There were a hundred, a thousand reasons why, but I
couldn't think straight. "Give me time to think.... I
don't know, right now I don't know." And then the words
that must have been spoken so many times in the past by
women far less surprised than I: "This is all so sudden!"

He bent and kissed my hands, one after the other.

"Of course, my love, but not more than couple of days.
I am being pressed already by Rosamund to name the
wedding date. Tonight is Tuesday; I'll meet you here for
your answer the same time on Thursday. In the meantime," he added, "I shall find it extremely difficult to
avoid grabbing you and kissing you in front of everyone!
I love you, my dearest...."

I staggered back to my room down the stone stairs in
a complete daze. At the bottom, by the light of a candle
I had left burning, I saw two pairs of eyes staring up at

me accusingly. Too much to expect that, between them, they didn't know exactly what had happened.

"I'm going to bed," I said firmly. "Right now. We'll talk in the morning, if you have anything you want to say."

The truth was that for a few precious hours, just a few, I wanted to hug to myself everything he had said, everything he had done, without dissipating the secret joy a jot by sharing or discussing it. If you leave the stopper off a vial of perfume it soon evaporates, and this love potion I had received tonight was the sweetest perfume in the world, and I had every intention of staying awake all night to conserve and savor every drop. . . .

"Breakfast," said the Wimperling succinctly, "is outside the door. As we didn't turn up for breakfast, they brought it to you."

I opened bleary eyes, for a moment lost to the day and hour. Then I remembered. But surely I couldn't have fallen asleep—

"What time is it?"

"Getting on for two hours after dawn, I reckon."

So much for spending the night awake, relishing the declaration of Gill's love! I must have fallen asleep almost at once and been tireder than I thought, for now I was grouchy, headachy, scratchy-eyed. The storm that had threatened last night hadn't broken after all and, like most animals, I still felt the oppression in the air, like a hand pressing down on the top of my head. And there was so much to do, so much to think about. . . .

We ate, what I don't remember, but I know the others had most of whatever it was. All the while the thoughts in my head danced up and down, round and about, like a cloud of midges, and as patternless.

"I'm going for a walk," I said abruptly. "You can come or stay as you wish."

We left the courtyard and passed the cluster of huts below the wall. Ahead stretched the long, straight road that led through the fields and orchards, past the fringes of the forest, to the gates of the demesne. I walked, not even noticing the surrounding landscape, just thumping my feet down one after the other, my mind a hopeless blank. It was an unseasonably hot day and at last sheer discomfort made me turn off to the shade of one of the still-unpicked orchards. I sank down on the long grass, leaned back against one of the gnarled trunks and sank my teeth into one of the small, sweet, pink-fleshed apples they probably used for cider. The Wimperling wandered off in search of windfalls, and the breeze brought faint and faraway the sound of the chapel bell ringing for noon.

Even Growch knew what that meant. "We've missed the midday meal," he said plaintively, sucking in his stomach.

"I know," I said unsympathetically.

"Ain't you got nuffin with you? Bit o' crust, cheese rind?"

"No. You had most of my breakfast, remember? Go away and look for beetles or bugs or something and don't bother me. I need to think," and promptly fell asleep once more, to awake only when the lengthening shadows brought with them a chill that finally roused me from sleep. The Wimperling lay by my side, the freshening breeze lapping his hide with the dancing shadows of the leaves above; Growch was lying on his back, snoring, his disgraceful stomach, pink, brown and black-patched, exposed to a bar of sunshine.

I sat up, suddenly feeling rested, alert, alive once more. I stretched until my bones cracked and twanged, then bounced to my feet and snatched another apple, sucking at the juice thirstily, then another, not caring whether I got stomachache. Time to walk back, or we should miss another meal, and now I felt hungry.

I realized I was enjoying the leisurely walk back, and spoke without thinking. "It'd be nice to be back on the road again. . . ."

Then began the Great Campaign, as I called it later, though the first few words were innocuous enough.

"Nice enough when the weather is like this," said the Wimperling. "But it's autumn already. All right for those with stamina and guts."

"Remember how cold it was last winter?" said Growch. "His Lordship—beggin' your pardon, lady—caught a cold what turned to pew-money?"

"Certainly doesn't like cold weather," said the Wimperling. "His sort are used to riding: never liked walking far."

"Remember how he used to complain about his feet?" said Growch. "Used to whinge about the food, too. . . ."

"That's the trouble with knights," said the Wimperling. "Only trained for one life. Give them a sword, a charger, a battle, and they're happy. In civilian life they can loose a hawk, sing a ballad—"

"Or flatter a lady . . ." said Growch.

"Easy enough for them to get accustomed to being waited on, having the best of everything—"

"Soon enough blame anyone what robs 'em of it—"

At last I realized where all this was leading, refused to listen, stopped up my ears. How *dared* they try and influence what I was going to do! It had nothing to do with them, it was between me and Gill.

The trouble was, their words remained in my consciousness, as annoying and insidious as the last of the summer fleas and ticks. And what they had said, exaggerated as it was, still held a grain of truth. Gill *had* grumbled a lot—but then he had had a right to. But would choice make it any easier for him to bear a simple life? Yes, he did catch cold easily, yes he was a bit soft, but he hadn't been used to the traveling life. Would he be any better prepared now? A small voice inside me whispered that it had been a new way of life for me, too, though perhaps I had made a better job of it, but I brushed the thought aside impatiently: everyone was different.

It was true, too, that the only life he had known was that of a knight, and that in spite of his brave words he would find it difficult to turn his hand to anything else. And that bit about flattering ladies: were the words he had spoken to me merely the courtesies he thought I would like to hear, not meant to be taken seriously? If he found it so easy to be turned from his betrothed,

would a week or so in bad weather have him feeling the
same way about me?

I got through the rest of the day somehow or other,
but at dinner that night I found myself studying Gill's
face for signs of what he was really like. Was his chin
just a little bit weak, compared with his father's? Had he
always looked so petulant when something displeased
him, as it did that night when a particular dish was empty
before it reached him? And if he now disliked his fiancée
so much, why was he paying her such great attention?
His fine new clothes certainly suited him: that was the
third new surcoat I had seen him in. Who would carry
all his gear if we were on the road once more?

That night I couldn't sleep at all. Hoping a little fresh
air would help, I crept up the spiral stair to the walls
again, but just as I drew back the bolts, greased earlier
in anticipation of my meeting with Gill on the following
night, I saw that the walkway was already occupied,
although it must be near midnight. A man and a woman
stood close by, talking softly. I was about to descend
again when something about her stance made me believe
I recognized the woman, and curiosity kept me where I
was.

". . . that makes it so important to risk being seen?" I
couldn't identify his voice, and he had his back to me.

"I had to see you! As things are, I have to be with
him all the time. . . ." Rosamund's face was as pale as
the moon that rode clear of cloud as she turned fully
towards the man before her. "Robert, what are we going
to do? I'm at least two months pregnant!"

CHAPTER
TWENTY-EIGHT

I couldn't help a gasp of horror as I realized the implications of what she had just said, but they were so intent on each other that they didn't hear. Once again I knew I should retreat without further eavesdropping, but how could I? This concerned Gill's and my future so closely I *had* to listen.

"Two months, you say?" said Gill's father, after a pause. His voice never faltered: he might have been discussing the gestation period of a favorite horse.

"I have missed two monthly courses, yes. One could have been ignored perhaps, but I have always been as regular as an hourglass, and now there are further signs. . . ." A shrug of those cloaked shoulders. "It will start to show soon."

"Let me think. . . ." He started to pace up and down the walkway, up and back twice, his arms folded across his chest. How like Gill he walks, I thought. He came back to face her. "You were no virgin when I took you," he stated flatly. "How do I know . . . ?"

"Of course it's yours! You know it is. Whatever I did in the past has nothing to do with it."

He regarded her broodingly. "Maybe not, but you were already a practiced whore when you came here.

315

You seduced me with sighs and words and gestures, and I believed you knew what you were doing, that there would be no harm in it. I am not in the habit of soiling my own midden."

"You were as eager as I," she said sulkily.

"Maybe . . . How come you never got caught before?"

"Medicines, herbs; they are not available here."

"Then it was either intentional, because you thought my son would never return, and you wished me to keep you as my mistress—"

"It was an accident. Do you think I wanted to spoil my figure on the chance you would accept the child? No: like you I gave way to something I could not help." She spoke with conviction, and apparently he accepted it.

"Then there are two ways to deal with this—three, if you count being sent home in disgrace. But I shall not do that. Your dowry has been paid, and some of it already spent. The second way is to seek out the witch in the wood, and try one of her potions—"

"I have already tried that. The maid you gave me was pregnant by one of the grooms, so I sent her for a double dose. It worked for her but not for me. Your child is lusty, Robert: it wants to live."

He thought for a moment. "Then it has to be the third way, and no delay. No one knows about this but us, so let's keep it that way, but I shall want your full cooperation. . . ."

She nodded. "You have it."

"Right. The first thing is to get my son to your bed now, tonight—no, listen to me! I will give you a potion that I have sometimes used when my wife has failed to excite me. Make sure he drinks it, and if you cannot tempt him to your bed, then visit his. He will be so befuddled he will not know whether he has or has not performed. He will sleep without memory, but make sure you are there beside him when he wakes. He is a simple man: he will believe whatever you say."

"And the child?"

"There are plenty of seven-month babes. And he could

be away. . . . There are many errands I could send him on."

"But your wife . . . She would know."

"She will say nothing. Her only thought is of Gill, what would make him happy. She may suspect, but once the babe is born, she will accept it. And once he, and everyone else, is persuaded he has slept with you then the wedding can take place within the week."

"The sooner the better . . ." She moved forward and rested her hands on his shoulders. "You think of everything. I had rather it had been you, but I promise to make your son a good wife." She was smiling like a pig in muck. "And your son—*our* son—will be the next in line, after Gill. Quite something, don't you think?" She leaned forward and kissed him, and I noticed he didn't draw back, but rather folded his arms around her and returned her embrace. "And perhaps, another time?"

"Get away with you, hussy. . . ." but he didn't sound displeased. "Remember, my son mustn't suffer over this."

"Of course not! I am really quite fond of him. There will be no complaints from that quarter, I swear. I know some tricks that even that girl he traveled with would not know—which reminds me: I fancy he became quite close to her, and I would not wish her to distract him from what we have planned. I have caught him looking at her a couple of times as if he were quite ready to disappear with her again—and we can't have that, can we?"

Oh, Gill, you idiot! I thought, shrinking back into the shadows as far as I could go. She is much cleverer than you thought. . . .

"She shall be disposed of, if you play your part. By tomorrow morning I want to see everyone convinced that my son will be the father of your child."

"Disposed of?"

"An accident, a disappearance: what do you care? No problem. It will be in my interest as well as yours, remember? But first, you must do your part. Tomorrow I will take care of Winter, or Summer, whatever she calls herself. . . . Meet me in the chapel in ten minutes and I will give you the potion."

I started back down the stairs, carefully closing the door behind me, shocked and horrified by what I had just heard. First their arrant duplicity regarding Rosamund's pregnancy: what could I do? Rush and find Gill, tell him what I had heard? I didn't even know how to find him and if I did, would he believe me? I doubted it. Whatever happened, I realized that Gill's dream of running away with me was gone forever. If his father's plan succeeded, by tomorrow morning he would believe he had seduced a virgin, his betrothed, and would be honor bound to marry her as quickly as possible; in cases like these his knightly training would give him no choice, however much he fancied someone else. And had I the right to try and stop it, even if I could? That baby could not be born illegitimate; I was myself, and I knew how it felt, not to have a father and to be jeered at because my mother was a whore. It would be worse in the sort of household Gill's father ran, and I believed both he and the perfidious Rosamund would bring the child up as Gill's. He need never know, and I was sure he would make a good father.

So now the choice I had thought would be so difficult was taken from me. Why was it that with no decision to make, I now felt a great sense of relief? Did that mean that what had happened was for the best, that Gill was not, never had been meant for me? I should always remember his declaration of love, I thought, but now I need never discover he would change, or I would as we traveled the roads. It was as if he were dead to me already: I should just remember the best, and nurse a few sentimental regrets.

"Infatuation," said the Wimperling at my elbow. "Nothing like the real thing. You wait and see."

"What are you doing! You made me jump out of my skin!"

"Just wanted to remind you that we'd better not tarry—yes, I was listening to your thoughts—because I reckon they mean you harm. . . ."

Of course! How could I have forgotten. I had to be got out of the way, and that didn't mean a bag of gold and a lift to the nearest town, I knew that. Headfirst down the nearest well, a stab in the back, perhaps a deadly potion ... It would have been better to leave right away but I wanted to be sure, quite sure, that there was no chance Rosamund had failed in her plan. I knew in my heart she would succeed, but something within me wanted to twist a knife in the wound already so sore in my heart. Besides, Sir Robert had said he would do nothing until the morning.

During that long night I packed everything securely into two bundles, one for the Wimperling, one for me. The only money we had left were the few coins tossed down for our performance before Gill's miraculous appearance on the first night, but I wasn't worried. The countryside was still full of apples, late blackberries, enough grain to glean to thicken a stew, fungi and mushrooms. Besides we could always give a performance or two.

The last thing I did was to write to Gill: I felt he deserved some explanation, even if not the true one, and it might also serve to put his father off trying to pursue us. I tore a blank page from the back of my Boke and thought carefully.

"Gill:— I am sorry to leave without a farewell, but it is time I was on my way. Besides, I hate good-byes. Perhaps I should have confided my hopes to you earlier, but I have not had the chance to speak with you alone. . . ."

That should allay their suspicions, I thought.

"I am going back to Matthew, and will now accept his proposal. It will be a good match for me."

I paused, flicking the end of the quill against my cheek. Yes . . .

"Please thank your family for their hospitality. I wish you and your betrothed every happiness, and many sons."

I signed my name "Someradai" as it had been written in the church register at home. After some thought I scratched out "Gill" and substituted "Sir Gilman." There, that would do. I rolled it carefully and tied it with one of the ribbons Gill's mother had given me. I would leave it on the table.

Satisfied that I had done all I could until dawn, I snatched a couple of hours sleep, but was up and ready as soon as the kitchens opened. We might as well take something with us, so I made up some tale about spending the day out-of-doors, missing meals, etc., but everyone was only half-awake, so it wasn't difficult to help myself to a cold chicken, some sausages, a small bag of flour and a string of onions.

After taking these back and packing them, I slipped into the Great Hall for breakfast, as if everything was normal, the Wimperling and Growch with me as usual. We should have to eat as much as we could, for the other food would have to last some time.

I watched carefully as the family appeared, one by one, on the top table. First Sir Robert, yawning hugely, downing two mugs of ale before touching any food. He never even glanced in my direction. Next came Gill's mother, who picked listlessly at a manchet, dipping it in wine, her eyes downcast. Where, oh where was Gill?

At last he appeared, but I would not have recognized him. Even on our worst days on the road he had not looked so disheveled, haggard, outworn. Unshaven, tousled in spite of his cropped head, it seemed as though he had thrown his clothes together in a hurry, and as soon as he sat down next to his mother, he grabbed her arm and started whispering in her ear; no food, no drink, nothing. He didn't glance in my direction either.

Then came Rosamund, and as soon as she appeared she made the position quite clear. In an artfully disarranged dress, she yawned, rolled her eyes; her hair was unbound, her cheeks flushed, and as she made the obligatory curtsy to Sir Robert and his wife she pretended to stagger a little. She sat down next to Gill, and to everyone's fascinated gaze, proceeded to examine her arms and neck for imaginary bruises, smiling contentedly all the while. Above the neckline of her low-cut shift were strawberry bruises; love-marks. She could not have placed them there herself. She appeared to notice Gill for the first time, and her hands flew to her mouth and she gazed away as though she were ashamed.

It was a consummate performance, and it quite halted breakfast. Eating and drinking were temporarily suspended as elbow nudged elbow and nods and winks were exchanged. The message was quite clear, even to those on the bottom tables, and there was a sigh of envious relief as she suddenly swamped him in her arms, pouting, grinning, cuddling up, murmuring in his ear. He looked half-awake, bemused, bewildered, but she leaned across and spoke to his parents, then she nudged him and, prompting as she went, she made him say what she wanted.

I had seen enough, and even as Sir Robert rose to announce that his son's wedding would take place a week hence, the animals and I were making our way back across the courtyard. Now the plotting was confirmed, I had no intention of finding myself suffocated in the midden or letting the Wimperling crackle nicely on a spit; Growch would escape anyway, but what use was that to the pig and me?

I loaded up the Wimperling and myself as quickly as I could and made our way to the gate. We were in luck; two carts were about to go down to the cider-apple orchards, farthest away from the house, and we accepted a lift; no one questioned our right to leave, though all the talk was of the coming wedding and who would be invited. It had been less than a half-hour since Rosamund's performance, yet it seemed everyone had a topic of conversation to last for days. I tried not to listen.

We were only a quarter mile from the forest when the wagon halted. Getting down I thanked them for our lift, and at a nudge and thought from the Wimperling, asked for the quickest road to Evreux, making sure they remembered the direction I had asked for.

"Now, make for the gates as fast as possible," said the Wimperling and within a quarter hour, breathless, we were on the road again. A couple of foresters were at work clearing the undergrowth, and once again, on the Wimperling's prompting, I asked the road to Evreux. Once out of earshot I asked him why the insistence on that road.

"Because if they come after us, they will waste time looking along that way," he answered tranquilly. "We will take the other road west just to throw them off the scent."

"I see. . . . In the note I wrote to Gill I said we were going to Matthew's, so everything is consistent. Clever pig!"

"But your knight won't get the note."

"Why not?"

"If he had done, then he wouldn't bother any further, and the road would be clear for his father to pursue you uninterrupted. Without it he will worry, perhaps insist he goes out with a search-party. . . . Sir Robert won't have it all his own way, and it will give us a better chance."

I hadn't considered this: the Wimperling was cleverer than I thought. He must also know who I was writing to. How did pigs know things like that?

"But what did you do with the letter?"

"I ate it. Ribbon and all."

"Did it taste nice?" asked Growch interestedly.

"No."

"Oh."

"But why should anyone come after us now?" I questioned. "Sir Robert and Rosamund have everything as they want it, surely?"

He didn't answer for a moment, then he said: "Just suppose you had been bothered by a mosquito all night, but hadn't caught it? Then in the morning you saw it again, ready to swat? Would you leave it, on the off chance it would disappear, or would you annihilate it there and then, so there was no further chance of it biting?"

"I see. . . . At least, I think I do."

"All that matters to Sir Robert now is that his son is born legitimate, and no one to question it or deflect his son's interest. He is a very proud man, and to ensure this he would do almost anything, believe me."

The Wimperling wouldn't even let us stop to eat at midday; instead we had to march on, chewing at the chicken. I was getting crosser and crosser as we approached the fork in the road we had turned off before, the right-hand fork leading to Evreux, the left to the west. I was about to demand a rest when we came across a swineherd grazing his half-dozen charges along the fringes of the forest.

By now I knew what question we were supposed to ask. He pointed the way to Evreux, but as soon as we left him at the turn in the road the Wimperling directed us into the trees to double back.

"Why? Can't we leave it a little longer? This is a good road, and so far no one had come after us. . . ."

"You've still got a lot to learn about human nature! Do as I say. . . ."

We crept back through the trees till we were almost opposite the fork in the road again, and skulked down behind some bushes. Ahead I could see the swineherd patiently prodding his pigs.

"Now what?"

"We wait."

Nothing happened for five, ten minutes, a quarter hour. Then I heard them: hooves thudding down the road from the De Faucon estate. A moment later two horsemen clattered by, wearing swords but no mail. They halted by the swineherd and one called out: "Seen a girl on the road with a couple of animals?"

The swineherd pointed in the direction we had supposedly gone, but when asked how long ago he looked blank; time obviously meant little to him. The horsemen rode off in the direction of Evreux and in a moment were out of sight.

I stood up. "Gill might have sent them. Why should we hide?"

"They would hardly have come seeking you with an invitation to the wedding armed with swords and daggers! Be sensible. It's as I said; Sir Robert wants to be rid of you."

I had the sense to become frightened. "Then, what do we do?"

"Once they find you are not on the road they have taken, they will come back and take the western road. And if they don't find us, others will be sent out. So, we go back to the estate."

"You must be mad! That's straight back into danger!"

"Not at all. The last place they would look is on their own doorstep. Come on: there's a good five miles to go before sundown!"

CHAPTER
TWENTY-NINE

So, using the road, but dodging back into the forest when we thought we heard anything, we made our way back to the estate. We had one more narrow escape: Growch was fifty yards ahead, the Wimperling the same distance behind, and their danger signals came at the same moment. Luckily I had time to hide, only to find that the first couple of horsemen had ridden back, to meet up with a fresh contingent of four who had come straight from Sir Robert. They halted so near my hiding place I could smell both their sweat and that of their lathered animals.

"Find anything?" asked the leader of the second band.

"They took the road to Evreux, according to a peasant we met, but we went a good five miles down and no sign of them. Another fellow coming back from the town reported a wagon going the other way, but we saw no sign of it."

"Fresh instructions: Sir Robert found a door or something leading up to the walk-away, and has reason to believe the girl may be wise to the pursuit. Go back the way you came, search along the way for more clues. We are taking the western road. Orders are the same: lose 'em, permanently!"

"Jewels still missing?"

"So the lady says."

"How's the boy taking it?"

"State of shock. Can't believe it. I fancy he was sweet on her. Can't say as I blame him: know which one I'd've preferred."

And they rode off in the direction of the fork in the road, leaving me in a state of disbelief. So that was Sir Robert's excuse: I was supposed to have stolen some jewels! I realized that it would have made no difference what I had written; valuables would still have disappeared, and I should have been to blame. So now there was a price on my head, and death the reward. No turning back, however much I might have wanted to.

I wondered when the jewels would conveniently turn up again—or would Gill's father believe it worth the game to leave them buried or whatever, and buy Rosamund some more?

Once we reached the demesne, the Wimperling led us along deer tracks through the forest, at a convenient distance from the manor house. We described a great loop around the demesne, going short of food because I couldn't light fires, though the Wimperling and Growch were quite happy with raw sausages. On the third day the Wimperling declared us free of the de Faucon estate, and we found a road of sorts.

At the first village we came to, two days later, I threw caution to the winds, and spent far more than I intended on bought food, luxuriating on pies and roasted meat. In the next village and the next I recouped some of the results of my spendthrift ways with a performance, but villagers have little enough to spend at the best of times, and now the winter was fast approaching.

Which led to the question of where we were headed.

All I had thought about up to now had been escaping Sir Robert, but now was the time to consider our future. I knew Growch had said he wanted a warm fire, a family and plenty to eat, and I had set off on this whole enterprise with the thought of finding a complaisant and wealthy husband, but as far as I could see, neither of us were nearer our goal, once I had refused Matthew's offer. And what of the Wimperling? He had never asked for a destination, had seemed content to follow wherever we went. But we couldn't just go on wandering like this: if nothing else we had to find winter quarters, and soon.

The question of which way to go came up naturally enough. One morning we stood at a crossroads; all roads looked more or less the same, and I had no particular feeling about any of them, except that south would be warmer, and it might be easier to over-winter in or near some town.

"Which way?" I asked the others, not really expecting an answer, for Growch was a follower rather than a leader, and the Wimperling had never expressed a preference. Now, however, he did have something to say.

"Er . . . I'd rather like to discuss that," he said diffidently. "Perhaps we could sit down?"

"Lunchtime anyhow," said Growch, looking up at the weak sun. "Got any more o' that pie left?"

"We finished that yesterday. Cheese, apples, bean loaf, cold bacon—"

"Yes."

The Wimperling chose the apples and I munched on the cheese.

"Right, Wimperling, what did you have in mind?"

He still seemed reluctant to ask. "When—when you so kindly rescued me," he began, "I said I would like to tag along because there was nowhere special I wanted to go. . . ."

I nodded encouragingly. "And now there is?"

"There wasn't then, but there is now. Yes." He sat back on his haunches, looking relieved. "Let me explain. When I was little I was brought up as a pig and believed I was one—in spite of the wings and the other bits that didn't quite fit." He held up one foot, and looked at the claws, much bigger now. "See what I mean? Well, ever since then as I have been growing I have felt more and more that I wasn't a pig. What I was, I didn't quite know, though I had my suspicions. Then, that night when we

crossed the border, I thought I knew. And the feeling
has been growing stronger ever since."

"Can you tell us?"

He shuffled about a bit. "I'd rather not, just yet. In
case I'm terribly wrong . . . But I should like you to come
with me, to find out. You might find it quite interesting,
I think."

I looked at Growch, who was practically standing on
his head trying to get a piece of rind out of his back
teeth. No help there.

"Of course we will come, Where do you want to go?
How far away is it?"

"One hundred and twelve miles and a quarter west-
southwest," he said precisely. "Give or take a yard or
so."

I flung my arms about his neck, laughing, then planted
a kiss on his snout.

"How on earth can you be so—"

But before I had finished my sentence an extraordinary explosion took place. The Wimperling literally
zoomed some twenty feet into the air vertically, then
whizzed first right and then left and then in circles,
almost faster than the eye could see. As he was now
considerably larger than I was, I was tumbled head-over-
heels and Growch disappeared into a bush, rind and all.

The whole thing can only have lasted some fifteen
seconds or so, but it seemed forever. I curled up in a
ball for protection, my fingers in my ears, my eyes tight
shut, until an almighty thump on the ground in front of
me announced the Wimperling's return to earth.

I opened my eyes, my ears and finally my mouth. "You
nearly scared the skin off me! What in the world do you
think you're *doing*?" I asked furiously. Then: "You're—
you're *different*!"

He looked as if someone had just taken him apart and
then reassembled him rather badly. Everything was in
the right place, more or less, but the pieces looked as if
they might have been borrowed from half a dozen other
animals. His ears were smaller, his tail longer, his back
scalier, his snout bigger, his chest deeper, his stomach

flatter, his claws more curved, and the lumps on his side where he hid his wings looked like badly folded sacks. He looked less like a pig than ever, while still being one, and his expression was pure misery.

My anger and fright evaporated like morning mist. "Oh, Wimperling! I'm so sorry! You look dreadful—was it something I said? Or did?"

His voice had gone unexpectedly deep and gruff, as if his insides had been shaken up as well. "You kissed me. I told you once before never to do that again. . . . Remember?"

I did, now. "Sorry, sorry, sorry! It's just that—just that when one feels grateful or happy or loving it seems the right thing to do. For me, anyway." I thought. "It didn't have the same effect on Gill. And, come to that, I've never kissed Growch. . . ."

"Who wants kisses, anyway?" demanded the latter, who had crept out from his bush, minus rind, I was glad to see. "Kissin's soppy; kissin's for pups and babies an' all that rubbish!" Something told me that in spite of the words he was jealous, so I picked him up and planted three kisses on his nose.

"There! Now you're one ahead. . . ."

He rubbed his nose on his paws and then sneezed violently. "Gerroff! Shit: now you'll have me sneezin' all night. . . . Poof!" He nodded towards the Wimperling. "An' if that's what a kiss can do, then I don' wan' no more, never!"

I turned back to the Wimperling. "Better now?"

He nodded. "Think so . . ." His voice was still deep, and if I hoped he would regain his old shape gradually, I was to be disappointed. "As I was saying, before all—this—happened—" He looked down at his altered shape. "I should like to go to the place where it all started. The place where I was hatched, born, whatever . . . The Place of Stones."

This sounded interesting. "And is this the place that you said was a hundred miles or so to the west—something?"

He nodded.

I wasn't going to miss this, hundred miles or no. "Will you set up your home where you were born?" "Hatched" still sounded silly. Pigs aren't hatched.

"No. It will merely be the place from where I set out on a longer journey, to the place where my ancestors came from."

"A sentimental journey, then," I said.

"An essential one. Without going back to the beginnings I will not have my coordinates."

"Yer *what*?"

"Guidelines, dog. Itinerary to humans."

Growch scratched vigorously. "Me ancestors go back as far as me mum, and I doubt if even she knew who me dad was, and as for me guidelines . . . I follows me nose." And he accompanied the said object into the bushes, his tail waving happily.

"And how far is it to where your ancestors came from?"

"Many thousands of miles," said the Wimperling. "A journey only I can take. But I should be glad of your company as far as the Place of Stones. . . ."

"You have it," I said. We sat quiet for a moment, and I suddenly realized that my conversations had been, for a long time, on a different level with the Wimperling than with the others. He didn't just "talk" in short sentences about the food or the weather, he communicated with me as though we were two equal beings, talking about feelings and emotions, even philosophizing a little. He wasn't really like an animal at all—

"And then you will be free to seek that husband of yours," continued the Wimperling, as though I had just said something. "Will you tell him your real name?"

I gazed at him blankly. "My *real* name? What do you mean? My name is Summer—well, Somerdai."

"The name on the register, as you keep telling yourself. Your birth was recorded by the priest but he never knew the exact date. So he wrote 'Summer day,' only he ran the letters together and misspelled them because he was an old man. . . . But when you saw it written down you

seized on the name, as a convenient way of burying deeper
the hurt when you learned your real, given name. . . ."

I was stunned. How did he know about the register?
But it was my name, it was, it was! If I'd had another,
then my mother would have called me by it instead of
"girl," or "daughter" as she always did.

"I know because the memory is still there inside you,"
he said, "hurting to get out. Thoughts like that escape
sometimes when you are asleep because they want to be
out in the open. I have become used to your thoughts
in the time we have traveled together. You have tried to
kill the memory because you are ashamed, but let it go
and you will feel better. I know, because I am not what
they called me, Wimperling, and when my new name
comes I shall be a different person."

A nasty, horrid picture was forming in my mind, however hard I tried to stifle it, cry "Go away! I don't want
to remember. It happened to someone else, not me!" A
child, a girl of four or five, a fat little girl, was playing
on the doorstep as one of her mother's clients came to
the door. And the mother said to the child: "Go and play
for a while, girl. . . ." And the man said: "Why don't you
call her by her given name?"

". . . and my mother said: 'How can I call that shape-
less lump with the pudding-face *Talitha* when she is neither graceful nor beautiful, nor will ever be? I was
pregnant when—when her father died, and he had made
me promise to give her that name if it were a girl. Of
course I agreed, never expecting she would be so plain
and clumsy!' " I was crying now, hot tears of shame and
remembered humiliation. "How could you remind me! I
had forgotten, I didn't remember, it *hurts!*"

"And that is why you stuffed the memory away for so
long, just because you were afraid of the hurt. But it was
a long time ago, and things—and people—change. Now
you have let it out, you will heal, believe me, and be
whole." He hesitated. "I will not be with you much
longer, so please forgive me. I did it for you."

"Yes, yes, I know you did. . . ." I tried the name on
my tongue. Now I remembered my father had chosen

it, it seemed right. "I feel better already. Thanks, Whimper ... But you said you weren't. Aren't ... you know what I mean! What is *your* real name?"

He shook his head. "That's the exciting thing. I don't know yet. It comes with the change, the rebirth if you like. All I know is that I took a form and a name that was convenient at the time, in order to survive. That's how I remember how far it is, counting the steps we traveled when they took me away. And that is how I can guide you there."

"Then what are we waiting for? Let's get going. Come on Growch, wherever you are: we are going to a place full of stones, and you can christen every one!"

"Oh, I don't think so," said the Wimperling. 'These stones are—different."

We were now in the last couple of weeks of October, and the weather stayed fine. We made leisurely progress, ten or twelve miles a day, but the terrain changed dramatically with every turn of the road. Villages became smaller, more isolated, there were fewer farms and no great houses or castles. The land became rocky, wilder, less hospitable, and now, instead of dusty lanes, there were sheep tracks, moorland paths, great stretches of heather, thyme, gorse and broom. A barren land as far as crops went, but with a wild beauty of its own.

The winds blew with no hindrance, whirling my hair into great tangles and carrying in their arms gulls, buzzards, crows, peregrines and merlin. The undergrowth hid fox, hare, coney, stoat, weasel and an occasional marten; under our feet the ground was springy with mosses, lichen, heather, bilberry, juniper, cotton grass and bracken, the latter the color of Matthew's hair, Saffron's cat-coat. Away from the paths the going was tough; wet feet, scratched legs and turned ankles the penalty for trying a shortcut.

We came upon a small village, some seven days before the end of the month, and the Wimperling advised me to stock up. They had only had a small harvest, but were eager to have coin to buy in some grain, so I used what little I had left and was rewarded with cheese, salt pork, honey, turnip, onion and small apples, till I could hardly stagger away under the weight. Once away from the village however, the Wimperling insisted I load most of it on his back.

"My strength is much greater now I approach the end of my journey."

"So is your size," I said, for now he was truly enormous: over twice as big as me, length and breadth.

"Ah, but I have much to hide. . . ."

"If you hides it much longer you'll burst," said Growch. "If'n I had that load abroad I reckon me legs'ud be worn to stumps."

"Really? I was under the impression that is what had happened already. . . ."

The next day we topped a rise in the land and there were the Stones in the distance. Not just ordinary stones, but ones of great size and power, even from miles away. I could feel them now from where I stood, both repelling and attracting at the same time. We had already passed the odd standing stone and the stumps of plundered circles, but there for the first time was a veritable forest, a city of stones: circles, lanes, avenues, clumps; grey and forbidding, they pointed cold stone fingers at the sky, now whipped by a westerly into a roil of rearing clouds. Down here at ground level it was still relatively calm, but the heavens were racing faster than man could run.

The Wimperling heaved a great tremble of anticipation and satisfaction. "The Place of Stones starts here. Half a day's journey and we are there."

Briefly I wondered how we were going to find our way back to civilization without our guide, but I held my tongue, sure he would have a solution.

That night we sheltered in a dell, the freshening wind creaking the branches of the twisted pine and rowan above our heads, the latter's leaves near all gone, the few berries blackened. I fell asleep uneasily, with Growch tucked against my side, to wake half a dozen times. And each time it was to see the Wimperling standing still as the stones, his gaze fixed westward, the wind flapping his small ears, his snout questing from side to side and up and down, as though reading a message in the night only he could comprehend.

In the morning the wind had swung to the northwest and it was noticeably chillier. After breakfast, as I strapped the Wimperling's burdens to his back, I noticed how hot his skin felt, as if he was burning from some internal fever; I made some silly quip about burning my fingers, but I don't think he even heard. His gaze was fixed on the journey ahead, and he didn't seem ill in any way, only impatient to be off.

The further we went, the more stones; some upright, others broken, a few lying full length, yet more with a drunken lean like the few trees in this bare landscape, which all grew away from the prevailing westerlies, like little hunched people with their hoods up and their cloaks flapping in the breeze.

More and more stones, and yet we never seemed to get near enough to them to touch. There they were to left and right, ahead, behind, distinguishable apart by their different shapes, height, angle, markings and yet as soon as I headed towards one I found I had mysteriously left it behind, or it had grown more distant. I even felt as though I passed the same monolith a dozen times as if we were walking in circles through a gigantic maze, but the Wimperling still trotted forward confidently and the ring was quiet on my finger.

At last we came to a great avenue of stone, and there in the distance was a huddle of ruined buildings on a small rise. The Wimperling stopped and looked back at us. "There it is," he said simply. "Journey's end."

It didn't look like much to me, and looked less so the nearer we approached. It was the remains of what had obviously been a small farm—cottage, barn, stable and sty—and the buildings were rapidly crumbling. The thatch had gone, apart from some on one corner of the cottage, the broken-shuttered windows gaped like missing teeth and all walls and fencing had been broken down. The place was deserted, no people, no animals and, perhaps because it was the only sign of civilization we had seen in a couple of days, the desolation seemed worse than it probably was.

"And all this in less than a year," said the Wimperling, as if to himself. "They angered the Stones. . . ." Then he turned to us. "You must be hungry and tired. And cold, too. Come with me and don't be afraid. I promise you will feel better in a little while."

I hoped so. Just at that moment I felt I had had more than enough of the mysterious Stones: all I wanted was to find some cozy corner inside where I could curl up and forget outside.

He led us to that part of the cottage adjoining the barn where there was still a corner of roofing. The room itself was about twelve feet square, with a central hearth, but I dragged over enough stones to make another fireplace under the remaining thatch. There was plenty of wood lying about, and I soon had a cheerful blaze going, the smoke obliging by curling up and disappearing without hindrance. I found a stave in one corner and, binding some heather to the end, made a broom stout enough to sweep away the debris from our end of the room. Then I went out and gathered enough bracken to make a comfortable bed for later. The Wimperling showed me where a small spring trickled away past the house, and I filled the cooking pot and set about dinner.

I had the bone from the salt bacon, root vegetables and onion, and was just adding a pinch or two of herbs when the Wimperling strode in with a carefully wrapped leaf in his mouth. Inside were other leaves, some mushrooms and a powder I couldn't identify, but on his nod I added them all to the stew, and the aroma that immediately spread around the room had me salivating and Growch's stomach rumbling. I had a little flour left so put some dough to cook on hot hearthstone. I tasted the stew, added a little salt, then walked outside to join the Wimperling and Growch, who were variously gazing up at a waxing moon, some three or four days off full, riding uneasily at anchor among the tossing clouds, and searching the old midden for anything edible.

"Will it rain tonight?"

"Probably," said the Wimperling. "But we have shelter."

"Is it—time? Are you going tomorrow?"

"No, the time is not quite right. A day or two."

"We haven't got much food left. . . ."

"Don't worry. The food will last."

And that night it seemed he was right. However much we ate—and Growch and I stuffed ourselves silly on a stew that tasted like no other I had ever come across—the pot still seemed full. The Wimperling said he wasn't hungry, but he did have a nibble of bread.

As we sat round in the firelight, the fire damped down by some turves of peat I had found in the barn, I felt sleepier than I had for ages; not exhausted but happily tired, the sort of tiredness that looks forward to dream. Growch was yawning at my feet, stretching then relaxing, his eyes half-shut already.

"Gawdamighty! I could sleep fer days. . . ."

"Why not?" said the Wimperling.

"He'd die of starvation in his sleep," I said, laughing, and stifled a yawn.

"Not necessarily. What about those animals who sleep all winter?"

"Good idea," I said. "Wake me in March. . . ." And as I wrapped myself tight in my father's old cloak and lay down on the springy bracken bed, Growch at my feet, I gazed sleepily at the glowing embers of the fire, breaking into abortive little flames every now and again, or creeping like tiny snakes across the peat, till all merged into a pattern that repeated itself, changed a fraction, moved away, came back. Soothing patterns, familiar patterns, patterns in the mind, sleep-making patterns . . .

When I finally came to I found it was already mid-afternoon, and Growch was still snoring. The fire smoldered under a great heap of ash that seemed to have doubled overnight. I broke the bread, stale now, into the stew, and put it on to heat up. Then I went outside to relieve myself and look for the Wimperling, but he was nowhere about. I went down to the spring for a quick, cold wash, for I still felt sleepy, then combed out my tangled hair. Still no sign of the Wimperling. He couldn't have gone without saying good-bye, surely?

It had obviously rained overnight, for the ground was damp and the heather wetted my ankles as I lifted my skirts free from the moisture. After calling out three or four times I shrugged and went back to dish out the stew, leaving a good half for our companion. I cleaned out the bowls, banked up the fire and went outside again. The wind was still strong, but it seemed to be veering back towards the west and the biting chill had gone.

Something large trotted out of the shadows. "Were you looking for me?"

"Wimperling! Where have you been?"

"Around and about ... Did you sleep well?"

"Like a babe! Your supper is waiting."

"I'm fine without, thanks." He gazed up at the sky, where the moon seemed to bounce back and forth between the clouds like a blown-up bladder. "Tonight I can sup off the stars and drink the clouds. . . ."

"And what about the moon? I teased, looking up at where she hung, free of cloud at last. "A bite or two of—Oh, my God!"

I felt as if I had been kicked in the stomach. "I don't understand!" Suddenly I was afraid. "Last night when I went to sleep the moon was three or four days short of full. And now . . ."

And now the moon was full.

CHAPTER
THIRTY

"Yes," said the Wimperling, following my gaze. "You have slept through four days. 'Like a babe' is what I think you said."

Just like that. Like saying I overslept. Or missed Mass.

There was still a clutch of fear in my stomach. "I don't understand! Magic? How? Why?"

"No magic, just a pinch of special herbs in your stew. They slowed down your mind and your body, therefore you needed less breath, less food, less drink. As to why . . . As you said, there was little food left, and I had some things to do while you slept."

I still felt scared that anyone's body could be so used without their knowledge and permission; suppose, for instance, the dose had been too strong? And did one age the same while in that sleep? Did one dream? I couldn't remember any.

As usual, he knew what I was thinking.

"I wouldn't hurt you for the world, you know that. The dose was carefully measured. All it meant was that you and the dog had a longer rest than usual, that's all. And saved on food. No, you haven't gained time and yes, you did dream. One has to. But you don't always remember."

"What—things—did you do?"

"I will show you. When—when I am gone, if you travel due west for two days, you will come to a road that leads either south or east. You will have enough food to last till you come to another village. As to coinage—Follow me!"

He led us back to the room we had slept in, and there, in a heap on the floor, were twenty gold coins.

"It takes time to make those," he said.

I ran the coins through my fingers. "Are they real?" They felt very cold to the touch.

"As real as I can make them. More solid than faery gold, which can disappear in a breath. But you must be careful how you use them. As long as they are used honestly for trade they will stay as they are, although each time they change hands they will lose a little of their value. A coating of gold, you might say. But if they are stolen or used dishonestly, then the perpetrator will die."

"How are they made?"

"White fire, black blood, green earth, yellow water."

None of which I had ever come across, but I supposed anything was possible with a flying pig-not-a-pig. A large flying pig. Very large. Now he almost reached my shoulder: those four days sleep of mine had made him almost twice as big again.

"You will soon be too big for your skin, you know," I said jokingly.

He looked at me gravely. "I hope so. . . . Come and see what else I have been doing. You'd better make up the fire, while you're at it."

"I've been letting it die down. I can light it again for breakfast. It's not cold."

"Don't you remember what your mother taught you? On no account let the house fires go out on the eve of Samhain, lest Evil gain entry. . . ."

"Samhain? All Hallows' Eve?"

He nodded, and I suddenly realized that it had been exactly a year ago that I had made a funeral pyre of our house for my mother and had set out on my adventures.

A year, a whole year ... Somehow it seemed longer. That other life seemed a hundred years and a million miles away. I couldn't even clearly recall the girl I had been then: this Summer was a totally different person. For one thing she had a name—two names, in fact. For another, this person would not have been content to sit by the fire and dream, and eat honey cakes till she burst. In fact, I couldn't now remember when I had the last one. This girl now talked to animals, tramped the roads, thought less of her own bodily comforts and more of others, and had learned a great deal that was not taught in books. And hadn't used one single item of her expensive education that she could recall ...

I threw a couple more logs on the fire and then followed the Wimperling out and across the yard to where the pigsties had once been, an unusually subdued Growch tailing us. The Wimperling stepped over what had once been one of the walls of the sty, and now in the middle, rising some six feet high, was a newly built cairn of stones.

"Did you build this?"

"Takeoff point," he said.

I looked at him. He seemed so different from the little persecuted pig I had stolen from the fair and run off with tucked under my arm. Not just the size, which was phenomenal; he had also grown in confidence over the months I had known him. He was mature, patient, wise, and had saved us more than once with courage and good advice. I had lost my little piglet to an adult one, and wasn't sure whether to be glad or sorry.

"What are you going to do?"

"You will see. First let me tell you a little of what happened when I was young. . . ."

I sat down on part of the old wall and listened, Growch at my feet.

"This is where I was born. The very spot I hatched." "Hatched" again, as though he truly believed he had come from an egg. "I was raised, as you know, among a litter of innumerable little piglets, although I didn't grow exactly the same and stayed the runt of the litter. As I told you, I would probably have made a fine dish of suckling pig if the farmer hadn't discovered my stubs of wings, and sold me. After weeks of torment you found me, and the rest you know."

"But if you were unhappy here, and pretending to be something you were not, why come back?"

"Because this place is a Place of Power. It was arranged that I start my breathing life here, and also meant that I eventually leave from here for the land of my ancestors. The fact that a farmer built a pigsty over my hatching place was an accident that couldn't have been foreseen. However, once I had been sold, the Stones made sure they left and destroyed what remained of the farm. The Stones are my Guardians, they have watched and waited for a hundred years for my birth and then the Change."

"What?" I couldn't believe what I was hearing. He was fantasizing. "You waited to be born—for a *hundred* years?"

"Legends have it as a thousand, but that is an exaggeration. A hundred is the minimum, though, but the warmth of the sty above me accelerated things somewhat and I only had ninety-nine years. This hadn't given my personality enough charge to resist the nearness of the other piglets, so I adapted their bodily conformation to give myself time to acclimatize before the Change. Exactly a year, in fact."

I was utterly bewildered. I had lost him somewhere. Hatching, a hundred years, Stones of Power, a "change," guardians . . . I seized on one question. "You say the stones around us are Stones of Power? What does that mean?"

"Listen. Listen and feel. Where we are now is the centre of it all, like the center of a spider's web. If you hung like a hawk from the sky you would see the pattern. This is not the only Center of Power, of course: they exist in other countries as well. Because of their special magic they have been used since understanding began for birth, breeding, death, religions, sacrifice, healing. I say again: listen and feel. . . ."

I tried. At first, although the night was still as an empty
church, I could hear nothing special. Then there was a
growl from Growch and I began to feel something. A
low, very faint vibration, as though someone had plucked
the lowest string of a bass viol, waited till the sound died
away, then touched the silent string and still found it
stirring under their finger. I put both hands flat on the
ground and found I could hear it as well, though the
sound was not on one note, it came from a hundred, a
thousand different strings, all just on the edge of hearing.
I felt the sound both through my body and in my ears
at the same time, both repelling and attracting, till I felt
as if I had been a rat shaken by a terrier. Beside me
Growch was whimpering, lifting first one paw then the
other from the ground—

"Understand now?" asked the Wimperling, and with
his voice the noise and vibration faded and was still.
"That is why I had to come back. Had my life been as
it should, my hatching taken place at the right time, had
I not become part pig, I should have needed no one.
But you were instrumental in saving my life, you have
fed and tended me, and now I need you as the final
instrument to cut me from my past. I cannot be rid of
this constriction without you," and he flexed and
stretched and twisted and strove as though he were
indeed bound by bonds he could not loose.

"Anything," I said. "Anything, of course. How soon—
how soon before you change?" I wanted to ask into what,
but didn't dare. I didn't think I wanted to know, not just
yet, anyway. In fact, just for a moment I wished I was
anywhere but here, then affection and common sense
returned: nothing he became could harm us.

He glanced up at the sky. The moon was calm and
full and clear and among the stars there ran the Hare
and Leveret, the Hunter, his Dog and the Cooking Pan.
There were the Twins, the Ram, the Red Star, the Blue,
the White. . . . No wind as yet, night a hushed breath,
as if it, too, waited as we did.

Around us the ruins of the farm, all hummocks and
heaps, farther away the Stones, seeming to catch from

the moon and stars a ghostly radiance all their own, casting their shadows like fingers across the heath, so the land was all bars of silver and black like some strange tapestry bearing a pattern just out of reach of comprehension. And yet if one looked long enough . . .

"Five minutes," said the Wimperling. "When the shadow of the cairn touches the nearest Stone. Climb up with me and you will see. . . . That's right. See, there is room for us both at the top."

Growch yipped beneath us, and scrabbled with his claws at the stone but could get no further.

"This is not for you, dog," said the Wimperling. "Be patient." He turned to me. "Do you have your sharp little knife with you?"

"Of course." I touched the little pouch at my waist where it always lay, wondering why he wanted to know.

"Then it is farewell to you both, Girl and Dog. My thanks to you, and may you find what you seek soon." He took a deep breath. "I had not thought partings would be so hard. . . . Are you ready, Talitha?"

"Yes," I said, wondering what was to happen next. The shadow was creeping nearer and nearer to the Stone. . . . "At least I think I am."

"Then take out your knife, and when I count to ten, but not before, cut my throat. One . . ."

CHAPTER
THIRTY-ONE

"Two . . ."

"What are you *talking* about?"

"Three . . . Four . . ."

"I'm doing no such thing! How could I possibly hurt you?"

"Five—"

"Listen, *listen*! If I dig this knife into you—"

"Six—"

"—you will *die*! I thought you said you were going to—"

"Seven!"

"I won't, I can't!"

"Eight!"

"Wimperling, Wimperling, I can't kill you!"

"Nine! Do it! You *must*!"

"I love you too much to—"

"Do it *now*, before it's too late! Ten . . ."

And there was such a look of agonized entreaty on his face that I brought the knife out and drew it across his skin. The tiny gash started to bleed, a necklace of dark drops in the moonlight, and I couldn't do any more. I had rather cut my own throat.

"Talitha, Summer—there are only a few seconds left!" His voice was full of an imprisoned anguish. "*Please . . .*"

"I *can't*! Stay a pig: I'll care for you always, I promise!" and I flung away the knife, threw my arms around his neck and kissed him.

There was a tremendous bang! like a thunderbolt, a great blast of hot air, and I was toppled off the cairn. The moon and stars were blotted out and I lay stunned, conscious only of a huge tumult in the air, as if a storm had burst right over my head. I could hear Growch yelping with terror, but where was the Wimperling?

I sat up, my head spinning, and saw an extraordinary sight. The body of the flying pig was hurtling around the cairn like a burst bladder, every second getting smaller and smaller. Pony-size, man-size, hound-size, piglet-size, until at last it collapsed at my feet, a tiny bundle no bigger than my purse, and the moon appeared again.

Crawling forward I picked up the pathetic little bundle and held it to my breast, rocking back and forth and sobbing. Once again I had been asked to help, once again it had all gone wrong. At least I had never physically harmed any of the others, but there was my precious little flying pig burst into smithereens, and all I had left was a split piece of hide with the imprint of a face and a string of tail, four little hooves and two small pouches where his wings had been—

"Look up! Look up . . . !" The voice came from the air, from the clouds that were now massing to the west, from the Stones—

The Stones! They were alight, they burned like candles. One after the other their tips started to glow with a greenish light as if they were tracking another great shadow that glowed itself with the same unearthly light as it swooped, banked and turned, dived in great loops from sky to earth and back again. The sky was full of light and there was a smell like the firecrackers I had once seen, and a beating sound like dozens of sheets flapping in a gale.

Again came the voice: "Look up! Look up!" but I could only hug the remains of the Wimperling, little cold pieces

of leather, and cry. Growch crept to my feet from wherever he had been hiding, whimpering softly.

"Great gods! What was it? Where's the pig? Are you
all right? C'mon, let's get back inside. . . ."

But even as he whined there was a sudden rush of air
that had me flat on my back again and there, balancing
precariously on the cairn above us, wings flapping to
maintain balance, clawed feet gripping the shifting stones
was a—

Was a great dragon!

I think I fainted, for darkness rushed into my eyes and
I felt my insides gurgling away in a spiral down some
hole, like water draining away and out down a privy,
and there was a peculiar ashy smell in my nostrils. Then
everything steadied, I decided I had been seeing things
because of the terror of the night, and cautiously opened
one eye. . . .

It was still there.

The great wings were now quiet at its sides, and the
scaly tail with the arrow-like tip was curled neatly around
its clawed feet. The great nostrils were flared, as if
questing my scent, the lips were slightly curved back
above the pointed teeth, but the yellow eyes with the
split pupils seemed to hold quite a benign gaze. I could
see its hide rise and fall as it breathed.

I had never seen a dragon before, but it closely resembled the pictures I had seen, the descriptions I had read,
so I knew what it was. Perhaps if I stayed perfectly still
it would go away. It couldn't be hungry, for it had obviously eaten the Wimperling. So I waited, scarcely daring
to breathe, conscious of Growch trembling at my side.

It cleared its throat, rather like emptying a sack of
stones.

"Well?" it said, in a gritty voice. "How do I look?"

I swallowed, surprised it could speak or that I could
understand. But of course the ring on my finger . . .
Come to think of it, why wasn't it throbbing a warning?
To my surprise it was still and warm. Perhaps after all,
dragons didn't eat maidens, in spite of what the legends
said.

"Er . . . Very smart," I said, my voice a squeak. "Very . . . grand."

It stretched its great wings, one after the other, till I could see the moon shine faintly through the thin skin, like a lamp through horn shutters. "Still a bit creaky, but they haven't dried properly yet," said the dragon. "Everything else seems to be stretching and adjusting quite nicely. Of course I shall have to take it in short bursts for a day or two, but—"

"What have you done with the Wimperling?" I blurted out. "He was my friend, and all he wanted was to return to his ancestors! He never harmed anyone, and—and . . . If you've swallowed him, could you possibly spit him out again? I have his skin here, and I could sew him up in it and give him a decent burial. And if you're still hungry, I have some salt pork and vegetables left. . . ."

He stared at me, and for a moment I thought if he hadn't been a dragon, he would have laughed.

"You want your little pig back?"

"Of course. I said he was my friend. Now I am alone, except for my dog. He—he's somewhere about. . . ." Hiding, I thought, as I should have been.

"You offered me salt pork. . . . Pork is pig."

"Not—not like the Wimperling. He was different. He wasn't a *real* pig. You want some? Wait a moment. . . ." and I dashed back inside and emerged with the cook pot and put it on the cairn. "I'm afraid it's only warm. . . ." But there was no sign of the dragon. "Don't go away! It's here," I called out.

"So am I," said a small voice. "But I can't reach it there," and a tiny slightly blurred piglet was at my feet, just the same size as the Wimperling when I first met him. I bent to scoop him into my arms, my heart beating joyously, but as my hands closed over him he was gone, only the scrap of hide I had earlier cuddled in my fingers. Then I was angry. I shook my fist at the sky.

"I don't care who or what you are!" I screamed. "You cheated me! Just eat your accursed stew, and I hope it chokes you. *Where's my Wimperling?*"

A man stepped from the shadows behind the cairn, a

tall man wearing a hooded cloak that was all jags and
points. I could not see his face and my heart missed a
couple of beats. I snatched up my little sharp knife, the
one I had thrown away only minutes ago, and held it in
front of me.

"Keep away, or I'll set my dog on you!"

"That arrant coward? He couldn't—Ouch!"

Apparently Growch was less afraid of strangers than
he was of dragons, for he darted from the shadows and
gave the man's ankle a swift and accurate nip before
dashing back, barking fiercely.

"Mmmm . . ." said the stranger. "I could blunt all your
teeth for that, Dog!" He addressed me. "I mean you no
harm, so put that knife away. You weren't so keen to use
it five minutes ago, to help your friend."

So he had seen it all. I wondered where he had been
hiding. I tried to peek under his hood, but he jerked his
head away.

"Not yet. It takes time. . . ."

I didn't know what he was talking about. Just then the
rising wind caught the edge of his jagged cloak and a
hand came out to pull it back. I stared in horror: the
hand was like a claw, the fingers scaled like a chicken's
foot. What was this man? A monstrosity? A leper? He
saw the look in my eyes.

"Sorry, Talitha-Summer. I had thought to spare you
that. See . . ." and held out a hand, now a normal, every-
day sort. "I told you it would take time. Better with a
little more practice. And it's all your fault, you know. . . .
If you hadn't kissed me—not once, but the magic three
times—I would have appeared to you only in my dragon
skin. As it is, I am now obliged to spend part of my life as
a man." He sighed. "And yet it was that last kiss of yours
that set me free. If you had but kissed me once there
would have been a blurring at the edges every once in a
while, human thoughts. Two kisses, a part-change now and
again and a definite case of human conscience—which
hampers a dragon, you know. But the magic three . . ."

"*Wimperling?*"

"The same. And different." He came forward and one

hand reached out and clasped mine, warm and reassuring. The other threw back the concealing hood and there, smiling down at me, was at one and the same time the handsomest and most forbidding face I had ever seen.

Dark skin and hair, high cheekbones, a wide mouth, a hooked nose, frowning brows, a determined chin. And the eyes? Dragon-yellow with lashes like a spider's legs. Under the cloak he was naked; his hands, his feet, were manlike, but at elbow and knee, chest and belly, there was a creasing like the skin of a snake's belly. Even as I looked the scaly parts shifted and man-skin took their place.

"You see what you have done?"

"Does it hurt?" I asked wonderingly. Down there, at his groin, he was all man, I noted, with a funny little stirring in my insides.

"Changing? Not really. More uncomfortable, I suppose. Like struggling in the dark into an unfamiliar set of clothes that don't fit and are inside out."

"How long can you stay? When did you know what you were meant to be? When—when will you change back? Er . . . Do you want the stew?"

He laughed, a normal hearty man's laugh. "How long can I stay? A few minutes more, I suppose. Until I start changing back into my real self and my dragon-body. When did I know I was meant to be a dragon? Almost as soon as I was hatched, but the piglet bit fazed me a little. I was sure again that night when we crossed the border and I set the forest on fire with dragon's breath—" Of course! The question I had forgotten to ask at the time. "The stew? No, from now on my diet will be different. Here," and he lifted it down from the top of the cairn.

"Like what?" said Growch, already accepting the situation and sniffing around the stew pot. I tipped some out for him.

"Well, back east where my ancestors come from, there is a land called Cathay, and there—"

"And there they has those enticing little bitches wiv the short legs and the fluffy tails!" said Growch, the stew temporarily forgotten. "*That* was the name they used: Cathay!"

"And men with yellow skins and a civilization that goes back a thousand years! You have a one-track—no, two-track mind, Dog: food and sex. There are other things in life, you know...."

"Not as important. Think about it, dragon-pig-man: reckon in some ways as I'm cleverer than you."

Sustenance and propagation, with the spice of fear to leaven it: he could be right.

But the Wimperling-dragon-man ignored him and took my hand. "Let's walk a way. I don't know how long I can stay like this. Trust me?" And we strolled towards the nearest Stones, an avenue shimmering softly in the moonlight, a soft green, nearly as bright as glowworms.

As we walked I became gradually aware of his hand still clasping mine, of the contact of skin to skin, and my whole body seemed to warm like a fire. There were tickly sensations on my groin, tingly ones in my breasts and I'm sure my face burned like fire. I had never realized that palm-to-palm contact could be so erotic, could engender such a feeling of intimacy.

He stopped and swung me round to face him. "Well, Talitha-Summer, this is journey's end for us. Where will you go?"

"Wait a minute!" I didn't want to say good-bye, and couldn't think straight. "You know my name, but what is yours? We called you the Wimperling, but that was a pet name, a piglet name."

He laughed. "In Cathay they will call me the One-who-beats-his-wings-against-the-clouds-and-lights-the-sky-with-fire, but that is a ceremonial name and you'd never be able to pronounce it in their tongue. My shorter name is 'Master-of-Many-Treasures,' and that does have a Western equivalent: Jasper."

"Like the stone," I said. "Black and brown and yellow ... I don't want you to go!" Gauche, naïve and true.

He didn't laugh, just took both my hands in his.

"If I were only a man, my beautiful Talitha-Summer, I would stay."

But that made me angry and embarrassed, and I pulled my hands away. "Now you are laughing at me! Don't mock; I am fat and ugly, not in the slightest bit beautiful. . . ." I was close to tears.

"Dear girl, would I lie to you? Look, my love, look!" And in front of us was a mirror of clarity I couldn't believe. I saw the reflection of the man-dragon beside a woman I didn't recognize. Slim, straight-backed with a mass of tangled hair, a pretty girl with eyes like a deer, a clear skin, a straight nose and an expressive mouth—a woman I had never seen before.

"You're lying! It's some fiendish magic! I'm not—not like *that*!" I gestured at the image and it gestured back at me. "I'm ugly, fat, spotty. . . ."

"You were. When you rescued me you were all you said, but a year of wandering has worn away the fat your mother disguised you with. She didn't want a pretty daughter to rival her, so she did the only thing she could, short of disfigurement: she fattened you up like a prize pig, so that only a pervert would prefer you. Now you are all you should be. Why do you think Matthew wanted to marry you? Gill leave all behind and run away with you? You're beautiful, Summer-Talitha, and don't ever forget it!"

I reached out my hand to touch the reflection and it vanished, but not before I had seen the Unicorn's ring on my finger reflected back at me. So, it was true.

"Look at me," said the dragon-man, the Wimperling, Jasper. "Look into my eyes. You will see the same picture."

It was so. Dark though it was, I could see myself in the pupils of his eyes, a different Summer. I shivered. Instantly he put his cloak around both of us and pulled me towards him, so I could feel the heat of his body.

"Too much to comprehend all in one day? Don't worry: tomorrow you will be used to being beautiful. And now I must go: it will take me many days and nights to—"

"Don't! Please don't leave me. . . ."

"I must, girl. From now on our paths lie in different

directions. Go back to Matthew, who will love and care for you, take the dragon gold to a big city and find a man you fancy, travel to—"

"I want you," I said. "Just you. Kiss me, please. . . ." and I reached up and pulled his head down to mine, my hands cupped around his head. Suddenly he responded, he pulled me close, as close as a second skin, and his mouth came down on mine. It was a fierce, hot, possessive kiss that had my whole being fused into his and my body melting like sun-kissed ice into his warmth.

Then, oh then, we were no longer standing, we were lying and—and I don't know what happened. There was a pain like knives and a sharp joy that made me cry out—

And then I was pinned to the ground by a huge scaly beast and I cried out in horror and scrambled away, my revulsion as strong as the attraction I had felt only moments since.

"You see," said the dragon, in his different, gritty voice. "It didn't work. For a moment, perhaps, but you would not like my real self. Don't hurt yourself wishing it were any different."

I swallowed. "But for a moment, back there, you forgot the dragon bit completely. We were both human beings." I felt sore and bruised inside.

He was silent for a moment, shifting restlessly. "Perhaps," he said finally: "but it shouldn't have happened. It gave me a taste for . . . Never mind. Forget it. Forget me. Bury your remembrances with that scrap of hide you kept. Go and live the life you were meant to lead.

"And now: stand clear!"

He flapped his great wings once, twice, as a warning and I scrambled back to safety, watching from behind one of the Stones. He flapped his wings again, faster and faster, and it was like being caught in a gale. Bits of scrub and heather flew past my ears till I covered them with my hands and shut my eyes for safety, There came a roaring sound that I heard through my hands and a great whoosh!, a smell of cinders, my hair nearly parted from my scalp and I tumbled head over heels.

Once I righted myself and opened my eyes, my dragon was gone. A burned patch of ground showed where he had taken off and in the sky was a great shadow like a huge bat that circled and swooped and filled the air with the deep throb of wings. To my right—the east—the Stones had started to glow again, a long avenue of them, like a pointer.

The shadow swooped once more towards the earth then shot up like an arrow till it was almost out of sight, then it steadied and hovered for a moment before heading due east, following the direction the Stones indicated, head and tail out straight, wings flapping slowly. I watched until its silhouette crossed the moon, then went wearily back to the ruined farmhouse.

I wasn't even annoyed to see Growch with his head inside the now-empty cook pot. I was too tired. His voice sounded hollow.

"I saw you! Doing naughties, you was!"

"Naughties? What do you mean?" But even as I said it I realized what it must have looked like to an inquisitive dog. *Was* that what had happened?

"You know . . . you didn't do naughties with the knight or the merchant with the cat and the warm fires: why with *him*?" He pulled his head out of the pot a trifle guiltily and his ears were clogged with juice. "Sort of fell over it did; din' want to waste it. . . . Why don' we go to that nice place for a while? Likes you, he does, and it's too cold to stay outside all winter. Just for a coupla months . . ."

"Matthew?" I was deadly tired, confused, bereft, couldn't think straight. I must have time to sort myself out, and better the known than the unknown. "Yes, why not?"

CHAPTER
THIRTY-TWO

Easier said than done. It was the beginning of November now, and we were all of three or four hundred miles from the town where Matthew lived, north and east. It took us two weeks to get anywhere near a decent, well-traveled road, and those people we met were usually traveling south as we had done the year before, so we were heading against the flow of traffic. Company and lifts were few and far between and I was burdened with all the baggage, now there was no Wimperling, and what I would have expected to travel before—ten or twelve miles a day—was now only five or six: less if we were delayed by rain.

For the weather had changed with the waning of the moon: cold, blustery, with frequent rain showers. We seldom saw the sun and then only fitfully, and too pale and far away to heat us. To ease my burdens I made a pole sleigh—two poles lashed together in a vee-shape, the tattered blanket acting as receptacle for the rest of the goods—but the majority of the roads were so rutted and stony that the sleigh either kept twisting out of my hands, or the ends wore away and the poles had to be renewed.

Thanks to a couple of good lifts, by the end of November

354

we were over halfway, but every day now saw worsening weather, and at night sometimes, if the wind came from the hills, we could hear wolves on the high slopes howling their hunger. Mostly we slept in what shelter we could find by the way—an isolated farmhouse, a barn, a shepherd's croft—but sometimes I paid for the use of a village stable or a place beside a tavern fire. Careful as I was, the cost of food and lodgings was so high in winter that almost half the dragon gold had gone when disaster struck us.

One night in a tavern I had being paying in advance for a meal when my frozen fingers spilled the rest of the gold from my purse onto the earthen floor. I scooped it up as quickly as I could, but three unkempt men at a corner table were nodding and winking at one another slyly as I did so. That night I slept but little, although the men had long gone into the dark, and in the morning my fears were justified.

Growch and I had scarcely made a couple of miles out of the village when the three men leapt out from the bushes at the side of the road, kicked and punched me till I was dazed, snatched my purse, pulled my bundle apart and flung Growch into the undergrowth when he tried to bite them. They were just pulling up my skirts, determined to make the most of me, when there was the sound of a wagon approaching and they fled, taking with them my blanket, food, cooking things and my other dress.

The carter who came to my rescue was from the village I had just left, and he was kind enough to help me gather together what little I had left and give the dog and me a lift back. I was in a sorry state: my head and arms and face bruised and swollen and my clothes torn, but poor Growch was worse off, with a broken front leg. The tavern-keeper's wife gave me water to wash in, needle and thread to mend my torn skirt and sleeve and a crust of bread and rind of cheese for the journey and I made complaint to the village mayor, but as the thieves had not been local men there was nothing they could do, and

I was hurried on my way with sympathy but little else, lest I became a burden on the parish.

Once out of the village I bound up Growch's leg, using hazel twigs wrapped with torn strips from my shift, and poulticing it with herbs from the wayside to keep down the swelling and aid the healing, using the knowledge I had and the feel of the ring of my finger to choose the best. Of course now I would have to carry him, so I discarded any nonessentials, leaving me a small parcel to strap to my back, and my hands free for Growch.

By nightfall, hungry and depressed, I reached a tumbledown hut just off the road. As I walked through the scrub towards it I saw various articles strewn by the way: a man's belt, a rusty knife, a tattered blanket—surely that last was mine? I shrank back into the undergrowth ready to run, but Growch sniffed, wrinkled his nose and demanded to be put down. My ring was quiet, but cold, so I let him hobble forward on three legs to investigate further.

He came back a few minutes later. "We're not dossin' down there tonight, that's for sure. They's all dead an' it stinks to high heaven."

I crept forward, but even before I reached the hut I was gagging, and had to hold my cloak across my face. There, huddled on the earth floor, were the men who had robbed us only this morning, dead and smelling as though they had been that way for weeks. The contorted bodies lay in postures of extreme agony, mouths agape on swollen tongues and bitten lips, arms and legs twisted in some private torture, a noisome liquid oozing from great suppurating blisters on their blackened skin. Surely even the plague could not strike so quickly and devastatingly?

Then I noticed a little pile that was smoking away in a corner, like the last wisps from a dying fire. It was from here also that the worst stench came. Carefully stepping over the bodies, I walked over to investigate. There, dissolving in a last sizzling bubble, were the remains of the coins of dragon gold the then-Wimperling had left for me. I remembered what he had told me:

given or used for trade they were perfectly safe; stolen, they brought death and destruction. I shivered uncontrollably, but not from cold.

That night we spent in the open, the first of many. With no money but my dowry left, which coins the country people would not accept, not recognizing the denominations and being suspicious of strangers anyway, I was reduced to begging, to stealing from henhouses, a handful of grain from sacks, vegetables from clamps. It was a wonder I was never caught, but with a dog who could no longer dance for his supper what else could I do? I did find the occasional root or fungi and gather what I could of herbs and winter-blackened leaves, but every day I grew weaker. Growch's leg healed slowly, but he probably fared worse than I did, for I could no longer find even the beetles and grubs that he would eat if there was nothing else. I even tried to trap fish, as I had been taught as a child, but with the frosts the fish lay low in the water and it all came to nothing, even the frogs having burrowed down under the mud.

There were one or two remissions, like the time I came upon a late November village wedding—none too soon from the look of the bride's waistline—and I stuffed myself stupid in return for a handful of coins and a tune or two on my pipe and tabor which I had providentially kept. I took with me a sack of leftovers that lasted us for a week.

But that was the last of our good luck. The weather got even worse and our progress slowed to a crawl. Lifts, even for a couple of miles, were few, and the stripped hedgerows and empty fields mocked our hunger. A couple of times, dirty and disreputable though I now was, I could have bought us a meal or two by pandering to the needs of importunate sex-seekers, but somehow I just couldn't. I do not believe it had anything to do with morals, nor the off-putting stench of their bodies: it was something deeper than that. I had been infatuated with Gill—the Wimperling had been right about that—I had had an affection for Matthew, and—But I would think no further than that. The recent past I blotted out from memory. Sufficient that it stopped me from greater folly.

I have no clear recollection of those last few days. I know I was always hungry, always cold. My shoes had fallen to pieces but my numb feet no longer hurt on the sharp stones. I was conscious of a thin shadow that dogged my heels as a limping Growch tried to keep up, and I do recall him bringing me a stinking mess of raw meat he had stolen from somewhere and me cramming it into my mouth, trying to chew and swallow and then being violently sick. I also remember a compassionate woman at a cottage door, with half a dozen children clinging to her skirts, sparing me a mug of goat's milk and a few crusts, and finding rags to bind my feet, but the rest was forgotten.

It started to snow. At first thin and gritty, hurting my face and hands like needles, then softer, thicker, gentler, drifting down like feathers to cover my hair, burden my shoulders, drag at my skirt, but provide a soft carpet for my feet. I think it was then that I realized I wasn't going to make it, although some streak of perversity in my nature kept me putting one foot in front of the other. I remember falling more than once, stumbling to my knees many times, and on each occasion a small hoarse voice would bark: "Get up! Get up! Not far to go now ... We ain't done yet. ..."

But at the end even this failed to rouse me. The snow was up to my knees, above them, and I could go no further. Even Growch, plowing along in my dragging footsteps and then trying to tug at my skirt to pull me forward, failed to rouse me.

"Come on, come on, now! A little further, just two steps, and two more! Round this corner, that's right! You can't give up now. ... Now, down here a step or two— don't fall down, don't!" Another tug at my skirt, and this time a nip to my ankle as well. I tried to thrust him away, but he was as persistent as a mosquito. I staggered a few steps, fell again. The snow was like a featherbed and no longer cold and forbidding. If I could just lie down for a few minutes, pull up the covers and sleep and sleep and sleep . . .

"Get up! Don't go to sleep! Up, up, up!" Nip, nip, nip . . .

"Go away! Leave me *alone!*" For the last time I got to my feet and stumbled down the road. "Leave me, go away, I don't want you anymore!" and I fell into a snow-drift that was larger, deeper, softer, warmer than any before. Shutting my eyes I burrowed deeper still and drifted away, the last thing I heard being Growch's hysterical barking: "Yip! Yip! Yip!" but soon that too faded and I heard no more. . . .

"I think she's coming round . . . How are you feeling?"

A strangely familiar face swam into focus, an anxious, rubicund face with a fringe of hair like the setting sun. I shut my eyes again, opened them. Did angels have red hair? Assuredly I must be in Heaven whether I deserved it or not, for I was warm, rested, lying I suppose on a cloud, and no longer hungry, thirsty or worried about anything. Except—

"Growch? Where's Growch? Is he here too?"

"She means the dog," said someone, and something walked up my feet, legs, stomach and chest, then thrust a cold wet nose against my cheek and I smelt the familiar, hacky breath.

"Been here all the time—'cept for breakfast 'n' lunch 'n' supper—thought at one time as how you wasn't goin' to make it. . . ."

I put up a strangely heavy and trembly hand to touch his head. *Did* they have dogs in Heaven, then? I'd think about it later. Just have a little sleep . . .

"Fever's down," said another voice I thought I recognized. "By the morning she'll be fine."

And by morning I was at least properly awake, conscious of my surroundings and hungry, though not exactly "fine" just yet, for all the damaged parts of me that had been exposed to the bitter weather started to smart and ache, and I was still very weak.

Of course I had ended up at Matthew's house, thanks

to Growch. He had led us both over the last few miles, scenting food and warmth and comfort, and luckily my final collapse had taken place just outside the merchant's house, though it had taken Growch a long time to rouse them from sleep and he had ended up voiceless, for a few hours at least.

At first they were convinced I was dead, so pale and cold and lifeless I had become, but providentially for me Suleiman had been staying with Matthew once more and he found a thin pulse and proceeded to thaw me out.

"Not by putting you in hot water or roasting you by the fire, as my dear friend would have me do," he said. "That would have killed you of a certainty. Instead I used a method I learned when a boy, from the Tartars my father sometimes traded with in hides. A tepid bath, oil rubbed gently into the skin, a cotton wrapping, then the natural warmth of naked bodies enfolding you. The servants took it in turns. Then the water a little warmer, and so on again ... It took many hours until you were breathing normally, though once I saw you could swallow, though still unconscious, I gave you warm sweet drinks.

"Unfortunately there was a fever there, waiting for your body to warm up, but with one of my special concoctions and poppy juice to keep the body asleep, we managed to pull you through, though it was a close thing. The bruises and cuts will heal soon, but you have two broken toes, and I have bound those together; you were lucky you did not get frostbite as well."

After I had done my best to thank him, I asked about Growch's broken leg.

"Ah, you did a good job there. He still limps a little, but I have removed the splints and renewed the healing herbs. He will be as good as new."

Once I started to eat again properly I made rapid progress and was soon allowed up to sit by the fire in the solar, with a fully mobile Growch at my feet, luxuriating in the idleness, and Saffron, the great ginger cat, actually venturing his weight on my lap, though he was singularly uncommunicative, even when he realized I could talk to him. Of course I was petted and pampered and cosseted by Matthew, who seemed delighted to have me back. Both he and Suleiman could hardly wait to hear of my travels and find out what had happened to "Sir Gilman", so I gave them an edited, but nevertheless entertaining, account of my wanderings.

I had had plenty of time while convalescing to think up a good story, for who would believe the real one? I told them about the ghost in the castle and about our sojourn in the artist's village, and they were suitably impressed, both believing in the supernatural and Suleiman having heard of the other artist's seminars in Italia. When I recounted our stay with the Lady Aleinor, I had a surprise, and further confirmation (to them) of the complete veracity of my story.

"I quite forgot to tell you!" exclaimed Matthew. "The lad who helped you escape, Dickon, came here eventually, he said on your recommendation. He seemed an enterprising sort of lad and brought news of you—though he did embroider the facts a little!"

"Something about you flying to safety on the back of that pig of yours," said Suleiman, but his eyes were speculative. "It was a good tale. . . ."

"Anyway, I decided to give him a chance, for your sake," said Matthew. "Sent him off on one of our caravans with a letter of introduction. He'll be away at least a year, and he may prove useful. We can always do with promising youngsters."

Of course I didn't tell them the whole truth about Gill. I made a great tale of our escape across the border and of the miraculous return of his eyesight, however, the latter gratifying Suleiman.

"A theory of mine proved. One blow to the head: blindness. Another knock, and whatever has been displaced in the brain is jarred back. I expect he will have recurrent headaches for a while, but all should be well."

Matthew looked uncomfortable, but after a while he asked: "And the young man's parents? They must have been glad of his return. . . . He—also had—others—who must have rejoiced?"

I nodded and said, my voice quite steady and unemotional, "His fiancée had almost given him up for dead. They celebrated their nuptials while I was there and Rosamund, a beautiful fair-haired lady, was already with child when I left, I believe. . . ." That at least was true.

"And the rest of your little menagerie?" asked Suleiman. "The horse, the pigeon, the tortoise and the—er, flying pig?"

"The pigeon flew away once his wing was healed and joined a flock of his brethren." Truish. "The tortoise I let loose in suitable surroundings." True, but short of the full facts. "The mare—she grew up into quite a fine specimen and went for breeding." Again, basically true, but not the full story.

But what is truth? I thought to myself. It is always open to interpretation. Even if I had told them everything it would have been colored by the telling, my subjectiveness, and they would have heard it with ears that would hear parts better than others, would remember some facts and forget others, so the story to each would be different. If someone asked you what you ate for breakfast and you answered truthfully: "eggs," that would be truth but still not tell the enquirer how many, how cooked and what they tasted like, though they would probably be quite satisfied with the answer.

"And the pig?" asked Suleiman. "The odd one out . . ."

"He—the pig, died." I said. Another sort of truth. "He just dwindled away. He doesn't exist anymore." I still had the little scrap of hide, shriveled still smaller now though still bearing the imprint of its owner's face and the remnants of his hooves. Stuffed, it would make a mini-pig, and child's plaything. My eyes were full as I remembered all that had happened.

"Well, it seems all turned out for the best," said Matthew comfortably. "Feel well enough for a game of chess, Mistress Summer?"

Through the colored glass of the window in the solar I watched the sun climb higher in the sky every day as the celebrations of Candlemas gave way to the rules of

Lent. Matthew and Suleiman still insisted on convales-
cence, so I brought out my Boke, one of the few things
I had managed to save, and wrote out my adventurings
as best I could, but the version for my eyes only. When
I had finished, the fine vellum Matthew had insisted on
buying stood elbow to wrist high and my fingers ached.
And even then the story wasn't complete.

It ended when the Wimperling "died," for there were
still some things I couldn't bring myself to write down,
or even think about.

Matthew and Suleiman brought out their maps, planning the year's trade and seeking a faster route to the
spices of the East. I studied the maps too, fascinated by
the lands and seas they portrayed, so far from everything
I knew. At one stage Suleiman mentioned the difficulties
of coinage barter and exchange between the different
countries and I bethought myself of my father's dowry
gift, bringing the coins to show him.

To my amazement and delight he recognized them all
and spread out the largest map in the house, weighing
it down at the four corners with candlesticks.

"See, these coins all belong to different countries: Sici-
lia, Italia and across the seas to Graecia. Then Persia,
Armenia . . ." and he placed the coins one by one across
the map so they looked like a silver and gold snake.
South by east, east, east by north, northeast; all tending
the same way. "Your father must almost have reached
Cathay. . . . He did: look!" And he held out the last and
tiniest coin of all, no bigger than a baby's fingernail and
dull gold. "Either that, or he was friendly with the traders
who went there. These coins follow our trade routes
almost exactly. . . . Don't lose them: they might come in
useful some day."

I offered the coins, my precious dowry, to dear, kind
Matthew when he tentatively proposed marriage to me
just before Easter, but he closed my hand over them.
"No, I have no need of them; you are enough gift for
any man. Keep them in memory of your father."

It was agreed we would be wed when he returned
from a two-week journey to barter for the new season's

wool in advance. He and Suleiman set off together one fine April morning and I waved them out of sight, clutching Matthew's parting gift, a purseful of coins, to buy "whatever fripperies you desire."

He had kissed me a fond good-bye, and as his lips pressed mine I remembered Gill's urgent mouth on mine. And another's . . .

"Well, then: that's settled," said Growch by my side, tail wagging furiously. "Home at last, for both of us. When's lunch?"

Part III
A BEGINNING

CHAPTER
THIRTY-THREE

"Gotcha!"

I awoke with a start to find Growch trampling all over me, tail wagging furiously. Night had fallen early with lowering cloud, but I was snug in the last of the hay at the far end of the barn, wrapped in my father's old cloak, and had been sleeping dreamlessly.

"D'you know how long I been lookin' for you? Four days! Four bleedin' days . . . Fair ran me legs orf I did. You musta got a lift. . . ."

"I did. Yesterday." I sat up. "How did you know which way I'd gone?"

"Easy! Only way we ain't been. 'Sides, I gotta nose, and that there ring of yours got a pull, too."

I glanced down at it. Warm, but pulsing softly.

"Got anythin' to eat? Fair starvin' I am," and he pulled in his stomach and tried to look pathetic.

I gave him half the loaf I had been saving for breakfast. "And when you've finished that you can turn right round again and head back where you came from!"

He choked. "You're jokin'!"

"No, I am not. I left you behind deliberately. I even asked Matthew in my note to take care of you while I was away. . . ."

A note he wouldn't find yet, not for a couple of days at least, and by that time I should be aboard a ship for Italia, cross-country to Venezia and ship again for points east. And then to find Master Scipio and present myself to the caravan-master as Matthew's newest apprentice . . .

Once the merchant and Suleiman had disappeared I had had plenty of time to think.

Before, there had always been someone hovering, in the kindest possible way of course, making sure I wasn't hungry/cold/thirsty/tired/bored. I hadn't realized how constricted I had felt until they were both gone: the first action of mine had been to run from room to room, down the stairs, round the yard and then back again, flinging cushions in the air and the shutters wide open. Free, free, free! I sang, I danced, I felt pounds lighter, almost as if I could fly. Growch thought I was mad, so did the cat and surely the servants.

Once I had calmed down I asked myself why I had acted like that, and I didn't particularly like the answers I came up with. One of them was obviously that a year or more traveling the freedom of the roads had left me with a taste for elbow room; another that I was obviously not ready to settle down yet. The third answer was, in a way, the most hurtful: I obviously didn't care enough for Matthew to marry him—at least I didn't return his affection the way he would have wished.

And why should you expect to love him? I could hear my mother's voice like a dim echo. Marriage is a contract, nothing more. You are lucky in that you don't actively dislike him. Just look around you, see what you will have! A rich husband who will grant your every wish, a comfortable home, security at last . . . A little pretense on your part every now and again: is that so much to ask?

Yes, Mama, I answered her in my mind. You had my father, don't forget, you knew what real love felt like. You, too, had a choice. Didn't you ever regret not flinging everything aside and following him to the ends of the earth and beyond? A cruel and unjust death took him away from you, but at least you had your memories. And what have I got? A taste, just the tiniest taste, of what life could really be like, what love meant.

If I married Matthew now, feeling the way I did, I should be doing him a grave injustice and he was too nice, too kind a man for that. He would know I was pretending. Whereas if I tried to find what I was seeking and failed, then I could return and truly make the best of things. If he would still have me, of course. And if I succeeded . . . But I wouldn't even think of that, not yet. Besides, the odds were so great, maybe ten thousand to one, probably more. But I was damn well going to try!

That letter to dear Matthew had been difficult to write, for I knew how it would hurt him.

I know you will be upset to find me gone, but I find I cannot yet settle down, much as I am fond of you and am grateful for your many kindnesses. I hope you can forgive me. I am not sure where I shall go, but I hope to return within a year and a day, all being well. By then, of course, you may well have changed your mind about me, but if not I hope I shall be ready to settle down with you.

I have taken the bag of coins you gave me so I shall not be without funds, although I know you intended them for more frivolous purposes. Thank you again for everything. Please, of your goodness, take care of my dog till I return. . . .

There were two things—three—that I didn't tell him. I had spent a few coins in kitting myself out in boy's clothes: braies and tunic, stockings and boots. Also, I had cut my hair short. At first I had been horrified at the result, for now my hair sprang up round my head in a riot of curls, but I soon became used to the extra lightness, and it would be much more convenient. I had taken the discarded tresses with me, for there was always a call for hair to make false pieces and they might be worth a meal or two.

Another thing he wouldn't know was that I had copied

his maps showing the trade routes, and the last way I
had taken advantage was to use his seal and forge his
signature to a letter of introduction to one of his caravan
masters, the same one who had engaged young Dickon.
Having memorized, unconsciously at the time, the sched-
ules of the routes, I now knew I had a couple of days
more to make the twenty miles or so to the first rendez-
vous. And now here came trouble on four legs just to
complicate matters. . . .

"I locked you in deliberately to stop you following!
You can't come with me! I'm not even sure where I'm
going. . . ."

"Why can't I come? S'all very well tellin' the servants
as you're goin' visitin', but I ain't stupid! They tried to
keep me in, as you ordered, but I jumped out a window,
I did. You ain't goin' nowheres without me. You knows
you ain't fit to be let out on your own. Din' I get us to
that fellow's house?"

I admitted he had.

"Well, then! There's gratitude for you. . . . I don' care
where you're goin', I'm comin' too. Try an' stop me."

"I thought all you wanted was a comfortable home.
Matthew would take good care of you. And all that lovely
food . . ."

"I can change me mind, can't I? You have. Don' know
what you wants do you? Well, then . . . Where we goin'?"

I gave up. "To sleep, right now. In the morning . . .
east."

"Where the little fluffy-bum bitches come from? Cor,
worth a walk of a hundred miles or so . . ."

Nearer thousands, I thought, as I lay down again. It
was a daunting prospect, thought of like that. But otherwise how could my mind and body ever be rid of the
ache, the questioning, the unknown, engendered on that
never-to-be-forgotten night when my world had turned
upside down?

Growch had been wrong there: I did know what I
wanted.

Somewhere a dragon was waiting. . . .

POUL ANDERSON

Poul Anderson is one of the most honored authors of our time. He has won seven Hugo Awards, three Nebula Awards, and the Gandalf Award for Achievement in Fantasy, among others. His most popular series include the Polesotechnic League/Terran Empire tales and the Time Patrol series. Here are fine books by Poul Anderson available through Baen Books:

If not available at your local bookstore, you can order all of Poul Anderson's books listed above with this order form. Check your choices and send the combined cover price/s to: Baen Books, Dept. BA, P.O. Box 1403, Riverdale, NY 10471.

Name _____

Address _____

City _____ State _____ Zip _____

BUG YOUR BOOKSTORE

We've said that a sure-fire way to improve the selection of SF at your local store was to communicate with that store. To let the manager and salespeople know when they weren't stocking a book or author that you wanted. To special order that book through the bookstore, rather than order it directly from the publisher. In order to encourage you to think about these things (and to satisfy our own curiosity), we asked you to send us a list of your five best and five worst reads of the past year. And hundreds of you responded.

So we got to thinking, too. Below you will find what we think are our top fifteen reads on our current list (in alphabetical order by author). If your bookstore doesn't stock them, it should. So bug your bookstore. You'll get a better selection of SF to choose from, and your store will have improved sales. To sweeten the deal, if you send us a copy of your special order form and the book or books ordered circled on the coupon below, we'll send you a free poster!

THE WARRIOR'S APPRENTICE, Lois McMaster Bujold, 0-671-72066-X, $4.50
BARRAYAR, Lois McMaster Bujold, 0-671-72083-X, $4.99
THE PALADIN, C.J. Cherryh, 0-671-65417-9, $4.99
HAMMER'S SLAMMERS, David Drake, 0-671-69867-2, $4.95
STARLINER, David Drake, 0-671-72121-6, $5.99
METHUSELAH'S CHILDREN, Robert A. Heinlein, 0-671-65597-3, $3.50
REVOLT IN 2100, Robert A. Heinlein, 0-671-65589-2, $4.99
BARDIC VOICES: THE LARK AND THE WREN, Mercedes Lackey, 0-671-72099-6, $5.99
THE SHIP WHO SEARCHED, Anne McCaffrey & Mercedes Lackey, 0-671-72129-1, $5.99
SASSINAK, Anne McCaffrey & Elizabeth Moon, 0-671-69863-X, $5.99
THE DEED OF PAKSENARRION, Elizabeth Moon, 0-671-72104-6, $15.00
THE MAN-KZIN WARS, created by Larry Niven, 0-671-72076-7, $5.99
MAN-KZIN WARS II, created by Larry Niven, 0-671-72036-8, $4.99
MAN-KZIN WARS III, created by Larry Niven, 0-671-72008-2, $4.99
PRINCE OF MERCENARIES, Jerry Pournelle, 0-671-69811-7, $4.95